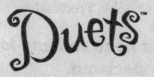

**Two brand-new stories in every volume...
twice a month!**

Duets Vol. #61

Little wonder veteran Duets author Kristin Gabriel has
received two RITA Awards from the Romance Writers
of America for her fabulous, funny stories. This month
she delivers a delightful duo—the Kane brothers and
their adventures on the path to true love. Enjoy!

Duets Vol. #62

Voted Storyteller of the Year twice by *Romantic
Times*, Silhouette writer Carol Finch always "presents
her fans with rollicking, wild adventures...and fun
from beginning to end." Making her Duets debut this
month is talented newcomer Molly O'Keefe with a
fun story about the matchmaking Cook family—and
what can happen when there are *too many Cooks...!*

Be sure to pick up both Duets volumes today!

Mr. Predictable

"You just need to hang loose," Moriah declared.

"Our next hurdle is to get you to do something impulsive, something totally unplanned, unexpected and off schedule."

"Hey, I can be impulsive if I feel like it," Jake said, affronted.

"Couldn't prove it by me, Mr. Predictable," she teased him. "When was the last time you hauled off and did something totally out of character?"

He frowned pensively.

"Well?" she prompted.

"Don't rush me. I'm thinking."

"That's your problem."

He suddenly grinned. "You want impulsive do you?"

He leaned over, snatched Moriah off her horse and planted a kiss on her. It wasn't just a playful little peck on the cheek, either. It was a hot, steamy, burn-off-your-lips kind of kiss that demanded a response.

It was the most spontaneous thing Jake had ever done, and he liked it. A lot...

For more, turn to page 9

It was total sensory overload...

The last time Cecelia had been under a man this way was...well, during the Reagan administration. Her body short-circuited and with a kind of dreamy fascination she watched Ethan's mouth as he swore at her for trying to break his thumb.

"I'm going to kiss you," she interrupted. Her self-edit mechanism had been squashed under the weight of his body. She lifted her head off the ground and pulled on his hair until their lips met in a whisper of a kiss.

Ethan felt poleaxed. "Crazy city people," he growled. "Radiation, cell phones making them nuts..." He leapt to his feet and helped her up.

A breath away from her, he grabbed her head and kissed her in a way she had never dreamed of being kissed. Things spun loose in her, bones melted.

Then he pulled back, looked at her with hooded eyes, opened his mouth as if to say something, shut it and walked away.

"Oh my," Cecelia breathed.

For more, turn to page 197

HARLEQUIN DUETS

ISBN 0-373-44128-2

Copyright in the collection:
Copyright © 2001 by Harlequin Books S.A.

The publisher acknowledges the copyright holders
of the individual works as follows:

MR. PREDICTABLE
Copyright © 2001 by Connie Feddersen

TOO MANY COOKS
Copyright © 2001 by Molly Fader

This edition published by arrangement with Harlequin Books S.A.

® and TM are trademarks of the publisher. Trademarks indicated with ® are registered in the United States Patent and Trademark Office, the Canadian Trade Marks Office and in other countries.

Visit us at www.eHarlequin.com

Printed in U.S.A.

Mr. Predictable
Carol Finch

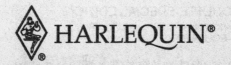

HARLEQUIN®

TORONTO • NEW YORK • LONDON
AMSTERDAM • PARIS • SYDNEY • HAMBURG
STOCKHOLM • ATHENS • TOKYO • MILAN • MADRID
PRAGUE • WARSAW • BUDAPEST • AUCKLAND

Dear Reader,

I'm delighted to be writing my third book for Duets, because I love romantic comedy! In this story you will meet a serious-minded workaholic who clashes with the fun-loving owner of a resort for stressed-out businessmen.

J. T. Prescott doesn't believe for one minute that he needs these two weeks of recreational therapy that his sisters arranged for him, and he stubbornly resists Moriah Randell's attempt to change his attitude, his unwavering routine and his lifestyle. This battle of wills becomes far more personal and complicated when their attraction to each other refuses to be ignored or denied. When unexpected emotions sneak up on J.T. and Moriah, they can't imagine what has hit them so hard and so fast...and just won't go away!

Enjoy,

Carol Finch

Books by Carol Finch

HARLEQUIN DUETS
36—FIT TO BE TIED
42—A REGULAR JOE

SILHOUETTE SPECIAL EDITION
1242—NOT JUST ANOTHER COWBOY
1320—SOUL MATES

This book is dedicated to my husband, Ed,
and our children—Jon, Jeff, Kurt, Christie and Jill.
And to our grandchildren, Blake, Kennedy
and Brooklynn. Hugs and kisses!

And a very special thank-you
to my editor, Priscilla Berthiaume,
and my agent, Laurie Feigenbaum, for all your help
and support. You are greatly appreciated!

1

JACOB THOMAS PRESCOTT squeezed his eyes shut to relieve the strain of staring at the computer screen for ten hours straight. Of course, that was nothing new, he reminded himself as he massaged his temples to ease the headache pounding in rhythm with his pulse. This, after all, was life as he knew it. Work. And more work. It's what he did six days a week—and sometimes on Sunday.

J.T.—as his three employees at his graphic shop and his sisters knew him—checked his watch. Six o'clock, right on the button. With robotlike precision, J.T. saved the file and transferred it to floppy disk so he could work on his laptop computer over the weekend.

When he shut down the computer, J.T. pushed away from his desk and worked the kinks from his neck and shoulders. He glanced sideways to note that his three younger male employees had already called it quits for the day and that they were smiling at him for no apparent reason.

"Is there a problem?" he asked as he surged to his feet.

"No," the young men chorused, still smiling enigmatically. "Have a nice weekend, boss."

J.T. nodded, then waited for the men to precede him out the door. He grabbed the plastic bag of clothes he planned to drop off at the dry cleaners, checked his watch again and then locked the door behind him.

Right on time, as usual, he noted as he stuffed the shop keys in the pocket of his black suit. He would swing by the cleaners at 6:11 p.m., just as he did every Friday, then drive to his apartment to pop in a microwaveable turkey-and-dressing TV dinner.

J.T. skidded to a halt on the sidewalk and his eyes popped when he noticed the two flat tires on the driver's side of his older-model gray sedan. "Well, damn," he muttered. This was going to throw off his regular routine by a half hour—maybe more.

Scowling at the inconvenience, J.T. looked up and down the deserted street, then frowned as the fire-engine red Jeep Cherokee—that seemed to come from out of nowhere at lightning speed—ground to a stop beside him. To his surprise, a smiling blue-eyed blonde, wearing a bright blue T-shirt that was plastered with stars and stripes, a pair of screaming red shorts and hiking boots, bounded from the vehicle like a jack-in-the-box.

"Is this your car?" she asked all too cheerfully for J.T.'s sedate tastes.

He appraised the female who looked to be in her mid-twenties. He wasn't sure if he should salute this personification of the American flag or answer her. He decided on the latter. "Er…yes, it's my car," he mumbled, focusing on the flat tires rather than the woman's flashy appearance and blinding smile. Flamboyantly dressed blondes with one-hundred-watt smiles and more energy than they knew what to do with didn't appeal to him—and for good reason.

"I'll give you a lift to the service station," she offered, then stuck out her hand to introduce herself. "I'm Moriah Randell."

Again, J.T. felt the ridiculous urge to salute. Instead, he shook her hand, marveling at her decisive grip. But then, he mused, her firm handshake really shouldn't surprise him. Bubbling spirit, vitality and independence—hence her American flag ensemble—fairly crackled around her. She was about as easy to ignore as a hurricane or earthquake, and she came on so strong that J.T. reflexively withdrew into his own space.

"I'm J. T. Prescott," he murmured as he resituated the pile of laundry, briefcase and laptop in both arms.

"Here, let me help you with that stuff," she volunteered.

Before J.T. could accept or reject her offer, Moriah scooped up his precious possessions.

A most peculiar sensation assailed him when Moriah confiscated his laptop and briefcase. It was as if she had suddenly amputated extensions of his hands. She juggled the objects as if they were insignificant pieces of junk and that didn't set well with J.T. "Hey, be careful with that stuff," he cautioned as she strode quickly around the side of her SUV. "Those happen to be my stock-in-trade—" His voice fizzled into a groan when she unceremoniously dumped both prized possessions on the back seat.

Moriah flashed him another dazzling smile that made her blue eyes sparkle like polished jewels. The thick ropelike braid of blond hair slithered over her shoulder as she plunked behind the steering wheel.

When she motioned for him to join her, he resigned himself to accepting the young woman's assistance. With a sigh, J.T. climbed into the brightly colored vehicle. He barely had time to shut the door before Moriah stamped on the accelerator and whizzed off. Jeez, he'd just climbed onboard with the female version of Evel Knievel, he mused as he hurriedly fastened his seat belt.

J.T. glanced over to appraise Moriah's fire-engine-red fingernails, red hoop earrings and jangling red-white-and-blue bracelets. He also noticed there wasn't a wedding ring on her finger, not that he cared one way or another, of course.

Who the hell dressed this woman? *Conservative* and *conventional* were obviously foreign concepts to her. He decided loud clothes were an essential warning that signaled the arrival of this female cyclone. She appeared to be the kind of individual who walked right in and took over. For sure and certain, she bustled J.T. off in whirlwind fashion!

"Would you mind slowing down?" J.T. requested as they zipped down the street. "I'd like to live to see my thirty-sixth birthday, if you don't mind."

"You don't find speed exhilarating? You don't like the feel of the wind in your hair?" she asked, still smiling radiantly.

Her perpetual smile was really beginning to bug him. *She* was beginning to bug him. She was too cheerful, too bouncy, too vibrant, too feminine, too reckless, too…everything! Plus, the alluring scent of her perfume was clogging his senses and the narrow confines of the Jeep didn't allow enough room for him to avoid breathing her in.

"Hey!" J.T. erupted as he glanced out the side window. "You buzzed right by the service station!"

She turned that high-voltage smile on him again. "I did it on purpose."

J.T. frowned warily as Moriah increased speed and sailed onto the ramp that merged with the interstate highway. "What the hell is going on here, lady?" he demanded to know that very second.

She grinned impishly. "The name is Moriah, remember?"

"Yeah, whatever." J.T. gnashed his teeth and braced himself when she switched over to the fast lane of rush hour traffic. "Am I being kidnapped? I should warn you that I'm not carrying much cash. I never carry much cash. Demanding a ransom for my return is a complete waste of time."

"You aren't being kidnapped. You're being escorted to Triple R," she said, as if that explained everything.

It didn't. Not to J.T.'s satisfaction. "What the hell is Triple R?" he demanded gruffly.

"Randell's Resort Ranch."

"Ranch? You work at a ranch and you dress like that?" he asked, then smirked.

One delicate blond brow arched as she spared him a quick glance. "You don't like my clothes?"

"Lady, I'm not sure I even like *you*, especially after you kidnapped me, so don't get me started on your clothes!"

She chuckled at the insult, then crossed two lanes of heavy traffic to roar down the off ramp. "I was told to expect this kind of reaction from you, Jake."

"The name is J.T.," he said through gritted teeth.

"J.T. sounds too stuffy. I prefer to call you Jake, if you don't mind."

"I do mind. And who the hell told you to kidnap me? My employees? Is that why they were grinning at me as if they were sharing some sort of conspiracy? They've been whining that I've been working them too hard lately. I should've known something was going on—"

"It was your sisters," she interrupted as she swerved

onto a two-lane road and headed north to only God, and this personification of the American flag, knew where!

"Kim and Lisa are responsible for this abduction?" he croaked in disbelief.

Moriah nodded as she set the SUV on cruise. The thick rope of braided blond hair rippled over her shoulder and curled against the swell of her full breasts. J.T. did his gentlemanly best not to dwell on her curvaceous figure and the long expanse of tanned legs.

It dawned on him that the impact of meeting Moriah—what with her flashy attire and cheery smile—served to momentarily distract a man from her very shapely, very feminine figure. But once you were enclosed in a vehicle with her, and spared her more than a casual glance, you couldn't help but notice her striking good looks and appealing physique, despite those godawful, bold-colored clothes. Yet, after seeing Moriah's representation of Old Glory, you couldn't help but wonder what she'd be wearing tomorrow.

"Kim and Lisa contacted me because I run a resort ranch that caters to businessmen who've forgotten how to slow their hectic pace and relax. According to your concerned sisters your life revolves around your graphic art shop. They're giving you a two-week, all-expenses-paid vacation at my ranch."

"What!" J.T. exploded angrily. "I don't want or need a two-week, all-expenses-paid vacation!"

Moriah grinned at him, undaunted by his booming voice and erupting temper. "Oh, and by the way, Kim and Lisa said to tell you happy birthday."

"Birthday?" J.T. parroted. Well, damn. Sunday *was* his birthday, come to think of it. He'd been so intensely focused on creating a spectacular Web site for his new client that he'd forgotten. But birthday or not, he wasn't spending the next two weeks at some ranch in the boon-docks that was run by this all too cheery, wild-driving female.

"Stop the damn car and turn it around," J.T. ordered brusquely. "I don't have time for a forced vacation. I have work to do and a business to run."

"Everything is going to be fine, Jake—"

"J.T.," he growled in correction.

"Just calm down," she soothed him. "I'm the rec-reation director at the ranch and I've been trained in stress management. I can tell that you're entirely too tense."

"Maybe I wouldn't be so tense if you'd slow this car down!"

Smiling in amusement—at his expense, he had no doubt—Moriah decreased her speed. "There now, Jake. Happy?"

"Not particularly," he said, and scowled.

"I understand that you're feeling a little testy. Stress does that to a person. After you kick back and relax for a few days you're going to be amazed how refreshed and rejuvenated you feel."

He glared thunderclouds on her sunny smile. "I am as relaxed as I ever intend to get!"

Her carefree laughter was getting on the one good nerve he had left. "Your voice is rising, Jake," she pointed out calmly.

"Well, so is my temper!" he all but shouted. "I have a business to run. My employees won't take work seri-ously if I'm not there to keep their noses to the grind-stone. I have no intention of allowing my shop to go down the toilet."

"But if you don't take time to get back in touch with your inner self and break your rigid routine, you'll be too stressed out to run your business effectively,'' Moriah said reasonably. ''You might find yourself snapping impatiently at your clients or employees. That certainly wouldn't be good for business, now would it?''

''My *inner self?*'' J.T. snorted derisively at that. ''My *rigid routine?*''

''Yes, let's start with that,'' Moriah suggested as she hung a sharp right turn and zoomed down a gravel road, taking J.T. farther into the outback of Oklahoma's wooded hill country. ''You've become a creature of habit and you've forgotten how to sit back and enjoy life.''

''I most certainly have not,'' he snapped in fierce denial. ''I know how to relax as well as the next person.''

''Really?'' she challenged, flashing him another of those annoyingly captivating smiles. ''Then let me ask you a few questions.''

''Hell, I didn't know there would be a test. Do I get time to study?''

Moriah chuckled in amusement, though he was striving for snide and sarcastic. But apparently nothing irritated Miss Rebecca of Sunnybrook Farm. It made him want to try harder to tick her off.

''What time do you get up every morning?'' she asked.

''Six o'clock. Is that a problem?'' he said defiantly.

''Only if you do it every single morning. Do you work on your business projects before you leave for your office?''

''Yes,'' he muttered grudgingly.

''Do you wake up at night, and also notice at various times of the day—like now—that you're gritting your teeth and have to force yourself to unclamp your jaw?

Do you find yourself tensely knotting your fists—like you are now—and have to tell yourself to unclench?''

J.T. glowered at her as he uncurled his knotted fists and slackened his jaw, but he refused to reply. Okay, so he was a little tense. Who wasn't?

"Do you eat breakfast?"

"Yes, at 7:42 a.m. I use the drive-through window at the doughnut shop to pick up coffee and a cinnamon twist. So you see, I do take time for breakfast," he assured her flippantly.

"Cinnamon twist and coffee every morning of the week? No deviation from routine? No variation of food whatsoever? You sound pretty predictable, Jake," she said as she tossed him a knowing smile.

Uh-oh, J.T. could see where this line of questioning was headed. Moriah was trying to point out that he was a stickler for a strict schedule. Well, so what if he was? When a man ran a business that was as successful as J.T.'s had been the past ten years, he had to organize his time wisely and follow a structured routine. Otherwise, he'd never get anything done—and he had a helluva lot to do, too.

"So…you arrive at your office and go right to work, I presume. What time is your lunch break, Jake?"

He shifted uneasily in the bucket seat. He didn't bother with a lunch break. Hadn't bothered in years, he suddenly recalled. But he sure as hell wasn't going to tell her that!

"I have a gourmet meal catered around high noon," he lied without compunction.

She shot him a glance that indicated she didn't believe him. So, what did he care? He *didn't* care, he assured himself. And furthermore, she wasn't going to get another straight answer from him. He wasn't going to give her the ammunition to analyze him to death.

"You exit your shop at six p.m. and drive home—except for today when your sisters purposely let the air out of your tires and asked me to personally escort you to the resort," she continued.

J.T. gnashed his teeth. His kid sisters were definitely going to pay for having him shanghaied. Damn it, he'd made one personal sacrifice after another for them for years on end. He'd cared for them, provided for them and consoled them after their parents died unexpectedly in a boating accident during a vacation. The tragedy had changed the entire course of his family's life, not to mention the excessive pressure put on him to assume full responsibility for Kim and Lisa.

"So, Jake, what do you do every day when you get home from work?" she prompted when he lingered too long in thought.

J.T. was really getting PO'd at the rapid-fire questions, with the entire turn of events that left him Miss Vivacious's prisoner in this speeding vehicle. Although he did follow a monotonous diet of TV dinners and canned food, he did jog, pump iron and then work on his business accounts in the evening. But he wasn't going to confide that he ate frozen chicken teriyaki on Monday and canned spaghetti and meatballs on Tuesday—and so on—to Moriah. In fact, he wasn't going to tell her the truth about himself or his daily habits because it was none of her business.

"I enjoy fabulous meals prepared by my housekeeper and cook. Her name is Stella," he said, improvising as he went along.

"Mmm," was all she said in response. He couldn't

tell for sure, but he thought Moriah had swallowed a snicker.

"Then I shower and change before I pick up one of my dates," he said, weaving a fairy tale of lies that would throw Moriah off track.

"You date a lot then?" she asked, eyes twinkling, lips twitching.

"Continuously," he said with a nonchalant flick of his wrist. "Different woman every night of the week. Variety is the spice of life, I always say."

"And what do you and your dates do for entertainment?" she inquired as she veered down another gravel road that circled around the steep hillsides, taking him deeper into the middle of nowhere.

"We have sex," J.T. told her outrageously. "Lots and lots of sex. Isn't that the best form of relaxation for stressed-out businessmen like me?"

He really knocked her for a loop, he thought triumphantly. Her bewitching smile faltered and she cleared her throat. J.T. was so enormously pleased that he'd managed to rattle his abductor that he pushed the tall tale to the limit. "Really kinky sex. Erotic sex. I love sex. The more the better. It recharges my battery, so to speak."

She made a strangled sound and kept her eyes on the road. "Interesting," she tweeted.

"Exceptionally interesting. After all that heavy breathing and wild, mind-numbing sex I usually soak in my hot tub for a half hour." He'd never taken time to soak in a hot tub in his life, truth be told. And the truth wouldn't be told to Moriah.

"And what do you think about when you allow your mind to wander, Jake?"

He thought about his accounts every spare minute of

the day, but he'd rather fire a couple of bullet holes into his foot than tell her because, sure as shootin', she'd make something of it. "I think of unique places and inventive ways to have sex. I try not to use the same position twice."

J.T. mentally patted himself on the back when Moriah's face turned a fascinating shade of pink. This, by damn, should teach her not to pry into his personal life. He did *not* need stress management. He did *not* need to relax and he damn sure did *not* need a two-week vacation out here in nowhereville! His sisters should have their heads examined for scheming against him, damn it!

"Ah, here we are," Moriah commented a few minutes later.

J.T. glanced out the window to survey ten, carbon-copy log cabins that were tucked beneath the canopy of shady cottonwood, elm and cedar trees. The resort was nestled beside a meandering river in a spacious valley between the rolling hills. A large stone-and-timber lodge sat in the middle of the well-manicured compound. A bunkhouse-style apartment complex sat off to the north side. A monstrous stable was butted up against a nearby hill.

The ranch was a cross between an isolated mountain retreat and the palatial plantations he'd visited as a kid during family vacations in Louisiana and Mississippi. J.T. did admit the area was panoramic and serene, but it definitely wasn't the kind of place J. T. Prescott wanted to waste time. And this was unquestionably a waste of his valuable time. He had things to do and he had no intention of doing them here—especially under the supervision of Miss Cheery and Chipper! The way he had it figured, if he smarted off often enough and put up plenty of belligerent resistance, Moriah would write him off as a lost cause and take him back to town so he could get back to doing what he did best—working relentlessly.

That was his plan and he was sticking with it.

"I'll introduce you to the staff before I show you to your cabin," she said as she bounded from the SUV.

J.T. frowned, wondering if Moriah always exuded this much bubbling energy and enthusiasm or if she put on an act for her stressed-out guests. His lips curled in objection when Moriah carelessly scooped his belongings off the back seat and made a beeline for the gargantuan lodge.

"I'll take those," he insisted. He followed quickly on her heels, willfully ignoring the hypnotic sway of curvy hips encased in trim-fitting red cotton. Instead, he concentrated on his mission of retrieving his delicate electronic equipment and floppy disks.

"No, sorry, Jake," she told him with another one of those megawatt smiles that he was really beginning to despise. "All electronic devices and briefcases are checked at the registration desk. Oh, by the way, I'll need your cell phone."

"Why? Are you planning on making international calls and charging them to my account?" he asked caustically.

"No, I'm cutting you off from civilization so you won't have contact with the world that's placed excessive stress on your life and your inner self."

J.T. screeched to a halt and glared at her good and hard. "No, you will not," he said firmly. "I make a habit of calling my sisters three days a week and this is one of those days."

"Your sisters are married and on their own," she reminded him gently.

"Yes, and I paid for their weddings and walked them down the aisle," he informed her tartly. "They're the two reliable relationships in my life and I will call my family if I feel like it!"

Moriah squared off against him, her smile still intact. Why was he not surprised? "Your sisters know exactly where you are and what you will be doing for the next two weeks. Furthermore, you're here to break habits." She outstretched her hand, palm up. "Give me the phone, Jake."

"The name is J.T." He sneered at her.

"I told you that sounds too stuffy and businesslike, *Jake,*" she repeated emphatically.

Their gazes locked and clashed. Jake was accustomed to giving orders and having them executed quickly. But Moriah, apparently, was accustomed to getting her way, too, especially while she was on her own turf. For the first time in forever, he felt his confidence waver. That determined look on Moriah's face indicated she wasn't the pushover he hoped she'd be.

"Don't make me send Tom Stevens out here to disarm you of your sacred phone."

J.T. smirked at the threat and drew himself up to his most imposing and intimidating stature. "Tom and whose army is going to confiscate my state-of-the-art cell phone?"

To his dismay, Moriah let loose with a sharp whistle that blasted his eardrums. Immediately thereafter a big brawny, muscle-bound hulk—who had a monobrow stretching over his deep-set hazel eyes, and was built like a professional linebacker—appeared in the doorway of the lodge.

"Trouble, Mori?" Tom asked as he crossed his brawny arms over his buffalo-size chest and took J.T.'s measure through a narrowed gaze.

"Am I having trouble, Jake?" she asked all too sweetly.

J.T. considered his options and decided he didn't have any. Damn it to hell! Muttering begrudgingly, he fished his cell phone from his suit pocket and slapped it into Moriah's outstretched hand. He should've known Miss Smiley would have plenty of muscle to back up her demands.

Moriah tucked the phone into the pocket of her shorts, then grinned at Tom Stevens. "This is Jake Prescott," she introduced. "Tom is our masseuse and weight trainer—"

"And your hired muscle," J.T. finished for her. "Gee, I thought the idea here was to avoid stress, not get me all tensed up thinking I'll have a serious fight on my hands if I don't meekly comply with your unreasonable demands."

Tom grinned, displaying a missing front tooth. J.T. would hate to meet the burly SOB who knocked out Tom's teeth.

"Nice to meet you, Jake. Come 'round and see me about a massage when you get settled in."

"Sure, Tom. Looking forward to it like you wouldn't believe."

He was looking forward to nothing of the kind!

When Tom disappeared back inside, Moriah smiled good-naturedly at J.T. He gnashed his teeth.

"It's not unusual for our guests to suffer electronic-gadget and caffeine-buzz withdrawal the first few days, but it won't be long before you realize there's life beyond your regular routine in the business world. You'll do fine here, Jake.''

Although he'd been defeated, he couldn't resist tossing a sarcastic rejoinder to soothe his offended pride. ''Yeah, I'll do fine as long as I get my daily recommended dose of sex.'' He checked his watch, hoping she wouldn't take *it* away from him, too. ''What time can I expect Lolita to show up at my cabin to scratch my daily sexual itch? I'd hate for her to come by during my usual yoga meditation session and deep breathing exercises.''

''Sorry, no Lolita,'' she informed him as she led the way into the lobby of the lodge. ''Maybe our cook, Anna Jefferies, will accommodate you. You can ask her.''

Anna Jefferies introduced herself to Jake a moment after he strode in the door. The stout, curly-chestnut-haired woman looked to be in her late forties. Judging by her leathery skin and wrinkled features, she'd spent a great deal of her life outdoors. She offered him a steaming cup of herbal tea and butter cookies while Moriah stashed his electronic devices in the safe behind the registration desk. J.T. didn't ask Anna for sex, of course, although Anna's conventional style of dress—a cream-colored blouse and faded blue jeans—held more appeal than Moriah's loud attire.

When he saw Moriah's lips twitching as her gaze bounced back and forth between him and Anna, J.T. muttered under his breath. Damn, he'd like to wipe that smile off Miss Chipper's lips—or kiss it off…. J.T. jerked upright so quickly he nearly spilled hot tea down the front of his white shirt.

Where the hell had that ridiculous thought come from? Oh sure, he found Moriah Randell attractive, even if he didn't approve of her bright clothing, her gaudy red fingernails, those huge hoop earrings and clattering bracelets. But, under no circumstances was he going to develop an interest in a woman who was his complete opposite during his *two-day* stay in the Oklahoma outback. *Two days,* he told himself resolutely, and then he was outta here!

"C'mon, Jake, I'll introduce you to the golf course manager and stable manager," Anna said, latching on to his arm to drag him along behind her. "Everybody's just finishing up supper. Moriah will bring your meal to your cabin since you arrived late."

While Anna shoveled Jake forward to make the acquaintance of the staff, Moriah filled out paperwork then grabbed the key to the available cabin. Her gaze drifted over the six-foot-two-inch, raven-haired man who'd given her a bad time during the hour drive to the resort. Sex, sex and more sex indeed, she mused, chuckling. She'd never heard such a crock of malarkey from one of her guests.

Of course, most of her guests came willingly, after a panic attack or some physical ailment that alerted them to their high-level stress. Jake Prescott, the King of Denial, had to be deceived into his two-week stay. His sisters were firmly convinced that Jake would never agree to come here on his own accord.

Moriah shook her head at the outrageous exaggerations Jake had concocted when she tried to make him aware that he'd become stuck in the rut of working nonstop without time off for relaxation. She didn't believe that nonsense for a minute because J.T.'s sisters had filled her in completely.

According to Kim and Lisa, their older brother had become entrenched in routine and went through each day like a programmed robot. He left his house at precisely the same time each morning, stopped for a pastry and coffee, worked through the lunch hour, then returned home with a briefcase full of work projects. He had no social life worth mentioning. The only dates on his calendar were the ones his concerned sisters set up for him in attempt to alter his monotonous lifestyle.

Moriah was sure Jake would be a hard-core case that demanded extra time and effort. He refused to open up to her, refused to admit he led a mundane, predictable life that was devoid of entertainment and pleasure. Of course, the first difficulty for Jake to overcome was *admitting* he had a problem that needed to be addressed. Considering the resistance he raised, it could take a week for him to realize he needed to kick back and relax.

It might be a very long week, Moriah predicted.

Moriah appraised her new guest while he glanced around the spacious dining room. Black suit, white shirt, and nondescript black tie. According to his sisters, Jake had a closet full of black suits and white shirts. They were his standard business uniform—no deviation allowed. No bright, cheerful colors to spice up his wardrobe. Amazing, since Jake was touted as a highly creative design wizard.

Obviously, there was an interesting, unique man trapped inside that black suit. Moriah wondered if he would emerge in two weeks. Jake was definitely going to be a challenge, considering his tendency toward the stubborn and contrary. But she'd find a way to teach him to relax and enjoy his vacation.

Again, her astute gaze flooded over his lean physique and eye-catching profile. Jake Prescott wasn't classically handsome. His features were a mite sharp and defined, and his displeased frown could be quite severe. She ought to know, having been on the wrong side of his displeasure during the long drive.

Moriah guessed Native American blood ran through his veins. His sisters bore a similar resemblance with their dark complexion and high cheekbones. Three peas from the same pod, and a family devoted to each other to boot, Moriah mused. Kim and Lisa were determined to save their beloved brother from his monotonous life, and Moriah was being well-paid to ensure the transformation took place—beginning now.

"Jake! Are you ready to settle into your cabin?" she called out to him.

He half-turned to stare down his nose at her. Yep, she definitely had her work cut out for her, she decided as she mustered another cheery smile to counter his aggravated frown.

2

MORIAH MOTIONED for Jake to follow her outside. When she stopped by the sport-utility vehicle to retrieve the suitcase he hovered over her, all but breathing down her neck.

"What's that?" he questioned grouchily.

"Your sisters packed casual clothes for you," she reported, handing him the luggage.

Moriah bit back a giggle when he stared at the baggage as if it were a live cobra. The reality that he *was* staying and that he needed several changes of clothes obviously hit him full force. The poor man was in for a shock when she left him at his cabin with his suitcase of casual clothes and nothing but free time on his hands. She sincerely hoped he didn't freak out.

Jake hefted up the luggage and tossed her a smirk. "It's a relief to hear you didn't pack for me. I wouldn't look worth a damn if I were impersonating a flag."

Another cheap shot about her attire, she noted. If he thought trouncing on her feelings would get him out of here sooner then he was mistaken. She had her reasons for dressing colorfully, not that it was any of his business why she did it.

"Your sisters packed jeans and bland-tan and hohum-green chambray shirts," she informed him. "I believe the term they used when referring to you was 'a drab dresser'."

He glanced sharply at her and frowned. "I believe the correct terms are *conventional* for me and *outrageously flamboyant* for you."

Moriah shrugged lackadaisically as she made the three-hundred-yard hike to cabin number seven. "Outside dressing is really of no concern here at Triple R," she assured him. "We aren't the least bit superficial and we're more interested in acknowledging and being kind to the true, inner self."

He snorted at that. He was nothing if not predictable, Moriah thought.

"So, who actually owns this place?" he asked, falling into step just enough ahead of her to indicate he refused to leave the impression he was being led around. "Some stressed-out corporate executive who needs an occasional hiatus to revive those inner juices you keep harping about?"

"No, I own the place," she informed him.

"You?" He glanced down at her. "You can't be over twenty-five. Is Daddy's money paying for this resort?"

"Actually I inherited the land when my mother died. My dad had a stroke three years ago because he worked constantly." She sent him a pointed glance, then a smile. "Dad lives in the apartment beside mine behind the lodge. I'm thirty, by the way, not twenty-five, but thank you for the compliment."

"It wasn't meant to be one," he didn't fail to remark.

Moriah grinned at him. "Really? I was so hoping you'd have one nice thing to say about me."

Before she could unlock the cabin door, Jake slapped a big hand on the doorjamb and stared her squarely in the eye. His expression was solemn, his onyx eyes intense. "We better get something straight from the get-go. I have no intention of being reformed by you or big

brawny Tom Stevens, or stout Anna Jefferies or the rest
of your staff. I like my life dandy-fine, thank you very
much. How about if you give my well-meaning but misdirected kid sisters their money back and save yourself
the wasted effort of cramming this compulsory R-and-R
down my throat? In case you haven't figured it out yet—
and, smart lady that you are, I'm sure you have—I'm
not planning to cooperate. In fact, I plan to be anything
but cooperative.''

Moriah nodded in mock seriousness as she stabbed
the key into the lock. ''I understand completely and I
realize this vacation will cramp your voracious and
kinky sex life. But the contract states there will be no
refunds, except in the event that you die of boredom.''
She grinned at his ferocious scowl. ''Then, of course,
your sisters will be cheerfully reimbursed.''

''Real cute, Miss Chipper,'' he muttered sarcastically.

''A compliment! Thank you kindly, Mr. Predictable,''
she gushed as she shouldered through the doorway.

''Good God…'' Jake halted on the threshold, his verbal sparring obviously forgotten. He stared at the interior
of the cabin in such frantic horror that Moriah nearly
burst out laughing at his reaction. ''There's no TV, no
radio, no phone, no…'' His voice gave out as his goggle-
eyed gaze circled the room to appraise the overstuffed,
sprawl-all-over-me couch and come-here-and-let-me-
rub-you-all-over massage recliner. Then his astounded
gaze leaped to the Murphy bed that folded down from
the cedar-paneled walls.

Moriah watched his comical reaction to the simply
furnished room that was equipped with soothing music,
designed to relax tense guests, and decorated with the
peaceful landscape paintings that depicted the timeless
essence of snow-covered mountains, a rippling seashore

and a rolling prairie. Most of her guests suffered minimal culture shock when they first arrived at the resort, but Jake reacted noticeably and made no attempt whatsoever to disguise his disapproval. Clearly, electronic-gadget withdrawal had hit him hard and fast.

He gaped at her, as if he'd been sentenced to two weeks in torturous hell. "You can't be serious!" he choked out. "What the devil am I supposed to do with myself in this cabin for two tormenting weeks? And don't give me that crap about tuning in to my inner self again or I'll have to strangle you!"

He looked so thunderstruck and dismayed that she reflexively reached out to give him a consoling pat on the arm. Moriah was astonished at the tension pulsing through him. Lord, the poor man had no idea how desperately he needed to escape the rat race.

"Everything is going to be fine, Jake. You aren't going to self-destruct in this unfamiliar environment, I promise."

"Yeah, right. I'm self-destructing as we speak," he said, and snorted.

"We have several activities scheduled to make your transition easier. We have a nine-hole golf course and the nearby river provides excellent fishing. There's horseback riding, a hiking trail, indoor swimming, canoeing, paddleboating, a spacious hot tub and horseshoe games."

He wrenched his arm free from her light grasp and then glowered laser beams at her. "I haven't played golf in ten years. I'm not going to watch a damn cork bob on the river while trying to catch a blasted fish. I have a pool in my apartment complex if I want to use it. I haven't ridden a horse since I was a kid, which is fine by me. And there's no way in hell that I'm taking up the game of horseshoes unless I can pitch them around your neck!''

His voice rose to a shout. Moriah winced and cautioned herself not to lose her temper. None of her other guests put up this kind of fuss. Jake had been goading her for nearly two hours, but that didn't matter. She wasn't going to let him rile her, she promised herself fiercely.

In a burst of bad temper Jake lurched around and stalked over to the designated kitchen area in the far corner. ''Great,'' he muttered sourly. ''Three feet of cabinet and counter space, plus a piddly little sink.'' He jerked open a drawer, then shot her another seething glance. ''What? No knife so I can slit my wrists and end this torture?'' He hitched his thumb toward the small bathroom, then leveled her with another glare. ''No soap-on-a-rope so I can hang myself, I suppose?''

She tried out another encouraging smile on him, not that it did a whit of good. If anything, it seemed to infuriate him further. Moriah was pretty sure Jake held her personally accountable for the anger simmering through him. ''No knives or ropes, but I do have a puppy to keep you company. Pets have a calming influence on people.''

He gave her one of those don't-even-think-about-it glowers before she pivoted to intercept Chester Gray, the golf course manager and groundskeeper, who strode up the wooden porch with the pooch cradled in his arms.

''Thanks, Chester,'' she murmured as she cuddled the pup against her chest.

''You bet, Mori. Tell Jake the movie starts in forty-five minutes and Anna has his supper tray heated.''

Scratching behind the pup's ear, Moriah pivoted to face Jake who growled ferociously. The puppy huddled fearfully in her arms.

"You expect me to take care of that spitwad of a dog?" he muttered crossly. "Think again, my dear Mo. You don't mind if I call you Mo, do you? It's not nearly as stuffy and sophisticated as Moriah."

Leave it to Jake to throw her words in her face. She angled her head and appraised the frown that caused his thick brows to form a V over his glittering obsidian eyes. "You really aren't taking this well, are you?"

"Gee, ya think?" he said, then snorted. "How many more times do I have to express my displeasure before you get it through your dense blond head that I want no part of this stress management crapola!"

Moriah willfully overlooked the dumb-blonde wisecrack, giving it the lack of recognition it deserved, and scratched beneath the puppy's chin. "As I was saying," she went on determinedly, "we take in the unwanted dogs from the animal shelter in town to serve as companions for our guests. According to statistics, animals have a soothing effect on—"

He waved her off with an impatient flick of his wrist. "Don't start with me. I *don't* want a dog. I *don't* want to be here. Do you hear me?"

Moriah smiled bravely in the face of his booming tirade. "Yes I do, but I'm not sure my guest in cabin number one heard you loud and clear."

He bared his teeth and flashed her the queen mother of all glares. She smiled—with considerable effort. "The dog food and bowls are on the floor of the closet. The pup is housebroken."

"Well, *I'm* not," he smarted off.

Moriah bit back a grin, then glanced sideways to see Anna Jefferies ambling up the stone walkway. "Ah, here comes supper. Anna must've given up on me."

"Supper?" he said caustically. "I figured Spitwad

and I were supposed to rough it tonight and share the dog food.''

Moriah set the pup on the floor and exited to take the tray Anna held out to her.

''I could hear him yelling at two hundred yards,'' Anna murmured, grinning. ''He's going to take special effort, I'd say.''

''He'll be fine once he calms down and accepts his fate.'' She hoped.

When Anna reversed direction and hiked off, Moriah carried the covered tray inside and set it on the small drop-leaf table. ''Here's your supper, Jake.''

''Ah, good. A reason to live. For a while there, I wasn't sure there was one.''

She ignored his wiseass remarks. She predicted she'd be doing a lot of that during his two-week stay. ''We'll be expecting you to join us for the movie this evening. You can meet the other guests.''

''And you can hold your breath waiting for me to show up,'' he snapped.

Moriah did her best to ignore his hostility—again. ''We don't watch highly intense adventure movies at the resort. Just lighthearted comedies and such.''

''No trashy porno?'' he asked. ''No, of course not. What was I thinking? We wouldn't want to get all these maxed-out businessmen fired up, would we?''

''No, we wouldn't,'' she agreed. ''It might upset the inner self.''

''You can take your psychobabble and stick it where the sun—''

Moriah promptly shut the door before he finished voicing his insult. Rightfully, she should be annoyed with her belligerent guest. Instead, she found him amusing, entertaining and very different from her older guests. She knew Jake was fighting back the only way he knew how—by lashing out at her in frustration.

And maybe there was a little fear involved here, too, she mused pensively. Fear of the unknown and the unfamiliar. Jake was also suffering from separation anxiety from his predictable life and from his close association with his sisters.

According to Kim and Lisa, Jake had devoted his life to raising them and making scads of money to provide for them. He'd taken family responsibility seriously and it led him into such a deep rut that he couldn't see his way out. Asking Jake to change his ways made him uncomfortable and defensive. Moriah understood that, even if Jake refused to acknowledge that he was feeling anything except annoyance.

Somehow or another, she was going to get through to this man. She was going to teach him how to relax, how to take life at a more leisurely pace, how to laugh and smile. The man took himself, and life, entirely too seriously. Jake Prescott wasn't the hopeless cause he wanted her to think he was. He simply had to be retrained to take a different approach to life.

If Jake didn't cooperate she might have to resort to konking him over the head and *knocking* some sense into him. Moriah grinned mischievously. That idea held tremendous appeal at the moment.

JAKE STARED DOWN at the fuzzball of a dog that sniffed at his shoes. The multicolored, pint-size mutt appeared to be a cross between a frizzy-haired miniature poodle, a Pekingese, a Chihuahua and who knew what else. The mutt was butt-ugly.

Sighing audibly, Jake glanced around the efficiency cabin once again, finding nothing comforting or appeal-

ing to him. What the sweet loving hell was he going to
do with himself out here in the boondocks? Already the
index finger of his right hand felt empty without a computer mouse resting beneath it. In addition, there was no
phone to call his demented sisters and rake them over
live coals for this horrendous betrayal. What the hell
were those two thinking? They weren't thinking, he decided. Of all the lamebrain ideas they'd ever concocted
over the years this topped the list!

Muttering several foul expletives, Jake plunked down
on the wooden chair to examine his evening rations. A
tantalizing aroma filled his nostrils as he uncovered the
plate that was heaping with smoked ribs, a baked potato,
corn on the cob and vanilla pudding. Until now, he'd
been too upset to realize he was starving. Jake plucked
up a sparerib and sighed in culinary anticipation. Anna
Jefferies might look like the female version of an army
drill sergeant but she could damn sure cook, he decided
at first bite.

Jake polished off the first melt-in-your-mouth sparerib, then glanced down to see the mutt staring hopefully
at him. "Yeah, well, that's all I figured a little beggar
like you would be good for anyway." He handed the
spitwad of a dog a chunk of meat. The mutt practically
grinned as he trotted across the tile to plop down on the
rug beside the sink. Jake watched the mutt chew his food
happily.

While Jake ate his meal, he pondered this pointless
hiatus. In the first place, he didn't need stress reduction.
No way, no how. He'd never suffered an anxiety attack.
Okay, so he did endure throbbing headaches, eyestrain,
shoulder strain and a few other job-related ailments, but
that went with the territory. Jogging and pumping iron
usually relieved his tension.

Secondly, who did that thirty-year-old bombshell think she was? A wanna-be psychologist? The next Dr. Freud? The way Jake saw it, Moriah was only colorful, attractive scenery at this haunt in the woods. For sure, she hadn't been able to pry useful information from him during their road trip. He hadn't told her a damn thing she could use to pick him apart and readjust his lifestyle—and that's the way it would stay.

Having finished the delicious meal, Jake opened his suitcase to see what his sisters had packed for him. Sure enough, there was an array of chambray shirts in muted colors, plus several pairs of prewashed jeans, shorts and T-shirts. Jake's eyes nearly popped from their sockets when he noticed the new string bikini briefs—in assorted bold colors and wild prints—that his ornery sisters had purchased for him. Hell! He favored the garden variety of white cotton underwear, not these skimpy scraps of fabric. The prospect of his kid sisters buying him this racy underwear made him cringe. Jeez!

Muttering and snarling in frustration, Jake shed his suit and donned a T-shirt, shorts and running shoes. He had no problem with casual clothes—the bikini briefs he wasn't so sure about—but he wasn't going to tramp over to the lodge to watch a flick with the old fogies from the other cabins. Furthermore, he was in no mood to see Moriah again. He was keeping his distance from the walking American flag. He wasn't sure why he felt it imperative to avoid her as much as possible, but some inner voice—Good gad! He was starting to sound like her already—kept warning him to watch his step with her. He was too reactionary around her.

Besides that, he didn't like blue-eyed blondes on general principle. His two-timing ex-fiancée was a blue-eyed blonde, so that was one strike against Moriah. Then there was the fact that Moriah dressed too outrageously for Jake's sedate tastes. He preferred subtle and subdued. Moriah Randell was one of those here-I-come-ready-or-not, in-your-face kind of females. Plus, she was nagging him to get in touch with his inner self—whatever good *that* was supposed to do. She wanted him to change his perfected routine and develop a carefree approach to life.

Bull! It was all a bunch of bull!

"Ain't happenin'," Jake told himself resolutely. He may be stuck here for two hellish weeks—an eternity as far as he was concerned—rather than two days, but nobody was messing with his attitude. It worked for him and he wasn't changing his ways at this late date.

When his parents died he'd moved back home to give Kim and Lisa the extra attention, security, guidance and support that a fourteen-year-old and sixteen-year-old needed at such a crucial time. He'd made a solemn commitment to his family and he'd stuck to it for ten years. It had cost him a fiancée and a social life. Hell, you couldn't bring home a babe and fool around when you had two impressionable teenage sisters underfoot who were trying to cope with a devastating loss, could you? How insensitive would that have been?

Oh sure, Jake had promised himself that once he raised his kid sisters he'd let loose and enjoy himself for a couple of years. But working and riding herd over his sisters had become such an ingrained habit that he never got around to breaking it.

Jake had occupied his time and mind by getting his graphic design shop up and running. He'd had more clients than he knew what to do with before he knew it. So what was wrong with that? He'd taken on the responsibility of his sisters and become financially and professionally successful. Was that a crime? Around

Triple R it was, apparently, he mused as he shoved his foot into the sneakers his sisters packed for him. If Moriah had her way, Jake would be strolling around the wooded hills, picking wildflowers and meditating. Not very damn likely!

Yeah, okay, so maybe he was transferring his frustration about the situation, and this feeling of betrayal to Moriah, when it rightfully should be vented on his sisters. But his sisters weren't within earshot—and he couldn't get his mitts on a damn phone to chew them down one side and up the other!

It was better this way, Jake convinced himself. Directing his irritation at Moriah was the safe thing to do. Fact was that, despite her vivid blue eyes and thick blond hair, despite her shockingly loud clothes and those aggravating smiles that nothing he said could affect, he was a teensy-weensy bit attracted to her.

A reluctant smile pursed his lips, remembering how her cheery smile had faltered when he kept yammering on and on about using sex, sex and more sex as a remedy to reduce stress. He'd rattled her, he knew. It was the most fun he'd had all day. Maybe all week…all month…aw, hell!

The disturbing thought that enjoyment wasn't an integral part of his everyday life put Jake on his feet and had him moving toward the cabin door. "C'mon, Spitwad," he commanded as he strode onto the porch. "Time to go jogging. And you better keep up or I'll leave you out in the woods to find your way home. Or get eaten by a bear—whichever."

The mutt stared at him, then glanced at the half-eaten chunk of meat between his front paws.

"If I've gotta hang out here in the boonies, then

you've gotta hang out with me, Fuzzball," Jake told the mutt. "Get off your lazy butt and let's go."

The pup defied him and went back to gnawing on the meat.

Jake stamped over to snatch the food away, tucked it in a napkin and then crammed it into his shirt pocket. Left with nothing else to do, the pup followed at Jake's heels.

Left with nothing else to do, Jake thought as he jogged along the footpath that wound through the hills. Boy, if that didn't just about say it all!

MORIAH HAD JUST returned to the lobby after chatting with the guest in cabin number three, when a baritone roar gushed through the open window. She had a pretty good idea who let out that booming shout. She made a beeline for cabin number seven.

Before she got within a hundred yards of the cabin the offensive smell of skunk closed in around her. Moriah covered the lower portion of her face with her hand, then glanced this way and that.

"Jake?" she called to the darkness at large.

"Over here, damn it to hell!" he bellowed like an outraged moose.

Moriah veered toward the hiking path, relying on the golden shaft of light that streamed through the cabin windows. She heard the pup's abrupt yip and Jake's muttered growl.

"C'mere, you idiotic mutt!" he snarled.

The bushes shook, then Jake, clutching the little pooch like a football, came into view. Moriah reflexively stepped back several paces when the foul odor grew more potent.

"What happened?" she asked without daring to take a breath.

"Spitwad thinks he's a damn bloodhound," Jake muttered irritably. "He flushed out a damn skunk and we both suffered a direct hit. You'll have to go into my cabin and fetch some clean clothes for me."

It wasn't a request, she noted. It was a direct order. She suspected Jake was accustomed to barking orders, which was probably why he balked and brooded after being forced to do as he was told at the resort.

"There's no way that I'm going to enter my cabin in these smelly clothes," he grumbled. "The whole place will stink to high heaven. I'll have to bathe in the river first."

"I'll be right back with clean clothes," she said as she whipped around and sprinted to the cabin.

Hurriedly, Moriah grabbed a blasé-brown shirt and blue jeans. She rifled through the luggage to locate underwear. Her sense of urgency screeched to a halt when she spotted the sexy bikini briefs. Moriah snickered right out loud, envisioning Jake prancing around in this leopard-print underwear—and nothing else....

Moriah quashed the tantalizing vision and stifled the alarming thought immediately. It shocked her to no end that she could so easily imagine what Jake would look like in this leopard-print garment. It also unsettled her to the extreme to realize that the initial attraction she'd felt—and tried to suppress—had come through for the second time today. Well, okay, she corrected grudgingly, for the fourth or fifth time today.

Of course, nothing would come of this flare-up of physical awareness, she reminded herself. She had no intention of getting personally involved with any of her guests. Most of the businessmen—and the occasional female executive—who came to her resort were in their sixties, so the problem hadn't actually arisen.

And then along came Jake, she mused as she headed toward the door, with his jeans and shirt tucked under her arm and those skimpy leopard-print briefs hooked over her index finger.

Okay, Moriah, she told herself on her way across the front porch, *you aren't going to get involved with Jake for several reasons. Number one: it goes against your personal rules and regulations. Number two: Jake is an intense workaholic, who's allergic to the concept of free time, and you advocate a carefree lifestyle.* The list went on, but Moriah wasn't one for making lists. That was probably one of Jake's habits.

She and Jake viewed life from entirely opposite perspectives. No, she wouldn't become romantically involved with Jake because she'd learned the hard way that she wasn't good at relationships unless they were built on the need and dependence of the other party— like recreational director to guest, or daughter to ailing mother or father. She had accepted the fact that love was not going to play a dominant role in her life and that she could make her contribution to humanity by providing recreational activities and hobbies for her stressed-out guests.

However, that didn't mean she couldn't have a little fun with the blustering Jake Prescott, she decided as she twirled his bikini briefs around her forefinger. The man needed to lighten up and learn to laugh and smile occasionally. Moriah made a pact with herself, there and then, to ensure Jake did exactly that!

3

JAKE INWARDLY GROANED when Moriah sashayed toward him, twirling the ridiculous underwear around her finger and grinning mischievously. He also noticed Moriah had a naturally provocative saunter when she let her guard down. "That happens to be my sisters' idea of a joke," he was quick to inform her.

Moriah halted a safe distance away. Not that he blamed her. The stench surrounding him had to be mega-offensive. Of course, Jake's olfactory senses were in traumatic shock, so he couldn't smell much of anything at the moment.

"You realize, I'm sure," she said with an entirely different kind of smile than he was used to getting from her, "that knowing you wear leopard-print bikinis will make it difficult for me to take all your snarling and growling seriously from here on out, don't you?"

"I wasn't aware that you were taking me seriously before," Jake murmured distractedly. He stood there, studying Moriah's enticing profile, which was enhanced by the backwash of light streaming from his cabin windows. He wasn't sure at what precise moment he became intently aware of Moriah—probably the first time he piled into the vehicle with her—but he could easily detect the difference between her neutral smile and the impish grin she was wearing now. He wasn't sure what this new smile meant, but it was doing crazy things to his pulse.

Jake stiffened—especially in places that had no business whatsoever getting stiff—and battled his attraction to Moriah. "If you'll leave my clothes draped over a bush near the river I won't have to touch them until I rid myself of this offensive smell."

"Sure, be glad to," she said, still twirling his undies and grinning devilishly. "I'll show you the best place to bathe without worrying about stepping into an unseen hole and going under."

With Spitwad tucked securely under his arm, Jake followed a safe distance behind Moriah. He didn't know why he was being courteous. He shouldn't be. He should share this stench with her, just for spite.

"I'm not going to have to fight off alligators and snakes in here, am I? The skunk was enough excitement for one night."

"No, you should be relatively safe. Here you go, Jake." She gestured to the narrow footpath that led to the sandy bank. "Soak to your heart's content."

Jake squatted down to remove his sneakers, then walked into the river. Although the October evening was unseasonably warm, the cool water gave him the shivers and made Spitwad squirm for release, but Jake submerged the mutt, nonetheless. When he resurfaced, he released the pooch to paddle around in circles.

"Toss me your stinky clothes and I'll launder them for you," Moriah offered. "I have a surefire product that will eliminate the stench."

Jake peeled off his socks and shirt, then hurled them toward a bushy shrub.

"Now take off your pants," she said, snickering.

"This is not amusing," Jake muttered as he shed his shorts and briefs.

"From my standpoint it is," she replied as she set aside his clean clothes. "I don't usually chitchat with naked guests, but I'm making the exception with you. This is the perfect chance for you to try deep breathing. Fill your lungs, and then let your breath out slowly and try to relax."

Jake glowered at her as she perched on a boulder near the river. "And if I refuse to cooperate?" he challenged.

She shrugged nonchalantly. "Then I take your clean clothes, your dirty clothes, your cabin key and leave you to prance around naked. Now breathe, Jake."

Begrudgingly, he breathed in the evening air and slowly exhaled. "There. Finished. Breathing exercises over. Go away, Mo."

She shook her head. Her golden hair glowed like a halo in the moonlight. Jake wondered how that thick mane would look if she set it free to flow over her shoulders and down her back. Damn but she was a pretty woman. He wished he hadn't noticed. Good thing he was waist deep in cold water. Otherwise, he might embarrass himself.

"I'm not going anywhere until we've spent quality time together," Moriah insisted. "Take another deep breath."

Muttering, Jake did as he was told. He scooped up the mutt to give the soggy animal a rest after swimming circular laps.

"The problem with developing a structured routine is that we don't take time off to enjoy life's simple pleasures," she commented. "We have to be impulsive occasionally. We have to figure out what makes us happy and reward ourselves with enjoyable pursuits. What makes you happy, Jake?''

He thought about that for a moment. To his dismay, he couldn't think of anything other than checking on his sisters. Good gad!

''Difficult question?'' she asked gently. ''Obviously it's been too long since you really let loose to remember what you like to do for leisure and entertainment.''

''No, it hasn't,'' he said defensively. ''I told you I like sex, plenty of sex with a disgustingly large number of different women to appease my obsessive penchant for variety and change of pace. I'm a card-carrying sex-aholic.''

''You might as well know your sisters already informed me that your only dates are the ones they manipulate you into taking out.''

''And they'll pay dearly for talking out of school,'' he said, and scowled.

''Kim and Lisa want to help you. *I* want to help you find yourself.''

''I'm not lost. I know exactly where the hell I am and you can help most by leaving,'' he snapped. ''The water is cold and I'd like to get out!''

''I'll leave when you admit to me, and to yourself, that it's time to change your predictable, monotonous lifestyle and open your mind to developing a few hobbies.''

''Fine,'' he grumbled. ''I need a hobby. Are you happy now?''

''No, because you're patronizing me.''

Jake sighed irritably. He was cold, tired and in no mood for this compulsory stress-reducing session. ''Is this the way you impose your carefree philosophy on your guests? You drive them into the river and baptize them with your devil-may-care theories?''

''I advocate living life to its fullest, most promising potential. It's not the same as devil-may-care,'' she corrected pleasantly. ''Most of my guests have acknowledged their problem before they arrive. You, however, require more drastic measures to open your eyes and see the light.... I'll be around in the morning to take you horseback riding.''

''What time?'' he asked.

She grinned. ''We try to avoid schedules because we're here to break routines. We'll be getting together at various times of the day.''

Well, so much for accusing *her* of establishing a routine, he mused sourly.

''I'll be back later with a glass of warm milk before bedtime,'' she said, rising gracefully to her feet.

''I don't drink milk, warm or otherwise,'' he muttered stubbornly.

''Would you prefer a small glass of wine instead?''

''What I would prefer,'' he said through chattering teeth, ''is to get the hell out of the river and go home where I belong!''

Moriah strolled down the riverbank to face him directly. Her perpetual smile vanished, he noted. She stood with feet askance, arms crossed over her chest. Her stance indicated that she meant business. ''You aren't going anywhere until I find a way to push your fun button.''

''I don't have a fun button,'' he retorted.

''Oh, yes, you do. I'm making it my mission in life to find it and to push it—hard and often,'' she said very determinedly. ''We're going to find something here at the resort that you like to do and you're going to do it—cheerfully!''

"Cheerfully choking you has exceptional appeal," he couldn't resist saying.

"Well, at least there's something that makes you happy. That's a good place to start." She plucked up his soggy clothes. "Later, Jake."

When she walked away, Jake headed for shore, trying to ignore the nip of his conscience. He was being extraordinarily hard on Moriah, he knew, but it felt necessary for some reason. Something about that woman put him on the defensive and kept him there. He didn't want to like her...but he did. He didn't want to be attracted to her...but he was.

Certainly, nothing could come of his interest because it was a dead-end street. He had his responsibilities and she obviously had hers. Whatever he was feeling—and he sure as hell wasn't going to examine it too closely—was just physical. He'd done without sex longer than he cared to admit and Moriah sparked awareness in him, was all. All his yammering about sex had simply brought it to his attention and escalated his awareness.

Jake shrugged on his clothes and walked barefoot up the sandy path. "C'mon, Spitwad. We've had enough excitement for the night. Don't go sniffing out some other varmint."

The mutt shook himself off, then trotted obediently at Jake's heels. The instant Jake entered the cabin he headed for the shower and slathered his body with soap. After scrubbing himself squeaky clean, he wrapped a towel around his hips and strode off to retrieve the scandalous briefs his mischievous sisters packed for him.

Jake pulled up short when he saw Moriah hovering beside the door, a short glass of wine in hand and a shocked expression on her face. Her gaze drifted over his bare chest, skidded over the damp towel, then shot upward and a tinge of color blossomed in her cheeks. Well, well, Moriah wasn't quite as immune to him as he thought she was, he noted.

"Like what you see?" he asked when her gaze made another sweep of his scantily clad body. "Is this one of those Kodak moments? Too bad you didn't come armed with a camera."

She jerked upright, then met his amused gaze. "Sorry. I...um...I thought I'd g-given you enough time to shower and dress b-before...um...delivering your wine," she stammered, her face aflame. "When y-you didn't...um...answer m-my knock at the door, I... uh...wanted to make sure you hadn't done yourself bodily harm."

Clearly, she felt awkward and uncomfortable. Devilishly, he wondered what she'd do if he dropped the towel and reached for those candy-apple red bikini briefs. He really should do it. After all, she'd been nagging him to do something reckless and impulsive, hadn't she?

"Is there anything else, Mo?" he prompted when she simply stood frozen to the spot, scrutinizing him.

"Er...no...um...I'll just set your wine on the table and give you some...uh...privacy." Like a shot, she zipped across the cabin. In her haste to leave the wine and skedaddle, she clanked the bottom of the stemmed goblet against the edge of the table. The goblet cartwheeled over the back of her hand. Wine splattered on the tiled floor and glass shattered in a gazillion pieces.

"Oh, damn, I'm sorry!" Moriah yelped in dismay.

Amused, Jake watched Moriah hunker down to pick up shards of glass. He noticed her hands shook as she cleaned up her mess. Male pride swelled to gigantic proportions, as he realized that he was having a tremendously unsettling effect on her. Her face was beet-red from the roots of her blond hair to the base of her neck and she was making a big production of *not* looking in his direction.

When the pup trotted over to slurp up the spilled wine, Moriah shifted sideways to block the dog and accidentally smacked her head on the sharp corner of the table. The blow caused her to teeter off balance. She reached down to brace herself—and embedded slivers of glass in her hand.

"Ouch! Damn it!" She recoiled and blood immediately spread across the heel of her hand.

"Leave the mess. I'll clean it up," Jake insisted, as he shooed the mutt out the door. "Come into the bathroom and let me have a look at the damage."

"I'll be fine," she mumbled as she reached up with her good hand to inspect the knot on her hairline. "I'm usually not this clumsy."

"Oh? What do you suppose caused it tonight?" he couldn't resist teasing her.

"If you had any decency you'd put your pants on," she muttered at him.

His brows furrowed in feigned confusion. "Not twenty minutes ago you ordered me to drop my drawers. Now you want me to put them on. Which is it, Mo?" he razzed her unmercifully.

She flashed him a fulminating glance. "I better leave before—"

Watching where he stepped, Jake grabbed the back of her shirt and hoisted her to her feet. Despite her objection, he shepherded her into the bathroom.

"Let's see how deep the cuts are," he said as he

turned on the faucet and then shoved her right hand beneath the stream.

"I-It's f-fine. I—I'm okay," she stuttered.

"Now who's in a state of denial?" he asked as he glanced sideways to see her gaze focused on the light furring of hair on his chest and belly. He really had her discombobulated and he was loving every minute of it.

Moriah inhaled a deep, cathartic breath, then exhaled. Jake noted she practiced what she preached when she found herself tensed up. And she was definitely tense. Why do you suppose that was? he thought wickedly.

"I…uh…don't think I'll bleed to death before I reach my apartment," she chirped, staring down at her injured hand—anywhere but at him.

"Well, I'm not taking any chances," he said, grinning. "After the fuss I put up about being abducted and held hostage here, I'll be the prime suspect if you're found in a pool of blood."

When he bent forward to examine her hand closely, his bare shoulder grazed her arm. He felt her flinch. "Hurt?" he asked, smothering a snicker.

"Er…no." Her voice wobbled noticeably.

Jake grinned, enjoying the effect he had on Moriah. He brushed her shoulder again—accidentally on purpose—and felt a tremor run down to her arm to her hand. When he saw her gaze drop, he glanced down to see what had diverted her attention. His bare hip was peeking from the split in the towel. Her face splashed with color as she snapped up her head and met his knowing grin in the mirror. He didn't think her face could turn redder. Amazingly, amusingly it did. Considering all the blood rushing to her face and ears, he wondered if her head was about to explode.

"Hold still a minute and I'll dig out the shards with

tweezers.'' He opened the medicine cabinet to retrieve the tweezers, antiseptic and bandages he'd noticed earlier.

Moriah, who had yet to be at a loss for words, and was usually in complete control of her composure in his presence, just stood there as if she'd been shot with a stun gun. Jake concentrated on removing the slivers of glass, but he recalled what Moriah had said about finding enjoyment. If he was honest with himself, he'd have to admit that verbally sparring with her during their road trip, having her lecture him on breaking old habits while she held him as a captive audience in the river, and watching her get flustered at the sight of him wearing nothing but a towel was the most fun he'd had since he couldn't remember when. He felt alive, different somehow. He felt more attuned to himself than when he was living his robotlike existence in the city.

''I think I removed all the glass,'' he murmured as he rinsed her hand. ''Now for the antiseptic and bandages. You'll be almost as good as new.''

Within a few minutes he had completed his first-aid ministrations. Moriah still hadn't spoken and her face was still blotchy with color. He noticed she'd taken a couple more of those cathartic breaths she was so fond of, in order to restore her composure.

The moment he released her hand she shot from the bathroom like a cannonball. ''Thanks, Jake. I need to check on my dad before I turn in. See you tomorrow morning.''

Chuckling, he watched her beat a hasty retreat. Humming softly to the tune playing on the canned music system, Jake squatted down to clean up the broken glass. All the while he kept replaying the scene with Moriah. She certainly had turned skittish around him this evening. Self-assured and confident as she usually was, he hadn't expected that. It made him wonder about *her* sex life—or lack thereof.

What kind of romantic relationship could she possibly have when she lived at the resort and cared for her father and catered to her guests? Not much of one, he figured. He wondered why. She was certainly personable, intelligent and attractive. So what was the deal with Moriah?

Jake went to bed that night with Moriah on his mind—and not a single thought of the graphic shop that had consumed the past ten years of his life.

MORIAH, feeling a little frazzled, hiked toward the stables to retrieve two horses. She hadn't slept worth a damn the previous night, thanks to her encounter with Jake—the ornery rascal! Every time she closed her eyes she kept seeing his appealing image in that skimpy towel that parted to expose his bare hip, not to mention the unhindered view of his broad chest, washboarded belly and muscular legs. Damn! Wasn't it enough that she'd had her hands on his racy bikini underwear? Then she'd seen him fresh from the shower, wearing a towel. Sheesh! She did not need to become more aware of him than she already was.

Well, she'd just have to forget last night happened, she told herself sensibly. Jake was her guest and he had a ways to go before he learned to adjust to a less stressful lifestyle. Plus, she had no interest in men who were so forcefully driven toward success that they couldn't devote time and attention to their significant others.

She'd noticed at the buffet breakfast earlier that morning that Jake kept checking his watch. She should've taken that away from him, too, she supposed, because he was too clued in to time schedules.

He hadn't mixed and mingled with her other guests at breakfast, just sat at the far end of the table with his gaze glued to his plate. She noticed he stuck a couple of slices of bacon in a napkin and tucked them in his pocket before he left the lodge. Snacks for the pup, no doubt. For all his grousing and complaining about the imposition of having the pooch underfoot, Jake was taking good care of the animal. Better care, in fact, than her other guests took of their temporary pets. It proved that Jake wasn't self-absorbed and focused solely on himself. She liked that about him.

"Hey, Mori, how's it goin'?"

She glanced up and waved at Kent Foster, the former rodeo star who had signed on to care for the livestock and guide her guests along the riding trails. Although Kent had broken several bones during his career as a bull rider, and walked with a noticeable limp, the wiry cowboy never failed to show up and put in a hard day's work. His love of animals was apparent in the way he tended the horses. He talked to them, petted them and pampered them as if they were his children.

"Things are going fine," Moriah replied as she halted beside Kent.

"Yeah?" Kent grinned as he adjusted his Resistol hat. "Word around the ranch is that we have a hostile guest on our hands."

"Jake is beginning to settle in," she said optimistically. "We're riding this morning. Have any of the other guests contacted you about going riding?"

Kent nodded, then brushed the blades of straw off his faded jeans. "Yup. Three of 'em," he drawled. "I thought we'd follow the path that meanders up to the lookout point that towers over the river. Nothin' like a

breathtakin' view of the great outdoors to start your
mornin' off right.''

"I better make my rounds before my guests scatter,"
Moriah replied.

"I'll fetch a couple of saddle horses for you." Kent
pivoted on his boot heels to retrieve the mounts. In less
than a minute he returned, leading a sorrel and buckskin.

"I don't know much about Jake's ridin' experience,
so I'll give him Ol' Sally. She's so easygoin' that you
can climb on the wrong side of her and she doesn't even
twitch her ears."

Moriah decided she could take lessons from the good-
natured sorrel. She'd become extremely twitchy while
Jake was ambling around the cabin in his towel, looking
so incredibly appealing that she couldn't keep her eyes
off him. When he brushed up against her, his arousing
touch and the scent of him bombarded her. The very last
thing Moriah needed was to become more aware of that
man than she already was. The prospect had *disaster*
written all over it in flaming letters.

Well, she'd just have to concentrate on keeping an
emotional distance, she lectured herself as she mounted
the buckskin.

Fifteen minutes later, Moriah tethered the horses beside Jake's cabin, then climbed up the steps. Before she
could rap on the door, it swung open.

Jake frowned curiously as she offered him the red rose
clasped in her hand. "What's that for?"

"I deliver a rose to each guest every morning," she
informed him with a cheery smile.

"Don't tell me, let me guess. We're supposed to take
time to smell the roses along the pathway of life."

"Very astute, Jake." She eased past him to retrieve a
vase from the cabinet.

Moriah glanced over her shoulder at the table, then blushed when she remembered the disaster she'd caused because she got so rattled when she walked in on Jake while he was draped with a towel. "Is the pup okay? He didn't suffer any glass cuts, did he?" she asked, striving for a casual tone.

"He's fine. No harm done. And by the way, why did I get this fuzzball of a dog for my companion when I noticed your other guests have more manly pets? I've seen a Doberman, a chow and a German shepherd trailing behind some of the guests. I get the wuss dog that has a thing for skunks. Thanks so much, Mo."

Moriah set the rose on the table and pasted on a smile. "Don't take it personally, Jake. The pup is a new arrival and so are you. Besides, those supposed watchdogs you mentioned turned out to be wimps. That's why their owners foisted them off on the animal shelter. You raise your voice to the Doberman and he cuts and runs scared."

Jake gave her the once-over as she headed for the door. "Nice outfit, Mo. I see you're impersonating a flower garden today."

"And you're wearing ho-hum green," she noted.

A wry grin pursed his lips and he waggled his eyebrows at her. "Only on the outside. Inside I'm hot-to-trot red."

Moriah felt heat rising to her cheeks. Having seen Jake in a towel made it infinitely easier to visualize him wearing his flashy briefs. That was not a good thing. "Well, that's a start in spicing up your life, I'd say," she said breezily. "Shall we go riding?"

"Can't wait," he enthused. "I feel the overwhelming need for the speed you're so fond of."

"I was planning a leisurely ride so we could get to know each other better."

"No, you're planning to lecture me," he said perceptively, then swept his arm toward the door. "Let's get this show on the road, Mo. We're burning daylight."

4

JAKE AMBLED toward the horses. "So what's up with your loud clothes? I've already figured out they're a disguise of sorts."

Moriah missed a step. "I beg your pardon?"

"Why are you begging my pardon? You haven't offended me in almost five minutes," he said flippantly.

"I just happen to like colorful clothes," she replied as she mounted the buckskin.

"Aw, c'mon, Mo. I'm not as stupid as I look." Jake swung effortlessly onto the sorrel mare. "For some reason, you don't want the male of the species to notice how attractive and well-built you are. That wild wardrobe is not so much an attention-grabber as a clever distraction. So is that perky, bubbling facade of yours. I wonder if anyone at Triple R has ever actually met the real Moriah Randell."

Moriah felt her temper rising when Jake tried to pick her apart. Then she realized she'd just experienced what he must be feeling when she tried to impose her unfamiliar beliefs on him. Willfully, she focused on remaining cool, calm and collected. "No need to worry about me. We're here to discuss methods of altering your routines and improving your life, remember?"

"How can I forget? You harp at me every chance you get. So what's your story, sugarplum?"

This man was going to be even more trouble than she

originally anticipated. Her other guests arrived here, keyed on themselves, anxious for suggestions and solutions to their stress. Not Jake, damn him. In an effort to keep the focus off him, Jake poked and prodded into her psyche. Well, if opening up to him promoted his willingness to relax and confide in her, then so be it. Refusing to answer his questions might leave the impression that she was as obstinate and unapproachable as he was. One mule-stubborn individual around here was plenty.

Moriah led the way to the path that skirted the river and formulated her thoughts. "My story is nothing earth-shaking," she began as she settled comfortably on the saddle. "I spent a great deal of time caring for my ailing mother during adolescence, while my father worked long days and made numerous business trips. When my mother died, my dad dealt with his grief by taking on even more projects that kept him away from home."

"So you didn't have the opportunity to run fast and loose as a teenager," he presumed.

"No, caretakers are rarely allowed that privilege," she agreed, smiling ruefully. "By the time I entered college I had a solid background in caregiving and nursing. I also liked to dabble in psychology and I developed an interest in stress management, after watching Dad run himself ragged. After I graduated I worked as the assistant director of stress management for several corporate firms in Oklahoma City."

"If you were doing what you were trained to do, why did you leave your job?" Jake asked, watching her astutely.

Moriah squirmed uneasily in the saddle. "Because I..." Her voice fizzled out. She drew a deep breath, ignored her humiliation and blurted out, "Because I got my heart broken and I wanted to make a new start."

"Good enough reason," Jake remarked. "Who was the jerk?"

Moriah relaxed enough to chuckle. After five years, she could be a little more objective. Plus, Jake took her side without question, which made her feel better about herself. "He was my boss. A blond Adonis who could charm women—especially the naive ones like me—into believing he was the quintessence of Mr. Right. He took advantage of my willingness to share the workload and handle paperwork, which made him look good to his corporate clients. I thought all the attention he showered on me meant he felt the same way I did."

"But…?" he prompted as he eased the sorrel up beside her.

"But he didn't," Moriah murmured. "Turns out he was bed hopping with three other women in the office. I was supplying him with all the spare time needed for his personal version of recreational pursuits. I realized that the only relationships I knew anything about, the only kinds I excelled at, were the ones built on *someone else's* need and dependence on *me*. I know I'm shamefully inadequate as a serious marriage prospect."

Jake glanced over at her and frowned. "How'd you arrive at that conclusion?"

Moriah shrugged. "Because it made sense. I was never really wanted for myself, only what I could provide in the way of help and assistance for others. In short, I grew up learning to *be there* for someone else."

He snorted in disagreement. "You're selling yourself short, Mo. Like I said, you've got the looks, brains and outgoing personality, despite those loud clothes."

"Maybe so, but I always end up attracting people who

depend on me for emotional and physical support. I'm like an ambulance to the rescue. My flashy clothes merely announce: Hey, here I am. What can I do for you today?''

Jake threw back his dark head and barked a laugh. It was a full rich sound that seemed to come from deep inside him. Fascinated, Moriah stared at him, watching his sensuous lips curve upward and his obsidian eyes sparkle with inner spirit. A warm, fuzzy sensation fluttered through her body when she realized she'd seen her first glimpse of the man trapped inside his rigid routine.

"You should do that more often, Jake. Laugher definitely becomes you."

"Well, I haven't had all that much to laugh about in a decade," he admitted. "When I lost my parents things turned serious in a hurry."

Moriah halted her horse to stare at the scenic view of the river, hoping Jake would experience the same sense of peace and tranquility that flooded over her. Apparently, he did. She noticed his grasp on the reins slackened and his gaze wandered admiringly across the river that glittered like mercury in the sunlight.

"I see you've managed to return the focus of the conversation back to me," he said, sparing her a brief but perceptive glance.

"Yes, well, as recreational director it's my job to urge guests to relax. Discussing the reasons for stress in your life makes you aware that you need to change your routines and habits. Whatever works, whenever it works, is my motto."

"You're shrewd, Mo," he murmured. "This is kinda like a cattle drive from days gone by. Cowboys moseyed the livestock along the trail at such a leisurely pace the dumb creatures never realized they were being led to slaughter.''

Moriah wrinkled her nose. ''I'm not sure I appreciate that comparison.''

''Yeah, well, I wasn't sure I wanted some wanna-be psychologist picking around in my brain and analyzing me six ways to Sunday, either. But hey, here I am, opening up to you when I had no intention of doing it.'' He tossed her a quick grin. ''That's progress for you.''

''Minimal progress,'' she qualified. ''You were about to tell me what your life was like when you assumed responsibility for your kid sisters.''

''Was I?''

''Yes, you were. If I can spill my guts to you, then the very least you can do is return the favor.''

Jake nudged the sorrel in the flanks and clomped down the path. ''I had two teenage sisters to raise, a fledgling business to run and a social butterfly of a fiancée who expected, and demanded, more attention than I could provide. She's a blue-eyed blonde, by the way,'' he called over his shoulder.

''Ahh…'' Moriah said insightfully. ''That's another reason why I kept getting vibes of resentment from you. You were transferring your frustration toward her to me.''

''Yeah, I suppose,'' he admitted. ''But thankfully, you're turning out to be nothing like her. Anyway, Shelly was jealous of my loyalty and devotion to my sisters. While I was trying to give my sisters special attention during a crucial time, Shelly found herself a sugar daddy who could provide the expensive gifts and fawning attention she thought she deserved, being the goddess she was and all.

''I walked in on her and lover-boy at her apartment

one night when I wasn't expected. By the time Shelly got through twisting the incident around, she made it sound like it was all my fault she looked elsewhere for affection and attention. That's when I figured out that I wasn't too good at relationships that didn't involve dependence from the party of the second part. The humiliating rejection stuck like a dart through the heart and deflated my male pride. Thankfully, I was smart enough not to make the mistake again. Besides, I had my sisters to raise and my business to run. I didn't have time or the inclination for anything else.''

So he understood what it was like to be jilted and to have people depending on him. They had more in common than she first thought. ''And since that time it's been you and your sisters against the world, until they married.''

Jake nodded his raven-black head. ''Pretty much. But at least Kim and Lisa turned out all right. My parents would be proud of them. My folks were devoted to each other and to us kids. It only seemed natural for me to follow the example of keeping the family united and strong.''

''But then, you got yourself stuck in a monotonous rut,'' she commented gently. ''It was your loyal and devoted sisters who came to *your* rescue.''

''They bound me over to you, the ungrateful little brats,'' he muttered sourly. ''Turncoats, is what they are. To think of all I've done for them!''

''They obviously care deeply or they wouldn't have made these arrangements,'' Moriah assured him.

''Yeah, so here I am, pussyfooting around at the resort, wondering if any work will get done at the shop during the next two weeks, pacing the floorboards with nothing to do but wait for you to show up and lecture me on the error of my robotlike ways.''

"But you're making headway," she encouraged him. "Twenty minutes ago you had a stranglehold on the reins. Now you're relaxed. That's progress. All we have to do is get you to let it all hang loose.''

"In this underwear? Are you kidding?"

Moriah snickered. "See there? You can even joke around and laugh at yourself. Yesterday that was an impossibility. You were too uptight and angry to do anything except bite my head off. Our next hurdle is to get you to do something impulsive, something totally unplanned, unexpected and off schedule.''

"Hey, I can be impulsive if I feel like it," he said, affronted.

"Couldn't prove it by me, Mr. Predictable," she teased him. "When was the last time you hauled off and did something totally out of character?"

He frowned pensively.

"Well?" she prompted.

"Don't rush me. I'm thinking.''

"That's your problem. You do too much thinking and planning and moving along according to routine," she told him.

He swiveled his head around to focus directly on her. "You want impulsive, do you?"

"Yeah, I do. Climb out of your rut for once in your life, Jake," she encouraged him. "It's okay to make time for yourself. Just go for it. Kick up your heels once in a while. Do something different. Do something impetuous, if only to prove to yourself that you can.''

"Fine. You want extemporaneous and impromptu? You've got it.''

He leaned over to snatch Moriah off the saddle and

planted her on his lap—facing him, her legs straddling his hips. He bent his head and kissed her. It wasn't just a playful little peck on the cheek, either. It was a hot, steamy, burn-off-your-lips kind of kiss that demanded a response—whether you meant to give one or not.

Moriah hadn't planned on wrapping her arms around his neck and pressing up against him. She hadn't meant to let him invade her mouth with a second plundering kiss that stole the breath clean out of her lungs. She didn't expect him to clamp his hands around her rump and haul her against the hard evidence of his arousal. She didn't expect to feel the blaze of desire frying her alive. But there they were, climbing all over each other on top of Ol' Sally who didn't so much as twitch her ears in objection.

The mare stood there docilely while Jake and Moriah got it on like a couple of hormone-plagued teenagers going at it in the back seat of a car. It was the damnedest thing Jake had ever experienced in his life. One minute Moriah was daring him to be impulsive, and poof! He dragged her to him and kissed her like a starving man devouring a feast. And worse, Jake couldn't seem to get enough of the taste and scent of her. Every time he came up for air he found himself craving more. He stared at her kiss-swollen lips—and she stared at his—and they came together again like fire and dynamite.

That long dry spell must've caught up with him, because he was so hot and bothered in the time it took to blink that he felt the insane urge to peel off his clothes and follow this wild impulse to its natural conclusion.

The feel of her full breasts mashed against his chest, the feel of her parted thighs resting on his own drove him right out of his mind. Mercy! He didn't need a caffeine zing when these sizzling sensations were bouncing through his veins like pinballs. Desire definitely had a stronger kick than coffee and chocolate combined.

His self-control hit the skids and his hands developed a will of their own. They mapped the full swells of her breasts, feeling her nipples harden against his prowling fingertips. Her nails raked over his back as he skimmed her ribs, measured the trim indentation of her waist and scanned the flare of her hips with his hands. Damn, she felt as if she were made to fit into his hands, fit against his aching male body.

Light-headed from panting for breath, Jake experienced the sensation that he was tumbling off balance. Too late, he realized he and Moriah truly were off balance. Ol' Sally had decided to step down the steep incline to have herself a drink at the river. When she lowered her head to slurp water Moriah and Jake were left with nothing to hold on to except each other. They somersaulted pell-mell over Sally's downcast neck and landed with a splat—their arms and legs tangled up worse than a pretzel.

Jake floundered upright, after swallowing a couple of gallons of water. He burst to the surface like a spouting whale, then glanced wildly around, trying to locate Moriah. She surfaced three feet away from him. Her long hair was plastered against the sides of her head and her eyes were as wide as serving platters. Sputtering, she struggled to catch her breath.

Gape-mouthed, she stared at him and he stared back, his jaw sagging on its hinges. She appeared astounded— as he was—by kisses and caresses that carried the impact of a nuclear blast.

He should say something, but his tongue seemed to be stuck to the roof of his mouth and his waterlogged brain had short-circuited. He wasn't sure what to expect from Moriah. Anger and indignation, probably. After all, he hadn't exactly *asked* permission to kiss her breathless and put his hands all over her. Jeez, he couldn't believe he'd done that! What the hell happened to his sense of decency?

"Hey, you said do something impulsive," he said before she could jump down his throat. "Besides, your flower garden ensemble needed watering."

Boy, that was totally lame, he thought with an inward groan. He expected her to rear back and slap him—it was what he deserved. Or at the very least, chew him out royally. Most women he knew would've been furious about getting their hair and makeup ruined by a dunking in the river.

"Well," she said eventually, "I did ask for impulsive, but that wasn't exactly what I had in mind. Next time I'll be more specific."

When Moriah took an impromptu swim he decided to join her. For sure, he needed to cool his heels—and other parts of his body that had overheated. He wondered if she was suffering the same need to cool off and put some time and emotional distance between that explosive kiss that they had just experienced.

Jake was more than a little relieved that Moriah chose to pretend the kiss didn't happen, because that was fine by him. She piled on her horse and started yakkety-yakking about ways to reduce stress so his life would become more well-rounded and personally fulfilling. Jake tried to pay attention, he really did, but the way her wet clothes clung to her voluptuous body like a coat of paint was one hell of a distraction.

MORIAH PULLED the cake from the oven, set it aside to cool, and then rifled through her cabinets for vanilla and a sack of powdered sugar. She had decided to make Jake's birthday an event that would bring her guests and staff together for a party in the lobby. The occasion would serve two purposes—celebrating Jake's birthday in a casual setting and creating time for informal conversation. There were no power lunches or business conferences at Triple R, and Moriah wanted her guests to function in laid-back settings. They needed to carry on conversations unrelated to business. One of their biggest problems was learning to broaden their focus of interests.

Plus, this shindig would ensure Moriah wouldn't be alone with Jake. Having discovered how wildly responsive she was to him had thrown her for a loop. After that scorching kiss, she'd needed a swim to get herself in hand. She'd told herself not to get involved with Jake. Yet, she'd stepped over the line—did a hundred-yard dash over it was more accurate! But damn, that man knew how to kiss and leave a woman burning—inside and out!

Moriah told herself to calm down when she realized she was whipping the icing so frantically that she nearly beat the finish off the bowl. She was tense and she almost never got tense because she practiced breathing exercises and relaxation techniques. Yet, here she was, reliving that incredibly amazing kiss and wishing for more of the same. What was she thinking!

"Relax," she told herself sternly. "Focus."

"Pardon?"

Moriah had been so distracted that she forgot she'd brought her dad over to her apartment for a private visit. He'd been making some electronic adjustments to his motorized cart and watching TV while she whipped up the cake.

"Nothing, Dad. Just talking to myself." She glanced over at her silver-haired father to note he was fumbling with the remote control. Her first impulse was to dash over to help him, but she stayed where she was. William Randell was learning to work around the partial paralysis in his left side and was determined to be as independent as possible.

"Whose birthday did you say we're celebrating tonight?" Will asked.

"Jake Prescott's."

"The new guy," he said with a pensive nod. "The one who put up the big fuss about being here. Is he doing better?"

"Uh…yeah. I saw him and his pup canoeing down the river this afternoon. I think he's settling in."

"Anna said another guest arrived a couple of hours ago to replace the guest in cabin two. From Saint Louis, right?"

"Right." Moriah washed the powdered sugar off her hands, then plunked down on the sofa. "Very demanding sort of individual."

"Gonna be trouble?"

"Probably. He's expecting an instant fix to stressful habits he's spent a lifetime developing."

"If anybody can teach him to relax and unwind, you can, hon," he said confidently.

Moriah leaned over to give her dad a peck on the cheek. "Thanks for your vote of confidence."

His hand folded over hers and she swallowed the lump that suddenly clogged her throat. For years they'd passed by each other like ships in the night without really knowing each other. Her dad had been a guest in his own home and Moriah never felt as if she understood him until he was forced into retirement and required her care.

It had taken Will a year to adjust to his limited life-style, but now he spent his time modifying and creating electronic gadgets, whizzing around the resort on his cart and relaxing. Even better, she and Will had grown close these past three years.

"Did I ever tell you how grateful I am to have a daughter like you?" he murmured appreciatively.

She leaned over to give him an affectionate hug. "Did I ever tell you how grateful I am to have you?"

He patted her shoulder. "Thanks, honey. Don't know where I'd be without you." He inclined his gray head toward the kitchenette. "Better finish up that cake before I get all blubbery on you. It'll ruin the hard-ass image I maintained in the business world." He tapped the remote against the armrest of his cart. "Damn gadget won't work right. What idiot tinkered with the design of these things anyway?"

Moriah chuckled as she bounded to her feet. "I do believe it was some of your technology that pioneered those gadgets. You were an electronic wizard in your day."

His eyes twinkled and he smiled, though the muscles in the left side of his cheek drooped noticeably. "I was, wasn't I?"

"Damn straight, Dad."

While Will turned his attention to the new remote he'd designed to control all the lights in Moriah's apartment, she iced the cake—and cursed herself soundly when her thoughts circled back to Jake. She couldn't keep avoiding him. She'd left a rose on his doorstep this morning and asked Tom Stevens to deliver the glass of wine the previous night. It wasn't like her to dodge awkward situations. She usually laughed and smiled her way through them.

Unfortunately, the tactic didn't work quite as well with Jake. She was entirely too aware of him, too attracted to him, too embarrassed that she'd climbed all over him and groped at him while they'd kissed each other breathless. Sweet mercy! That was totally out of character for her. She didn't do stuff like that—until Jake came along.

Moriah sighed in frustration, wondering what had gotten into her. She'd never reacted to a man like that before. She had to keep her distance and clear the air—sexually charged though it most definitely was—between them. Tomorrow she'd have a nonchalant visit with Jake, she decided as she slathered vanilla icing on the strawberry cake. They'd get past that impulsive kiss and things would be back on an even keel—she hoped.

JAKE PACED the floorboards, then checked his watch for the umpteenth time in two hours. This place was driving him straight south to crazyville! He'd had nothing to do all day and he'd had all day to do it. Sure, he'd checked out a canoe and paddled Spitwad on the river for an hour, and then he'd hiked up the hillside path to visually pan the plush valley below. Still, he felt edgy, restless and twitchy. He needed a computer mouse under his fingertips and a monitor screen to stare at. He needed to work to keep his mind off Moriah who'd been avoiding him since that sizzling kiss that made him uncomfortable in all the wrong places.

He needed to apologize—if he could manage to get her alone for more than five seconds. She'd breezed by once or twice, flashing that cheery smile, on her way to visit other guests, but she'd taken a noticeably wide berth around Jake.

He checked his watch again, then glanced down to

see Spitwad sprawled on the floor, sound asleep. Speaking of sleep, Jake couldn't believe he'd slept until eight o'clock this morning. Ordinarily, he was up and at 'em by six. He was pretty sure Moriah had added a sedative to the wine she had Tom deliver the previous evening. Surely his internal time clock and razor-sharp business edge hadn't deserted him on their own accord. There had to be a reason—like sleeping potions and tranquilizers and such, he decided suspiciously.

Whirling around, Jake headed for the door. He was going to find Moriah and get things squared away. She needed to know there'd be no more kissing, that he'd keep his hands to himself. She wouldn't have to feel wary or uncomfortable around him because he wasn't going to touch her again—ever.

Jake strode swiftly toward the lodge that was lit up like a Christmas tree in the darkness. He'd probably have to chitchat with the other guests a while before he managed to draw Moriah aside. He'd get the apology over with and then hightail it back to his cabin to play tug-of-war with Spitwad. The mutt had already chewed a hole in one of Jake's socks, so he'd tied the demolished sock in a knot and whiled away his time with the pesky pup. Amazing what lengths a guy would go to when he had to entertain himself—or risk going insane from boredom. In two weeks he'd probably be nuttier than a jar of Jif.

Jake was fifty feet from the lodge when Moriah appeared on the porch. The golden glow spotlighted and accentuated her eye-catching physique. She was wearing a jungle-print ensemble that featured zebras, tigers, colorful parrots and frothy ferns. Her blond hair was piled loosely atop her head by some invisible means of support he couldn't figure out. Damn, but he'd like to unwind that silky mass of hair and run his fingers through it, then pull her lush body against—

Jake gnashed his teeth and cursed himself soundly. Damn it, he had to get past this physical attraction and he better do it fast.

"Hi, Jake," Moriah called out, waving her arms like a cheerleader on the sidelines. "I was on my way over to see you."

"Yeah? What for?" Did he sound casual enough? Too snippy and uptight? He tried for a neutral tone that disguised his frustration. "So, what's up, Mo?"

"There's something I want to show you." She gestured for him to follow her into the lodge. "Come on inside and have a look."

5

JAKE HALTED in his tracks when he walked into the lobby to see nine guests, four staff members and Will Randell gathered around the dining table where a cake waited with his name printed on it in red icing. His mouth dropped open wide enough for a pheasant to roost.

"Happy birthday, Jake," the group said in unison.

Everyone had a beaming smile on his face, except the newcomer who seemed to think he was too good for a party where he wasn't the center of attention. Jake inwardly winced, wondering if he'd given the same offensive impression when he arrived, demanding to be released so he could go home where he belonged. He felt the need to apologize to the entire staff for being troublesome.

"Thanks," Jake murmured humbly. "Who made the cake?"

When he glanced at Anna Jefferies, she hitched her thumb toward Moriah. "Don't look at me. She's the one who took time out to bake."

Jake focused his attention on Moriah, but her smiling gaze was directed over his left shoulder, avoiding eye contact. Yep, he'd blown the companionable camaraderie he'd enjoyed the previous morning before he kissed her lips off and practically climbed all over her on the back of Ol' Sally. Sheesh! What was the matter with him? He must be cracking up.

"Have a seat, everyone, and I'll dish up the ice cream," Moriah said cheerily.

"So, Jake what's the age count?" the burly Tom Stevens asked as he sank down at the table and made room for Will Randell's motorized cart.

"Thirty-six."

"Well, aren't you the spring chicken around here," Joe Higdon, the frizzy-haired guest from cabin six, said with a snicker. "Took me until age sixty-one to realize I was a fanatic workaholic in need of relaxation."

Several other guests nodded their heads—which were in various states of balding.

"Do yourself a favor, Jake m'boy," Will Randell remarked as he grabbed a glass of decaffeinated tea. "Learn to take life a little easier now so you don't end up like me. Now I'm trying to make each day count and have some fun along the way."

"No, kidding, kid," Eugene Morris, the guest from cabin eight, chimed in. "I had to have myself a heart attack before I realized I was pressing too hard. Scared the bejeezus out of me."

"Yeah, well, try hyperventilating and collapsing at the podium while giving a speech at a corporate board meeting," Harold Pinkly, the guest from cabin nine, spoke up. "That will open your eyes in a hurry."

While Jake parked himself at the head of the table—being the guest of honor that he was—he heard testimonials from everyone except the sour-faced gent who made it apparent that he was a little too good to be bonding with a bunch of corporate-whiz has-beens.

While Jake devoured the moist, delicious strawberry cake and ice cream, he formed closer acquaintances with the men. He was surprised that Moriah's guests hailed from all parts of the country. Obviously her resort's reputation was known far and wide, because Joe was from Dallas, Harold from Omaha and Eugene from Detroit.

Immediately, the cogs in Jake's brain started cranking. He could create an incredible Web site to promote Moriah's resort, one with enticing scenic pictures, peaceful music and all the necessary blurbs to advertise her myriad of recreational activities. Add to that a few testimonials praising positive results, a couple of tips for relaxation, and Moriah would have stressed-out businessmen clambering to her cabins in the panoramic valley.

"If you don't mind, I'd like to skip the fun and games and have a look at my cabin," Robert Fullerton demanded as he stared down his nose at Moriah. "I've had a long drive from Saint Louis, after all."

"Sure thing." Moriah vaulted from her chair, her cheerful smile intact. "I'll show you to the cabin."

Jake was unprepared for his agitated reaction to Fullerton's snippy attitude toward Moriah. It was fine for him to fling barbs at her, but let someone else come down hard on her and it ticked Jake off royally. Jeez, he had no right to feel possessive or protective. He'd only been here a couple of days and kissed her once. He didn't have any rights whatsoever...but that didn't stop him from feeling the urge to put in his two cents' worth. With great effort he kept his trap shut and ate his birthday cake.

When the party crowd migrated to the living area to watch Will demonstrate his new electronic gadget that controlled the lights and catch the evening news, weather and sports, Jake took a long hard look at the other guests. It dawned on him—hit him like a lightning bolt, actually—that he was staring into his own bleak future when he gazed at these older men who'd worked themselves into anxiety attacks, heart seizures and strokes. He could be back here in twenty years, learning to take a more laid-back approach to life.

Jeez, Louise! He might become a burden to his sisters who, by then, would have children of their own and additional family expenses. He'd be the shriveled up, burned-out uncle stuffed in the corner and his nieces and nephews would have to veer around him on their way out the door to enjoy life. He'd probably have to be spoon-fed meals because carpal tunnel syndrome would cause his hands and wrists to function improperly.

Damn, he needed to chill out a little, he decided. He needed to find a hobby that he enjoyed and work it into his business routine.... He needed to take some time to stop and smell the roses....

The epiphany made him bolt upright and take another look around the room at the older men who were drumming their fingers on the armrests of their chairs, tapping their feet, twitching nervously and squirming restlessly in their seats. Holy cow! He realized his fingers were clenched around his glass of iced tea and *he* was tapping *his* foot. He forced himself to relax and unwind.

Okay, so maybe he was wound up tighter than a spring. He could fix that if he stayed the full two weeks and dedicated his time to recreational activity. Just because he made a pact with himself, there and then, to take his life at a less hectic pace didn't mean he had to give up his devotion to his sisters and their new husbands. He could fulfill his professional responsibilities and keep a close family bond and still drop what he was doing when his sisters needed him. That would never change. Kim and Lisa would always be top priority because he'd made a commitment—financially and emotionally—to be there for them when needed. But he sure as hell didn't want his sisters and brothers-in-law to have to care for him when he stumbled over the edge because he worked himself into an early collapse! After all, he was only good at relationships where others were dependent on him, same as Moriah was. He couldn't function as the dependent in a relationship. It would feel too unnatural.

Jake surged from his chair and strode purposely toward Tom Stevens who was lounging in the La-Z-Boy recliner. "Tom, I'd like a massage, first thing in the morning. Can you work me in?"

Tom glanced up, his unibrow soaring up to his hairline. "No kidding? Good for you, Jake. Sure thing. How about right after breakfast?"

Jake nodded. "I'm there."

After Tom gave him two thumbs-up and flashed a toothy grin, Jake wheeled toward Kent, the bowlegged wrangler in charge of the stables and livestock. "Sign me up for a ride after my massage," he requested. "And don't put me on Ol' Sally again. I want a horse with enough stamina and spirit to hold up for a two-hour ride."

Kent chuckled at Jake's newfound enthusiasm for recreation. "You bet, pardner. Want some company or is this a solo ride?"

"Solo," Jake requested. "I plan to absorb the scenic countryside and do some in-depth personal meditation, if you don't mind."

Kent shrugged. "Sure, whatever you need, Jake. I used to do some serious meditation after one of those crazed rodeo bulls launched me through the air, then tried to trample me when I hit the dirt. That's why I'm here instead of ridin' the suicide circuit. I woke up in the hospital one day with my ribs busted and my knee twisted from its socket. I realized there had to be an easier way to make a livin'.''

"Ain't that the truth," Tom agreed as he massaged his bulky shoulder. "I used to be an offensive tackle for the Dallas Cowboys until a bruiser, who was bigger and meaner, laid me out and knocked me unconscious. He also separated me from a few teeth. I decided I was getting too old and brittle to butt heads and fly all over the country, living out of a suitcase."

"Same for me," Chester Gray commented as he twisted in his chair to glance up at Jake. "I attacked the pro golf tour like a maniac for years. Got to where I couldn't remember where I called home and booze was my most reliable companion." He shook his sandy head and smiled ruefully. "Thanks to Moriah, I'm doing what I love and helping other folks take up the game of golf for pleasure and relaxation. Nothing makes me happier than giving a few pointers and then seeing one of the guests drive the ball down the fairway, after they'd whiffed it a few times without my help."

Jake didn't know where Moriah had found this motley group, but obviously she was a decent judge of character when it came to handpicking her staff. No doubt, she'd taken them under wing and worked her recreational magic on them as well. He suspected these relationships she had developed with her staff had originated from need and dependence and progressed to friendship and loyalty. Everyone around here seemed to think Moriah hung the moon and made the sun shine.

Well, Jake fully intended to take advantage of this resort, now that his eyes were open and his head was on straight. Yessiree, he'd have hobbies galore when he returned to his world. His sisters would stop fretting over him, because he'd no longer be Mr. Predictable who was stuck in a rut. He'd be Mr. All-Around from here on out.

Resolved to making life-altering changes in his behavior, Jake hiked off to tend to his first order of business—apologizing to Moriah. His attraction to her was going to be at the bottom of his list of things to do at the resort, he promised himself. He'd view her only as a recreational director and friend. No more getting sidetracked by her enchanting face and tantalizing figure wrapped in those outrageous and wildly colorful clothes. He'd divert his interest and attention to one hobby after another. Hell, he'd *be* Mr. Hobby. No more fierce intensity and one-track business mind for him. He was a changed man!

Jake was jostled from his thoughts by a feminine squawk that came from the area near cabin two. He sprinted through the darkness, dodging trees, to determine what had happened. He skidded to a halt and gnashed his teeth when he saw two silhouettes wrestling with one another.

"Hey! What's going on here!" he boomed.

Jake's arrival allowed Moriah to shove Robert Fullerton back into his own space. The man had followed her outside for his version of slap and tickle, after she'd managed to dodge his advances in the cabin. Damn, this jerk had a lot to learn about backing off and calming down.

Oh sure, some guests flirted with her from time to time and she had her own way of sidestepping unwanted advances. Robert, however, didn't respond as readily to the lack of interest she paid to his suggestive innuendoes. If the domineering chump didn't back off she'd send

Tom over to have a man-to-man talk with him. Tom had been called in a couple of times the past five years—usually with miraculous results.

"Buzz off, pal," Robert scowled when Jake advanced on him. "Sorry, birthday boy, but you'll have to wait your turn. Moriah and I are getting acquainted right now— Whoa! Calm down, man!"

Moriah gasped in surprise when Jake clenched his fists in the front of Robert's dress shirt and jerked him clean off the ground. "That isn't necessary," she assured him, trying to step between the two men.

"Yeah, it is," Jake contradicted in a growl, never taking his eyes off the fifty-eight-year-old businessman. "Listen up, Bobby-boy, you behave yourself around Ms. Randell or I'll be all over you like a bad rash. Are we clear on that?"

Robert shoved himself away and made a big production of smoothing the wrinkles from his silk shirt. "Look, bozo, I happen to be very influential in—"

"I don't give a flying f—ig where your influence lies in the world outside Triple R," Jake snapped brusquely. "Around here, you're a guest and Ms. Randell is your recreational director. You treat her with the courtesy and respect she deserves. Starting now. Apologize."

Robert's square chin shot up defiantly. "No, she was stringing me along."

Moriah opened her mouth to deny the preposterous claim, but Jake beat her to the punch.

"No, she didn't," he snarled ferociously. "Apologize!"

When Robert stubbornly refused, Jake pounced like a cheetah to twist the older man's arm up the middle of his back.

"Ouch, you son of a—"

"Now!" Jake growled down the man's neck.

"Fine…Ow!…I'm sorry," Robert yelped.

Jake pushed him away, as if he found physical contact offensive. Moriah knew that feeling exceptionally well. She'd shivered with repulsion when Robert tried to slobber all over her. She had the unmistakable feeling Robert considered himself a regular ladies' man. No doubt, Robert used his power of position to hit on women in the workplace—and anywhere else he could make a pass.

"Now, beat it, Full-of-Yourself," Jake demanded.

"The name is Fullerton," Robert said hatefully.

"I think you and I need to take a long ride up the mountain in the morning," Jake insisted.

"Be careful you don't knock him off the mountaintop," Moriah advised, lips twitching.

Jake grinned wickedly. "Not to worry, Ms. Randell. I'll make it look like an accident."

Robert turned tail and scampered, lickety-split, into his cabin. Jake waited until the door slammed shut before he pivoted toward Moriah. "C'mon, I'll walk you to your apartment."

"That's okay. I know the way," she said, uncertain if she wanted his company at the moment. She wasn't sure she had a secure grip on her emotions. Watching him rise to her defense like her personal knight in shining armor made too great an impact on her. She wasn't accustomed to anyone standing up for her unless she specifically requested help—and that was always her last resort. Independent though she was, she kinda liked the way Jake defended her honor and discouraged future offenses.

Moriah told herself not to get used to the gratifying feelings that flooded through her, because Jake wouldn't be around long. He was one of her guests and that was the extent of their short-term relationship, she reminded herself for about the fiftieth time.

He took her arm and steered her toward the lodge. "I'm walking you back so I can apologize all over myself for being an ass when I got here and for…um…that kiss yesterday."

Moriah missed a step, then hurried to keep up with his long, swift strides. "That's okay, Jake. I know you didn't come here of your own free will. As for the other incident, I challenged you and you simply proved to me that you could be a little reckless and impulsive."

"Apparently, I can be too reckless and impulsive where you're concerned," he grumbled. "That's not a good thing. But I plan to be on my best behavior from here on out and change my rigid lifestyle."

Moriah pulled up short and peered into his shadowed face. "It sounds as if you've been doing some soul-searching."

"I have," he confirmed with a decisive nod. "My inner self and I had a chat and we've decided I need to change my habits and lose the overly structured routine. I'm going to develop a hobby that's unrelated to work."

"That's wonderful!" she enthused.

He tugged her alongside him. "In a week you won't recognize me as Mr. Predictable."

"Good. Your sisters will be enormously pleased."

"They'll get their money's worth," he promised as he circled around to the back of the lodge. "Now, about Bobby-boy. If he tries to give you any lip—verbal or physical—you let me know and I'll straighten him out again."

Moriah chuckled at his vehement tone. "That won't

be necessary. Tom usually handles incidents like this when I ask him to.''

Jake's brows jackknifed. ''This happens on a regular basis?''

''No, only a couple times when corporate-executive Don Juans think I should be part of their recreational activities.'' Moriah sailed past him to climb the wooden deck that led to her apartment. ''Well, thanks for the help. I'll see you tomorrow, Jake.''

She glanced back to see him standing there with his hands stuffed in the hip pockets of his jeans, his gaze intense. A shiver—born of a source she refused to acknowledge—rippled through her body. She had the impulsive urge to hug the stuffing out of him for coming to her rescue and gallantly walking her home. But she knew she couldn't stop with an appreciative hug. It was becoming alarmingly evident that her feminine body threw off sparks when she got within ten feet of him—which was good reason to keep her distance. Something deep inside her called out to him, needing and wanting things—like desire and passion and romance—that had been missing in her life.

Gad, she was being ridiculous! She didn't need those things to make her happy. Her life was rewarding and fulfilling, just the way it was. Stiffening her resolve, Moriah reminded herself that she intended to have a talk with Jake, too, so they could return to solid footing.

''Come in a minute,'' she invited as she pushed open the door.

''No, I don't think that's such a hot idea,'' he mumbled.

Frowning, she glanced over her shoulder at him. ''Why not?''

He shifted restlessly from one booted foot to the other,

then stared up at the moon, as if it suddenly demanded his undivided attention. "Because, for all my good intentions, I'm still attracted to you. Seeing Bobby paw at you made me feel too protective, territorial and possessive, even when I felt like a damn hypocrite for practically giving you a tonsillectomy…and the other stuff… yesterday morning."

Moriah felt herself moving instinctively toward him, even when that warning voice inside her head yelled, *Keep your distance! You know these kinds of relationships can get tangled up if you let them. Besides, you don't know squat about interactions and social dynamics between a man and woman. You flunked Romance 101, remember?*

She also reminded herself that men occasionally mistook affection for gratitude when she coaxed them into kicking back, relaxing and developing hobbies. Usually, the affection was more along the lines of substitute daughter to father, which included friendly hugs and such. But Jake was only six years older and she was definitely attracted to him—now there was an understatement if she'd ever heard one! The look, feel and scent of him played havoc with her senses, though she tried to maintain physical and emotional distance. Everything about him was different. *She* felt different when she was with him.

When Moriah halted directly in front of Jake and stared into his shadowed face, she knew her resolve had failed her completely. Before she could even think to stop herself she pushed up on tiptoe and kissed him, right smack-dab on the lips. And wham! Desire hit her like a grand slam, emptying the bases of her self-control. Jake clamped his arms around her and his lips came down hard on hers. Need roared in her ears while she kissed him for all she was worth.

Moriah couldn't fault him for brushing his hands all over her, leaving her achy and breathless, because she had her hands all over him, too. She arched against the evidence of his arousal, pressed her tingling breasts against his muscled chest and lost the ability to think, only to feel and enjoy.

"Aw, jeez," Jake said roughly against her lips. "Here we go again...."

And then he kissed her so ravenously, so thoroughly, she feared her legs would buckle beneath her. Every erogenous zone on her body was pulsating with intense need and the sizzle in his touch nearly electrocuted her. She groaned in frustrated desire when Jake nudged her feet apart and ground his hard flesh into the cradle of her thighs. Moriah clung to him, moving instinctively against him, baffled by her wild abandon, craving more of the delicious sensations pounding through her.

"Damn it to hell!" Jake suddenly stepped away and Moriah staggered for balance, wondering why desire hit her so hard so fast and launched her self-restraint into orbit around the planet Pluto. *How* could this keep happening? *Why* was it happening?

Jake raked his hand through his thick raven hair and blew a ragged breath. "I'm not sure these impulsive actions you advocate are good things for me. I came to apologize for kissing you the first time and the kicker is that all I could think about was kissing you again. Now look what's happened. I'm so screwed up I can't control or trust myself around you!"

"I started this," Moriah reminded him unsteadily. "You don't deserve the blame for what just happened. I asked for it."

"Yeah," he said, then gave a self-deprecating snort. "And I delivered. I'm sorry, Moriah. G'night."

Moriah watched him disappear around the corner and then cursed herself soundly. She'd known Jake Prescott was going to be trouble—a dozen different kinds of trouble—an hour after she met him. Sure 'nuff.

Moriah staggered up the steps, closed the door and stood there staring at her empty apartment. The silence in there was deafening. Needs she'd spent years ignoring were exploding through her body like popcorn. She was magnetically drawn to Jake, hypnotized by those intense chocolate eyes, mesmerized by the needy desire he ignited in her. She couldn't even begin to describe or categorize the sensations that bombarded her when he kissed her and caressed her. Damn, she must've been a harlot in a previous life, because she'd wanted to rip off his shirt and get her hands all over that sleek muscled flesh she'd seen the first night when she'd accidentally walked in on Jake while he was practically naked.

Moriah gulped when she realized her body was still sizzling and her heart was thumping like a nail gun. She remembered, with vivid clarity, how it felt to be wrapped in Jake's powerful arms, their bodies meshed intimately together, his hands skimming over her feminine contours, her hands exploring his masculine body.

This was not good! This was insane! She barely knew the man, yet she wanted to take their relationship to a deeply intimate level and she *never* felt that obsessive need hammering at her before.

Good grief, did some latent feminine hormone kick in at age thirty to cause a woman to freak out, despite the good sense she'd cultivated for three decades? For heaven's sake, she knew she was lousy at romantic relationships. She didn't know diddly about attracting and holding a man's attention. For all her extensive education she had some serious deficiencies when it came to relating to a man her own age.

Senior citizens she could handle, no sweat. Jake made her sweat—and that was the *least* of her reactions to him!

Ordinarily, she kept things lighthearted and casual with her guests. She could joke around with the best of them. But with Jake—

"But nothing. Go make your rounds, then go to bed, Mo," she ordered herself sharply. "Just because this is Jake's birthday, you didn't have to kiss his lips off this evening. You baked his cake. That should've been good enough!"

Moriah blew out her breath, then lurched around to return to the lodge. She had warm milk and wine to deliver to her guests. She may have the hots for Jake, but it would pass when he returned to his world and she welcomed another guest to take his place.

She wasn't sure she wanted to delve into the reason why she was anxious for time to whiz by at supersonic speed. She suspected it had something to do with the fear of developing heart trouble. She had to take the necessary precautions to ensure she didn't contract the dangerous ailment.

MORIAH FROWNED when she returned from hiking with one of her guests to see Tom, Kent and Chester motioning her to an isolated spot beneath a sprawling shade tree. "Something wrong?" she asked worriedly.

"Yeah, 'fraid so," Kent mumbled as he swept off his Resistol hat and raked his fingers through his smashed hair. "It's about Jake."

Moriah stared at the men in alarm. "What's wrong with him?"

"Well, for the past week he's attacked every leisure sport on the premises," Chester Gray reported, lips twitching. "He got all huffy the first time he showed up to play golf and I told him we didn't set pars for the course and we didn't allow scorecards because it makes the game competitive and we don't encourage competition at Triple R. He played twenty-seven holes of golf, nonstop. He wouldn't have quit then, but his golf cart ran out of charge and I had to tow him to the shed. It's the same drill each time he arrives at the course to play a round."

"He comes to me for a massage to work out his kinks after all his physical activity," Tom reported. "He's always tied up in knots and it's a wonder I can get him to relax."

"He shows up at the stables to take a daily ride," Kent informed her. "He's usually gone so long I'm afraid somethin' happened, so I go to check on him. Guess what he was doin' today?"

Moriah was in no mood to guess. "I give up. What was he doing?"

"He was timin' himself like a barrel racer. He was thunderin' around designated trees rather than barrels. He took one spill that I witnessed and who knows how many I didn't see. It's a wonder he didn't break a few bones."

"One of the other guests saw him down at the river yesterday afternoon with four rods and reels going at once. Fish were biting as fast as he unhooked them and tossed them back," Tom said, shaking his head. "Man, talk about a complete turnaround in attitude! Jake's going to be exhausted when he returns to his world. Haven't you told him to enjoy himself *in moderation?*"

Moriah shifted uncomfortably. Fact was, she'd been avoiding Jake. She made sure whatever activity they shared was in full view of other guests or the staff. She simply couldn't trust herself alone with Jake and she was careful to keep her casual persona in place. She preferred to deal with Robert Fullerton, even if he was a royal pain in the butt. But at least she had no vulnerable, uncontrollable feelings for that sour executive who held a grudge against her after Jake lit into him.

"I'll talk to Jake after supper," Moriah promised.

"Good," Chester said, snickering. "Much as I like Jake, he's taking leisure sports too seriously. I wasn't that devoted when I was practicing for the pro tour."

"You're going to have to take those rods and reels away from him and give him a cane pole and a shovel to dig worms," Tom advised. "He's not practicing for a national fly-fishing tournament, you know. But good luck convincing him of that."

Kent scratched his head, then plunked his hat in place. "It's like he's on some kind of fiendish crusade to cram as much physical activity into each day as possible. First you couldn't drag him from his cabin and now he never stays in it. You need to explain to him what R-and-R stands for. He thinks it means *Rundown* and *Ragged.*"

"I'll take care of it," Moriah assured them. "But you keep reminding him that relaxation is the name of our game, too. He needs to hear it from all of us."

"Oh, and while we're tattling to you, I think you should know that Fullerton character from cabin two instigates trouble every chance he gets," Chester reported. "The jerk hit into the twosome of golfers ahead of him and nearly smacked Pete Sanders in the shoulder with a

ball. When Pete and Geoffrey told Robert to back off he
insisted they let him play through because he was better
at the game and played a lot faster.''

"Honest to God, I don't know how that man carries
around that ego of his," Kent muttered. "It's gotta
weigh a ton."

Robert was hostile and upset because he'd been
through a nasty divorce. Moriah wondered if his faith-
lessness was the cause of it—though Robert was too
proud and closemouthed to explain the situation.

"Robert is really stressed out right now," she said.
"I'm trying to encourage him to unwind."

"The jerk is getting on our collective nerves," Tom
said. "Haven't had a guest of his annoying caliber
around here for a couple of years. The man's spoiling
for a fight and I'd like to accommodate him."

"Yeah, and we'll help," the other two men volunteered in unison.

"I'd prefer to avoid a lawsuit," Moriah cautioned.

"Damn lawsuits and attorneys lookin' for an extra
buck," Kent said, then scowled. "You can't swing a
dead cat anywhere in society these days without some
money-grubbin' creep threatenin' to sue your pants off
with little provocation."

"I'll try to convince Robert to calm down and modify
his aggressive attitude. Then I'll see if I can slow Jake
down before he collapses from attacking his new hobbies
with fiendish zeal," Moriah said.

Damn, *she* needed a vacation. Her guests were drain-
ing her energy faster than she could recoup.

"You look tired, Mori," Chester observed. "You
could use a rest."

"I'll give you a massage to relieve your tension,"
Tom offered helpfully.

"I'll plan a group expedition of horseback ridin' so you can have some spare time to yourself," Kent spoke up. "Go take a break."

"I could use a little R-and-R," she agreed. "A few hours of privacy sounds heavenly."

"Yeah, you gotta be careful you don't form habits of overexertion when you're trying to get your guests to break their obsessive routines," Chester reminded her with a wink. "You could use an assistant to take some of the pressure off you."

Moriah nodded and smiled tiredly. "I know, but we're all working double duty. Our budget won't allow for extra help. Maybe in another year."

"By then *you'll* be a guest here," Tom prophesied.

"Nag, nag," she teased.

"Hey, doll face, you're our family and we care about you," Kent added. "No tellin' where we'd be, if not for you."

"That's right, Mori," Chester continued. "When I was down-and-out, you pulled me upright, dried me out and gave me back my self-respect and offered me a job. None of us want to lose the good deal we've got going, so you take care of yourself, hear?"

"I hear." Moriah pivoted toward the lodge. "I'll kick back and relax for a few hours."

"Good," they chorused as she walked away.

6

THIS WAS WORKING. It was working damn well, Jake congratulated himself as he tilted his sunburned face into the shower mist and sighed tiredly as water trickled over his aching body. He'd kept himself busy for days on end and he'd only thought about Moriah a few thousand times. Distraction was the ticket. Thank goodness Moriah hadn't dropped by for lengthy visits. If he could hold out a few more days he'd be gone and temptation would be out of sight—and hopefully, out of mind.

Of course, Jake didn't think he needed Moriah's encouragement to relax now that he was knocking himself out, racing from one recreational activity to the next. And thankfully, Moriah didn't linger more than two minutes when she delivered her rose each morning and wine at night. He'd kept conversation light and casual, subtly assuring her that he could, and would, control this attraction that couldn't go anywhere anyway. She had her life and responsibilities here at Triple R and he had his business and his family obligations elsewhere. He didn't think he or Moriah would be comfortable having an affair. So where did that leave them?

Nowhere.

Scrubbed clean, Jake stepped from the shower and dried hurriedly. He didn't want to be late for the chow line because all this physical activity left him ravenous by mealtime. And man, he hadn't enjoyed such good eats since Kim or Lisa invited him over for supper occasionally.

Anna Jefferies could damn sure cook, he mused, salivating at the thought of her hearty feasts. Her ranch-style cooking had him stampeding to the table every chance he got.

Hurriedly, Jake donned the skimpy briefs—another pair of those leopard prints his sisters packed—then slipped on his clothes. He noticed Spitwad had confiscated one of the socks he'd laid out and he went in search of the gnawing little pest. Spitwad had the sock torn in two pieces, chewing happily on the remains. Jake had half a mind to scold the pup, but what the hell, he decided. It was just a sock. Better that than a pair of jeans or hiking boots.

When Jake arrived at the supper table he noticed Moriah was nowhere to be seen. Ordinarily, she was there to greet her guests. She was always ready with a cheerful smile and she was the first one to speak. She had a knack of making each guest feel special and wanted, he recalled.

Since Moriah wasn't there, Jake assumed her duty as social director and asked each arrival if they'd enjoyed their day of activity. The only guest who didn't respond amicably was Robert Fullerton. Of course, Jake expected no less after their confrontation. Mostly, Robert steered clear of Jake—and hopefully of Moriah. If not, the creep could expect a visit from Tom and Jake. He didn't have any rights where Moriah was concerned, but he felt possessive, regardless. He's spent years looking out for Kim and Lisa and watching out for Moriah was becoming a natural reflex to him.

Jake chewed on a bite of moist, juicy grilled chicken,

then glanced over at William Randell. "Where's Moriah this evening? Settling in a new guest?"

Will shook his silvery head. "Nope. She's resting. I keep telling her she needs to designate one night a week for socializing in town." He glanced over at Jake and grinned. "One of these days I'd like some grandchildren to spoil." His expression sobered considerably. "I wasn't around much when Moriah was growing up and I regret it now that I've come to realize how much I missed. Always too involved with business to spend time with my family. Now my wife is gone and Moriah is taking care of me. If I had it to do over again…"

His voice trailed off and his pale-blue eyes misted over. Jake glanced around the table, wondering how many men in attendance had neglected their families in their quests for the almighty dollar. Jake promised himself that when Kim and Lisa had kids he would play a dominant role in their lives. Not just gifts and toys, but time spent wallowing around on the floor with plenty of hugs and smooches to go around. He'd be at Little League games, basketball games, school plays—the whole nine yards. He wasn't going to wind up at age sixty like Will Randell, looking back on his life, wishing he'd done things differently.

Feeling inspired and revived, Jake finished his meal then bounded up to scoop his plate and silverware from the table.

"Hey, that's okay, Jake," Anna said with a wave of her hand. "I'll take care of cleaning up."

"Nope. I think it's time we men cleaned up after ourselves and gave you a break."

Anna stared at him as if he'd sprouted a rack of antlers.

He chuckled at her astounded expression. "Okay,

guys, who wants to scrape plates and load the dishwasher? Thanks, Bob,'' he said, although Robert Fullerton didn't volunteer. ''Pete, you and Geoffrey can gather the plates.''

The two men nodded their bald heads agreeably.

''After we've spiffied up the place, who's interested in a friendly game of poker? All proceeds go to purchasing food and chew toys, *especially* chew toys, for these canine companions that are overrunning the place.''

The comment drew several snickers and inspired conversations about the various breeds of dogs that were loping around Triple R.

While the other men tended KP duty, Jake wiped the table clean, and then strode over to refill Anna's coffee cup. Decaffeinated, of course. There was no other kind at Triple R.

''Boy, you've really made a change in attitude,'' Anna commented as Jake filled her cup. ''I've seen Mori work miracles a dozen times, but you—'' She shook her frizzy chestnut head and grinned. ''You're an overnight convert.''

''What can I say? I've seen the light and I'm a changed man,'' he declared.

''Yeah, except you've taken it to the extremes from what I've heard. You're wearing yourself out rushing from one activity to the next.''

He cocked his head and winked at her. ''Never can have too much fun, you know, Anna.''

She shot him a wry glance. ''Actually, all play and no work can be bad news, too. If you don't believe it, just ask me. I wasted my life on two husbands who drank themselves half-blind and turned junkyard-dog mean. I finally wised up and left. Of course, I didn't have anywhere to go until Mori found me and offered me a place to live and work.''

Anna stared at him over the rim of her coffee cup. "Of course, I like to enjoy leisure activities myself. Are women allowed in this poker game?"

"You bet." Jake grinned when she snickered at his pun. "I advocate equality for one and all."

"Good. I'll fetch the cards."

To Jake's amazement, Anna could play poker like a pro—must've learned from those two losers she married. In fact, she knew the names and rules to a variety of games he'd never heard of. Although the group was only playing for pennies and nickels, Anna had a stack of coins resting beside her right elbow when Jake called it quits for the evening.

"How about horseshoes tomorrow before supper?" Jake suggested as he watched Anna rake up the winnings for the collection plate.

"All the cash still goes to the Fund for Canine Companions, right?" Tom asked, chuckling.

Jake nodded. "I can't afford to lose too many more socks to that fuzzball dog I'm sleeping with. We definitely need chew toys."

When the group adjourned, Jake headed for the bookshelves in the corner of the living area. Since he'd missed his evening jog, he needed a book to distract himself from forbidden thoughts of Moriah's cheery smiles, her bubbling laughter, her outlandish attire. Damn, that woman stuck in his mind like glue.

Whistling, Jake ambled across the freshly mowed compound, then slowed his step when he saw Moriah, wearing a leopard-print blouse that was the exact match to his skimpy underwear. Her blond hair lay in shimmering waves over her shoulders and cascaded down her back. He hadn't realized how long and gorgeous her hair was until she left it unbound.

Jeez, he'd love to plunge his hands into that thick, shiny mass of hair, love to inhale the fresh, clean scent he knew was waiting to consume his senses. He wanted to get his hands all over her—

Whoa. Down, boy. Don't go there!

Jake wrapped his self-control—which wasn't as reliable as he used to think it was—around himself and strode resolutely toward his front porch where Moriah was cooing and stroking the fuzzball of a mutt.

"Feeling better, Mo?" he asked as casually as he knew how.

She glanced up and he tumbled into the depths of those captivating eyes that reminded him of the crystal waters on a Caribbean coastline. Damn it, why'd she have to be more incredibly attractive than the day before? With each passing day she became even more attractive to him. Hell, he just couldn't catch a break when it came to this woman.

"Hey, Jake." She smiled and hot, hungry sensations pelted him repeatedly. "Yes, I do feel better. Thanks for asking."

"You missed a tasty dinner," he said, for lack of much else to say—except, *I'm wearing myself out trying to keep my distance from you and here you are, tempting the hell out of me all over again.*

"Anna brought me a tray." Moriah rose gracefully to her feet to follow him inside. "Do you mind a little company?"

"No." He'd prefer it wasn't Moriah's company because, damn it, after days of trying *not* to think about her, she still weighed too heavily on his mind.

Moriah sank onto the couch and propped those long,

tanned legs on the edge of the coffee table. Jake plunked down on the opposite cushion—as far away from temptation as he could get.

"You really don't need to bother joining me for recreational activities anymore." Jake stared straight ahead at the mountain landscape painting, searching desperately for his *querencia*—that place Moriah referred to as a person's private, serene haven. "I've taken to this life of leisure like a duck to water."

"That's the thing, Jake. You've gone overboard," she said gently.

He swiveled his head around to stare at her—and wished he hadn't. Damn, she had the most kissable lips ever planted on a feminine face. He knew for a fact they were lush and soft, just like the rest of her shapely body.

Give it a rest, man! Concentrate on something else!

"So, you're saying I didn't take time to smell the roses before I arrived and now I'm smelling too many roses?" he asked a little too defensively.

She nodded and smiled. It was one of those neutral smiles, and suddenly that wasn't good enough for him. He wanted to coax out one of those blinding smiles that was a natural response to something amusing he said or did. He wanted a true reaction from her—a reaction of a woman to a man, not recreational director to guest.

"There seems to be something else going on here besides your apparent enthusiasm for sports and relaxation techniques. Am I right?"

Jake fiddled with the book in his hand, glanced at the title page. "I credit you with enormous intelligence, Mo. I think you know what triggered my recreational-activity spree." He sighed audibly. "Look, I told you I'm having a little problem with this attraction to you."

When she tried to interrupt he held up his hand like a traffic cop. "I'm trying to work through it for your sake and mine. You can't always convince contrary male hormones to calm down, even when you know you'll be gone soon."

"Jake—"

"And it's not like I'm not aware of your policy of keeping things on a casual level, because I'm in total agreement with it. Besides, I have my responsibilities and you have yours. Things wouldn't work out anyway."

"Jake, could you stop yammering and let me get a word in edgewise, please?"

Jake slumped on the sofa, raked his fingers through his hair and put a stranglehold on the book in his lap. "Okay, fire away."

She scooted closer. He really wished she'd stayed where the hell she was. The scent of her perfume reached out like octopus tentacles to grab his attention. The warmth of her body so close to his put him on red alert.

Hell! He'd spent hours on end distracting himself. Now here she was, a foot away, cramping his comfort zone, filling up his senses until wanting her became an impulsive throb drumming through his too attentive body.

"We definitely have a problem here," she murmured as she reached out to smooth the hair that drooped over his forehead. "I've worked myself into exhaustion trying not to think about you."

"Mo, don't," he said through clenched teeth.

She laughed softly and the sound went all through him, igniting fires in his bloodstream and nerve endings.

"Funny, but that's what I told myself while I soaked

in the tub for an hour during my meditation," she admitted. "*Don't* get in over your head. *Don't* get too attached. *Don't* get too involved."

"Smart woman. You keep chanting those mantras," he said, his voice husky.

He made the crucial mistake of glancing at her while she was up close and personal. Aw damn, he could feel his body inching toward hers, see her inching tentatively toward him.

"This is another mistake," Jake growled, his lips a hairbreadth from her luscious mouth.

"A mistake of gigantic proportions," she agreed, staring at his lips as if she wanted to devour him.

He knew that feeling all too well.

"Damn, I'm dying for another taste of you," he said raggedly.

"Same goes, Jake," she whispered. "What's wrong with us?"

"I don't know. I was hoping you could tell me."

"I'm clueless."

"No, you're positively irresistible."

His mouth slanted over hers and the dam of restraint broke like unleashed floodwaters when she opened her lips and welcomed him. The impact of tasting her thoroughly sent his willpower up in flames and he was fully aroused in one red-hot minute.

Internal combustion, he reckoned. He'd been on a slow burn too long. That was the problem with internal combustion. Everything below the surface was already hot and smoldering before the flames erupted. Then you had a devastating blaze on your hands and no effective means of extinguishing it promptly. When the fire of desire erupted and took on a life all its own, there was nothing you could do but let it burn.

Jake roped his arms around her, crushing her to him, fitting her lush curves and swells into his aching contours. When her arms fastened around him, as if she, too, were holding on for dear life, he just lost it. There were one hundred and one reasons *not* to take this relationship to an intimate level and only one reason to. Wanting. Uncontrollable wanting that distorted sensibility into flimsy, inconsequential excuses.

Before Jake knew it he had Moriah on her back and he was pressing her into the sofa cushions. He was as hard as diamonds and his breath was coming in gasping spurts, because his heart was pounding against his ribs like a sledgehammer. He had his hands all over her and she returned the favor enthusiastically. One kiss blended into the next and Jake didn't come up for air until his lungs threatened to burst from oxygen deprivation.

While he was exploring the curvaceous terrain of her body with eager hands, he was sinking into her yielding softness, cursing the cotton and denim barrier between them. He strung greedy kisses over the pulsating vein in her throat, along her collarbone and nuzzled his face in the knit fabric that covered her breasts. His hand glided up her leg, his thumb sliding beneath the hem of her shorts. He lifted his head to recapture her lips in a devouring kiss while he cupped his hand between her thighs, gently stroking her through her panties.

"Jake…stop!" Moriah gasped and pushed him away.

He groaned in unholy torment, but he acknowledged her request to back off. Much as he wanted her—and he did, badly—he had too much respect and admiration for her to use his physical size and strength to manhandle her. Although it took considerable willpower, Jake pried himself away—though his male body was screaming some pretty raunchy curses at him for being so damn honorable.

Pushing upright, Jake gave Moriah room to sit up and adjust the leopard-print blouse that was riding just below her breasts. As for his leopard print, the speckled fabric was stretched tightly below his belt buckle, leaving him decidedly uncomfortable. He wondered what the chances were of a man, as hot and bothered as he was, dying of sexual deprivation. He had to be in the high-risk category, for sure.

He wanted to throw back his head and howl in frustration when Moriah climbed to her feet and wobbled unsteadily toward the front door. She was leaving and he knew it was for the best, but you couldn't convince his male hormones of that. They were in full-scale riot, pounding at his insides like battering rams, demanding release.

Jake was still struggling to get his breathing under control when Moriah closed and locked the door with a decisive click. He glanced up when she switched off the overhead lights. The night-light cast a faint glow across the room, outlining her arresting figure and the glimmer of gold in her hair.

"Moriah?" he whispered uncertainly.

"Make no mistake, Jake. I *never* do this with my other guests. It's imperative to me that you know that," she murmured as she walked deliberately toward him. "You're the…um…first. But there comes a time when it just feels too right and necessary. Sometimes you have to take a risk, to live in the moment and reap as much from the *now* as you can get. I've had a really hard time with this, but I've made my decision and I believe it's the right one."

He grinned wryly. "Woman, you have no concept of what a hard time really is," he assured her.

When she chuckled, he took her hand in his, drawing her down beside him. Jake had spent his life looking to the future, toeing the line as he went. He'd accepted his responsibilities without considering his own wants, needs and desires. Now here he was, ready to say to hell with everything and everyone for just one night with Moriah. Because, right now, he couldn't see past this moment or the intense, obsessive craving that consumed him, mind and body.

"You should know I'm not very experienced," she whispered against his lips.

"You should know I'm out of practice," he whispered back.

"Really? What about all that wild kinky sex you claimed you had with all those different women?" she teased playfully.

He grinned. "I might have overexaggerated—a lot."

He felt her smile against his mouth as she looped her arms over his shoulders. She said, "After seeing you traipse around in your gaping towel—and I swear you did that just to get me all worked up—I've had the most erotic dreams you can imagine."

"They can't possibly be as erotic and disturbing as mine," he insisted huskily. "Mine are in Technicolor and Surround Sound."

Jake lost all interest in conversation the moment his roaming hand closed around the full mound of her breast. He felt her tremble, then melt against him. He brushed his thumb over the pebbled peak beneath her blouse and heard her ragged moan of pleasure. The intriguing sound encouraged him to discover all the muffled noises she'd make when he explored each curve, swell and flaring contour of her body.

He fumbled momentarily with the clasp of her bra—cursing his lack of practice—then he slid his palm over her ribs to acquaint himself fully with the satiny feel of her flesh. He pulled off her blouse and bra with his free hand, then lowered his head to flick his tongue against her dusky nipples. She hissed breath through her teeth and nearly came off the sofa. Jake grinned triumphantly at her wild response. There and then, he vowed to summon more passionate noises as he took her nipple between his thumb and forefinger and tugged gently. Sighing raggedly, she arched upward and writhed restlessly. He suckled her, kneaded her silky flesh and whispered hot, carnal descriptions of what he wanted to do with her.

Boy, that really set her off, Jake noted in roguish satisfaction. She practically tore off his bland-tan chambray shirt in her eagerness to get her hot little hands on his chest. She raked her nails over him like a playful kitten, then slid the heel of her hand down his belly until she encountered the fly of his jeans and the rigid flesh beneath. Jake groaned in pleasure, then he cursed in torment when she withdrew her hand, as if she thought he disapproved of her bold caresses.

"Do that again," he urged her. "You have my permission to get your hands all over me. Don't be bashful, sweet pea. Everything I have is yours to explore. No holds barred here tonight."

She snickered impishly as she unfastened his belt, then tossed it recklessly across the room. "Remember, you asked for this."

"No," he contradicted as his hand glided leisurely across her concave belly and his gaze lingered appreciatively on her bare breasts. "I'm *begging* for it and I'm putting myself in your competent hands."

Jake forgot to breathe, couldn't even recall why he needed to, when her fingers folded around his throbbing length—leopard print and all. He was entirely too receptive to her caresses, he realized as a barrage of pleasure pummeled him. He was straining shamelessly toward her hand before he could stop himself. She stroked him repeatedly and the friction caused by her caressing hand drove him wild.

Placing himself in Moriah's hands—literally—was too distracting. Much as he liked her provocative touch, he had his own fantasy to live out. He wanted her naked under his hands and lips and he couldn't think straight when she was arousing him at warp speed.

Jake twisted away to peel off her shorts and panties, giving devoted attention to every silky inch of skin he exposed. When his hand skimmed between her thighs he felt the moist heat of her desire beckoning him closer. He felt her quiver, heard her raspy moan and swore he wouldn't be satisfied until he knew every part of her lush, receptive body by taste, scent and touch.

His thumb glided over her softest flesh and she gasped, then clutched desperately at his shoulders. Her nails bit into his skin hard enough to leave marks but he barely noticed. He was too captivated by her shimmering response. He dipped one finger inside her and felt liquid fire shimmer on his hand. He stroked her and felt shock waves of sensations ripple through her, but it still wasn't enough to satisfy him. He bent his head to trace her softest, hottest flesh with his tongue and felt her legs go lax against his shoulders. He kissed her intimately, caressed her with lips and fingertips and felt the wild uncontrollable spasms of desire vibrate through her body and echo into his.

"Jake?…Ahhh…No!" she whimpered in panted breaths.

Her body quivered with urgent need and he tugged frantically to free himself from his jeans and briefs but they tangled around his knees and crisscrossed over his ankles. Moriah was clutching at him, urging him to hurry. He wanted to be there for her at that precise moment when she wanted him to the point of mindless desperation.

Oh, hell! he thought suddenly. He needed protection. Damn, he had to locate his wallet—and fast! Jeez, why hadn't he thought of that earlier? Because his brain had shut down and his male body was on automatic pilot, that's why!

"Jake? What's wrong?" Moriah asked breathlessly.

"I need my wallet."

"You aren't planning to pay for this, are you?" she teased.

He chuckled as he crammed his hand into his pocket to grab his wallet. "I thought resort owners charged for every little thing."

"Believe me," she said, staring pointedly at the bad boy from south of the border. "This is no small thing, Jake."

He grinned scampishly, then scowled as he fumbled to locate a foil packet. "Hell, these things don't have expiration dates, do they? I'm gonna slit my own throat if they do!"

It finally dawned on Moriah what he was referring to. It was a wonder anything dawned on her when she felt so dazed and out of control. Lingering sensations were still humming through her ultrasensitive body and she could barely find her voice to reply.

"Expiration dates?" she repeated. "I have no idea!"

"Just give me a sec here," he whispered when she reached for him.

"I don't have a sec. I'm dying here, Jake," she panted.

While he was preoccupied with his foil packet, Moriah clasped the hot rigid length of him in her hand, drawing him to her. Touching him familiarly excited her beyond belief. Each stroke of her hand made the ache inside her more pronounced.

"Jeez, woman," he wheezed, his breath hitching.

Realizing she was also disturbing him to the extreme, she stroked him again, urging him ever closer. "Hurry up. I need you now!"

"For a week you've been telling me to slow down. Now you want me to hurry up. Damn, there's no pleasing you."

"You could be if you'd stop fooling around!" she teased.

She glanced up to see Jake looming over her, ripping open the foil packet with his teeth. She wanted to laugh at the overanxious expression on his face. She wanted to screech at the tormenting delay. She was on fire and impatient and he couldn't move fast enough to appease the urgent need pounding through her.

"Here we go," he murmured as he swept her caressing hands out of the way to don protection. "Okay, okay, everything's cool—"

"No, it isn't! I'm burning alive." Moriah surged toward him, wanting to experience the ultimate pleasure she sensed awaited her. "Come here, Jake. Now!"

He braced himself above her and gently nudged her

legs apart with his knees. He uncurled above her and plunged his hips forward, filling the empty ache left in the wake of his arousing kisses and caresses. She grimaced slightly, trying to adjust to the unfamiliar penetration of this passionate possession.

Jake stopped dead still. His wild-eyed gaze locked with hers, his teeth clenched in restraint. "Moriah?" he chirped, stunned.

She forced herself to relax rather than resist the intense pressure bearing down on her. She held Jake to her, wanting and needing to rediscover that pinnacle of ecstasy he'd taken her to earlier. "I told you it was the first time," she reminded him as she rocked her hips gingerly against his.

"Yeah, but I thought you meant… Oh, hell, I'd have taken things slower and easier if I'd known. You should've told me in plain English."

She stared at him in frustration when he continued to hold himself perfectly still—as if *that* would help! "This isn't all there is, is it, Jake?" she wheezed. "Please tell me it isn't."

He shook his tousled head and stared down at her from beneath long black lashes. She couldn't explain the unfamiliar expression that spread across his face. Nor could she interpret the hint of a smile that quirked his lips. Why was he looking at her like that?

"No, sweet pea, this isn't all there is," he whispered softly. "There's plenty more. I'll show you."

He reached between their linked bodies to stroke her in some magical way that caused sensations to explode like the special effects in a sci-fi movie. Then he was gliding forward and withdrawing in slow, hypnotic rhythm, sinking deeper and deeper until she couldn't determine where his passion ended and hers began. They moved as one in tempo with a melody playing some-where in the distance. The erotic crescendo built, taking her higher, holding her suspended like a rhapsody drift-ing on the wind.

Suddenly Moriah felt the world crumble beneath her and she spiraled downward into a dark abyss where sen-sation after incredible sensation marked the passage of time. He drove into her with such frantic urgency that she was swept into the heat of indescribable passion all over again. She was burning alive in wild, breathless abandon. No part of her mind, body and soul seemed exempt or untouched by the raging fire of passion that engulfed her. Blazing flames, scorching heat, scalding steam and infinite pleasure consumed her, stole her breath until she nearly passed out.

When Jake clutched her to him, groaned and shud-dered in release, Moriah followed him over the edge of oblivion again, marveling at the aftershocks of rapture pulsing through her. She was pretty sure Jake's solid, muscular body was the anchor that prevented her from floating weightlessly away, like scattered ashes in the wind. She savored the feel of his arms holding her tightly, possessively. She marveled at the innate sense of rightness and belonging that whispered through what was left of her mind, body and soul.

A long while later—at least a century by her calcu-lations—Jake raised his head and nibbled at that unbe-lievably sensitive spot beneath her ear. "You wanna ex-plain to me how this happened?"

"Because I'm attracted to you. Uncontrollably at-tracted to you, apparently," she clarified in a ragged voice.

"Glad to hear that, especially since I seem to be suf-fering from the same mindless affliction. But I was referring to the fact that you managed to live thirty years as a…er…without having…aw, hell…How is it that I'm the first to discover that you're the best-kept secret in Oklahoma?''

Moriah chuckled at Jake's roundabout way of asking why she was still a virgin. ''I told you my mother was in ill health and I was responsible for her care. That didn't leave time for a social life, aside from a few casual dates that lost interest because I couldn't go out on a regular basis. I lived at home during college to stay with Mom because Dad was on the road or in his office so much. Thankfully, my first adult infatuation never progressed to the intimate stage before I discovered Stuart was a corporate Romeo. Then I devoted myself to establishing this resort. Generally, I only come in contact with men who are old enough to be my father.''

''Until I came along and was closer to your age?'' he asked wryly. ''Thanks, sugarplum, it's nice to know I'm wanted for my convenience and close proximity.''

Moriah swatted him on the shoulder. ''Yeah, that's it, stud muffin. This has everything to do with your compatible age, your accessibility, your incredible body and nothing whatsoever to do with the fact that I actually *like* you.''

Jake grinned slyly. ''Careful, dumplin', you're starting to sound a tad sarcastic.''

She batted her long lashes at him. ''Gee, I wonder where I picked that up? Huh?''

Jake shifted sideways on the narrow confines of the sofa, then tucked Moriah possessively against him. Knowing he was her first lover bombarded him with mixed emotions. On one hand, he was enormously pleased because he'd never been anyone's first time. On the other hand, being Moriah's first experience with passion provoked feelings he wasn't sure he wanted to sort out. He had an old-fashioned sense of values that made him uncomfortable with what had transpired—but not so uncomfortable that he regretted one single, glorious, mind-boggling moment of making love with Moriah.

Furthermore, he knew that satisfying this phenomenal craving, just once, wasn't going to cut it. All Jake had to do was take one look at Moriah's bewitching face, run his hand through that silky mass of golden hair and feel her exquisite body meshed to his, and wham! He wanted her like hell blazing—again.

He should've known nothing would be simple and uncomplicated with Moriah. Hell, he wouldn't be where he was right now if she didn't stir something deep and compelling inside him—way down in those places he'd sealed off and protected for years. He'd worked himself into a strict routine that didn't allow for anything except the needs of his family and business. But Moriah had reached inside him to unlock feelings and set emotions free.

He liked her. He really liked her. He liked what she stood for, and against. He liked her concern and devotion to her guests, her father and her staff. She was a kind, caring person with a heart of twenty-four-karat gold. He liked her sense of humor, her intelligence, her personality, and he loved her uninhibited responses to him.

"You're awfully quiet," Moriah murmured as she traced the curve of his lips with her forefinger.

"I'm thinking." He kissed her fingertip, then nipped at it gently, playfully.

Moriah propped upon her elbow and the waterfall of wavy hair tumbled around her like a cape. She was breathtaking, he thought. Blue-eyed blonde or not, she was the most beautiful woman he'd ever seen, ever touched.

"Don't do a lot of thinking, Jake," she requested, smiling the kind of smile that made him go hot all over again. "I know you're going back to your world soon and I'll still be here in my world. That's a given. So, for the rest of your stay could we just let whatever will be, be?"

She was offering him the easy out, so why didn't he feel comfortable and satisfied taking it? A casual fling for Moriah? He really didn't think she was the type, given her track record in bedroom gymnastics—or rather, the lack thereof.

"Fine, if that's the way you want it." What was he supposed to say? What man in his right mind would turn down incredible sex with an incredibly beautiful woman who didn't make demands on him? Yet, the fact that she *wasn't* making demands left him wondering if what he felt for her was more intense than what she felt for him. Jake had been down that road before with his fiancée. To this day, he remembered what humiliating rejection felt like—and it wasn't something he wanted to experience again. Jake's troubled thoughts scattered like buckshot when he heard clomping footsteps on his front porch.

"Oh, damn," Moriah muttered, scrambling from the couch with more speed than grace. She flung Jake a horrified glance as she groped to gather her scattered clothes.

Jake tried to vault to his feet but his legs got tangled in Moriah's. They fell, cattywampus, and landed with thuds and muffled curses. Jake, however, managed to brace himself the split second before he squashed Moriah flatter than a shadow.

''Jake?'' A deep, persistent voice followed the sound thump that rattled the door. ''Are you asleep? Hey, open up!''

Damn, talk about your untimely interruptions! Jake and Moriah gaped at each other in alarm. They were about to be caught red-handed. And worse, stark-bone naked—*together!*

7

___

Jake didn't know whether to pretend to be asleep or answer the summons. Moriah looked terrified of the prospect of being discovered, and no way did he want her to be humiliated so he kept his trap shut.

"Jake? Yo!"

"It's Tom," Moriah whispered apprehensively.

Jake swore colorfully.

"Hey, Jake. You got a call from your sisters and I can't find Mori to ask her whether to let you return the call or not."

"Just a minute," Jake called out.

It was second nature to leap into action when his sisters needed him. They obviously needed him or they wouldn't be calling, expecting him to handle whatever emergency had arisen.

Jake's hand shot toward the closet, indicating Moriah should stuff herself in it. With a quick nod, she scooped up her clothes and streaked across the darkened room in a waddling crouch.

Jake grabbed his breeches and put them on. He hated going commando but he had no idea where the skimpy, leopard-print underwear had gone to. He glanced quickly at his illuminated watch. It was nine o'clock. Barefoot, he darted to the door.

Spitwad and Tom were standing on the porch. The

burly masseuse thrust out his hand to give Jake a note with a phone number scribbled on it.

"Sorry to bother you, Jake, but your sisters said this was important and couldn't wait." He frowned fretfully. "Have you seen Moriah in the last half hour?"

Oh, yeah, he'd seen a lot of Moriah, but he figured Tom would take him apart with his bare hands if he knew what he and Moriah had been doing in his darkened cabin. "I haven't seen her recently," he lied straight through his teeth. "But she came by earlier to talk to me about slowing down my frantic recreational pace."

Tom stared at Jake for a long, pensive moment "Well, I guess she's okay then. She must be visiting with one of the other guests or something."

Or something, thought Jake.

"Mori usually delivers wine or milk around this time of night. Guess I'll try to track her down while you make the call in her office."

"Thanks." Jake let Spitwad inside, closed the door and switched on the lamp.

When the footsteps receded, Moriah slithered from the closet. Her leopard-print shirt and shorts were inside out and her hair was in wild disarray. She looked both comical and gorgeous at once.

"Er...you better skedaddle to the bathroom," he suggested, grinning. "I don't think that ensemble was meant to be reversible. Somebody might get suspicious if they see you dressed like that."

Moriah gasped in dismay when she glanced down her torso. "Yeah, good idea. Go on over to the lodge and make the call. I hope everything is okay with your sisters."

Jake nodded solemnly. "I'm sorry about this."

She waved off his apology. "Don't hitch a ride on the guilt-trip express, Jake. What happened was by mutual consent. Now go!"

Jake stuffed his feet in his boots, snatched up his shirt and dressed on the way out the door. He hoped that one of his sisters hadn't met with calamity while he wasn't on his perpetual watch. Although his loyalty had always been to his sisters, he didn't like feeling as if he'd abandoned Moriah moments after making love to her for the first time. He didn't want their evening to end—period. Unfortunately, the interruption had ruined the moment. But then, Jake wondered if fate had intervened and it was for the best. He couldn't make a habit of this, he lectured himself sternly as he hotfooted it across the compound. No matter what he felt for Moriah, this was still an ill-fated attraction. There were too many obstacles in their path to develop a lasting relationship.

If he had the sense God gave a goose he wouldn't let himself forget that.

MORIAH TURNED her clothes right side out, reached into her pocket for a clip to secure her wild tangle of hair and checked her reflection in the bathroom mirror. She felt like a teenager who'd been sneaking around doing things she wasn't supposed to be doing—and nearly getting caught at it. Never let it be said that *reckless* and *impulsive* didn't have its consequences, she mused as she strode toward the cabin door.

The consequences of her intimate encounter with Jake were severe. For a while now, she'd suspected that she was a little bit in love with Jake—given the amount of time she spent thinking about him and wanting him to the extreme. Why else would she have given in to her fierce attraction to him? Although she was fully aware that she was unskilled and incompetent when it came to romantic relationships, that hadn't stopped her from eagerly participating in the momentous milestone in her life. Yes, she was in love with Jake and she knew she'd get her heart broken when he left Triple R.

Moriah had enough psychology classes in college to know that once you'd analyzed the problem then you could make the necessary adjustments and get on with your life. She decided that since she was only allowed to go round once in life she was going to enjoy the remarkable passion she'd discovered in Jake's arms, enjoy the pleasure of his company…and then she was going to let him go.

She knew his first priority was to his sisters. Tonight was proof of that. She didn't fault him for it, because she lived by the same values of loyalty and commitment. She took care of her father and her unique family here at Triple R, providing homes for her staff who had no other family support groups of their own. The staff members had become her extended family and she'd walk through fire for every last one of them.

All things considered, Moriah decided that the only rule she'd apply to this short-term affair with Jake was that there *were* no rules, no strings attached, no expectations and regrets.

Her mind wrapped firmly around that resolution, Moriah walked off into the darkness. She cared deeply for Jake and she believed he cared about her—in his own limited way. She was going to live for today without stewing about tomorrow, because Jake was the best thing that had ever happened to her and she wasn't going to let happiness and pleasure pass her by.

Some people never discovered the magic she found with Jake. Their passion was incredible. Their playfulness and companionship were rare and cherished. They simply clicked. Together, they sparked amazing chemistry. Moriah smiled contentedly and clung to the warm, giddy sensations bubbling inside her as she trotted toward the lodge to gather the wine and milk for her evening rounds.

ANXIOUSLY, Jake dialed the familiar number to Kim's home phone, then waited for his sister to pick up. He hadn't realized how totally relaxed and satisfied he'd become…until the tension suddenly thrummed through him. He inhaled a cathartic breath, unclenched his teeth and loosened his grasp of the phone.

"Hello?"

"What's wrong, Kim?" Jake asked without preamble.

"Nothing's wrong."

He frowned, bemused. "I was under the impression that calls to the resort were limited to emergencies." For the first time in forever, Jake was impatient with his sister, specifically because he preferred to be lying in Moriah's arms, reveling in the pleasure she aroused in him.

Of course, Tom Stevens was probably turning the ranch upside down to locate Moriah. The possibility of spending the remainder of the night with her was slim indeed.

"So what's up, Kim?" Jake asked, uncomfortable with the fact that his newly awakened personal whims and desires were standing directly between him and his unswerving loyalty to his sisters. The feeling was foreign and unwelcome.

"Golly, J.T., you sound tensed up. Isn't your recreational vacation working for you? You aren't still mad at Lisa and me, are you?"

J.T.? He wasn't sure he was the same J. T. Prescott who'd arrived ten days ago. The name and the image didn't seem to fit quite right—neither did his skin. He felt like a snake during shedding season. A transformation had taken place in his life and his focus and direction had become fuzzy and unclear. He wasn't sure how he felt about that.

"I was irritated as hell, but I got over it. You and Lisa were right. I was stuck in a rut and I needed to break my routine. I can see that now. So, are you going to clue me in on what this call is about or do we have to play twenty questions?"

"Hold on a minute," Kim insisted. "I want Lisa to pick up the extension phone."

Jake heard Kim yelling at the top of her lungs—just like the old days.

"Hi, bro!"

"Hey, kiddo," he said, smiling at the sound of Lisa's peppy voice. In some ways Moriah reminded him of Lisa.

"We have big news," Kim and Lisa said in unison. "We're pregnant!"

Jake nearly dropped the cordless phone that he'd tucked against his shoulder. Thrown off balance, he reached out to steady himself against the edge of Moriah's desk. "What? Both of you?" he bleated. "Jeez, I know the two of you are close, but did you plan this? In my mind, you aren't even old enough to be doing the stuff that makes babies!"

"We're married, J.T.," Lisa reminded him, chuckling.

"I know. I was there for both ceremonies." Jake kerplopped in Moriah's chair then glanced at the old family photo of her and her parents. Damn, such a cute kid. Too bad she'd had adult responsibility thrust on her at an early age and missed out on the customary social life during adolescence. At least, he'd had that, but he wished the same normalcy for Moriah. "Congratulations. So when are my nieces and-or nephews due to arrive?"

"March," they chorused. "March twenty-first."

Jake jerked upright in his chair, his eyes popping. "The same day?" he croaked. "How is that possible? Just a coincidence?"

"No, you know we've been on the same menstrual cycle since puberty," Kim said.

Jake grimaced at Kim's plainspoken comment. He remembered, with vivid clarity, the mood swings, PMS, adolescent rebellions, boyfriend troubles and various and sundry other traumas he'd coped with while raising two kid sisters.

"We simply did our calculations and planned conception—"

"Hey, I don't need to hear all the details," Jake interrupted Kim. "Thanks to the two of you, I already know more than I want to know about all that female stuff."

"We had it confirmed by our doctor today," Lisa said, chuckling. "Then our hubbies took us out to dinner to celebrate. That's why we're late giving you the call. We just couldn't wait to tell you the great news, J.T. Hope we didn't interrupt your leisurely activities this evening."

They'd interrupted far more than your run-of-the-mill leisurely activities, he mused. But he was delighted with the news. "Congratulations, you two. I'm excited about being an uncle," he enthused. "Glad you called."

Damn, he was going to be an uncle! Wasn't that something? He'd have to keep close watch on the little tykes, because they'd probably be his only exposure to infants. Plus, he wanted to contribute money to college funds—no sense waiting until the last minute for that. Higher education didn't come cheap these days. He shuddered to think about the catastrophic bills that'd be rolling in when his nieces and nephews entered Yale or Harvard. Nothing but the best for his sisters' kids.

"We better let you go," Kim said. "We need our rest, you know. This morning sickness that lasts all day is the pits."

"No joke," Lisa agreed. "I can't cook certain foods without making a dash to the bathroom to bow to the porcelain god."

"Don't start!" Kim yelped. "Just the thought of the smell from cooking bacon is enough to make me nauseous."

Jake felt himself tensing up again. The very idea of his sisters being queasy and ill tormented him. "Are my brothers-in-law being as considerate and helpful as they should be? Put those two clowns on the line right now," he demanded.

Lisa snickered. "Calm down, J.T. We'll be fine. The guys are pampering us, so not to worry."

"Yeah, and sometimes they pamper us to annoying extremes," Kim added. "We just wanted to share the good news with you. Night, J.T. Happy belated birthday. Love ya."

"Me, too," Lisa was quick to add.

Jake hung up, then scrubbed his hand across his face. Damn, Kim and Lisa didn't seem old enough to have kids of their own. When had they grown up and what were the chances of him ever treating them like mature, responsible adults when he'd been both brother and parents to them for a decade?

His mind spinning like a Tilt-A-Whirl, Jake ambled outside to inhale a breath of fresh night air. He recoiled reflexively when he noticed a shadow looming by the stone wall. "Jeez, Tom, you scared ten years off my life."

Tom's monobrow formed a V over his narrowed hazel eyes. "Better scared off than *whipped* off," he growled threateningly.

Jake had the unshakable feeling that good ol' Tom wasn't as oblivious to Moriah's whereabouts as he'd let on. "Are we gonna open a can of whoop-ass, right here, right now?"

"My can's already open, pal," he muttered ominously as he slammed his right fist into the palm of his left hand. "I may be a former football player who got his melon cracked one time too many on the gridiron, but I ain't blind and I ain't stupid. Furthermore, I've been around enough blocks in my time to know what I'm seeing when I see it. You had *The Look* when I came to your cabin. Now where is she, damn it?"

"Making her rounds is my guess," Jake replied, remembering the old sports injury on Tom's bulky shoulder that Tom had told him about. He figured he could get off the first punch and run like hell, then sic Spitwad on this fuming brute. His ferocious guard dog would scare off Tom. Yeah, right.

"She's family," Tom snarled as he loomed formidably in the darkness. "You've got kid sisters, don'tcha? You know what it feels like to be protective of family."

"Yeah, I know," Jake said, holding his ground—although he wasn't sure that was the wisest thing to do. But neither would he turn tail and run like a damn coward. He wasn't ashamed of how he felt about Moriah.

"I don't think she's very experienced, if you know what I mean," Tom muttered.

Nobody knew that better than Jake. "What do you expect me to say, Tom?"

The has-been tackle knotted his beefy fists and bared his teeth—minus a couple. "That you won't hurt her, for starters."

"I won't hurt her," Jake accommodated, watching those meaty fists carefully, bracing himself in case he needed to sidestep to avoid a mind-scrambling punch. "But who's going to keep her from hurting me, Tom?"

Obviously Tom wasn't expecting that. He frowned and his fists dropped to his sides.

"Since you claim you aren't blind and stupid, you tell me how I'm supposed to resist a generous, kind-hearted woman who bubbles with vitality and spirit and cares about her friends the same way they care about her? Maybe most of the other guests around here are so focused on themselves that they can't look past Moriah's wild attire and see the all-too-irresistible woman behind that cheery smile, but I can."

"Yeah, I'll admit she puts up a good front and that she's too attractive for her own good," Tom mumbled.

"Don't you think I can't see that her life revolves around this staff, her father and her guests? You think I haven't worn myself out with physical activities, in hopes of battling the attraction and keeping a respectable distance? Hell, I even tried to convince Moriah to let me go home so I wouldn't have to fight temptation. This isn't exactly what I planned, either, you know, Tom."

Jake stared Tom squarely in the eye. "There, I've had my say. If you still wanna take your best shot, then go for it. Moriah is worth a black eye and swollen jaw, so don't think a lot of bullying is going to make me back down.''

Tom glared meat cleavers at him. "I really wanna hit you, Jake," he seethed.

Jake prepared himself to feint left, dart right and land a quick counterblow. "Go ahead and try, if it'll make you feel better."

Tom cocked his bulging arm. "If it's just sex, I'll punch the living daylights out of you."

"It isn't. It would be easier if that's all it was. I tried not to care, not to get involved," Jake admitted. "But I'm sure as hell not ashamed of what I feel for Moriah."

Tom stared him down for a long moment, and then he uncocked his arm. "I mean it, Jake. If she's unhappy, then I'm unhappy."

"Well, that makes two of us." They exchanged significant glances and Jake waited, wondering if Tom wanted a promise, signed in blood, that he wasn't using Moriah as a convenient outlet for sex.

"Come in for a massage in the morning," Tom ordered gruffly.

Jake's brows shot up and he chuckled. "Not a chance." No way was he going to stretch out on a table and put himself at the mercy of this muscled hulk that openly admitted he wanted to beat Jake to a pulp.

Tom nodded. "You're right. Better wait a couple of days to make sure I've adjusted to the idea of you fooling around with Mori. It's gonna take some getting used to, but I'll never approve of it!"

Jake wheeled around and walked off. Whew! For a minute there he wasn't sure he'd live to see the birth of his nieces or nephews. But neither could he allow Tom to think that he was taking advantage of Moriah. No, there was much more to it than that. There were dan-

gerous, vulnerable emotions swirling beneath the surface. The incredible sex was an outward expression of
the feelings he'd tried to hold in check, feelings that
refused to be ignored or denied.

He wanted Moriah to the point of desperation, to the
point that he'd thrown caution to the four winds. He
liked being with her. He liked the way she made him
feel when he was with her. And, as she said, it was a
mutual, explosive and overpowering attraction that wrote
its own rules as it went along.

Jake broke stride and cursed Tom soundly, repeatedly.
The clever old fox had maneuvered Jake into putting his
sentiments for Moriah into words, which made it impossible to deny what he was feeling to anyone else,
especially to himself. Well, hell!

Moriah's spellbinding image rose above him in the
darkness and remembered sensations swamped and buf-
feted him. More than anything he wanted to be waiting
at Moriah's apartment after she made her rounds, wanted
to take up where they left off before they were interrupted. But he figured Tom would be guarding the door
and breathing fire.

When wanting Moriah intensified another twenty de-
grees, Jake quickened his step. He was going to take a
cold shower. Anything else was out of the question, even
when he knew that one night with Moriah was never
going to be enough to satisfy him.

Jake strode into his cabin and his gaze instantly landed
on the sofa. Tantalizing memories swirled around him
like a thick fog. The scent of her perfume still permeated
the room.

Jake sighed heavily. Damn, it was going to be a long
tormenting night filled with erotic dreams.

ALTHOUGH MORIAH WAS dragging bottom, because of her late-night drive into the nearest hamlet to gather a few supplies, she plastered on her customary smile to greet her guests at the breakfast table. Robert Fullerton was still complaining about the food on the buffet—and ended up going head-to-head with Anna who suggested that he help her cook if the meals didn't suit him. But Robert became invisible to her when Jake walked through the door and filled up her world.

Pretending nothing earthshaking had happened between them wasn't easy, but Moriah projected her air of cheerfulness when Jake nodded a greeting. She noticed belatedly that her staff was giving Jake the evil eye. She had the unmistakable feeling they knew something no one else was supposed to know.

Damn! Just what she needed—four mother hens clucking to beat the band. Worse, they were allowing personal resentment to affect their attitude toward Jake. He didn't deserve their hostility.

Moriah knew the best way to defuse trouble was to nip it in the bud. She intended to call a staff meeting immediately after breakfast and lay down the law. She was having none of this cold-shoulder routine that her staff directed toward Jake.

Ignoring Robert, who was whining that the scrambled eggs weren't fluffy enough to suit him, and Anna who was in his face again, Moriah took the empty seat beside Jake. Anna was flipping Robert's eggs upside down with a spatula, then waving the kitchen utensil in his face. Moriah considered breaking up the spat, but she had to admit that Anna and Robert looked as if they were enjoying their squabble. Maybe they needed to vent their frustrations and decided they were perfect sparring partners. Whatever. She wasn't going to intervene unless food or fists started flying.

"Is everything okay with your sisters?" Moriah asked Jake.

The smile that etched his features made Moriah's heart flip-flop in her chest. "I'm going to be an uncle, twice, in fact," he announced proudly. "Kim and Lisa are expecting in March, on the same day."

Moriah didn't have to ask if he was pleased by the news. She could feel the excitement and pleasure radiating around him.

"I guess this means I'll have to stop treating them like they were still teenagers," he said between bites of waffle swimming in syrup.

"I would've thought that giving them away in marriage would've done the trick," she remarked, then munched on her toast.

"Yeah, you'd think. But having babies ought to do it. I've got all sorts of plans to make for the little squirts."

His involvement in his sisters' lives touched her deeply. Yet, it hurt to know she'd never be his top priority, that there were only a few days left—and counting—for her to savor the feelings and sensations Jake aroused in her.

"I made a trip to a convenience store in town last night," she murmured.

Jake glanced at her curiously. "Just how far is the nearest town?"

"Ten miles west," she informed him.

"So what was the purpose of your late-night run?" he asked.

Moriah squirmed awkwardly in her chair and felt a blush bleeding across her cheeks when she noticed the staff was monitoring her conversation with Jake like four eagle-eyed chaperons. "Um...I picked up some packets," she whispered confidentially. "Since I don't have a frame of reference, I bought the extralarge size."

Jake choked on his waffle when he tried to laugh and swallow simultaneously. "That should cover it," he wheezed, then grinned wryly.

The innuendo prompted Moriah to snicker, but she managed to camouflage her mirth behind a cough. "My place tonight...oh, say, nine o'clock?"

Jake cut the four looming chaperons a brief glance. Obviously he'd noted their hostility right off. "Okay, if I'm allowed to live that long. I've got a news flash for you, Mo. Those need-and-dependent relationships you first established with your staff have evolved. You have four bodyguards prepared to defend you with their lives." He glanced toward the buffet line to note the lethal glare Anna directed at him. "She's the one who worries me most because she's in a position to poison my kibble."

"Don't worry about any of them," she insisted. "We're going to have a chat after breakfast."

"I already had one last night with Tom who obviously spread the word. Would you prefer that I talk to them?"

That he was willing to spare her the embarrassment and awkwardness made her want to hug him. "No, I'll leash the human guard dogs. But thanks for the offer."

Jake polished off his hearty breakfast, then climbed to his feet to visit with each guest. Moriah raised a brow, marveling at Jake's rapport with the other men, listening to them chuckle at his quiet comments. Obviously, some male bonding had occurred while she wasn't around the previous evening. With the exclusion of Robert, Moriah noted. He was too aloof and distant to connect with anyone at the resort.

When the guests filed from the lodge, Moriah turned toward her staff, squared her shoulders and said, "I know what I'm doing, even if you don't think I do, so please back off."

Her request was met with four grim stares.

"This isn't a good idea, Mori," Chester told her. "You haven't known Jake very long. We've no choice but to murder him. We're trying to decide whether to poison, shoot, stab or hang him." He hitched his thumb toward Kent. "He wanted to hang him high, but we figured the other guests might notice."

"No one is going to murder him," Moriah insisted. "This is my life and my decision. Jake is still a paying guest here and you should treat him courteously and respectfully."

Her staff grumbled and shifted restlessly from one foot to the other.

"I mean it," Moriah said firmly. "The hostility toward Jake is thick enough to slice with a machete."

"Just answer one question," Kent requested. "Where do you see this going?"

Moriah angled her chin upward. "Who says it has to go somewhere?"

Four mouths dropped open and eight eyeballs bulged. She'd accomplished her purpose by leading them to believe that *she* was the one who didn't want strings attached.

Maybe they were right. Maybe she hadn't known Jake very long, but damn it, she felt as if she'd been waiting forever for him to show up in her life. She admired him. She respected him, he amused her and she was in love with him. Just because their separate lives were too complicated to make a long-term commitment relationship plausible didn't mean she didn't want to spend every spare minute with Jake until he packed up and left.

"You'll get hurt, Mori," Tom prophesied bleakly.

Her chin tilted a notch higher. "He makes me happy and we have fun together. Don't begrudge me that. I don't need your approval but I'd like to have it, nonetheless... Well?"

"Ah, hell, Mori," Tom grumbled. "We just want what's best for you."

"He's the best," she told them honestly.

The staff sighed collectively, then ambled off to work. Moriah's shoulders slumped, relieved to have that conversation behind her. She wouldn't be the least bit happy if she found Jake in the river, wearing concrete boots. Moriah spun around to leave then noticed Anna had propped herself against the kitchen door.

"Let me give you a piece of advice, hon. Since I've been married to a couple of no-good deadbeats I've learned a thing or three about men."

Oh, great, thought Moriah. Miss Cynical speaks. "Yes, Anna?"

"Don't fall in love. There's not a man alive who's worth the trouble he can put you through."

Moriah smiled feebly. Anna's advice had come too late. The love bug had taken a bite out of her heart. "What about that old proverb that says it's better to have loved and lost than never to have loved at all?"

Anna snorted derisively. "It's pure crap is what it is," she said before she turned a one-eighty and walked away.

Hoo-kay, four against her taking a chance with Jake, she mused as she strode outside. Maybe she was a dozen kinds of fool for risking her heart. Maybe she was going to crash and burn. But for a few days she was going to love, laugh and live life to its fullest. She still believed that if you didn't seize the moment and take a few risks, then you might miss that one glorious instant that could make you feel whole and complete and immensely happy.

Moriah stamped on a cheery smile and hiked off to her fishing expedition with Eugene Morris. Then she'd go horseback riding with Joe Higdon. She glanced down at her watch and smiled secretively. In twelve hours she'd rendezvous with Jake. She sincerely hoped her staff took her request to heart and that Jake lived long enough to show up at her apartment.

8

JAKE SLOWED his step as he approached the stables. Kent was glaring at him from beneath the brim of his hat. The bowlegged wrangler radiated hostility and perceived himself as Moriah's protector, same as Tom.

Jake halted in front of Kent. "Thought I'd take an afternoon ride."

"Well, at least it'll be on the back of a horse this time," Kent said snidely. "I'll bring a horse around. Give me a minute."

Annoyed by the wisecrack, Jake waited while Kent took his sweet Texas time saddling a mount. He frowned warily when Kent led an unfamiliar horse from the barn. "New pony?"

"Nope, I've been trainin' this geldin' while I lead our guests along the ridin' trails," Kent replied. "You told me once that you didn't like ploddin' mares, right?"

Jake knew a dare when he heard one. Chances were this Appaloosa was a little green and a lot flighty, but Kent was spitefully challenging Jake to give the gelding a whirl—as penance for messing with Moriah last night.

"Right," Jake murmured as he took the reins.

Kent didn't ask if he wanted company—which he didn't—but the usual offer wasn't forthcoming. No question about it, Jake was at the top of Kent's hit list. Damn, talk about overprotective!

Jake noted how Kent plastered on a smile when three

other guests approached. The wrangler was suddenly good cheer and politeness. Moriah had no clue how protective her extended family had become now that they deemed Jake a threat.

As Jake reined away from the stable on the sidestepping Appaloosa, he asked himself if he'd been that surly when Kim and Lisa's high school dates showed up on the doorstep. Probably. He'd been pretty overprotective when it came to caring for what was left of his family. And come to think of it, he'd done some checking when his sisters announced their engagements. Oh, yeah, Jake could relate to Kent and the rest of the staff. They placed Moriah on a lofty pedestal and no man would ever be good enough for her.

It had taken Jake a year to decide his brothers-in-law qualified as good marriage material. After that, he decided his sisters had made good choices for lifelong mates.

It didn't take Jake long to figure out the Appy had an annoying habit of brushing up against nearby fences in an effort to scrape off a rider. The ornery creature needed considerable training to lose his bad habits. The Appy trotted along the trail at a bouncing clip, refusing to remain in a walking gait. Jake figured his insides would be scrambled by the time he returned to the stables.

Jake glanced across the lawn and chuckled when he noticed Will Randell whizzing around in circles on his malfunctioning motorized cart. Spitwad must've thought it was a game because the mutt was right behind Will who was shouting at Chester to help him turn the blasted thing off. Apparently, one of Will's electronic gadgets had gone sour.

When Jake suddenly veered off the trodden path and zigzagged through the canopy of trees, taking a cross-country route, the Appy became tentative. This was no leisure ride, to be sure. He was probably breaking the rules by leaving resort property, but when Jake had learned the nearest hamlet with a convenience store was only ten miles away, he'd acted on the idea he'd been toying with for the past few days.

In order to repay Moriah for helping him adjust his attitude, Jake intended to create a Web site to advertise Triple R. To do that he needed photos—lots of photos—before he returned to his shop. The only way to keep his gift a secret was to ride horseback to the convenience store, purchase a couple of disposable cameras and flick some pictures of the breathtaking scenery, lodge, cabins, et cetera.

He'd been amazed at the inspirational creativity that bubbled inside him when it came to this project. For years now, creating Web sites, logos and designs for his clients had been simply one job after another—same ol', same ol'. But this special surprise for Moriah got him enthused.

''Whoa, damn it!'' Jake jerked back on the reins when the Appy tried to break into a run. No way was Jake going to try to hang on to this cantankerous horse while dodging trees.

The first hour of what he anticipated being a three-hour ride to town was a battle for control. Then the Appy settled into a tolerable gait in the ditch beside the graveled road. When the first vehicle whizzed by, kicking up dust, the Appy bolted, nearly catapulting Jake into the grass. Luckily, he managed to hold his seat on the jittery horse and anticipate the reaction to passing traffic.

Jake was sure the muscles in his arms would be sore after holding back on the reins constantly. But it was worth it because Moriah was worth it. He was going to design the most spectacular, innovative Web site ever created and the photos would set it off perfectly.

By the time Jake reached the convenience store in the laid-back hamlet, he'd drawn considerable attention from passersby. He received plenty of amused grins, waves and snickers when he tethered the Appy beside the unleaded gas pump.

The young store attendant snickered when Jake strode to the counter with two disposable, wide-angle cameras. "I probably shouldn't ask, friend, but in which end of that horse are you planning to stick the gas nozzle?"

Jake grinned good-naturedly at the mop-haired young man. "Figured I'd stick it up his butt, fill him up, get a little more horsepower out of him and see how he handles in high gear."

The attendant's eyes twinkled in amusement. "How many miles do you usually get to the gallon?"

"Don't know for sure." Jake smiled wryly as he dug cash from his wallet. "This is the first time I've had to fill up since I got him."

"Next time you bring him in for a fill, I'll be curious to know how many miles you get on a full tank."

By the time Jake exited a crowd of farmers had gathered at the pump to appraise his mode of transportation. The crowd tossed out comments similar to the ones Jake received from the attendant, and he played along to let the crowd have a good laugh.

It dawned on him a mile later that he hadn't tried to inject lighthearted amusement into his employees' workday. He hadn't even considered it until he'd seen Moriah in action. Her ready smile, playful demeanor and enthusiasm were what made Triple R a success. He'd have to remember her techniques when he returned to his shop.

The thought of leaving Triple R lost the appeal it once

held for Jake. The first few days he'd have given anything to leave the resort. Now, he woke up every morning—later than he'd slept in years—and anticipated seeing Moriah. Damn, his perspective had changed, especially after his passionate interlude with Moriah.

Jake glanced at his watch as he trotted alongside the graveled road. This evening he'd be rapping on Moriah's door—despite the objections of her overprotective staff. Tonight he'd take his time with her, enjoy her thoroughly.

The erotic thought was arousing and Jake decided that wasn't a good idea when he was sitting on the saddle, staring down at the pommel. If he didn't pay attention on this goosey horse his male apparatus might not be in good working condition, come nine o'clock.

Willfully, Jake wrapped his mind around details for Triple R's Web site and tried not to get worked up by thinking about Moriah. He definitely wanted to show up on her doorstep in one piece, with all body parts functioning at peak capacity.

MORIAH WAS looking forward to seeing Jake at nine, but the afternoon she'd spent with Robert Fullerton had been equally gratifying. She'd tried to get him to open up to her while they were paddling a canoe downriver. At first he'd snapped and growled defensively when she hit one raw nerve after another. But since he couldn't vault to his feet and stamp off in a huff Moriah urged him to confide his frustrations in her.

Although she didn't consider herself a trained psychologist, she tried to help Robert figure out why he'd become so tense and oversensitive. He'd finally admitted that his inability to satisfy the woman he'd married had left him with feelings of inadequacy. From the sound of things, Robert was stressing out, trying to overcome feelings of rejection and security. His ex-wife had withheld sex to control him and hammered at his pride constantly, claiming that he didn't measure up as a man.

The poor man had turned as cynical on love as Anna. Moriah had suggested that Robert might want to seek counseling when he returned home. In the meantime, Robert promised to use his time at the resort to develop outlets for his frustration and seek inner peace rather than venting aggression—as he had during the incident on the golf course.

Amazingly, Robert volunteered to apologize to Pete and Geoffrey the first chance he got. He was finally beginning to see the error of his ways.

When Moriah steered the canoe to the dock, Robert gallantly held out his hand to assist her to her feet. Before she could caution him about two people simultaneously standing in the canoe he hoisted her upward. The canoe tipped precariously and Moriah yelped when she cartwheeled into the moss-covered cove. Robert howled in surprise when he was catapulted into the water and ended up doing a belly-buster.

Moriah floundered to her feet in the waist-deep water. Her head was covered with gunk and her shoes stuck like glue in the gooey mud. She watched Robert grab the capsized canoe then maneuver it upright. She waited, wondering how he'd react to the accidental spill they'd taken. His face was beet-red and his mouth was compressed in a flat line and he looked as if he were waiting for Moriah to rant and rail at him.

She arched a slimy brow and smiled. "Well, there's nothing more invigorating than a swim in the river, is there?"

The apprehension drained from his expression as he

appraised Moriah's disheveled appearance. He grinned for the first time since she'd met him. "You're really something, Moriah, you know that?" He chuckled as he reached over to pull a clump of goo off her soggy head. "Had you been my ex-wife, she'd have screeched like a banshee, insisting I was an incompetent, blundering ass. But you take accidents in stride."

Moriah wiped the soggy leaves from the shoulder of his polo shirt and grinned. "We have to learn not to be so quick to find fault and lay blame," she reminded him. "It's an unproductive waste of time. When you fell overboard, you actually took a giant leap forward, Robert."

He arched a brow and frowned, bemused. "How do you figure?"

"You aren't taking yourself as seriously as you did a few days ago. You also discovered that not everyone holds a grudge or delights in belittling you. I don't think less of you because we took an unexpected spill. Believe it or not, this sort of thing happens occasionally at Triple R. In fact, this is the second time I've been dunked recently and there was no harm done."

Moriah found herself smiling when she recalled the tumble she and Jake had taken off Ol' Sally. She wasn't likely to forget it because it was the first time Jake impulsively kissed her. She'd needed a dunking to cool down after that dynamite kiss that had caused emotions to explode inside her.

"I'm sorry I gave you so much grief when I first arrived," Robert murmured as he trudged ashore. He ducked his head guiltily. "I'm especially sorry I tried to get fresh with you. If I could take that back, I would, I assure you."

"It's forgotten." Moriah hoisted herself onto the dock to secure the canoe. "I'm glad you're beginning to settle in and enjoy your time at the resort. Since we missed supper in the lodge, I'll bring a tray to your cabin. We'll practice those breathing exercises and relaxation techniques I showed you.''

Robert nodded his soggy head. "Thanks for everything. I'm really sorry about upending you.''

"No problem. As I said, it's harmless spills that keep life interesting. We have to learn to roll with the punches.''

He smiled knowingly. "I plan to do that on a regular basis from now on.''

"Good, then you're on your way to beating stress and putting enjoyment in your life.''

"Yeah, as soon as I cast off the anchor that was my wife and make a new start. Don't know why I ever thought I could make her happy in the first place. I guess I thought loving her was enough.''

Moriah swallowed uneasily as she and Robert strode up the path in the gathering darkness. That was the second time today she'd heard it said that love wasn't everything it was cracked up to be. Anna's two marriages were disastrous, and so was Robert's. But Moriah reminded herself that she hadn't fallen in love with the wrong man. The problem was that his life and career were separate and distant from hers.

Don't let it drag you down, Moriah lectured herself. She was taking each day, each stolen moment with Jake as it came and she wasn't expecting forever. She was going into this short-term affair with eyes wide open, aware of the limitations. She'd fallen for him. She wanted him. That had to be enough to satisfy her.

Moriah glanced at her watch. It was seven-thirty. Before she knew it Jake would arrive at her door and they'd spend the evening together. If she hurried, she could shower, change, grab a bite and make her rounds before Jake showed up.

Anticipation put a smile on her lips and left a warm glow in her heart as she hurried to her apartment.

"WILL YOU behave yourself?" Jake snapped at the contrary Appy.

The horse threw his head, rolled the bit in his mouth and tried to bolt forward the instant they reached Triple R property. Jake suspected the animal could smell feed in the stable and was anxious to hotfoot it to his stall— and didn't appreciate it that Jake was making him trot.

"Damnation," Jake muttered as the Appy lunged forward, then half reared in protest when Jake yanked hard on the reins.

There was nothing Jake would've liked better than to race back to his cabin to shower and change for his date with Moriah. But no way was he going to zig and zag through these dense trees at a dead run on the back of this devil mount that seemed to have it in for him!

Jake thought he'd managed to assure the stubborn animal who was boss—until the setting sun glinted off a few empty aluminum beer cans. The sunlight glared off the aluminum and reflected in the Appy's eyes, startling him. Snorting, the horse bolted sideways, as if he'd been bitten by a snake, then lunged forward before Jake could catch his balance. Jake was totally unprepared when the Appy's head shot straight down between his front legs and his back hooves went sky-high.

The horse took two flying leaps that would've done a raunchy rodeo bronc proud. As rodeo rides went, Jake was proud to say he held on for more than the customary eight seconds. He clenched the reins in one fist and put a stranglehold on the pommel with the other. As the

Appy slammed down on all fours simultaneously Jake's rear end collided with the saddle—hard—jarring his teeth and causing him to bite his tongue.

He barely had time to register the pain when he caromed sideways, startling the flighty horse. The Appy plunged forward in an all-out run and Jake wrapped both arms around the steed's neck to prevent being dumped on his butt.

"You're glue, buddy," Jake growled in the horse's laid-back ear. "Whoa! I said *whoa*, damn it…! Oh, hell…" Jake realized a moment too late that he was on a collision course with a low-hanging tree branch. He tried to flatten himself against the Appy's flank—it didn't help. The cursed horse scraped him off.

Jake yelped in pain when his right foot hung up in the stirrup as he went down—hard. His knee was nearly wrenched from its socket as he squirmed desperately to free his foot and prevent being dragged all the way to the stables and ending up looking like an incompetent horseman.

Free at last! Jake breathed in relief as he dislodged his foot. He skidded across the ground and the air left his lungs in a forceful *whoosh*. While the Appy thundered toward the stables, as if the devil were nipping his hooves, Jake lay there, gasping for breath, assessing bodily damage and waving his fist at the horse from hell.

Hoo-kay, he was alive. That was good. He levered onto his elbows to stare at his right leg. It hurt like a son of a bitch, but it didn't appear to be broken. That was encouraging. Things could've been worse. Gingerly, he crawled onto all fours, gave the demon horse a thorough cursing for good measure, then tried to stand up.

"Ow! Damn, that hurts!" Jake roared when he put pressure on his leg.

Great. He'd gone AWOL from Triple R—on a horse that was only familiar with the resort's riding trails. He was an hour away from his cabin by horseback—and who the hell knew how long it'd take to return on a bum leg that strenuously objected to bearing weight. Wasn't this just peachy?

Jake glanced around to locate a fallen branch to serve as a crutch. He hopped over to grab a sturdy-looking limb. Holding on to his makeshift cane, he took one step…and cursed two blue streaks. If not for those shiny beer cans reflecting the sunlight the Appy wouldn't have come unglued and Jake wouldn't have come up lame and been forced to walk to his cabin. Hell's bells, of all the rotten luck!

Okay, relax, breathe, Jake told himself. He was a reasonably intelligent guy, right? He could improvise when necessary. He looked around to find a couple of short branches that would serve as splints to stabilize his injured knee and ankle. Balancing on one leg, he yanked off his belt to secure the makeshift splint around his ankle, then peeled off his shirt to tie the branches to his thigh. Primitive but effective, he decided as he put experimental pressure on his right leg.

The pain was tolerable—if you didn't dwell on it, didn't count the light-headedness and bouts of nausea. He could walk. Sort of. A tortoise would make faster progress, but hell, he was mobile and not completely helpless. Things could be worse, right?

Too bad he hadn't grabbed a candy bar at the convenience store to curb the hunger pangs gnawing at his belly. Damn, what he wouldn't give for one of Anna's scrumptious feasts right about now—

"Ah, jeez…hell and damnation!" Jake swore ferociously when he tripped over a fallen log concealed beneath a pile of leaves. Pain blazed down his right leg like wildfire. Since he was alone and injured he treated himself to every crude, offensive oath he knew, plus a few he coined to suit the situation.

Huffing, puffing and cursing, he uprighted himself and glanced at his illuminated watch. He'd never make it back to the lodge by nine o'clock. The good news was that Moriah would come looking for him because he was punctual to a fault. The bad news was that his erotic fantasies for the evening had gone up in a puff of smoke. It wouldn't have mattered if Moriah purchased a lifetime supply of condoms. He wouldn't be up to even one rollickingly romantic encounter in this condition. His leg was so tender that the slightest touch or jarring motion was enough to send him right through the roof.

Jake hobbled through the trees and glanced at the gathering clouds, wondering if fate had intervened again and was trying to nab his attention. Yeah, he knew that he and Moriah didn't have the time needed to develop a lasting relationship. And okay, you betcha, there were about a hundred obstacles in their path—including his job, her job, his family, her family and her guests. Never mind that it was an hour and a half drive from his apartment doorstep to hers—more, if you got caught in heavy rush-hour traffic.

Then, if you took into account that Moriah probably *wasn't* as emotionally involved as he was, Jake would end up repeating the mistake he'd made with Shelly. Plus, Moriah could simply be caught up in newly discovered passion, seeing how she'd recently lost virgin status, and didn't feel the deeper connection he'd felt. In addition, Jake had noticed the way her perpetual smile faltered at breakfast when he got carried away, yammering about his sisters and how he was making plans for being an uncle.

It was a good bet Moriah didn't want to get involved with a man who devoted considerable time to his family, considering *she* was laden with more responsibility than *she* could shake a stick at. Shelly had objected to Jake dividing his time between her and his sisters. Moriah might feel the same way and he didn't want to shove his affection for his sisters down Moriah's throat. It wasn't fair to her.

Between the pain, the hunger and the uneasy feeling that he should've looked before he leaped into this reckless fling with Moriah, Jake felt pretty doggone lousy. He questioned his impulsiveness and wondered if he should back away from these dangerously vulnerable feelings he'd developed for Moriah.

He should've listened to that quiet voice that warned him to maintain his distance from Moriah until he left the resort. Instead, he'd tuned in to the screaming voices of roiling hormones and he'd succumbed to Moriah's constant prompts about being reckless and impulsive for once in his life.

Where had that gotten him? In too deep, that's where. He was on the staff's hit list and he'd been bucked off a cantankerous horse—and that had to be some kind of serves-you-right omen. He had to hobble to his cabin on a lame leg in the dark. Considering his run of bad luck he'd probably encounter another skunk, or maybe a wolverine or a bobcat. Who knew what varmints and predators skulked these woods after dark, waiting to gobble him alive?

Thunder boomed overhead and lightning zapped the low-slung clouds. Sheesh! Could anything else go wrong? His day had gone from sweet to sour so fast it made his head spin like a roulette wheel. Panting, Jake propped himself against a tree to take a needed breather. Rain poured down in torrents, soaking him to the bone in nothing flat. Fan-freakin'-tastic! Wasn't this just the glaring example of what befell a man who fancied himself a little bit in love? The sky had fallen in on him—literally!

Jake glanced up at the scudding clouds and flinched when a fat raindrop smacked him on the forehead. "Okay, I can take a hint," he muttered as he pushed away from the tree. "I'll save myself from humiliation and rejection before it's too late."

Moriah's staff wanted him to back away, so he'd back away. He'd bury those vulnerable, untidy emotions he'd allowed to seep between the cracks of his protective armor. He'd tell himself, repeatedly, emphatically, that Moriah was a reckless mistake and he'd rectify it by ensuring their wildly passionate tryst began and ended the same night.

Yeah, he could do that—would do that—because it was logical and sensible and reasonable. He didn't want to face the possibility of another rejection. He had a perfectly good life in the city. It had worked for him for ten years. Sure, he'd change his rigid, predictable routine, take a little time off for himself and dote over his sisters' kids. He'd be fine. Peachy keen, in fact. He'd suffered through some pretty difficult times and he'd survived. He'd survive—again.

Moriah was just an unattainable star in a faraway galaxy, a refreshing breeze that touched his life momentarily. He'd remember her fondly, thank her kindly for teaching him to break his structured routine. But let's face it, they weren't meant to be.

Resolved, Jake limped through the pouring rain toward the distant lights of the lodge, knowing he'd made the sensible choice. Damn good thing he'd caught himself before he fell head over heels in love, wasn't it? He was an experienced survivor, but he wasn't sure he could survive *that*.

MORIAH PLUNKED into her recliner to catch her breath. She'd been buzzing around nonstop to make herself presentable. She'd wriggled into the sexiest dress she owned—a leftover from those days when she thought she had a chance of attracting Stuart's interest. The slinky, form-fitting red dress swooped low at the neckline to show cleavage and the hem hit her midthigh. Moriah thought she looked pretty good, even if she did say so herself. She'd carefully applied makeup and left her hair down the way Jake seemed to like it. She was all set for her first official date with Jake.

When Moriah glanced at her watch, she was surprised to discover Jake was ten minutes late. Jake? What was he doing? Proving to her that he'd learned to thumb his nose at time schedules?

Moriah drummed her fingers on the armrest, while rain pattered against the windows, then she made herself relax. He'd be here. After all, her Mr. Predictable was reliable—or had been until she hounded him to loosen up and lighten up.

When he arrived they'd make out right off and appease this craving that'd been building all day. Then they'd sip some wine, listen to some mood music and get to know each other better before they wound up back in her bedroom again. She wanted to know his tastes in music, in food, his political views and his religious affiliation. She wanted to know everything he liked, and disliked—besides her loud clothing.

Well, she didn't think Jake would find fault with this hot little number. It had Take Me I'm Yours written all over it in screaming neon letters.

Moriah glanced at her watch again. Nine-thirty and still no Jake? Where was he?

An unsettling thought snapped Moriah erect in her chair. Damn it, if her staff had conspired to keep them apart she was going to strangle every last one of them. That had to be it, she decided. Jake had mentioned that morning his worst fear was Anna seasoning his food with arsenic—or something equally lethal. Knowing Anna's cynicism of love, the older woman might've defied Moriah's request and ensured Jake was indisposed—temporarily, at least—so they couldn't enjoy a night of passion.

Fuming, Moriah stuffed her feet into her hiking boots and stalked out in the rain. She made a beeline to Jake's cabin, found it empty, then slopped through the mud to reach the bunkhouse-style apartment complex that housed her staff. Assuming Anna-the-cynic was the mastermind of this conspiracy, she pummeled on the cook's door first. Anna appeared, then did a double take when she noticed Moriah's shrink-wrap dress.

"Good gawd, girl, what are you advertising!" Anna croaked then cast a distracted glance over her shoulder, causing Moriah's suspicions to flare to life.

Moriah bounded on the porch to see who Anna was hiding in her apartment. "What did you do to Jake? Is he in there?"

"No. I didn't do a thing to him, but I'd like to get my hands on that Casanova," Anna muttered bitterly. She shot out her arm abruptly when Moriah tried to barge inside. "You can't come in."

"Who's in there—?" Moriah's mouth dropped open

when she peered around Anna's shoulder to see Robert Fullerton half-sprawled on the couch. Anna and Robert were fooling around? Her astounded gaze leaped back to Anna. "I thought you advocated banning love worldwide," she accused.

"Love, yeah," Anna agreed. "But I never said a thing about middle-aged divorcées giving up sex, did I? You gotta know the difference. *I* do. *You* don't. By the way, a postage stamp would cover you better than that dress!"

"What's going on out here?" Tom asked as he craned his neck around his partially opened door. His eyes popped when he noticed Moriah's hot, *wet* red dress. "Holy cow, girl! Where's the rest of your clothes?"

Moriah wheeled around to skewer Tom with a mutinous glance. "Never mind about my dress. What did this vigilante posse do with Jake?"

"Didn't touch him, but I'd like to pound on him," Tom said, scowling.

"What's all the racket out here?" Chester poked his head outside, then gasped when he saw the dress. "Whoa, where'd you get that spicy number?"

Moriah ignored the wide-eyed stare. "Where's Kent? Is he holding Jake hostage? Or is Jake sprawled in the middle of nowhere, tossing his cookies because Anna sabotaged his meal?"

"I did no such thing!" Anna piped up. "Wanted to. Thought about it but didn't. Jake didn't come to the horseshoe-pitching contest he scheduled this evening. I thought the two of you were fooling around again because you didn't show up for supper at the lodge, either."

"I was canoeing with Robert," Moriah said, and glared at Anna, as if she should've known, seeing how Robert was in the apartment. Apparently Anna and Robert hadn't spent time discussing who missed supper at the lodge. They were too preoccupied going at it on the couch. "I haven't seen Jake all afternoon."

"Good," Anna said. "You're better off if you keep your distance. You'll get your damn-fool heart broken."

Moriah zeroed in on Chester and Tom. "Where is he, damn it?"

"Haven't seen him," they mumbled in unison.

Moriah swore ripely. The threesome gaped at her as if she had devil's horns sprouting from her head. "I'm old enough to curse if I feel like it and right now I'm swearing mad because I think you have something to do with Jake's disappearance!"

Glaring at her staff, Moriah stalked over to pound both fists on Kent's door. When he appeared, Moriah grabbed the collar of his western shirt and hauled him out into the rain.

"Damn!" Kent hooted. "Where'd you get that dress?"

Moriah ignored Kent's stunned stare. "All right, now somebody better start talking because I want answers and I want them now! What have you done to Jake?" she all but shouted in frustration.

"We haven't done anything to him," Chester replied.

"Hell, we all figured he was with you. Didn't *like* it, but that's what we thought," Tom said, staring disapprovingly at the dress that clung to Moriah's body like a coat of latex paint.

Moriah was so frustrated she wanted to scream. Obviously she was mistaken in thinking her staff had conspired against Jake. So why hadn't he kept their date? Where the devil was he? "Jake was supposed to be at my apartment at nine, but he didn't show up. Where could he be?"

No one ventured a guess, just kept staring at her hot-to-trot dress.

Muttering, Moriah whirled around and stormed off to recheck Jake's cabin. She was halfway to Jake's cabin when she saw the bare-chested silhouette emerging from the row of trees. "Jake! Oh, my God!" Moriah took off at a dead run in the rain to reach Jake, who halted, looking like a war survivor limping home from a rain-drenching battle. "What on earth happened to you?"

"I got hurt," he said stiffly. He stared at her body-hugging dress, then wiped the dribbling rain from his hair-matted chest.

Moriah frowned at his curt tone. She didn't think his anger was directed at her, but she supposed she was in the line of fire and his obvious pain was playing hell with his disposition.

"Just wait here," Moriah instructed. "I'll run over to the shed and bring a golf cart."

He nodded his tousled head and stared at the air over her left shoulder. Moriah noticed leaves sticking from his hair and wondered what he'd been doing when he suffered injury. She lurched around and cannoned across the lawn to reach the golf shed. Hurriedly, she unplugged the charger to the nearest cart, then zoomed off. When she reached Jake he half collapsed on the padded seat beside her.

"Damn, I gotta tell ya, Mo, my leg hurts like hell blazing."

"Where?" she asked as she drove toward his cabin.

"All over. Knee. Ankle… Damn it, slow down!" he yelped. "Every bump feels like a spike driven into my leg…. Helluva dress, especially wet. But those muddy hiking boots don't suit your sexy ensemble."

"I know, but I was pressed for time when I came

looking for you.'' Moriah slowed the cart to a crawl and made an effort to dodge uneven terrain and puddles on the lawn. ''What happened to you?''

''When? Before or after I bucked off that demon horse and landed in a tangled heap?''

''Start with bucking off and proceed from there,'' she requested.

Jake offered her the condensed version of his rodeo ride, his subsequent fall and his torturous trek to the resort. When they reached his cabin, Moriah assisted him up the steps and shooed Spitwad out of the way before the soggy mutt tripped up Jake.

Moriah quickly unfolded the Murphy bed, then eased Jake down to unstrap his makeshift splint. Impulsively, she brushed her lips over his, wishing a kiss would make him feel better. Then she untied his wet hiking boots and carefully removed the right one. Jake grimaced in pain, but he didn't make a peep.

''Can you help me remove your jeans? Lift your hips,'' she ordered.

''I can do—oh, hell. Okay,'' he grumbled as he unzipped his fly.

Moriah tossed him a bemused glance, wondering why he was reluctant to drop his pants in front of her. It wasn't as if she hadn't seen him in all his splendor and glory the previous night. They'd been naked together, as close as two people could get, after all.

Gently, she slid his soaked jeans down his legs, noting the skimpy zebra-striped briefs, and then she focused her attention on his swollen knee. Her gaze drifted to his ankle, which was turning a putrid shade of purple.

''Damn, that's gotta hurt,'' she murmured sympathetically.

''You're telling me,'' Jake said. ''Besides that, I'm

starved. Go get some ice packs and some food. And don't forget to feed Spitwad. He's probably hungry, too.''

Moriah shook her head, amazed at how quickly Jake reverted to spouting orders. But she also noticed how he insisted on seeing to the pup when he needed immediate medical attention himself. And to think he'd snarled and growled about having to care for this fuzzball of a pooch. She doubted her other guests would've given their canine companions another thought if they were injured and in pain.

Moriah spun toward the door. ''I'll be back in a flash.''

''If you don't have fast-acting painkillers then bring the booze,'' Jake commanded. ''Plenty of it!''

''We don't drink to excess here, Jake,'' she reminded him.

He glared at her, then said very deliberately, very emphatically, ''There is no way in hell I can sleep in this condition. I plan to pass out.''

''But—''

''Bring the friggin' booze!'' he yelled at her. ''I plan to tie one on!''

Moriah told herself he was snarling at her because of the pain. She told herself that his lack of response to her kiss was the manifestation of his extreme discomfort. She wanted to believe he wasn't being standoffish toward her, but there was something about Jake's demeanor that shouted unapproachable. She sensed he was emotionally withdrawing and she didn't understand why.

Well, she'd give him a couple of days to recover. Maybe this cool attitude toward her would thaw out when he was his old self again.

Moriah bounded into the golf cart and sped to the

lodge, lickety-split. Personally, she didn't see how Jake's plan to get drunk out of his gourd was going to ease his pain. A hellish hangover, compounded with a wrenched knee and sprained ankle, would be murder in her book.

But hey, if it was booze he thought he wanted then booze he'd get. She supposed he was entitled, given the rough night he'd endured, limping around in the dark and getting drenched with rain.

9

JAKE PURPOSELY avoided direct eye contact and conversation when Moriah returned with ice packs, food and two bottles of wine, wearing that body-hugging wet dress. Whoa, mama! Now that he knew what he'd missed tonight, what he'd sworn to back away from, he wasn't sure he had the willpower to resist. But he had to, damn it. It was for the best.

He let her fuss over him, getting him comfortable—as if *that* was possible. His leg was throbbing from hip to toe and he was in no mood to listen to Moriah instructing him to relax and give in to the pain—whatever the hell that meant. She had her methods of countering agony and he had his. He tipped up the wine bottle and guzzled. The liquor hit his empty stomach and fizzed in his chest like an overdose of Alka-Seltzer.

"You better slow down with that stuff," Moriah advised.

"Why? I'm not driving." Defiantly, he chugalugged.

"At least eat the roast beef sandwich first."

Jake took another slug. His head spun like a Ferris wheel and he waited impatiently for the blessed numbness to counteract this hopeless attraction to Moriah. She'd let her hair down and, wet though it was, it tumbled over her shoulders to brush against the showcased swells of her breasts like a lover's caress. Damn, he wanted to touch her, hold her.

No, wait! That wasn't what he wanted, was it? Hadn't he come up with a sensible plan a couple of hours ago to back away and protect himself from getting hurt? Yeah, he was striving for emotional detachment, he remembered.

The wine went to his head and his thoughts fogged over. His nose tingled and his tongue wasn't functioning properly. Well good, he'd drink to that—and to anything else that came to mind.

"Jake, please," Moriah murmured as she grabbed the bottle.

He flashed her a hard stare, noting his vision was fuzzy, blurring her enticing image. Ex…cellent. That prevented him from getting lost in those hypnotic blue eyes or reaching out to run his fingers through that glorious mass of blond hair. "Back off, Mo," he ordered thickly.

When she stuffed a bite of sandwich in his mouth, he chewed and swallowed, then helped himself to a gulp of hooch.

"You can leave now," he slurred out, limply flicking his wrist in the general direction of the door. "I'll be fine."

"I plan to stay here all night, in case you need me."

"I'm not dependent on you, like everybody else around here," he said, then scowled. "The bottle's the only friend I need right now."

In a brief moment of clarity he figured out how to send Moriah running—for his self-preservation. She liked to think like a shrink so he'd outsmart her at her own game. Given his woozy condition—and getting woozier by the minute—she'd think he'd made a Freudian slip, triggered by his overindulgence in wine.

Jake, you're a damn genius, he congratulated himself.

He took another swizzle of wine, looked up at Moriah's fuzzy image and said, "Go 'way, Shelly. I tried to make it work again, but it won't. I can't do this...."

He thought he heard Moriah's sharp intake of breath. Of course, with that dull buzzing in his ears he couldn't be certain. But then she stepped away from him and he figured the comment had accomplished its purpose. Moriah would assume—as he wanted her to—that he was still carrying a torch for his blue-eyed blond ex-fiancée and that he'd projected suppressed affection to Moriah.

Damn, he was brilliant. Sigmund Freud had nothing on him. He should've majored in psychology in college and poked around in people's minds for a living. He was a damn genius...had he said that already? It sounded familiar. Jake took another slug. No matter. Mission accomplished. He heard the front door shut behind Moriah.

She was gone for good, outsmarted by her own sharp intelligence and presumptions. He'd drink to that, too. Hell, he'd drink to everything!

Sluggishly Jake reached for the sandwich beside him and took a bite then a drink. He'd dodged the bullet tonight, saved himself from his ill-fated craving for Moriah. He'd be out of here tomorrow, back to his own world and she wouldn't object because, one: he was injured and a recreational resort was no place for an injured man. And B: Moriah would think he was using her to replace his old flame.... Um... Now, where was he? Oh yeah. And three: kindhearted and understanding that she was, she'd think he was controlled by repressed emotions, triggered by Moriah and Shelly's similar appearance, and he'd substituted Moriah for his lost love—

Aw jeez...now his head was starting to spin in lopsided circles. That complex psycho-mumbo jumbo was a bit too much on top of the wine, the pain and the empty feeling that settled somewhere in the region of his heart. But this was for the best, he assured himself for the forty-eleventh time.

When Spitwad hopped onto the bed to finish off Jake's sandwich he stared at the mutt. "I'm doin' the righ' thing 'ere, aren't I, Spi'wad?"

The mutt just snarfed up the roast beef like it was going out of style.

Of course, Jake hadn't expected a reply. If he'd gotten one, he'd have known for sure that he'd lost all his marbles.

That was his last sane thought before he keeled over and passed out.

MORIAH POUNDED on each of the four bunkhouse doors with both fists. She was hurt and crushed and angry and...she didn't know what else. Emotions were converging so swiftly she couldn't separate them and deal with each one individually. Consequently, she was frustration personified, seeking a target to vent this maelstrom of emotions.

Four heads appeared around the edges of the respective doors. Moriah stalked over to where she could easily be seen by her entire staff.

"Staff meeting. My place. Five minutes. Move it!" she bugled, then wheeled like a soldier on parade and marched off.

Coping with the tormenting fact that Jake still harbored deep feelings for his ex-fiancée who'd cheated on him and rejected him sent Moriah's emotions reeling. Knowing he'd transferred his anger, resentment and eventually physical gratification to Moriah left her heart twisting into a tight knot in her chest. She should've seen this coming. But no, she'd allowed her personal attraction to overshadow sensible logic. Jake had told her right off that he disliked blue-eyed blondes. He'd also said that Moriah wasn't like Shelly, after he'd gotten to know her a little better.

Obviously he was still harboring the trauma of losing his parents, his fiancée and the overwhelming obligations to his kid sisters. Jake's suppressed feelings had lain dormant…until Moriah shook, rattled and rolled into his life, forcing him to change his attitudes and habits.

She'd shaken him up, all right. She'd triggered and unleashed his buried affection for Shelly. Those emotions had tangled in Jake's mind and then went flying like Pandora's opened box of devilish delights.

To Jake, Moriah represented what he wanted to see in Shelly—someone who accepted him as the man he was, someone who didn't make unreasonable demands, someone who surrendered in wild abandon to his embrace. Her innocence and responsiveness was the validation needed to heal his battered male pride and strengthen his self-esteem.

The problem was Moriah got stuck in the middle of his emotional shakedown. She was left to nurse *her* battered pride and deflated self-esteem and to question her inadequacies as a woman. Of course, she should've known, being a total zero in romantic relationships, that she couldn't hold Jake's interest. This disaster reinforced what she knew to be true: she didn't know beans about capturing and holding a man's affection.

"Well, duh, there's a no-brainer, Mo," she muttered at herself as she stormed into her apartment. "This really is the last time. I'm not wearing my heart out on another man—ever!"

When Moriah realized her fists were knotted and her jaw was clenched, she kerplopped in her chair to relax and regroup. Her staff would be here in a few minutes and she wasn't going to transfer her simmering humiliation and frustration to them because she'd recently learned she'd become the substitute for the woman Jake had chosen to marry and had lost to another man.

True, she was annoyed with her staff for being unnecessarily protective of her, but they didn't deserve to be pelted by the flying debris from her private emotional explosion.

When her staff filed inside, Moriah motioned for them to park themselves on her sofa. Moriah told herself to be calm and rational—or as close to rational as she could get when she wanted to race into her bedroom, slam the door and throw a super-duper-deluxe screaming-meemies fit.

She directed her unblinking stare at Kent who rested his elbows on his knees and propped his chin in both hands. "I found Jake," she reported. "He was bucked off his horse, twisted his leg and had to walk to his cabin in the rain, in the dark. What time did Jake request a horse?"

"'Bout one o'clock or so. I didn't bother to check for sure. I had other guests arrivin' for a guided tour into the hills," he mumbled.

"I see, and it didn't occur to you that there might be a problem when Jake didn't return within a reasonable amount of time. Hmm?"

"No," Kent mumbled. "When I walked into the barn the horse was standing there, waiting to be unsaddled. I figured Jake returned while I was out riding with some of the other guests."

Moriah frowned suspiciously. "What horse was he riding, Kent?"

He dodged her probing stare. "The...um...Appy."

"What!" Moriah erupted in outrage. "That horse's manners are still under construction! You told me so yourself. You purposely saddled the Appy, expecting Jake to have a rough time of it, didn't you?"

"Well, he could've refused the mount. His choice," Anna piped up in Kent's defense.

Moriah's irritated gaze swung to Anna. "Jake never should've been placed in the situation and you damn well know it. If he were any other guest he wouldn't have been on the Appy. But, given the fact that I have an interest in Jake, the four of you decided not to like him, even though you liked him fine and dandy yesterday!"

When she realized her voice had risen several decibels, she breathed deeply and glanced over at Kent. "Didn't it occur to you to check on Jake when you found the horse in the barn?"

"No," Kent replied. "Guests leave horses for me to unsaddle all the time. It's standard procedure and you know it. I just figured Jake was with you and you'd already told us not to interrupt *that.*"

"But there is something you should know." Tom shifted uncomfortably and couldn't quite meet Moriah's narrowed gaze. "Um...your dad overheard us talking and we sort of let it slip that you and Jake...well, you know. Your dad was none too happy with Jake, either."

Moriah closed her eyes and groaned in dismay. Was there anyone here at Triple R who *didn't* know she'd slept with Jake? Her dad, too? Jeez! She might as well post the news flash on the bulletin board in the lobby!

"I'm sorry if Jake got hurt on the Appy," Kent said, staring at the toes of his scuffed boots. "But I just assumed he returned the horse and went on his way."

"I don't profess the ability to foretell the future, but

my guess is Jake will insist on leaving first thing in the morning so a qualified doctor can examine him, then go home where *you* want him," Moriah predicted. "I can't take him because I have other guests leaving and arriving. One of you will have to transport Jake while the other three take up the slack."

She stared at Kent. "You're elected as chauffeur. You can apologize for putting Jake on that flighty horse during the drive."

"I'd rather not, thanks just the same," Kent declined.

"Tough cookies, pardner," Moriah snapped, then glared at the other staff members. "This should teach you a lesson. Don't meddle in someone else's private affairs without permission."

Moriah vaulted from her chair. Her arm shot toward the door, as if her staff was too dense to figure out where it was and what purpose it served. "You might feel threatened by Jake because he means something special to me and you think that might infringe upon our friendships, but you're wrong. I have plenty of room in my heart for all of you." She blinked rapidly when tears misted her eyes. "And just so you know, whatever might have been between Jake and me is over and done. I hope that makes you happy. Next time you decide to do me a favor for my own good, don't!"

Moriah managed to hold her composure until the bodyguard brigade trooped out and quietly closed the door behind them. Then she treated herself to a wailing, blubbering, self-pitying fit that ended in a fitful slumber.

JAKE PRIED OPEN one bloodshot eye, raised his head, then let it drop back on the pillow. God, he felt awful. Worse than awful. *Dead* had to feel better than this. Sunshine blared through the open windows and slammed into his hellish headache like a wrecking ball. He groaned miserably. This was a humdinger of a hangover. When he shifted on the bed his right leg screamed at him in agony—like he needed a reminder of his injury.

"Ah, jeez," he bleated. In a twisted sort of way he was glad he felt horrible. The pain and agony demanded his full attention, preventing him from focusing on the feelings of loss and regret that put a stranglehold on his aching heart.

"Jake?" Moriah's voice was as soothing to his ears as it was painful.

"I wanna go home," he wheezed without reopening his puffy eyes.

"I've already made the arrangements," she murmured. "I packed your suitcase, laptop, briefcase and phone in the Jeep. I brought some crutches from the supply room. Your sisters will be refunded for the entire two weeks. Kent will drive you to your apartment...."

Her voice trailed off and she gently ran her fingers through his rumpled hair to smooth it away from his pounding forehead. He moaned at her touch and she immediately withdrew her hand. "Sorry, I know you must hurt all over," she said compassionately.

"Mmm," was all he managed to get out.

"I brought you some tea and toast to settle your stomach. And aspirin if you think you can keep it down after consuming so much wine."

Her alluring scent infiltrated his senses as she leaned close to press a kiss to his puckered brow. "Take good care of yourself, Jake," she whispered. "Take time out to relax and unwind occasionally."

He didn't open his eyes until she turned to stride across the room. He smiled feebly at her loud, colorful attire—a Halloween print with bright-orange pumpkins, black cats and scarecrows. Damn, who would've thought he'd come to appreciate her outlandish clothes? Yet, he missed them already and wondered what she'd be wearing while he was back in his black-and-white, ho-hum world.

"What about Spitwad?" he rasped, wondering if all that wine had rusted his vocal cords. Apparently. He sounded like a sick bullfrog.

Moriah pivoted, her cheerful smile and persona in place. "Not to worry. I'll take care of the pup."

"No, he's coming with me," he insisted in a squeaky voice.

"Are you sure?" When he nodded affirmatively, Moriah shrugged. "Then I'll load the pup in the Jeep before you leave."

Her smile faltered momentarily before she turned away. Then she was gone. He'd severed all ties. It was for the best, Jake told himself, repeatedly.

Sluggish, Jake levered onto a wobbly elbow to munch the toast, chase it with tea, and swallow down the pills. By the time he struggled into his jeans and shirt—and that was no small feat, considering his leg ached something fierce—Kent rapped on the door.

Kent stepped inside, head downcast. "I'm sorry," Kent mumbled. "It was spiteful of me to give you the Appy. I didn't know you'd been hurt or I would've come looking for you."

"Forget it. I didn't have to take that horse," Jake replied. "If the reflection off the beer cans hadn't spooked the Appy I wouldn't have been bucked off." Jake didn't mention that he'd ridden off resort property and probably got what he deserved.

"Anything I can do for you, Jake, I'll do it. You name it and it's done," Kent offered magnanimously.

Jake wasn't beneath calling in the favor because he was badly in need of one. He grabbed the disposable cameras off the table. "I want you to take photos of everything at the resort. Every breathtaking view from the hilltops to the river. I want photos of the cabins, lodge, pool, stables—inside and out from various angles. Then mail them to me—PDQ."

Kent's woolly brows rose like exclamation marks. "What for?"

"Because I want to repay Moriah the only way I know how for changing my life," he explained. "I'm going to create a Web site to draw more guests, as a surprise gift to her."

"For nothing?" he asked, astonished. "No maintenance fee, either?"

Jake tossed the cameras to Kent. "I figure I owe all of you a debt because I acted like a world-class jerk the first few days I was here."

Kent stared at him for a long moment. "I guess you're an okay guy, after all, and I'm really sorry you got hurt. Been there, done that at rodeos."

When Kent held open the door, Jake hobbled outside on crutches to see the Jeep parked beside the front steps. With Kent's assistance he folded his battered body into the vehicle, then adjusted his throbbing leg. With Spitwad curled up on his lap, Jake gave Kent the go-ahead to drive off.

Jake glanced out the side window to see Moriah ambling alongside Harold from Omaha who was toting fishing poles. Jake watched Moriah covetously until she was no more than a colorful blur in the distance. He slumped in his seat, closed his eyes and wished like hell that doing the sensible thing didn't make him feel more miserable than he already did.

Getting over Moriah wasn't going to be easy, but he'd do it, he promised himself. He wondered how long it'd take to fulfill that promise. He hadn't been gone five minutes and he missed her—big time.

MORIAH PULLED up short in the doorway of cabin seven. Seeing the now-empty space Jake had occupied hit her right where she lived. She didn't even have to close her eyes to visualize him moving around the cabin, to hear his rich, baritone voice echoing in her mind. He'd left his memory behind and Moriah felt her eyes flooding with tears.

Even though he'd touched her, made love to her, pretending she was his ex-fiancée, she still cared deeply for him. That was the thing about love, she decided as she stripped the sheets from the bed and scrubbed the room within an inch of its life. Love didn't ask permission to intrude in your life, didn't follow logical time schedules. It defied common sense and rules. Sometimes it hit hard and fast and knocked you clean off your feet—like now, with her. And now Jake was gone forever, and wishing on every star in the Milky Way wouldn't bring him back.

Clutching the rumpled sheets in her arms, Moriah burst into tears. That's how Anna found her, blubbering like an abandoned child with nowhere to turn for comfort and consolation.

"Gimme those, girl," Anna demanded as she lumbered across the cabin. "I'll have the cleaning lady spiffy up for the next guest. You go take a load off."

"No, I want to work off my frustration by doing it myself," Moriah said between hiccuping sobs. "I'll feel better when I've disinfected the place, cleared out his scent and rearranged the furniture to distort his memory.

I'll—'' Her voice broke and she blotted her dribbling eyes with the hem of the sheet.

Anna threw up her arms and let them drop limply by her sides. ''You went and did it, didn't you? Confound it, I warned ya not to. Didn't I tell ya that falling in love was the curse of a woman's life? Well, didn't I?''

Moriah nodded and cried another bucket of tears.

''Didn't I tell ya there wasn't a man alive who was worth the misery and torment? Didn't I tell ya that sex was one thing, but love will get your heart broke? You never, *ever,* give your heart to a man, understood?''

Moriah hiccuped, sobbed and nodded.

''And see what you got for your trouble? Now go walk off his memory or swim it away—whatever. Just let the cleaning lady do this, hon.''

''I can't wish him away, not here,'' Moriah wailed. ''He's touched everything that's in my life!''

''Sheesh, pipe down, girl! You want your guests to think *you*'ve cracked up?'' Anna muttered at her.

''Well, maybe I have cracked up,'' she blubbered.

''Naw, this is just what phase one feels like. It gets worse before it gets better, lemme tell ya,'' said Miss Gloom and Doom.

''Then I'm shutting this place down for a couple of weeks, soon as the other guests leave this weekend. I'll reschedule our future guests,'' Moriah decided impulsively as she swiped at her burning tears. ''Will you keep my feelings for Jake a secret? Will you take care of Dad if I bail out for a while?''

Anna nodded. ''Sure thing, sugar. Go as far away as you need to. The staff will do the painting and remodeling you've mentioned. But if you think I can keep my big mouth shut about your feelings for Jake, forget it.

The others need to know why you're moping around.
Now, skedaddle!''

Moriah handed the wad of sheets to Anna, then bolted
from the cabin. She just couldn't face being here without
Jake. Not yet. Not until she had time to get herself in
hand and accept the undeniable fact that he hadn't really
wanted her for herself. He'd wanted her because she
reminded him of his ex-fiancée—the one true love of his
life.

It dawned on Moriah, while she was making her rain-
check calls to would-be guests, that she had it bad for
Jake if she could turn her back on this resort that had
become her life and walk away from her dad and her
devoted friends.

"This surprises you?" Moriah muttered to herself,
then smirked. "Love doesn't get any worse than running
away to hide from yourself and your feelings. Where
can you possibly go that your emotions can't find you,
huh?''

Just hold yourself together a few more days, she
chanted silently. You can cope, Moriah. So do it, damn
it!

After giving herself that much-needed lecture, she
pulled herself together, plastered on a smile and strode
off to help her remaining guests organize their lives
properly. Now there was a laugh. She couldn't put her
life back together, so how was she going to encourage
anyone else to be cheerful and relaxed?

JAKE DIDN'T NOTIFY anyone of his early return. He
camped out in his apartment with Spitwad and worked
off his torment by creating the most incredible Web site
he'd ever designed—a masterpiece of computer wiz-
ardry. It had all the bells, whistles, graphics and wild

colors Moriah favored in her wardrobe. There was peaceful music, spectacular photos that opened up with the click of a computer mouse to take an Internet surfer on a tour inside every building at the resort. With technical hocus-pocus, Jake even gave the illusion of an underwater swim in the pool and turned Kent's photos into action scenes that displayed fishermen pulling their catches from the glistening river.

Since Kent had generously purchased three extra disposable cameras and taken dozens of pictures, Jake's designs were a virtual-reality tour that gave Jake the sensation he was still there—if not in body, then in mind. His body, of course, was still on the mend and he couldn't put weight on his right leg without grimacing in pain. But all he needed was a little more time and he'd be as good as new—he tried to assure himself, and half-believed it.

As soon as he was able Jake dived headfirst into work at the graphic shop, falling into his robotlike routine, denying time for himself because he didn't want to *think* or *feel* or *regret* that Moriah was out of his life forever.

He doted over his sisters by phone and in person, but he kept putting them off when they tried to schedule his belated birthday party. Using what little spare time he granted himself, he shopped for baby toys and nursery furniture. According to his calculations he'd purchased enough baby paraphernalia to last his nieces and-or nephews until they celebrated their fifth birthdays. For sure, he wouldn't be having children of his own to fawn and fuss over. The only woman he wanted to father his children had more than enough responsibility without taking on Jake and his family.

Besides, he thought, by now Moriah probably didn't even remember his name. Another stressed-out executive was benefiting from her recreational resort, occupying her time and thoughts. Moriah didn't miss him, didn't need him complicating her complicated and busy life.

Considering the new Web site and promos Jake sent out to all his clients, Moriah was probably inundated with calls and requests for accommodations at Triple R. Maybe Jake couldn't give love and expect love in return, but he could give her all the business she could handle.

ALTHOUGH JAKE TRIED to maintain a positive attitude, he hit one of the all-time lows in his life. He'd repeated hundreds of consoling platitudes, kept himself busy, but the bottom dropped out of his heart, nonetheless.

He returned from work one evening, set aside his briefcase and wham! It hit him right between the eyes that he'd slipped back into a monotonous life and he couldn't stand it another day. His world had been clearer, brighter and sharper when he was with Moriah. He'd felt a thousand times more alive.

Moriah had spoiled every expectation of his life. Now everything around him, with the exception of his sisters, had become unimportant and meaningless and tormentingly predictable. He missed Moriah's outlandish clothes, her disarming smiles that made her blue eyes sparkle with a mystical inner light. He missed her intimate touch until hell wouldn't have it. He felt so lonely and isolated in his misery that he wanted to scream down the walls. He just couldn't take this robotlike existence anymore, because those traitorous emotions for Moriah kept boiling up at unexpected moments like a volcanic eruption about to blow sky-high.

"I can't do this anymore," Jake told Spitwad.

The ugly mutt looked up at him and wagged its stubby tail. A ragged sock dangled from the pup's mouth.

"Nothing is working out right," Jake muttered as he paced from wall to wall, then back again. "I can't forget her, damn it!"

"J.T.!"

He pivoted to whip open the front door. Kim, Lisa and their husbands stood on the steps, holding a birthday cake, colorful balloons and dorky cardboard party hats. Damn, he was nowhere near a party mood.

"Surprise!" the foursome trumpeted.

"We've waited long enough to celebrate," Kim declared as she breezed past him with cake in hand and made herself right at home.

Lisa glanced down at Spitwad as she barged inside, carrying cups and a plastic jug of punch. "That is one ugly mutt, J.T."

"Leave Spitwad alone," Jake said in the dog's defense. "He can't help the way he looks." No more than Jake could help the way he felt about Moriah.

His brothers-in-law, Steve and Brent, sent him pitying glances when he defended the fuzzball of a pooch, but Jake paid no attention, just opened the door and let Spitwad outside to tend his business after long hours of confinement.

Kim braced her hands on her expanded waistline and gave Jake the once-over. "You've lost weight. You've got circles under your eyes. What's happening to you? I thought your recreational vacation would give you a healthy glow."

"Yeah, bro, you're starting to look like death on a dim flame," Lisa chimed in. "And by the way, I received a check in the mail as a refund from Triple R. What's up with that?"

Jake forced a toothy smile. "I was an exceptionally

cooperative guest. I won all the awards for most improved so my stay was on the house.''

Kim frowned suspiciously. ''You paid for the vacation yourself, didn't you? You asked Moriah to return our money.''

Jake made a sound that could've meant anything—or nothing—then wheeled toward the kitchen. ''Let's have cake. I'm starved.''

While Jake wolfed down his cake and guzzled punch, he watched the interaction between his sisters and their husbands. It dawned on him in mid bite that his relationship and responsibilities to his sisters had changed dramatically. After his parents' deaths his role in life had been clearly defined. Now his sisters had grown up and established lives of their own, pursued their chosen careers. They looked at their husbands with devotion and affection. They were happy and it showed.

Jake studied Steve and Brent astutely. Same went for the two young men. They exchanged familiar touches and intimate smiles with their wives. Respect, commitment and devotion were floating around his apartment like an invisible fog. His sisters and their husbands had their shared lives ahead of them and were anticipating the arrival of their children. These two loving, companionable couples didn't need him the way they once had. They were family units standing alone, separate from him.

''J.T? Are you okay?'' Kim questioned in concern. ''You look like someone hit you between the eyes. Your face is really pale. Are you ill?''

''No, I'm fine,'' Jake insisted, flashing a smile. ''I was just thinking.''

''Well, don't do it again, because it doesn't seem to agree with you,'' Lisa teased playfully. Her eyes widened abruptly and her hand flew to her rounded tummy. "Oh, my God. I felt the baby move!"

The foursome practically went berserk. Everyone's hands settled on Lisa's abdomen, waiting with baited breath for another kick, punch, hiccup or whatever babies did to nab an expectant mother's attention.

Another mind-boggling revelation grabbed hold of Jake and shook the stuffing out of him. New lives and a new generation were growing inside his sisters while his mundane life was passing him by—day by tormenting day. Damn it to hell! He wanted the right to place his hands on the mother of his child and feel the nudge of tiny knees and elbows. He wanted what Kim and Lisa's husbands enjoyed. A family of his own. A shared life, not a predictable, monotonous routine.

My God, was it too late to return to Triple R where he'd left his heart? Was it too late to start all over again with Moriah and determine if the passion she felt for him could transform into the kind of love his parents had known and his sisters had discovered?

Jake inwardly groaned. He'd screwed up royally when he allowed Moriah to convince herself that he'd used her as a substitute for his ex-fiancée. Damnation, he'd blown it! For fear of being rejected and hurt, *he'd* decided how Moriah felt about him and how she'd react to the possibility of Jake dividing his attention between her and his sisters. He hadn't *asked,* only *assumed* that Moriah wouldn't want to get involved in his life. Furthermore, he hadn't *asked,* only *assumed* Moriah's newly discovered passion wouldn't evolve into love, given time.

Now, five weeks later, Moriah had probably written him off as a disaster and had gotten on with her life. If he even had an icicle's chance in hell of getting her back, how long would it take to convince Moriah to give him a second chance to win her love?

Jake surged to his feet. Well, it didn't matter what time frame he had to deal with. He didn't want to live without Moriah, didn't like his meaningless, empty existence. He wanted her—wild, colorful clothes and all! He couldn't wait a couple hundred years for his soul-deep feelings for Moriah to fade away. He wanted to live each day as it came, right beside her, sharing her joys and heartaches and her responsibilities. He wanted to make her life easier, to make her happy, because, damn it, seeing her happy made him deliriously happy.

"J.T.? What are you doing?" Kim chirped when he dashed abruptly into his bedroom.

"I'm going back to Triple R," he called out.

"Right now? In the middle of your party?" Lisa squawked. "You're acting weird, J.T. I'm beginning to think you need a psychiatrist, not a recreational director."

"I'm sticking with the recreational director," he said as he dragged a suitcase from the closet and crammed casual clothes into it. His hand stalled over the racy bikini briefs that were tucked beneath his no-nonsense cotton underwear. "Oh, hell, why not?" He scooped up the colorful garments and stuffed them in his suitcase.

His wide-eyed, worried sisters hovered in the doorway. Their husbands stood protectively behind them.

"J.T., have you gone insane?" Kim tweeted.

"If you equate *in*sane with *in* love, then yeah, maybe I have gone off the deep end."

"In love?" the foursome crowed. "With whom?"

"Moriah Randell." Jake snapped his suitcase shut.

"The owner of Triple R who wears those wild, colorful clothes?'' Kim hooted then stared pointedly at his black suit, white shirt and black tie.

"You're nothing alike,'' Lisa blurted. "She's bubbly, cheerful and—''

"And she was my wake-up call,'' Jake interrupted as he shouldered through the human barricade that blocked his bedroom door. He snatched up his briefcase and laptop. "Maybe I can't make her love me back, but I can sure as hell try.''

Kim got all defensive when he said that. "Well, she's nuts if she doesn't love you back, J.T. You're the best brother a sister could ever have!''

Jake smiled wryly on his way to the door. "I'm not looking for sisterly love here, kiddo. I want what the four of you have, babies and all.''

"How long will you be gone?'' Lisa wanted to know.

"As long as it takes to convince Moriah that I'm the man she needs. It could take weeks, months, maybe a year, but I'm not backing off. I'll be in touch.''

Kim nodded, lips twitching, as Jake closed the door. "He's finally crawled out of his rut and went over the wall.''

"Looks like,'' Lisa agreed, grinning in satisfaction.

Kim snickered and gave Lisa a high five. "About damn time, if you ask me.''

"Same goes,'' Lisa seconded as Jake walked out of his predictable, mundane old life and went looking for an exciting new one.

10

MORIAH SLOUCHED in her office chair and stared half-heartedly at her computer monitor. Her dad had tried to cheer her up by demonstrating the new gadgets he'd designed while she was away, but even his electronic marvels—and one malfunctioning thingamabob he'd attached to his coffeepot—didn't amuse her. Despite her glum mood, she needed to update her accounting files before five new guests arrived. She preferred to stagger the arrival times so she could devote a few hours to each guest. She couldn't believe the number of inquiries that had poured in since she returned from her two-week vacation in hell. She hadn't had one bit of fun, just sat around feeling sorry for herself and moving her tent from one Oklahoma campground to the next.

The emotions she tried to outrun were swift of foot and caught up with her. The rainy spell had cramped her style. She'd just huddled in her tent, listened to the patter of raindrops and thought about Jake.

Now, here she was, scheduling arrivals and juggling time slots for the following month. She didn't even want to think about the stack of correspondence piled up on the edge of her desk.

She frowned when she glanced at the letter from a CEO in Chicago who'd seen her Web site.... Moriah snapped to attention, rubbed her eyes and stared at the letter again. What the hell…? She didn't have a Web site!

Hurriedly, she typed in the web address given in the letter on her computer. To her astounded disbelief, soothing music floated through her speakers and panoramic photos drifted across the screen. At the bottom of the screen was the tag, Designed by J. T. Prescott. Jake had designed this elaborate site for her? Why? Had he remembered calling her by his ex-fiancée's name and decided to make amends by creating this fabulous site, complete with fascinating graphics, photos and sound links?

Moriah half collapsed in her chair. Tears floated in her eyes. Why couldn't Jake have gone to all this trouble because he *loved* her? Why did it have to be the electronic version of an apology?

"Here's your supper tray," Anna said as she barged into the office. "You need to stop skipping meals and get more sleep. The circles around your eyes are as big as Saturn's rings and you're losing weight you can't afford to lose." She slammed down the tray in front of Moriah. "Eat, girl!"

Moriah did as ordered, without tasting a bite of Anna's to-die-for smoked brisket, melt-in-your-mouth hot rolls and scrumptious grilled potatoes.

"What's that?" Anna asked, peering over her shoulder.

"A Web site designed by Jake Prescott."

Anna's jaw scraped her chest. "Wow, he's pretty darn good, isn't he?"

"The best." Moriah pointed to the stack of correspondence cluttering her desk. "I think we can credit him with this influx of reservation requests."

"I wondered what caused it," Anna murmured as

Moriah scrolled down to click on the photo of the lodge, then watched and listened to the door creak open to take them on a tour of the interior.

"How'd he do that?" Anna asked, astonished.

Moriah smiled ruefully as tears flowed down her cheeks. "Magic. High-tech, computer-wizard magic."

"Hey, Anna, can you come here a minute?" Tom requested as he craned his head around the doorjamb.

"Sure." Anna pushed upright, then stabbed her forefinger at the tray. "Finish that meal," she ordered sharply. "Don't make me shove it down your throat. And don't think I can't or won't, girl. I mean business here."

Moriah crammed a slice of brisket in her mouth to shut Anna up and hurry her on her way. She wiped away the tears with the back of her hand and pondered the masculine image floating in her mind. "Why couldn't you have loved me, Jake? I don't need a wizard, I just want you!"

JAKE SET Spitwad on the ground, then bounded from his new four-wheel-drive, sunshine-yellow SUV to see Triple R's staff members forming a blockade in front of the lodge. He didn't have time for this nonsense. He was on a mission. He thrust his arm through the vehicle's open window and laid on the horn. After four loud blasts, he drew himself up to his most imposing stature and marched forward with a bouquet of red roses in one hand and a suitcase in the other.

He broke stride when Moriah stepped through the door and halted behind her staff. He drank in the long-awaited sight of her. She was wearing the same American flag outfit she'd been wearing the first time he laid eyes on her. There were dark circles under her dull blue eyes and she was thinner than he remembered. Still, she was the most beautiful, captivating creature to walk the face of the earth.

"You wanna call off your guard dogs or do I have to fight my way through them to talk to you, Mo? I'm not leaving here until we have a private conversation."

Anna stepped off the porch and ambled toward him. "Nice shirt, flash," she said, then winked—which surprised the hell out of him.

Tom gallumphed forward. "'Bout time you showed up, ace."

Kent moseyed down the steps. "Took you long enough, slick."

"Finally wised up, did you, sport?" Chester commented.

Jake blinked when the staff parted like the Red Sea, then lined the pathway leading to Moriah. What was with the staff? It was as if they liked him again. Why? He figured he'd have to kick ass to get Moriah alone.

"What changed your minds?" Jake murmured as he strode past.

Tom hitched his thumb toward Moriah. "You can take one look at a woman who's now the shadow of herself and ask that? You turned her world upside down, damn you."

Jake squinted into the angled rays of sunset, wondering if the tears he saw glistening in Moriah's eyes meant she was happy or sad to see him.

"We voted to give you one week to get your butt back here before we came after you," Kent murmured as Jake strode past.

"She's been miserable," Tom added. "Make her happy again."

"Won't eat. Can't sleep," Anna added. "I'm making

an exception about love, just this once. Break her heart again, and you're dead meat.''

"I'll take a golf club to your head if you don't snap her out of the doldrums," Chester threatened—but with a smile.

Feeling more encouraged with each step, pretty sure he wouldn't be pounced on when his back was turned, Jake approached Moriah.

"These are for you," he announced, offering the bouquet to her. "I've been smelling the roses all the way from town. Now it's your turn."

He took her arm and steered her through the door.

"Hi, Will. Nice to see you again," Jake said when he saw Moriah's father rolling forward in his motorized cart. "Any new inventions?"

"Nothing earthshaking. You're about two weeks late, buster," Will replied. He glanced briefly at Moriah, then zeroed in on Jake. "Not as bright as I thought you were when I first met you, *obviously.*"

"No," Jake agreed as he shepherded Moriah to her office. "I was brain-dead a couple of weeks. Luckily I got better."

Will grinned, then flashed two thumbs-up. Jake breathed a sigh of relief. From the sound of things, his enemies had turned friendly. Now all he had to do was convince Moriah to give him the time needed for her to fall in love with him. He'd heard that adage stating you couldn't make a heart love somebody, but he was here to give it his best shot.

Jake closed the door to ensure privacy and gestured toward the monitor. "I see you located the Web site."

"Yes, just a few minutes ago, in fact. Thank you." She took a whiff of the roses, but it didn't seem to improve her blue mood. Tears still shimmered in her eyes and dribbled down her pale cheeks as she appraised his eye-catching Hawaiian shirt that boasted enough pine-apples to feed an army.

"I thought you said you wouldn't be caught dead in flashy clothes," she said in a wobbly voice.

"Well, I'm not dead, am I? So, technically, I didn't contradict myself."

She smiled wanly at his attempt to tease her into better humor, but her smile vanished when she met his gaze directly. "It's okay, Jake. Although my staff turned a complete one-eighty when you returned, they don't understand the dynamics of our relationship."

"I have something to say and I'm not used to saying it, so don't throw me off track." Jake dragged in a deep breath. "I love you. You push *all* my buttons, Moriah." There, he'd said it. Now his feelings were right there between them. "I don't want a refund. I want the last few days of R-and-R you owe me. I'm the best of who I am when I'm with you and I want the chance to convince you that you might come to love me, too, if you'll give me a second chance."

Moriah wanted to collapse at his feet and bawl her fool head off, but she willfully stood her ground. If Jake truly felt what he'd *convinced* himself he felt for her she'd be the happiest woman ever to draw breath. But he didn't, so she wasn't.

"As an armchair therapist, let me explain how you actually feel about me and why," she murmured.

He dropped the suitcase at his feet and leaned leisurely against the wall. "Fine, Miss Freud-in-training, get inside my head and tell me what *you* think *I* think."

Moriah inhaled a steadying breath and formulated her thoughts. "You have persuaded yourself that I can be an adequate substitute for the one great love of your life because I'm blond and blue-eyed and I respond eagerly to your passion. You're seeking validation, after being rejected by Shelly. You're striving to bolster your injured libido. You transferred and projected suppressed emotions that have been looking for a place to land all these years. When I insisted that you change your lifestyle and attitudes, your subconscious stirred up repressed emotions. These latent feelings are like a helicopter that's been in a holding pattern for ten years and have finally touched down. I'm no more than a convenient landing strip that looks like a familiar landmark.''

Jake chuckled in amusement. ''An intriguing theory. I'm sure Sigmund would be pleased. But the truth is that, although my mind was saturated with wine the night I called you Shelly, I still had enough brain power to pretend that slip of tongue.''

She shot him a dubious glance. Clearly, she didn't believe him.

''The truth is I don't have any leftover affection for Shelly that I subconsciously projected to you. Shelly is history. I only wanted *you* to *think* I still wanted her in my life.''

Moriah frowned, confused. ''Why?''

Jake shifted uneasily. Now they were getting to the nitty-gritty, the touchy stuff. ''Because I figured you wouldn't be interested in having me as a permanent part of your life, that what you felt for me was the newness of passion. And, like Shelly, you wouldn't want me to devote time to my sisters who'll always be a part of my life. Neither did I want to heap more responsibility on you when you have a strong sense of obligation to your dad, your staff and guests. I'm my family's caretaker and you're yours. I didn't want to force you to accept my sisters as part of your family. I cared too much about you to face the prospect of hurt and rejection—been there, done that, didn't like it—so I devised a way to send you running. I let you analyze the situation as I predicted you would. Being the amateur therapist you are, you did exactly what I figured you'd do.''

When Moriah stared at him, as if she were trying to analyze his convoluted rationale, Jake strode deliberately forward. He framed her face in his hands and brushed the pads of his thumbs over her lush lips. ''I don't want the life I had before I met you, Moriah,'' he whispered. ''That life was empty, meaningless and monotonous. I missed your smiles, your laughter and your touch...until I just couldn't take another day without you in it. All I'm asking is for you to see if your attraction to me can grow into something deeper. I want you to love me, because I want forever with you, if you'll have me. I want a family of my own, with kids underfoot. The works.''

Moriah hardly dared to hope Jake meant what he said. ''Are you absolutely certain I'm the one you want?''

He smiled tenderly and his onyx eyes burned with molten fire. ''Absolutely, positively certain,'' he confirmed. ''Will you give yourself a chance to find out if you feel the same way I do?''

She shook her head and his hopeful smile wobbled around the edges. Before she could tell him she didn't need time to develop intense feelings for him, he said, ''Before you answer hastily, you need to remember I've changed my attitude toward life. This blaringly loud shirt is just an example of the flashy new wardrobe I bought for my new lifestyle.'' A slow, wicked smile pursed his lips. ''And you really need to take a gander at the new underwear I purchased with you in mind.''

"New underwear?" she asked as her heart swelled with so much pleasure she feared it would burst.

He nodded. "Red-hot red with white hearts pierced with Cupid's arrows." He flashed her another rakish grin that nearly made her swoon. "I'm tellin' ya, sweet pea, you've gotta see to believe."

Moriah set aside the roses and looped her arms around his neck. "Well, since you've fussed with these new clothes, maybe we should adjourn to my apartment so I can have a look-see at those bikini briefs."

"Yeah? You're willing to do that?"

When she nodded agreeably, Jake scooped her into his arms and wheeled toward the door. "Hot damn, things are progressing faster than I dared to hope—"

His voice dried up when Moriah reached out to open the door—and sent the eavesdroppers, who'd pressed their ears to the portal, tumbling into a heap on the floor. Will Randell sat in his cart, grinning in amusement at the sprawled and entangled bodies that cluttered the floor.

Jake raised a dark brow and shot the snooping committee of five a reproachful glance. "Find out everything you think you need to know?"

"Pretty much," Will Randell said unrepentantly. "You gonna do right by my daughter or do I have to run over you a couple of times with my motorized cart and zap you with one of my electronic gadgets?"

Jake glanced at Moriah. "She's the one holding up the show, not me," he reported. "You'll have to ask her."

"Is there any chance of getting some privacy around here?" Moriah asked her nosy family. "Don't you have someplace you need to be?"

Thankfully, her father and her staff cleared a path so

Jake could carry her through the lobby and out the door. She glanced curiously at the yellow SUV in the driveway. "What happened to that boring gray sedan you owned?"

"Sold it," Jake said as he carried her around the corner of the lodge. "Not enough pizzazz for the new man I am."

Moriah unhooked her right arm from around his neck to open her apartment door for him. She watched Jake appraise the colorful decor that carried a Caribbean theme, replete with bright-yellow walls, vivid-blue carpet, flower-print furniture and an abundance of live plants.

"Why am I not surprised?" he said, chuckling.

He pivoted toward her bedroom. "Damn, this is better than I thought possible." He studied the frothy ferns, wicker furniture and tropical-print bedspread. "It's like being marooned with you on a desert island." Devilishly, he tossed Moriah in the middle of her bed, as if it were the middle of an ocean. "A fantasy come true!"

Moriah gestured toward the open window. "Close the drapes, will you?"

He shook his raven head and stretched out beside her. "Nope. I want to see every exquisite inch of you," he assured her as he deftly unbuttoned her blouse. "I want you to watch me watch you so you'll realize it's *you* I want and need, not some egotistical, attention-seeking, narcissistic ex-fiancée. I'm glad she's out of my life and good riddance to her." He peeled off her shorts and his fingertips skated over the elastic band of her panties. "I just want you, Moriah," he said softly, sincerely. "Because you're *you* and being with you makes me feel whole, complete and alive."

He angled his head toward hers as he drew the gaping

blouse from her shoulders and made short work of removing her bra. His hand glided over the creamy slopes of her breasts as he deepened the kiss, imitating the intimate pleasures to come.

When Moriah moaned beneath his kiss and arched into his hand, desire hit Jake like a runaway locomotive. His male engine was already revved up and *vrooming* through his body, demanding swift satisfaction. But he vowed to take it slow and easy with Moriah, to convince her with every reverent kiss and worshiping caress that he was whispering his love all over her, that he wanted to know every soft, silky inch of her not only by touch but by heart. Because she *was* his heart and his soul. She'd taught him to laugh and smile again. Taught him not to take life so seriously that he overlooked the most vital elements of existence—love and happiness. Moriah provided both for him and he wanted, more than anything, to have those feelings returned so they could share and enjoy them together.

When Jake abandoned her ripe dewy mouth to flick his tongue against the pebbled peaks of her breasts, Moriah's body quivered in helpless response. He smiled against her skin, assured that he still had the power to demolish her self-control in the heat of passion, even if he had yet to engrave his initials on her heart and bind her to him for all time.

Patience, Jake told himself. She might come to love you when she realizes you're never going to go away again.

As his hand skimmed over her abdomen and he slipped his fingertips beneath the leg band of her panties, Moriah's breath caught in her throat. He caressed her tenderly, feeling the moist heat of desire he'd called from her. When he would've traced a row of hot greedy kisses down her belly, she grabbed a handful of his hair and brought his head back to hers.

"I love you, Jake," she whispered raggedly. "I loved you before you left, I love you now that you're back and I loved you every moment in between. I don't need time to figure out how I feel about you. I already know you're all I want and need to make me happy."

He stared into her passion-drugged blue eyes, knowing desire put those words to tongue, but for now it was enough. "It's okay, sweetheart."

"Jake, you're hearing me, but I don't think you're *listening* to me."

He smiled indulgently. "I'm listening, honey, but I know passion is new to you and sometimes it's easy to mistake love for desire. We'll go from here and in time—"

His voice evaporated when Moriah abruptly shoved him on his back and hovered over him, wearing nothing but her lacy panties and a determined smile. Damn, she was a glorious sight with that arresting figure, that beguilingly beautiful face and that mass of golden hair that had come unwound from the hapless top-knot on her head.

"Now, Mr. Self-Acclaimed Psychiatrist," she said as she unbuttoned his Hawaiian shirt, jerked it off his shoulders and flung it across the room with a dramatic flair, "you need to keep in mind that some things are true, whether you chose to believe them or not. So let *me* tell you how *I* feel, rather than how you *think* I feel about you." She reached down to unzip his jeans. "Better yet, I'll *show* you how I feel about you—whoa!" Her delicately arched brows shot up when she saw his racy bikini briefs and the hard, aching flesh beneath it. She flashed him an impish grin. "Those really are attention-grabbers, aren't they?"

"Wait till you see what I have in store for your looking pleasure tomorrow, and the day after that, sugarplum. We're talking flash and sizzle—ah…"

Jake derailed from his train of thought when Moriah's hand enfolded his throbbing length and she bent to whisper her moist breath over his hard flesh. She stroked him with tenderness, suckled him, nipped playfully at him until he was ready to scream in tormented pleasure. Her roving hands and teasing lips were never still for a moment, making it difficult for him to draw air into his collapsed lungs.

Hot, fiery sensations converged, pelting him, arousing him so rapidly that his self-control was on the verge of being shot down. Jake clenched his fist in her hair, dragging her face back to his.

"Careful, honey, you're about to detonate a time bomb," he wheezed.

"Am I?" She stared boldly at the evidence of his desire and her eyes twinkled with devilry. "Good, I want you completely out of control and at my mercy."

"I'm already there…." His voice broke when she laid her hands on him again.

"Ex…cellent," she murmured as she grazed her lips over his aching flesh, then twisted to bring her mouth back to his.

Jake tasted his desire for her on her lips and tongue. His control snapped like a frayed rope. He hooked his arm around her waist and rolled her to her back. "Damn it woman, don't you know what *stop* means?"

Smiling, she shook her head. Her shiny blond hair rippled across the bedspread like waves on the sea. "Apparently not. I couldn't *stop* loving you when I thought you looked at me and saw your ex-fiancée. I couldn't *stop* wanting you during these agonizingly hellish weeks without you. I'll never be able to *stop* loving you and I won't even try.''

He stared into those mystifying blue eyes that glowed up at him and he believed with all his heart and soul that she knew her own mind and meant what she said. Relief tried to wash through him, but desire had no intention of relinquishing its dominance over his pulsating body.

''What'd you do with that lifetime supply of protection you bragged about buying?'' he asked as he slid the scrap of lace from her hips, then shucked his jeans and briefs.

''Tossed them. I didn't think I'd ever see you again and I wasn't about to substitute my love for you by fooling around with someone else,'' she told him.

''And if we make a baby before we can restock?'' he asked as he eased between her legs to stroke her moist sensitive flesh.

Her eyes glazed over when he aroused her to the extreme. A sigh escaped her parted lips. ''Fine by me,'' she whispered.

''Ditto,'' Jake murmured as he came to her and felt her close hot and tight around him. He glided forward, then sensuously withdrew, gauging her reaction by the expression on her face as their shared pleasure intensified. He wanted to watch Moriah come apart before his eyes, wanted to cherish every wild moment of this incredible passion that blowtorched through her and blazed over him.

''Jake!'' she cried out when the first wave of ecstasy engulfed her. She reached desperately for him, clutching him close.

She shimmered around him, dragging him down into the swirling depths of ungovernable passion. Shudders of seismic proportions shook his body and he clung to her as tightly as she clung to him.

Well, so much for taking it slow and showing his love for her one erotic step at a time, he thought, gasping for breath. Next time. Maybe.

A LONG WHILE LATER, Jake looped his arm around Moriah's waist, then dropped feathery kisses to her lips. "Okay, sweet pea, here's the deal."

She grinned playfully. "There's a deal, too? Heck, I thought we were just going to have sex, sex and more sex to relieve our stress and tension."

"Listen up and be serious for a second," Jake ordered, smiling. "I'm selling my graphic shop so I can help you with the resort and your dad."

Her smile vanished in a heartbeat. "No, that's your life, Jake. You're incredibly talented at what you do. We can work out a schedule so we can be together several nights a week."

"*Schedule?*" he squawked. "I can't believe that word passed your lips!" He shook his head emphatically. "Uh-uh. Nope. Ain't happenin', sugarplum. I told you I'm here to stay and I mean what I say."

"But, Jake—"

He pressed his index finger to her lips to shush her. "As it turns out, my three employees took care of business just fine while I was away and things ran smoothly. I've made arrangements to sell part interest to them. I'll still work with them. I can do designs here and e-mail information back and forth, no sweat. I'll make a weekly drive to the city to personally handle business and visit my sisters."

"And the deal is?" she asked curiously.

"That we tie the knot, build a home here and I invest part of my profit in the resort so we can build more cabins and hire more staff members."

Moriah gaped at him. "Man, you've obviously been giving this considerable thought while I was wallowing around here in self-pity."

He nodded and grinned. "Even made myself a list of things to do."

"Figures," she said, smiling.

"So what do you say to a guy like me and a gal like you merging our business and sharing our responsibilities and living happily ever after? I'm telling you here and now—and you can write this down, sweet pea—that I'm offering a lifelong commitment to making you happy." He grinned devilishly. "Plus, I'll throw in all the wild, kinky sex you want, anytime you want. For free. You snap your fingers, and I'm there for you."

"Yeah? Anytime and any place?" she questioned playfully.

"You'll never have to ask me twice, because you are my number one priority and I want to be yours. Deal?"

Moriah stared into those dark, obsidian eyes, fanned by long sooty lashes and fell all the way to the bottom of her soul. The expression on Jake's face indicated he was dead serious about making a commitment to her, to them.

Now what woman in her right mind would dare question the sincerity of Mr. Predictable when he declared his love and promised to spend his life making her happy, sharing her dreams and offering to let her share his?

Certainly not *this* woman! And what was wrong with breaking her personal and professional rule about getting involved with one of her guests, so long as she fell in love with the only man who could make her life fulfilling and complete?

"You've got yourself a deal," she murmured as she glided her hand over his muscular chest and leaned down to kiss him oh so slowly and thoroughly. "I love you, Jake."

"Same goes for me, sweet pea," Jake assured her as he wrapped his arms around her and held on to Moriah as if he never meant to let her go—because that's exactly what he intended to do. She was his life and his love and everything was coming up roses in his world.

Jake smiled in satisfaction when the sensations Moriah called from him exploded in bright neon colors, consuming him, satisfying him beyond belief. Ah, life was good, and from now on, the only thing *predictable* in his world would be this remarkable love he shared with Moriah.

Too Many Cooks

Molly O'Keefe

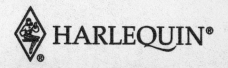

TORONTO • NEW YORK • LONDON
AMSTERDAM • PARIS • SYDNEY • HAMBURG
STOCKHOLM • ATHENS • TOKYO • MILAN • MADRID
PRAGUE • WARSAW • BUDAPEST • AUCKLAND

Dear Reader,

What a thrill this is! *Too Many Cooks* is my first book, and I couldn't have asked for a better experience! For years I've enjoyed reading Harlequin novels, and it's truly fantastic to provide a little love and laughter to the other romance readers out there.

I'm from a small town with about a dozen families just like the Cooks—big, loving and, for better or worse, constantly in each other's business. There's no way to avoid a mother and a couple of brothers who want only the best for the members of their family, and will stop at nothing to get it!

Falling in love with someone also means falling a little in love with their family. For some of us it's a breeze. For Cecelia Grady, who's from the city, it means making her peace with horses, snakes and plenty of manure.

I hope you enjoy Cecelia, Ethan and the whole Cook family!

Happy reading,

Molly O'Keefe

To Mom, Dad and Tim
for the years of patience and laughter,
and for Adam. Thank you.

1

CECELIA GRADY answered her cell phone on the first ring.

In a midgrade state of panic she beseeched the person on the other end of the line. "Samantha, tell me you know where I am."

"Well, as far as I can tell by this map..." Samantha paused and Cecelia could hear the rustling of papers over the phone "...you are nowhere near the Morning Glory Ranch."

Cecelia slumped against the rental car and swore under her breath. It had already been a bad day and she could tell the worst of it hadn't even started.

"Cecelia, what I don't understand is that you have three detailed maps," Samantha said in an irritatingly reasonable voice. "How could you get lost?"

Cecelia loved Samantha. She loved the girl's efficiency, her sense of humor, her kindness and up until this particular moment, she especially loved all the efforts her assistant had made toward Cecelia's pet project.

But, had miles and mountains not separated them, she would have cheerfully throttled Samantha Cook.

"First of all, it is not established that I am 'lost.'" Cecelia made a vague quotations gesture with her free hand. "Second, your 'maps,' and I use the word loosely, include landmarks like 'turn left at the big oak' and 'if you go by the granite outcropping you've gone too far.' Maybe I need to remind you that my degree is in Social Work, not Earth Science.''

"Okay, point taken," Samantha conceded. "But, I made those maps myself—"

"Look, the maps are useless to me right now, can we move on?" Cecelia barked and immediately felt horrible. "I'm sorry, Sam," she apologized. "I'm just freaking out here." She looked at the forest in front of her as if the trees might attack her at any moment.

Cecelia heard Samantha inhale deeply and recognized it as a regrouping breath. Soon, Cecelia knew, Samantha would start numerating. "First things first," Sam said. "How is Nate?"

Cecelia turned and looked over the hood of the rental car at her eleven-year-old traveling companion, Nate Hernandez. Nate was on the edge of the trees ambitiously throwing rocks into the forest at anything that moved.

A rock skittered and smacked into the car.

"Watch it, Nate!" she shouted.

"Whatever," was his sneering reply.

"He's fine," Cecelia said brightly into the phone.

"How are you?" Samantha asked in quiet tones.

"I am," Cecelia thought about it and pinched the bridge of her nose, "running out of positive visualizations."

"But you still have your sense of humor," Samantha pointed out, hopefully.

"Barely," Cecelia said on a breath. "Just barely."

Cecelia's job as a social worker in Los Angeles had

taken her to a lot of interesting places, but the top of a mountain on a dead-end road in the wilds of Montana was a first in her colorful career.

It was her own doing, of course. She insisted on seeing out the final leg of her pet project: a ground-breaking initiative to save inner-city youth from gangs, violence and drugs.

She proposed that most of the kids in the city's juvenile halls and halfway houses were the products of a bad environment. If you took a good kid out of that bad environment and gave him a chance in a supportive, healthy environment without the influences of the people and things that were leading him to make bad choices, then the kid had a chance.

Nate Hernandez was the guinea pig. He was going to be relocated to a ranch in Montana for the summer, more specifically the Morning Glory Ranch. Samantha's parents owned the land and as the host family, they were the other component of the project.

Cecelia had worked her entire life for this chance. The Relocation Project was hers—success or failure—and now that she was lost in the middle of nowhere with only a cell phone and a juvenile delinquent between her and a total breakdown, she had never felt the pressure quite so keenly.

"Cecelia." Samantha's calming voice broke into Cecelia's downward spiral. "I know you must be stressing out up there, but Nate and my parents are perfect for this project," her assistant said sagely.

One year ago, after months of fruitless interviews with people only interested in the small stipend the government provided for host families, Cecelia had been disheartened. Many people lied, a couple of families didn't pass the criminal background check. One woman came in drunk.

Cecelia was ready to put her head down on her desk and weep, when Samantha approached her.

"My parents would like an interview," she said, smiling. "They're interested in your project."

Cecelia had felt hope bubble in her chest.

"Is your mom a drunk?" she had to ask.

Samantha laughed and shook her head.

"Has your dad done time for burglary?"

"Nope, they're ranchers in Montana."

Ranchers in Montana. Cecelia had a mental image of them all going to church and sitting down to dinner every night to discuss the day's work. Mr. and Mrs. Cook would retire to the porch after dinner and look out at their land and think noncriminal thoughts. They had probably never even seen a "gang banger" or thought about being carjacked.

A kid from South Central Los Angeles couldn't get more relocated than that.

Because the family was Samantha's and she was proof of what a loving and fantastic environment she had been raised in, Cecelia met with them immediately, but left out a lot of preliminary work. Like visiting the ranch before going there with Nate, which explained why she was currently lost.

But lost or not, Samantha's reminder had bolstered Cecelia's flagging enthusiasm and confidence.

"What I don't understand is, if you grew up here, roaming these mountains on your trusted pony, how could you draw three horrible maps?" Cecelia leaned away from the car, her sense of humor returning as she imagined the strong and stalwart Cooks.

"I could hang up and then you'd really be lost," Sam threatened.

"You're right, just get me out of here." While her assistant mumbled and fumbled around with her copies of the maps, Cecelia finally took in the view with an appreciative eye. It was magnificent—from the blue sky to the green carpet of trees that covered the valley to the purplish-black crowns on top of the mountains, what she saw was the purest of colors. She took a deep breath of clean, crisp air.

"You were lucky, Sam."

"How so?"

"Growing up here, your parents, everything," she said quietly, drinking in the view. "You were one lucky cowgirl."

"Yeah, I know." After asking Cecelia some questions about the roads she had been traveling on, Samantha figured out what Cecelia needed to do to get back on the right road to the ranch. Cecelia wrote down her new directions on the back of a fast-food napkin.

"How's the car?" Samantha asked after confirming the directions a dozen times. Cecelia turned to examine the wreck social services had rented for her. The twenty-year-old hatchback had seen better days that didn't include mountains. She and Nate couldn't drive with the air conditioner on and when they crawled up mountains they had to turn on the heater to cool the engine.

"It's going to break down any minute," she said, only half joking. "Hey, on the radio while we were on our way to," she looked around, "the middle of nowhere, before we lost the signal, they were talking about bear activity.''

"What did they say?''

"That there had been some. Actually, I think the words they used were 'significant,' 'widespread' and 'oddly vicious.' What exactly does that mean?''

"Well, I think it means that there are a lot of angry bears out there.''

"This isn't funny, Sam!'' Cecelia admonished.

"Who's joking?'' Sam asked. "Look around you at the trees. Do they look intact or do they look like a giant cat's scratching post?''

Cecelia looked around and was startled and dismayed to see that the evergreen forest actually looked like a forest of cat toys.

"They ah…they don't look good,'' she answered, scared of what that could mean.

"Well, then I suggest that you get back in the car and stay moving.''

"Great.'' Cecelia whistled at Nate to get in the car. He threw one more stone at a low-flying bird and did as she asked, grumbling all the way.

"Uh, Cecelia?'' Cecelia climbed into the car, only partially noticing that her assistant's confident tone had wavered into hesitancy.

Cecelia was going through the now familiar dance to get the car going. She shook the gear shift, wiggled the wheel and had to turn the key twice before the thing would start. "What is it, Sam?''

"You know that trip my parents went on a few days ago?'' Sam asked.

Once the engine was running, Cecelia turned the car

around and headed back down the mountain like Sam had told her to. The road was rough and the little car bounced around like a rowboat on rough seas. "Anniversary, right?" Cecelia pushed the phone between her shoulder and ear because she needed two hands to maneuver around a tree in the middle of the road. *They should have rangers or something to clean these roads up,* she thought.

"Right, well, there is a small problem."

"Problem?" Cecelia shouted, convinced her heart would give out under any more problems.

"They haven't, um, actually gotten back yet." The car dipped into a valley and the connection went fuzzy.

"Sam?" Cecelia shouted into the phone. "So, they're stuck in the Billings airport? They're visiting neighbors? What are you saying?"

"Bad weather has delayed their flight, they're still in Florida." Cecelia could barely hear Samantha through the static.

"For how long?" Cecelia shrieked.

"Two days, tops."

"Your brothers are there, right? They know we're coming," Cecelia said. While this was certainly bad news, it wasn't the end of the world. Samantha talked about her brothers as if they were saints and, in lieu of Mr. and Mrs. Cook, three saints were better than none.

"Yes, they are and they do and just about everyone is very excited to be a part of the project, except..."

"Except what, who?"

"Ethan. They haven't actually told Ethan yet and he could be trouble." Cecelia dodged another fallen tree and the phone slipped.

"How could they not tell Ethan that we were coming? Was he out on the range? Was he taking cattle to Abilene or Dodge or wherever cattle get taken these days?"

"No, he was home. He's just...trouble."

"Well, that's just great, Sam. I'm lost, there are angry bears following me, I already have 'trouble' in the passenger seat of this car—sorry, Nate—and now I have to deal with your big brother? I have not come this far to be bullied."

The static was getting worse and Cecelia was getting a cramp in her neck. She was keeping herself together through sheer single-minded optimism—one troublesome cowboy wasn't going to stand in her way.

"It's just that he doesn't know about you guys and he can be resistant to change."

"I'm not redecorating, I'm bringing a kid up to spend some time in the fresh air. Look, Sam. I need two hands on the wheel here, I'll call you soon."

Cecelia closed the phone and set out finding the Morning Glory by her own devices.

There weren't that many roads in Montana, and the ranch had to be on one of them.

"We're lost, aren't we?" Nate asked, sneering at her. It was a weak sneer compared to some of the champion kid sneers she had seen in her days as a social worker, but he was working on it.

"Nope," Cecelia replied. "Not anymore." She smiled at him and jabbed him in the side with her elbow. "Chin up, buckaroo. We'll find our bunks."

"You are so lame, Cecelia," he sneered again, better this time, then turned to stare out the window.

Cecelia ignored him and wished for the hundredth

time that their car had a radio—the stony silences were killing both of them.

"Look at that sunset," Cecelia said just to hear the sound of a voice. She was looking up at the sun sinking behind the Rocky Mountains. "You don't see that kind of stuff in Los Angeles."

"Same stupid sun we got in L.A. I don't see why I gotta travel six-hundred miles to see it here." Nate scowled. "Why do I gotta go to this ranch anyway?"

Cecelia took a deep, calming breath. She had answered this question a dozen different ways since climbing into the car with Nate at dawn this morning. The only thing that tempered her response was that she understood his feelings. He was surrounded by the unfamiliar and controlled by the social worker who'd taken him away from home.

As dangerous as L.A. was to him, it was still home.

"Look, your mom, you remember her? The woman who's in charge of you?"

"No one is in charge of me."

"I am."

"Yeah, right," he scoffed.

"Your mom doesn't want you to end up like your brother, Eddie." Nate paled and squirmed. Eddie was a sensitive subject and Cecelia zeroed in. "You were hanging out with members of his gang and you've been picked up by the police a half-dozen times."

"I wasn't doing anything," he said weakly in his own defense.

She raised her eyebrow pointedly. "I don't think that the owners of the cars thought it was nothing. Neither did the guy who owned the store."

It was testimony to the kid's natural goodness that underneath his tough veneer he looked ashamed. That glimmer of normalcy, of eleven-year-old virtue, was why Cecelia picked Nate for the project in the first place. Perhaps with her help, the streets of Los Angeles wouldn't chew him up and spit him out.

With all the hunger and hope in her, Cecelia wanted to grab on to this boy and run the gauntlet of inner-city adolescence with him. But she knew social workers weren't allowed to get that close. She was used to being feared and hated by the people she tried to help, and until she had received the okay for her pet project, she had settled for a sad and dismal success rate. The Relocation Project, she hoped, would change that.

"Your mom wanted you to be the first kid in the project. She wanted you to get off the streets," Cecelia explained, but she knew it was fruitless.

He looked out the window. "Big deal."

"You know," she glanced over at him, "you should think of this as a vacation. How many of your friends have ever been on a horse?"

He squirmed, shifted a little and tried to shrug, but it came off jerky.

Ah, Cecelia thought, *a nerve.*

"Have you ever been on a horse?" she asked, watching him carefully while pretending to be as nonchalant as he was. The consummate social worker.

"Nah." Nate was working on feigned disinterest. The consummate kid.

"Me either," she admitted, honestly. "You scared?"

"Of a stupid horse? No way."

Cecelia smiled and thanked her lucky stars that Mr.

Cook was an intimidating kind of guy. A cowboy in the truest sense of the word, he had the face of Clint Eastwood and the body of John Wayne. His eyes had long ago disappeared into his head from years of squinting into the sun. His hands were huge and firm and when he put one on your shoulder, it felt like a boulder landing on your body. He was perfect for a kid who held rappers and rich drug dealers in high esteem.

Mrs. Cook was perfect as well, though not nearly as intimidating. She looked like Mrs. Claus and had brought cookies to the office when they came to Los Angeles. But she was sharp—she had raised four kids, three of whom were sons. She knew how to keep boys in line, and she knew her way around a chocolate chip cookie.

Cecelia had loved them right away, but more important, she was impressed by their enthusiasm to help Nate.

Speaking of impressed, Cecelia was astounded by how quickly things got dark after sunset in Big Sky Country.

Must be all those mountains, she thought, trying to calm the acceleration of her heart which was directly tied to the sinking of the sun. She didn't want to be out here in the dark.

"Are we almost there yet?" Nate asked wearily. He rolled his head so it rested listlessly on the window.

The road dipped and turned and started a winding path up another mountain. Cecelia had been holding her breath half the trip as the car shook and shuddered its way up a dozen mountains.

"Here we go again," she said. Her heart started thumping and her hands became sticky on the wheel.

"We're almost there," she said with false cheeriness as the engine made a strange thunking noise.

"What's happening to the car?" Nate asked.

"Downshifting," Cecelia answered, not having the faintest idea what was happening to her car. She flipped on the headlights, hoping some kind of light would ease the tension in her shoulders, but in the eerie half-light every fallen tree, bush or stump looked like a bear getting ready to charge.

"Ohmygod!" Nate gasped, all coolness gone.

"What?" Cecelia shrieked. She sped up, thinking that she could outrun whatever was after them. "What did you see?"

Nate paused, squinted, peered into the dark edge of the forest and finally sighed, relieved.

"Nothing."

They each replayed that scene a dozen times as night fell deeper and the mountain grew steeper. Nervous tension had Cecelia torn between laughing at their paranoia and crying because she was well and truly scared of the possibility of a charging bear.

"I really do think it's on the top of this mountain," she said, looking at Nate out of the corner of her eye.

"This one or the next one?"

"Definitely this—" The average shuddering and thunking of the engine turned into something outstanding. Cecelia leaned back, her mouth agape at the orchestration of rattles and thumps that ended in a crescendo that shook the car and its passengers. With a mighty gasp of air and a last desperate attempt to stay moving, Cecelia's car stopped. Just stopped. She pushed harder on the accelerator. Nothing.

She thought about turning off the ignition and trying again, but in that moment the car started to roll backward, down the mountain.

"What's happening?" Nate asked, his eyes huge in the twilight.

"I...ah..." Cecelia lifted her hands from the wheel, trying desperately to remember if anyone had ever told her the best thing to do when your hatchback is rolling backward off a mountain. She put the car in Park and jerked up on the emergency brake and the car stopped. Momentarily, but then gravity took over.

"What's happening, Cecelia?" Nate asked frantically.

They were picking up speed. Trees thwacked the windows and scratched the sides of the car on its course down the mountain...and ultimately off a cliff. She looked at Nate and couldn't believe it as the words came out of her mouth:

"Open the door and jump."

Nate just blinked at her, so Cecelia leaned over him, opened his door, unlatched his seat belt and was getting ready to push him out the door when their car came to a crashing halt. Against a tree.

They were quiet for a moment, assessing the damage, as the dust settled.

"Are you okay?" Cecelia asked around the knot of fear in her throat. She put her hands on his arms feeling for any broken bones.

"Yeah, I'm fine. Get your hands off me." Cecelia ignored him and continued to check him over. Only when she was satisfied he was okay did she turn her attention to the car.

She turned the key in the ignition, waited a second and turned it back on hoping, despite previous evidence to the contrary, that nothing was seriously wrong with the car. Nothing happened. There wasn't even an encouraging rattle.

Cecelia climbed out of the car right into the forest. Immediately, her nylons snagged, an evergreen attacked her hair and her silk blazer was covered in dust. *Forget about professionalism.*

She climbed over a bush to check the damage to the back of the car. The bumper was dented and the small tree that had stopped them had a definite slant to it, but for the most part, things could have been worse. Cecelia wasn't sure how, but she had been saying that to herself all day long. So far nobody was dead. That had to count for something.

She was trying valiantly to keep her chin up—optimism, some positive visualization, would not be remiss. But positive visualization was difficult when tears of frustration were burning in her eyes.

"Now what are we going to do?" Nate asked, insolence and disgust so ripe in his eleven-year-old voice that Cecelia wanted to shake him. "You know, lady, this whole idea is stupid. It was stupid to fly up here and it was stupid..."

"Hey!" she barked, interrupting his tirade. "Remember those words you can't say in front of me?"

"Yeah." Nate's eyes narrowed.

"Well, 'stupid' is another one."

Nate was silent and Cecelia, having won one small

battle, turned her mind to the issue at hand. How was she going to get Nate, herself and all of their stuff to the Morning Glory Ranch in the dark, without a car and with no real idea of where they were? She tried to visualize all the bears in the area ignoring the presence of fresh city meat.

"Well, grab your bag, pardner. We're gonna hoof it." Her John Wayne accent went unappreciated.

"You've got to be kidding."

"No way, pardner." Cecelia started pulling stuff out of the car and reluctantly Nate joined in. They grabbed as much as they could comfortably carry and headed up the mountain.

"You got a flashlight?" Nate asked. She knew he was probably scared, but he would never accept any comfort from her.

"You bet." Cecelia squeezed the small flashlight on her key chain and a tiny pinprick of light illuminated barely an inch of the road in front of them.

She looked at him and shrugged. "It's better than nothing."

Nate grunted in response, hoisted his bag and led the way.

Cecelia said a quick prayer and set out beside him, holding her pin light up so she could illuminate the trail in front of them. They made their way silently up the road, and Cecelia kept her ears tuned for any sound that wasn't quite…human.

When the first noise came, she stopped in her tracks.

"Nate," she whispered.

"What?" he answered in a voice that sounded like cannon fire in the silent forest.

"Shhh!"

The snort came again, followed by the rustling of leaves. She saw Nate's eyes widen in disbelief and fear. Branches snapped directly behind her.

"Run!" she yelled. She and Nate took off in an awkward sprint, their bags banging awkwardly against their hips and legs.

"What was that?" Nate asked over his shoulder, lurching under the weight of his duffel bag.

"I don't know," she panted. Her sensible flats were sliding off her feet and she could hear the sound of the animal gaining on them. She turned to look over her shoulder just as her foot landed in something slippery. Her shoe went one way, her foot went the other, and she landed hard in something warm and smelly. The pin light flew into the bushes. Darkness and fear settled around them.

"Cecelia?" Nate called, startled by her yelp. He turned, but without the pin light he couldn't see anything. "Cecelia? Where are you?" Panic made his voice crack.

"I hurt myself, Nate." She was sure that at any moment the bear or wild boar or moose that was chasing them would come barreling out of the woods and attack them. "It's my ankle." She tried to stand, but stuck her hand in the squishy stuff she was sitting in and fell again, wrenching her ankle.

Panic and frustration got the best of her and a small sob escaped her throat. "Go, Nate. Keep going up this road until you find the ranch."

"But what...?" Nate's eleven-year-old mind could not understand what was happening.

"I'll be fine. Just go, Nate."

"I can't leave you here," he protested.

Cecelia was about to demand that he forget about her and save himself when a sound, very unbearlike, came from behind them.

It was a man, laughing.

"Hold up a second, kid," the man said, his voice deep and rich with barely suppressed laughter. A large flashlight flipped on and Nate and Cecelia were bathed in a pool of light.

"You two look like a couple of deer caught in headlights."

2

GRATITUDE AND FEAR warred in Cecelia's brain. In the city, strangers were not to be trusted and Cecelia and Nate depended on those kind of truisms to stay safe. So, while this man appeared to be their white knight, they had no way of knowing that he wasn't really an evil character straight out of *Deliverance.*

The man's flashlight waved madly through the trees as he dismounted from his horse. Cecelia, sitting in manure and Nate, poised for flight, continued to stare, peering into the darkness past the light for a glimpse of the man. Cecelia had a faint impression of high cheekbones and a cowboy hat.

He crouched next to them and Nate dropped his duffel bag, shot his hands in the air. Cecelia leapt to her feet, ignoring the sparks of pain in her ankle and assumed her karate-ready position.

The flashlight flickered over them as the man stood slowly, confidently. "You can relax, I'm not in the mood for killing," he said, waving the flashlight up and down Cecelia's body. "I thought you could use some help."

Cecelia had never been so agonizingly aware of how bad things were, and how her appearance reflected her situation. Her black hair had pine needles tangled in it, her demure and professional suit was ripped and her face was dirty. Some of whatever she had been sitting in had stuck to her skirt, and at that very moment, a clump of it slid down her leg and landed with a splat on the ground behind her. The man chuckled again.

"We do need help. We…ah…" Cecelia floundered, looking for words to properly explain the colossal situation.

"Aren't from around here?" he supplied.

"No, we aren't." She chuckled as if he'd told a funny joke at an office party; it wasn't as if she'd twisted an ankle trying to climb a mountain in flats or anything. "Our car…"

"Backed itself into a tree?" That he was finding humor in her situation could not have been more evident.

"Indeed, it seems to have done just that, and, well, we thought you…"

"Were a bear?"

"Hey, asshole, you gonna help us or not?" Nate yelled. "'Cause if you aren't why don't you get back on your horse and ride the hell out of here!"

"Nate!" Cecelia didn't raise her voice, but the steel in it was as effective as a gunshot. She turned her back on the stranger and stared at Nate. To her relief, she succeeded in staring the kid down. He threw his arms in the air and sat on his duffel bag.

"Sorry, mister," he mumbled.

Cecelia turned back, knowing she wasn't at her best. "It's been a long day," she said rather sheepishly, gesturing toward Nate by way of explanation.

"What are you doing here?" he asked.

"I'm looking for the Morning Glory Ranch. Do you know where it is?"

"Why?" the stranger asked, his voice hardening.

Surprised by the hard tone and interrogation by a stranger, Cecelia's suspicious nature reared.

"Why do you care?" she demanded.

"That's my family's spread."

"Oh," Cecelia said, relieved. "You must be one of the boys."

"I'm Ethan Cook. My folks didn't say anything about a woman and her kid coming to visit."

"Yeah, well." She shrugged and tried for a casual laugh. "I'm not exactly sure why no one told you about us. I'm Cecelia Grady and this is Nate Hernadez. We're expected."

Ethan took a step toward her, crowding her in the darkness. "Not by me," he growled.

That was a first for Cecelia. Men simply had never growled in her presence before. "There's obviously some miscommunication going on here," she said, plastering on her best confidence-inspiring face. "I'm sure if you could just take us to the ranch Mac and Missy will clear this up."

Ethan Cook's chuckle set her teeth on edge.

"That's going to be pretty difficult," he said. "They're stuck in Florida."

Cecelia took a few calming breaths and tried again. Her ankle was throbbing, she smelled like animal poop and she was not in any mood to discuss the situation in the middle of a dark road with a man she had thought was a bear.

"Right, rain delays."

"More like tropical storm delays. Edward has them locked down in Miami."

"Edward?"

"Hurricane Edward, the tropical storm that's been chewing up the East Coast for the past three days. Perhaps you've been in a cave." The tone in the man's voice turned up the heat on Cecelia's temper and she longed, absolutely craved, to let this man have it. But he was their white knight and a Cook to boot. So Cecelia figured it just didn't pay to piss off the cavalry.

"Look," she said through clenched teeth, "I understand that you may not have known we were coming, but we *are* expected. If you could just give us a lift to the ranch, we can get this all squared away."

There was a moment of silence, and Cecelia could not have known that Ethan Cook, known through parts of Montana as a man with *no* sense of humor, was working up to a punch line.

"Well, lady, the ranch is about a half mile up that road. You just keep on walking and you'll get there eventually." He flipped off the flashlight, pleased as punch to see the look of shock on the woman's face. Silent shock, that was even better.

Cecelia could see his grin, the sheen of his white teeth in dim moonlight. The sight of those teeth blew the lid right off her temper, and before she knew she was doing it, she yanked her manure-covered shoe off her foot and hurled it in the general vicinity of those gleaming, white teeth.

The splat it made as it landed on his stomach and Nate's chuckle behind her were highly satisfying. But then, silence. Nothing but angry silence. She opened her mouth to apologize but his growling laugh stopped her.

"Nice one, lady. For that, you get a ride back to the ranch." He picked her shoe off the ground and tossed it at her feet. "Leave your bags, we'll come back for them."

Nate crept up to her side. "We're not—" he swallowed audibly "—we're not riding *that* are we?" Cecelia watched Ethan swing himself up into the saddle. She and Nate leapt out of the way as the prancing horse moved toward them.

"Surely, you don't expect us both to ride with you on *that*?" She was in a skirt for crying out loud. "Couldn't you go get a truck or something?"

"Lady, *that* is Freddie, and you threw horse dung at me." As if that explained all his actions, he reached down a hand. "You're first, kid."

"Way to go, Cecelia," Nate mumbled under his breath, but he reached up and put his hand in the cowboy's. Before he could start complaining, Nate was in front of Ethan on the saddle.

"Come on, lady, you're going behind me." He held out his hand, and Cecelia found herself unable to put hers in his.

"Perhaps I'll just walk," she suggested. She tugged on the hem of her blazer and something in the action must have upset him, because the next thing she knew he had hoisted her up by the waist and practically thrown her on the butt of the horse. She would have slid right off the other side if it wasn't for the fist he knotted in the back of her jacket.

"Put your arms around me," he said in a voice that offered no opportunity to argue. Tentatively, trying to avoid the manure on his shirt, she slid one arm around his waist and with her other hand attempted to pull her skirt down.

With no warning he nudged the horse forward. Cecelia squealed and gave up the fight with her skirt to wrap both arms around him. They hadn't gone three steps before Cecelia realized her skirt was not the only inappropriate part of the incongruous position she was now in. As the horse swayed, her chest alternately brushed and flattened against Ethan's back.

Ethan's large, muscled back, she couldn't help but notice. He was a giant man; her head didn't even come to his shoulder, and the arm that she had snaked around his waist registered the fact that the big man had not an ounce of fat on him. He was all hard muscle.

She leaned back and tried to avoid contact, but she started sliding off the horse, so she pulled herself closer. But she realized that with her skirt almost around her waist, her thighs, with no comforting barrier of denim or even cotton blend, rubbed intimately against Ethan's muscled, denim-covered thighs. In fact, it wasn't really rubbing; it was more like cradling. So she tried to scoot away from him, but as the horse swayed, her head collided with his shoulder.

"Lady, you don't have anything I haven't felt before, so stop giving yourself an ulcer and relax."

In the span of a day Cecelia had been lost, covered in horse manure, attacked by a man-bear and now dismissed by the Marlboro man.

She simply had no dignity left. She relaxed against him and with every step of the horse she let her body settle against his. She was past caring.

What did a glimpse of her sensible cotton underwear mean in the grand scheme of her bad day? It wasn't as bad as a host family stuck in Florida; it wasn't as bad as a broken-down car or a smart-aleck kid who now had even more reason to dislike her.

So what if she rested her head against this stranger's back and gave in to a little self-pity? That was nothing compared to the lambasting her boss would give her. So what if she let a couple of those tears that were burning her eyes and the back of her throat go. She rubbed her face against the worn denim of his shirt, wiping away some of the tears that were slowly leaking from her eyes.

Crying against this man's shoulder was nothing compared to the loss of everything she had worked for.

"Lady, I don't mind you crying. But if you're wiping your nose on my favorite shirt we're going to have to talk."

She leaned her head away from him and concentrated on the stars above their heads, trying to find what was left of her self-control.

"What's she crying for?" Nate asked.

"Her ankle hurts," Ethan answered, before Cecelia could even comment.

MORNING GLORY RANCH was nestled in a small valley. Two streams cradled the property, providing all the water the lush grazing land needed. There was a large, two-story house and a vegetable garden the size of Cecelia's apartment building. The center of attention was the barn with three corrals around it. There was a scattering of other buildings throughout the valley: a bunkhouse, a smokehouse and even a chicken coop. Just a couple of chickens, but the building was still standing. The moon that had been hiding behind trees and mountains was unobstructed in the valley and the Cook's property was bathed in a cool light.

It was a magical light, clearer and brighter than sunlight. The landscape was painted in tones of brilliant black and white.

"Oh, my…" Cecelia gasped.

"Holy shit," Nate swore, as taken by the valley as Cecelia was.

"Watch your mouth, kid," Ethan said when Cecelia didn't respond to Nate's language.

Perhaps it was part of Cecelia's mood, but after the day she'd had the ranch looked unearthly. The light, the quiet, the mountains, the foreign sensation of a cowboy in her arms…it was a different world. And she was a different woman. With her skirt hiked to her waist, her ankle swollen and her hair a disaster, Cecelia had never felt so…unprotected. So unsure. So absolutely not herself.

Ethan rode up to the house and dismounted. He grabbed Nate by the armpits and put him on the ground before the kid even had a chance to be too cool, then put his arms in the air as if to say to Cecelia "jump and I'll catch you." It all seemed so simple to Cecelia, swing one leg around and then just…jump. So she swung her leg around, let go…and slid right off the other side of the horse and fell to the ground.

Nate and Ethan came to stand over her, both looking at her with concern, amusement and just enough derision to get her past humiliation and right into angry.

"God save me from useless women," Ethan said, pulling her to her feet. Before she could even register a breath to start yelling at him, a woman came flying out the front door.

"Are you okay?" the woman asked breathlessly. She ran right up to Cecelia and put her hands on her shoulders. Cecelia looked at the young woman, whose brown eyes were huge with concern, and knew immediately that this was a shoulder to cry on.

"I'm fine," Cecelia assured the stranger.

Ethan ignored Cecelia and spoke to the girl. "She hurt her ankle. Could you get us some ice, sweetheart?"

Sweetheart? Cecelia decided the leggy brunette must be Ethan's wife, and immediately blushed. Moments ago, she was cradling somebody's husband between her legs. She knew from Samantha that Ethan was thirty-two years old and the foreman of the ranch, but no one had ever mentioned a wife. Nothing, absolutely nothing was going as planned.

"Sweetheart" ran inside to get some ice while Cecelia limped over to the steps leading up to the porch and sat down heavily. Nate, with nothing better to do, sat down next to her. She took it as a meager sign of triumph. On a day like this she'd take what she could get.

"I'm part of an inner-city relocation project." She looked at Nate and fought the urge to put her arm around his shoulders to provide and receive a little comfort. There was none coming, though, so she did what she always did and sat up straighter and put her mind to the business at hand. "I work with your sister, Samantha."

The man only grunted at that bit of news.

"Your parents volunteered to be a part of a revolutionary idea and host Nate for the summer."

"Sounds like something they would do." Ethan

pushed his hat back on his head, and Cecelia got her first good look at their white knight.

Oh my, she thought, and all the breath seeped out of her body. Living in Los Angeles had given her a lot of experience with beautiful people—men with perfect bodies and chiseled jaws, both of which Ethan had. But there was something else about Ethan that took Cecelia's breath away. Perhaps it was the cowboy hat or the stubble on his jaw. It could have been the way he handled the horse or even the memory of her thighs pressing his. Whatever it was, combined with his dark hair and gray eyes, his high cheekbones and the fullness of his lips, Ethan Cook was a prime, number one heartbreaker.

Cecelia could only blink and wish she at least smelled good while meeting this specimen of manhood. This... this...cowboy.

"Your parents told me they were going on a vacation for their anniversary." Cecelia was really having this conversation with herself; Nate and Ethan just listened in. "They said it was only for a week. One week! Plenty of time to be back for Nate and me. Plenty of time unless there was some kind of tropical storm. Who gets caught in a tropical storm?"

"Millions of people," Ethan answered dryly, throwing wood on the fire of her temper.

"Millions of *other* people! Not ranchers in Montana! Doesn't your father have land or cows or something to take care of?"

"I'm minding things while they are gone." Ethan's brow knitted and Cecelia figured he was growing frustrated with the temperamental woman who threw manure-covered shoes, wiped tears on his shirt and was about as close to a nervous breakdown as any man wanted to witness.

"Well, that's great! You don't know anything about us, do you? Well, considering your bad attitude, no wonder no one told you about us. I'm not surprised!"

"Bad attitude! Lady, I just met you!"

"My name is Cecelia!" She stood up, and due to the added height of the step she was eye to eye with Ethan and she wasn't going to back down an inch. No matter how much he crowded her, which he was currently doing.

"I don't care what your name is, or who you work with or what deal you have with my parents. I'm in charge here."

"Oh, right. You're in charge of sneaking up on women and children and bullying people with twisted ankles...."

"You want to see bullying?" Ethan took several steps toward her until his boots came up against the porch stairs.

"Oh, bring it on, cowboy...."

"Ethan!" Sweetheart stood at the front door. "Leave the poor woman alone—she just fell off a horse."

ETHAN AND CECELIA stared at each other for a second.

"Go inside," Ethan said, brusquely. "Alyssa will find beds for you."

Before the woman could say anything else that might make him lose his mind, Ethan swung up on Freddie's back and rode off into the night. His temper was on fire, and as he remembered her lithe body brushing against him, certain other parts of his body warmed up as well.

What a night.

He had laughed so hard at the woman and the kid as they ran up the mountain that he almost fell off his horse. When he heard her tell the kid to go on without her, he had to bite his lip from hooting. He hadn't hooted in years.

He had intended from the beginning to help them out, no matter who they were, but there was something about the flash in her eyes and the tone in her voice that put his teeth on edge. That's why he'd made that crack about her walking and for a moment it had been so worth it. Then she threw that shoe and started crying and saying bad things about his family.

What a mess.

He believed their story about the relocation whatever. The whole ranch had been abuzz with something and it wasn't uncommon for Ethan to be out of the loop. He worked. He worked hard and all the time with little left over for anything else. Be that as it may, things were working out so that he'd have to baby-sit his parents' little charity project. It was bad enough that half that charity project was a punk kid, but the other half was a long-legged, loose-lipped, drop-dead gorgeous, useless city woman. A useless city woman whose clumsy bumping and brushing against his back had turned him on in a way that he hadn't been in a long time.

He had no intention of playing tour guide or surrogate father when he had a ranch to run.

As he rode back to the barn, Freddie picked up on Ethan's anger and began to dance nervously. Ethan pulled on the reins a little too hard and Freddie reared, pawing the air with his giant hooves. Ethan held on with his hard strong thighs and wished he could throw a similar temper tantrum.

He had no idea the eleven-year-old punk watched, his mouth agape.

"Nate?" Cecelia called from the doorway to the kitchen and Nate jumped away from the door. No one would catch him staring at that guy. Nate didn't care if Ethan was a cowboy or not, he was a jerk and while he sure could handle that horse, Nate would like to see him in South Central. He wouldn't get away with being an asshole there.

3

"WHAT?" NATHAN ASKED, coming into the kitchen. He was trying not to be impressed by the ranch and the beautiful woman, named Alyssa, who was putting together sandwiches. But he was having a hard time.

They were, after all, ham sandwiches. Thick ones with mustard and cheese. Nate tried not to stare.

"Are you hungry?" Cecelia asked in a friendly, though tired voice. Nate felt one of those thick pulls of shame he sometimes felt with Cecelia. He knew she wanted to help him, but things were so screwed up that they became complicated in his head. It was too hard to figure out what to do, so he did what he always did.

"Yeah, I'm hungry." He scowled and flopped down at the giant table that took up the middle of the kitchen. The kitchen, Nate guessed, was bigger than his mom's apartment. It was cool how you could see the wood and stones that built the ranch. No one would punch holes in these walls, and, Nate guessed, you wouldn't be able to hear any fights going on in the next room, or any of the other sad and scary sounds that seeped through the walls in his mother's tiny apartment.

Alyssa came back to the table and put a plate with a sandwich and carrots in front of him.

"What are you giving me this crap for?" Nate asked,

holding up a carrot stick. He couldn't remember the last time he had one, much less what they tasted like.

"NATE..." CECELIA was tired to the point of weeping and she didn't know if she had it in her for another stare-down with Nate.

"That's what we eat with ham sandwiches," Alyssa said, intervening. "If you don't want it, you can forget the sandwich." She put her hand on the edge of Nate's plate and waited for him to understand what she was saying.

The rules were different.

"Whatever," he mumbled and bit into the carrot.

"You guys have had a tough time of it," Alyssa said as she slid into the seat across from Cecelia. Her giant green eyes were soft with compassion and understanding. "I'm Lis Halloway."

"I'm Cecelia Grady," Cecelia started to explain.

"Oh, I know who you are. You're Samantha's friend. This whole hurricane thing must be a wrench in your works."

"Well, not necessarily. If Ethan will cooperate, the project can be salvaged. But I'm afraid after the fight we just had, your husband might not be feeling..."

"My husband?" Lis asked, laughter sparkling in her green eyes.

"Isn't..."

"Oh, no. Ethan and I aren't married. Thank God. He's entirely his own man. Entirely. I'm the cook." Lis bit into a carrot.

Cecelia felt a trickle of relief. She hadn't been cradling a married man after all. Not that she had lusted; really, it was just the horse-and-cowboy thing.

Okay, so she lusted, big deal. Hormonal flare-ups were the least of her problems. Dealing with the man who had stormed off more than a little peeved with her was far more pressing. How was she going to convince Ethan that she was not only sorry about throwing the shoe at him, but that she was, despite all evidence, a rational and reasonable human being?

On top of that small obstacle—a mountain on a mole-hill—she had the distinct impression that she and Nate would be sent home only to come back after the Cooks had weathered the storm.

That hitch could result in any number of bureaucratic backlashes. Her project was tenuous as it was and this kind of setback could knock the legs right out from under it.

She closed her eyes and felt the warm pressure of Lis's hand over hers.

"This is all going to work out, you'll see." She squeezed Cecelia's hand. "Ethan's not about to turn you two out, and the Cooks are sure to be back in a few days at the most."

"What I don't understand is why the Cooks neglected to tell Ethan that we were coming."

"Ethan can be…stubborn and when he's against something everyone knows it. Sometimes it's just easier to go around him."

"Cecelia threw her shoe at him," Nate said, his mouth full of ham. "It was covered in horse—"

Cecelia cleared her throat. But in the silence that followed she found she had no real explanation to defend herself. Luckily, instead of being horrified, Alyssa laughed.

"I'm sure that he deserved it. He can be downright...ornery." Alyssa put some more carrots on Nate's plate. "I mean it, Cecelia. Things are going to be okay."

Cecelia nodded numbly, not sure she could believe that.

Alyssa chatted on while Cecelia and Nate ate sandwiches, providing some background noise for Cecelia's thoughts. Lis was the ranch's summer cook, saving for university and a degree in veterinary science at the University of Montana. She had practically grown up on the Morning Glory; her parents owned the next spread over.

Cecelia listened, nodded and laughed as some of the stress of the day melted away under the good companionship. Cecelia found she really liked Alyssa Halloway. After feeding them and calming the frayed edges of Cecelia's nerves, she shuffled them into bedrooms, loaned them clothes to sleep in and tucked both of them in. And neither the full-grown woman nor the boy complained.

BY THE TIME Ethan returned, the house was quiet. The kind of quiet Ethan liked. The ranch and everyone on it was resting from a day of hard work and preparing for the hard work ahead. To say that Ethan liked his life on the ranch would have been a gross understatement. Ethan lived for it.

As soon as Ethan was conscious of happiness he knew his was tied to the Morning Glory.

He put the bags that Cecelia and Nathan had dropped on the road in the foyer and walked to the kitchen. A light was burning over the long table and Alyssa had left a note for him. He opened the refrigerator, grabbed a beer and twisted the top off as he looked at the note. Nate was in the guestroom and Cecelia was in his parents' room. Ethan took a swallow of beer. His parents had called and would call back at midnight.

He checked his watch. Eleven o'clock.

He kicked off his boots, shrugged off the shirt that still displayed the remnants of Cecelia's tantrum, and threw it down the basement stairs in the general vicinity of the washing machine. He idly scratched his bare chest and drank his beer while he walked into the den to wait for the call.

It was dark, but the furniture had been in the same place since Ethan was a kid. He skirted the chair, stepped over the ottoman, put one knee on the leather couch and slid, face first onto a body.

A screaming body that immediately started fighting, landing solid punches on his face and chest.

"Hey, lady…hold it." He deflected a punch that could have broken his nose. She bucked under him, shoved with both hands against his chest and Ethan collapsed onto the floor. He sat there in a puddle of beer, and touched the corner of his lip with his tongue.

He was bleeding.

He could hear Cecelia's breathing—hitched and fast, and then stop in a gasp.

"Oh, no," she moaned.

"'Fraid so," he mumbled. He stood, leaned over to the lamp on the end table and flipped it on. Mellow light bathed them. Cecelia put a hand to her mouth and gaped.

"What are you doing in here?" he asked. A slow burning was building in the back of his head.

"I was waiting for you." She struggled for another apology. "I wanted to apologize."

The burning spread, climbing across his temples.

What is she wearing? he asked himself and then wondered where that thought came from. Thin black straps crossed over her shoulders. A tank top.

Lord, Ethan, he thought. *You've seen a woman in a tank top before.*

Not this one, something in him answered. In the light, her olive complexion looked golden. She took a deep breath and Ethan's eyes wandered to the cotton covering her breasts. She took another deep breath, preparing to say something and Ethan's groin hardened.

What's going on? he thought. A red haze crept across the corners of his vision.

"...mistake. I'm sure we can work it out."

"Work what out?" he asked, tearing his attention from her body when she stood and the blanket she was wrapped in slithered to the floor. She was wearing a tank top and sweatpants, hardly a lust-inspiring wardrobe.

So, why was he so lustful?

She bent to pick up the quilt and Ethan found himself craning his neck for a peak down her shirt.

"The situation." It was that voice, that briefcase-and-business-suit voice that really had his guts in a knot. Women with breasts like hers had no business taking on that tone of voice. She should be flat chested and bony. She shouldn't be ripe and round and strong.

"Your family called while you were gone," she was saying. "I...ah...I'm not sure why they didn't tell you about us."

"I'll tell you why—because it's a bad idea. The Morning Glory is no place for a punk kid."

CECELIA BIT HER LIP and took a deep breath. Another appearance of her temper was not going to help matters. "Your feelings are duly noted, but don't have much bearing on the present situation."

And the present situation included a handsome, half-naked man with murder in his eyes. Cecelia tried very, very hard to keep her eyes above his neck, but they kept straying back to his bare flesh. Another hormonal flare-up brought on by the sight of a chest only seen in movies by women who weren't wearing sweatpants.

"I'm sure that you and I can come to some kind of workable compromise." She averted her gaze and her mind from the golden skin stretched across his chest.

"Compromise?" he repeated. "Lady, you've thrown horse shit at me, bloodied my lip and scared the life out of me. You're in no position to ask me to compromise."

This was worse than Cecelia had imagined.

"The original agreement says that I am to stay here for a week to make sure Nate is settled. Your parents said they would be back as soon as possible. That should leave us with only a few days to work through."

"I'm not working through anything," Ethan grumbled and sat down in the large comfortable leather chair. He eased back, kicked his feet up on the ottoman, and took a swig of beer. He looked like a man who was done talking.

"I'm not sure you understand what's at stake," Cecelia said.

"And I don't think you understand what you're asking."

Cecelia didn't really know how to answer that. She was reading him loud and clear—he didn't like her or Nate and wasn't welcoming them into his house. But, that simply wasn't going to work for Cecelia.

"You are putting four years of work in jeopardy, not to mention a program that could possibly save hundreds of kids' lives." Her voice rose and her shoulders went back as she defended what she believed in. "Nate is just a kid. Where he was born is not his fault. He's smart and he's scared and he wants to try but doesn't know how. And now, now when he's got a chance at things, you're ready to slam the door shut on him because you don't like kids."

"Actually, lady, the kid is fine. It's you I don't like." Ethan's slate-gray eyes were cold and hard over his beer bottle.

Cecelia's mouth opened on a gasp. She could feel herself turning red, burning up with the effect this horrible man had on her.

"You're fairly loathsome yourself," she said, pleased that her voice didn't crack or waiver. "I'm offering you a chance to help this kid for one week. Both of us will stay out of your way. You won't even know we're here. But if you send us home now, I'll sue your parents for breach of contract." Cecelia wasn't sure where that horrible bit of blackmail came from, but she stuck her chin in the air and saw it out.

If there was one thing Ethan understood it was hardball and there was something about the way this woman stood up to him that had him so turned on he couldn't think straight.

"You're something else, lady. Stay out of my way until my parents get back, and if you're lucky I'll forget you said that. If you or that kid get in anybody's way around here you're going right back where you came from."

They stared at each other until Cecelia, light-headed from a narrow victory, grabbed the blanket and walked out of the room, with her chin high and embarrassment in her heart. As exits went, she thought, it was pretty good.

ETHAN WATCHED her go, took another swig of his beer, and counted to one hundred so he wouldn't chase after her and kiss that prissy look right off her face.

The phone ringing next to his head had Ethan sitting up and blinking into the darkness. He had fallen asleep in the chair waiting for his parents' phone call. He grabbed the receiver.

"Yeah," he said into the phone. The static was so bad on the other line he could barely hear his father's voice.

"Son?" his father asked and immediately launched into an explanation that Ethan only got part of. "Cecelia…program…good kid…have…commitment….see it out." Ethan closed his eyes. It wasn't like he was *really* going to kick the woman out; he had no intention of doing that. But somewhere inside it hurt that everyone in his life thought he was such a jerk that he would kick them out. Even his dad. When did this happen? This change. He used to be nice, or at least nicer. Which wasn't saying much.

"Dad, I'm not going to kick her out," he shouted into the phone.

There was a rustle of static, which Ethan assumed was his father's sigh of relief.

"Thanks, son...we'll be home soon." The static flared and the line went dead.

Ethan put the phone down, flipped off the light and walked to his bed, wondering where everyone got off thinking he was a jerk. If you asked him it was that woman who was the jerk. He touched his lip where there was a small cut and smiled.

She was something else.

THE NEXT MORNING, Ethan walked into the kitchen, prepared to make the best of things. He didn't have to be a jerk. He respected the work Cecelia was doing and as for the kid, well, he didn't have to talk to the kid if he didn't want to. He knew he had started off all wrong and while there was no way to go back and change that—he could try to make up for it.

The smell of breakfast made him smile as he clomped into the foyer, kicking off the dirt from the barn that remained on his boots from the morning chores. Nothing put a man in a good mood like the smell of hot coffee and fresh sausage.

The smile faded as he turned the corner and found his brothers tripping over themselves for the benefit of Cecelia.

"Now, Cecelia, you need to elevate that ankle." His youngest brother Billy, who could charm the skin off a snake, was picking up Cecelia's foot and taking off her sock!

"Really, Billy, that's so…" Cecelia was laughing, embarrassed, but if the blush was any indication she was charmed. Of course.

Mark, the brother sandwiched between Billy, the charmer, and Ethan, the jerk, put some ice in a plastic bag, wrapped a dishtowel around it and gently placed it on Cecelia's ankle. Mark smiled at her, but couldn't make eye contact, which didn't seem to matter to Cecelia. She was obviously taken in by Mark's Jimmy-Stewart shy-guy approach.

"I missed you boys in the barn," Ethan said, breaking into the scene like the Grinch who stole Christmas. Cecelia immediately stiffened and Ethan reminded himself that he had no business feeling bad for ruining a flirt's good time when he had a ranch to run.

His brothers, used to Ethan's bluster, only smiled back at him.

"You could have told us Cecelia and Nate had finally arrived," Billy said to Ethan.

"What do you mean finally?" Ethan asked, walking over to the coffeepot and pouring himself a cup.

Everyone looked at each other conspiratorially until the lightbulb went on in Ethan's head. "You knew?"

Ethan scanned the room getting affirmative nods from his brothers and Lis. "Why didn't anyone tell me?" Ethan asked.

"Well, Ethan," Billy said, clapping a sympathetic hand on his big brother's shoulder, "you tend to be a little stubborn when it comes to matters of change, wouldn't you say, Mark?"

"Ornery," Mark answered. "I'd say ornery."

So, this is how it is, Ethan thought. His whole family believed he was an ornery, stubborn jerk who would throw this woman and kid out in a heartbeat. Well, that was just…about right. Ethan had to admit it. He was stubborn and he supposed in the last little bit since his divorce went through, perhaps he had been opposed to change. He owed Cecelia an apology, which made him even more ornery.

"So, where's the kid?" Billy asked, excited by the prospect. As far as he was concerned there was nothing like a little diversion from cows to spice up a morning.

Cecelia looked at the young man, who couldn't have been more than twenty-one, and wondered how he could be related to his sourpuss older sibling. All the brothers had the same chiseled cheekbones and lips. Billy's hair was darker than Ethan's and his eyes were lighter. Mark had golden hair and eyes such a clear blue they were almost eerie. But as the three stood side by side in the kitchen it was Ethan who drew the attention. They were all handsome, but Ethan was so commanding, so… masculine.

Cecelia had had a wonderful hour with them. She couldn't help but be charmed by the two brothers who traded banter and stories with her and Lis. Ethan, of course, ended all of that.

"How's your ankle?" he asked, leaning up against the counter to eat his eggs and sausage.

"It's fine," Cecelia assured him. "Your brother is exaggerating my condition."

"We can't have you injured," Billy said, flashing his grin and dimples to great effect. "Since you're here we're going to put you and the kid to work. Slave labor doesn't come around often.''

Cecelia laughed. "If you're counting on us for slave labor you're going to be disappointed.''

"How's the kid?'' Ethan asked, interrupting the laughter.

"Why don't you ask me yourself?'' Everyone in the kitchen turned to look at the bristling boy standing in the doorway wearing a giant T-shirt and shorts. He looked so heartbreakingly young that Cecelia's breath caught in her throat. If it weren't for the sneer on his face and the anger that radiated from him, all in the direction of Ethan, Cecelia would have picked him up and put him on her lap.

"Who are you guys?'' he asked Billy and Mark, as if they were the ones who didn't belong.

The kitchen erupted in conversation and while the rest of his family welcomed the kid, got him some food and sat him down at the table, Ethan slipped out the back.

Cecelia was the only one who noticed and oddly felt the lack.

Watching Nate grow comfortable in the warm kitchen filled with joking, loving adults was one of the high points in Cecelia's career. He never really smiled, but his eyes were shining with suppressed laughter. And that, Cecelia thought, was a real change.

"You guys are cowboys?'' Nate asked at one point, shovelling in another mouthful of scrambled eggs.

Billy laughed, pretending to be shocked and hurt. "Of course we are. What do we look like?''

"You look like a movie star,'' Nate said to Billy.

"Like you're in a movie pretending to be a cowboy."
Mark and Lis erupted in laughter.

"That hurts, kid, that really hurts." Billy stood up,
stretched his powerful body and slapped his hat on his
head. "I guess I have to prove my skills to you. Go get
dressed." Billy reached over casually, as if it wasn't the
most genuine and kind thing that a grown man had ever
done for that boy, and ruffled his hair. Nate bristled, but
Billy ignored it. "Let's go pretend to be cowboys."

Nate protested, as if it was the lamest thing he had
ever heard, but he ran to the bedroom he had been given
to change his clothes, sliding across the hardwood floors
as he went.

Cecelia turned to Billy to give him her undying gratitude, but he only smiled.

"Nice kid. Mark, do we still have that kids' saddle?"

"Yep." And the two men thanked Lis for breakfast,
tipped their hats at the stunned Cecelia and made their
way to the barn.

Cecelia sat dumbfounded, the ice melting on her ankle, as Lis said, "Welcome to the Morning Glory."

4

CECELIA HADN'T exactly planned on being part of ranch life. She thought she might get a tour of the land in some four-wheel-drive vehicle, and the rest of the time she would observe from the front porch, maybe learn how to make beans or biscuits or something else equally ranchy.

Nevertheless, she found herself enjoying the daily routine of a big breakfast, with lots of laughter over lots of coffee. The whole gang spent some time by the corral watching Mark with a new horse. Billy murmured frequently, propped his foot up on the fence and nodded his head. Cecelia and Nate followed suit, feeling more and more cowboy every minute.

Finally, Billy said it was time for "Horses 101" and a tour of some of the land.

"Don't you have an RV?" Cecelia asked, following him into the tack room.

"'Course," he said, pulling leather things off the walls. When nothing else was forthcoming, Cecelia turned to Nate, an optimistic smile on her face.

"What an adventure!" she said lamely.

When it seemed Billy had gathered all the leather things they needed, he led them through the stable, which smelled pleasant—warm and earthy. The animals greeted Billy with soft neighs and a language all their own. A couple of cats joined their entourage.

"What the…?" Nate stammered when three kittens jumped up to attach themselves to his jeans.

"Shake 'em off," Billy said without turning around.

Nate bounced, trying to dislodge the animals. Two cats fell out, but one only climbed higher, reaching the waistband of Nate's windbreaker. Nate checked to be sure Cecelia and Billy weren't looking and then tucked the kitten into his pocket.

A door at the far end of the barn opened and sunlight streamed in.

"Billy?" It was Ethan. "Could you give me a hand?"

Billy turned to Cecelia and Nate with a rueful grin. "I'll be right back. The horse you're looking for is Peaches. Her stall is on the left, go on in. Move slow and talk soft so she knows you're there. If she were any more mild-mannered she'd be dead, so you've got nothing to worry about. I'll be right back."

He smiled and left Nate and Cecelia wondering if this was some kind of ranch joke: *leave the greenhorns alone in the barn with horses, pitchforks and other contraptions that look like medieval torture devices.* Cecelia paused.

"Let's go get something to eat," Nate suggested after a moment.

"We just had breakfast." Cecelia had to force herself to stay on track while the cozy kitchen and another cup of coffee beckoned. "Let's go introduce ourselves to Peaches." She took off through the stables, reading the names on the stall doors as she went.

"Amigo, Mr. Bojangles, Casey, Renegade." She

paused in front of Renegade's stall and peered in. Easily done, considering the door had been smashed through and what was left of it hung drunkenly on its hinges.

"I'm glad we're not meeting Renegade today," she said and walked on. The next stall was Peaches.

Now, to Cecelia's mind, the name Peaches evoked an image of a certain kind of horse. A small kind of horse, with big brown eyes that a city girl could trust. The kind of horse that might wear a silly straw hat and pull a wagonful of little girls in dresses behind her in a parade.

The monster horse in the stall had no business being called Peaches.

Nate looked at the nameplate on the door. "No way," he breathed.

The horse shook his head. His black mane flew, revealing the white star on his forehead.

"This…uh. This is Peaches." Cecelia put her hand on the door of the stall. The horse's nostrils flared and he backed away, snorting and pawing the ground. Nate was making some kind of low moaning noise, but Cecelia ignored him and pressed on. She knew she had to set some kind of example. If she backed out, Nate would always have an excuse not to be a part of ranch activities, such as they were.

"Nice Peaches," she murmured. The horse quieted, but his eyes rolled madly in his head. "See, Nate? He's already calming down. Good horsey."

Cecelia lifted the latch slowly on the door, but before she could ease it open Peaches reared back and smashed through the stall, knocking Cecelia down. Pain shot from her hip and wrist. She rolled over onto her back to get up only to come face to belly with Peaches. Who, she could tell from this angle, was definitely not a "she."

Peaches stood over her snorting, his hooves inches from her face. He pranced nervously and Cecelia lifted her arms to protect her face. This was it, she was sure. Death by horse. Just when the horse's hooves were about to pulverize her, a hand grabbed on to the back of her denim jacket and dragged her out of the way.

Slowly she took her arms down and opened her eyes. Ethan. Of course.

He stood over her scowling. She looked at the horse, which was being handled by Mark, and Billy had Nate in hand. Nate was talking and pointing and, Cecelia guessed, blowing the whole story way out of proportion.

"You just keep on proving what a bad idea it is for you to be here," Ethan said through his teeth.

The work at the ranch was often unsafe, but he trusted that just about everyone on the ranch had the ability to take care of themselves. Not so with Cecelia. And it made a vein throb at his temple.

Cecelia scrambled to her feet.

"Your brother," she rasped, jerking her thumb at Billy. Adrenaline was streaking through her system and she wanted to take giant bites out of Ethan Cook. "Told me to go in. He said I had nothing to worry about." Visions of the horse's hooves flashed in front of her eyes. "He said Peaches was mild-mannered."

"That's not Peaches!" Ethan barked. "Peaches is in the corral. That—" he jerked a thumb at the quivering beast "—is Renegade." Cecelia and Ethan were nose to nose, thumbs in the air, each considering the incredible pleasure throttling the other would bring them.

"Renegade kicked through his door," Mark interrupted from behind them. "I didn't want him with the other animals so I switched stalls." He looked at them both intently. "I didn't know."

There was a moment of silence as the anger between Ethan and Cecelia diffused. Whatever it was about Mark, he had the ability to take all the unreasonable frustration out of a situation.

"Are you okay?" Ethan asked lamely. He reached out a hand as if he were going to check for himself, but she stopped him with The Look. Her frigid look worked wonders with guilty parents and at-risk kids. Maybe she couldn't call off a killer horse, but she could wither a person with this look.

Ethan's hand dropped.

"I'm fine," Cecelia said, then walked over to Nate and put her arm around him.

"You okay?" she murmured.

"Yeah." In all the excitement Nate apparently forgot he hated it when people touched him and let her keep her arm around him. He looked at her and Cecelia saw a different glint in his eye. "That was really scary," he said.

"You're telling me!" She tried to keep the tone light.

Nate's lip curled in a rueful half-smile.

Cecelia was stunned by the power of that smile. The victory of that smile. She wanted to laugh and pull Nate into her arms for a hug, but she knew that the ground he had put them on was shaky at best.

Ethan watched them, obviously wondering if they both might be a little crazy.

"I am so sorry," Billy said as he approached the two, clearly unsure what to do next.

Cecelia took the situation in hand, and with the power of Nate's magnificent smile she felt bold enough to press on.

"Don't worry, Billy, we're both okay." She took a deep breath. "Why don't you show us the real Peaches?"

The brothers stood in stunned silence as Nate and Cecelia, heads together and talking excitedly about their misadventure walked down the stable toward the open door.

"That woman's got guts," Billy said. "Not a lot of women would want to try that again." Cecelia reached back and slapped the dust off the seat of her jeans and Billy's eyebrows raised a notch. "And a great—"

"Come on, we've got work to do," Ethan growled, picking up what was left of the stall door, while Billy and Mark exchanged laughing glances behind their big brother's back.

Billy led Cecelia and Nate to the corral and there, asleep on her feet with hay in her mouth, was Peaches. Billy took his time explaining horses: how to saddle, mount, manage and otherwise not be trampled by your horse. Before Nate could even sneer, Billy hoisted him into the saddle. Peaches woke up, shook her mane and with a shuddering breath, took a step forward.

Billy walked beside Nate, occasionally putting a hand on the horse's neck or on Nate's leg. Cecelia waited with baited breath for an outburst from Nate, but it never came.

NATE WASN'T BREATHING at all. There was nothing in his life to prepare him for this. In futile attempts to befriend him, the guys his mom dated had picked him up and put him on their backs. That was lame. This…this was unreal. Horses breathed and they made noises and moved around, their skin twitched and hair flew, they even smelled. He wasn't sure like what, but they definitely had a smell.

This thing under him was alive and big, and for once he couldn't even disguise his feelings. He was scared and excited and freaked out. Laughter and screams bubbled inside of him, barely under his control.

For a moment he wondered what the guys from the neighborhood would do if they saw him, but as soon as the thought entered his mind, he got rid of it. He understood that to bring those guys into this would have made the experience less…cool.

Billy was talking to him, telling him to use the reins to control Peaches.

Control this giant, hairy, awesome thing? Nate gave it a shot and pulled in on the reins. Peaches stopped. Billy told him to use his heels against the horse's sides to get her moving again. After a moment Nate got the hang of controlling the horse, gently pulling on the reins one way or another. He learned how to sit to help the horse move. He even learned how to make the clucking noises Billy was making to the horse. He wasn't sure what they meant, but he was glad to know them.

Finally, when he had made the circuit around the corral with Billy by his side and once more without him, he came to a stop in front of Cecelia and Billy.

''I tell you what, kid. You're a natural,'' Billy said to

Nate, without even a glimpse of his movie star grin. Nate felt the overwhelming sensation of pride and it just about lifted him out of the saddle.

"You ready to give it a try?" Billy turned to Cecelia.

"I don't think…"

"You gotta try it!" Nate said, his lip curled in that rare half-smile, and Cecelia was sunk.

"Of course," she said gamely.

Nate dismounted and Cecelia stepped up to the horse. Peaches looked back at her with a faintly quizzical look on her face. "You sure about this?" she seemed to say.

Billy was beside her, telling her what to do. Just when she put one foot in the stirrup and lifted her other leg to swing herself over on the horse, there was a small commotion at the other end of the paddock. Ethan was feeding two other horses.

Obviously, if there was one thing Peaches loved, it was dinner—hers or anyone else's. So with uncharacteristic speed, Peaches trotted over toward Ethan and the possibility of a handout. The reins immediately slipped from Cecelia's fingers and she barely managed to hitch her leg over the horse's back. Perched precariously, she grabbed the horse's neck and hung on for dear life.

"Whoa!" she shouted right into Peaches's ear, which she flicked as if Cecelia was a pesky fly. She tugged on the horse's neck and pulled at her mane, but Peaches was single-minded when it came to food. With nothing left at her disposal, Cecelia gave the horse a little pinch right in the loose skin by her neck. Peaches stopped in her tracks, reached over, gummed some of Cecelia's hair into her mouth and pulled. Cecelia shrieked and let go of the horse, immediately falling to the ground.

Cecelia began to consider karma and what horrible thing she must have done in her previous life to deserve Ethan Cook, who stood smirking above her.

"I'm sure there's got to be something around here you can handle," he said, hands on his lean hips, gray-green eyes flashing. Cecelia leapt to her feet, prepared to show him how she would handle him, when Billy stepped in.

"What's the big idea, Ethan?" he asked, accusingly. "You knew we were here."

"I forgot," he said by way of explanation and turned away, dismissing Cecelia's second near-death horse experience. Cecelia took three menacing steps toward him.

"You're a total jerk, a complete a…"

Billy cleared his throat and jerked his head in Nate's direction. Nate was staring at her with wide eyes. Never once in the year he had been working with her had he ever seen Cecelia really lose her temper. The word "jerk" had never come out of her mouth, and now Ethan Cook had made it happen twice in less than twenty-four hours. Nate already didn't like the guy and his opinion wasn't going anywhere but down.

Cecelia took a few deep breaths and tried to positively visualize rivers and wildflowers and other calming images, but the only thing that really calmed her down was imagining Ethan staked to an anthill.

Billy tried to help her brush the stuff off her jeans, but she slapped his hands away.

"Is there anything we can do that doesn't involve horses?" she asked, uncharacteristically snippy.

THE REST OF THE DAY turned out to be a big improvement on the morning. Billy walked them around, introduced them to the other hands and generally kept them out of the way of any horses and Ethan. Ethan did, however, always show up when she least expected or wanted him. The chicken coop situation, for example, when that hen came out of nowhere and started pecking at her. Of course Ethan was right there to laugh at her for running away from a chicken.

It was the first time she had actually seen one with skin and feathers, outside of its natural cellophane-wrapped habitat. She had no idea they were so blood-thirsty, or so *fast*.

Late in the afternoon she went into the big house to go to the bathroom and, considering no one even warned her about snakes, she didn't think she was overreacting at all when she started screaming at the sight of a snake curled up in the bathroom sink. Who should come running, scowl and all, but the devil himself: Ethan Cook.

"Lord, woman, the poor snake's more scared of you than you are of it."

"Don't count on it, mister," she snarled at him as he picked up the snake, which wound itself around his arm.

"It's just a snake." Somehow he knew that would set her off.

"Just a snake!" Cecelia exploded. "You know something? This whole thing from the start has been nothing but a joke to you. Did you put that snake there to scare me?" She was screaming, using one hand to poke him in the chest and the other one to hold her pants up.

"Lady, I didn't put the snake anywhere." He stepped into her, crowding her and her jabbing finger. The snake lifted his head in interest at the new close scent. "You're the one causing the commotion. If I remember correctly, last night you said I wasn't even going to know you and the kid were here. Guess what?'' His eyebrows arched and that mouth, the mouth that belonged on a much nicer, quieter more manageable fantasy, smirked at her. He stepped in closer, until all that separated them was her hand, which she flattened against his chest in a lame attempt to make him back off.

She lived in a city where waiting next to someone for the bus amounted to an intimate relationship, but she had never been quite so disturbed by the proximity of another person before. Every sense exploded with awareness of him. She could feel his breath fan her cheek, the heat of his body against her hand. She got caught up in the flecks of green in his eyes, the stubble on his face that changed the grain of his skin. She breathed in as he breathed out and she could smell the coffee on his breath. She wanted a taste, just a little sample of that mouth.

As if in anticipation her lips tingled and her eyelids did something they had never done—they fluttered. *Oh my God, he's going to kiss me,* she thought dimly. *How utterly strange to want to kiss this man. Aren't I mad about something?*

''I know you're here,'' he said, his voice a whisper, menacing in all kinds of ways. ''And I don't like it.''

And with that, Ethan took the snake and walked out of the bathroom, just as Cecelia's pants fell from her limp fingers and slid to the floor.

ETHAN STORMED out of the bathroom and through the kitchen, breaking off conversations and gathering stares from everyone in the room. He kicked the screen door open and walked out into the warm late-day sunshine. He lowered the snake to the ground and stood back up.

He truly sympathized with the snake. The poor thing was just going about its business looking for a cool place to nap when along comes Cecelia to turn the snake's world upside down. He could truly sympathize.

"Where'd you find the snake?" Mark asked as he came to stand beside his brother.

"Bathroom sink," Ethan mumbled, watching the snake slither away into the bushes. "That woman found it and started screaming."

"Cecelia?" Mark asked, concerned and surprised. "She okay?"

Ethan thought for a moment. He hadn't even bothered to ask. Something about that woman rewired his normal responses so that all he wanted to do was growl and glare and strip the clothes off her.

"Yeah," he said, deliberately trying not to meet his brother's eyes.

"Some reason you're riding her so hard?" Mark asked casually. "Seems to me our parents invited her and you just keep making her feel bad." Ethan felt about four inches tall. Times like these he hated his brother, but he was tired of being the big bad wolf in every scenario.

Ethan lashed out at his brother. "Mark, in case you've forgotten, I'm trying to run a ranch here. We've got market next month, some kind of virus in the barn and Mom and Dad are conveniently in Florida! On top of all that, Billy's going to be baby-sitting for the next couple of days and you and I have to make up for it. Last thing we need right now are those two!" Ethan looked pointedly at his brother before making his way to the barn, feeling no better for having yelled.

Cecelia was far more together when she finally emerged from the bathroom, having had a stern conversation with the weaker parts of her anatomy. Lis prevented Billy from taking Cecelia out to the barn again and finding some other animal that she had to ride or admire or try to take eggs from. Lis had her stay inside and help with dinner. The relief was fantastic.

Kitchens had always appealed to Cecelia. They were the center of the home, the gathering place of families. Things she had read about and knew about, but never got to experience. Certainly never on the scale of the Cooks' kitchen. Men constantly came in and out, laughing, ribbing Lis and admiring the smells. It was loud and busy and when Lis put a cup of coffee in Cecelia's hand and told her to stir the pot of bubbling red sauce, she felt as if she were home.

Lis fed everyone at the table, thirteen men in all. Pots of spaghetti, bowl after bowl of green beans, racks of biscuits and no less than three chocolate cakes.

Nate was in the thick of it, avidly watching and listening. Whatever Billy did, Nate emulated.

Hero worship, Cecelia thought smiling. *How healthy.*

She sighed, so pleased with her work and the effect the day had on Nate that she was able to ignore Ethan glowering at her from the other end of the table.

Cecelia insisted she and Nate would help with dishes.

"Why do I gotta do dishes?" Nate whined, watching forlornly as the rest of the men walked out the door to the bunkhouse. Nate was itching to see the bunkhouse.

"You ate, didn't you?" Cecelia asked, slapping a towel in his hands.

"I saw you on Peaches today. You looked pretty good up there, pardner," Lis said solemnly, carrying dishes to the sink.

"Yeah." He grabbed a plate and began drying. "It was pretty cool. But riding a dumb horse isn't exactly the most important thing in the world."

When they were finished, Cecelia took the cup of tea Lis held out and followed her advice to look at the sky from the vantage point of the corral. The air was cool and the stars so plentiful it looked as if some might fall to earth due to overcrowding. She leaned back against the rough wood of the corral, took a deep breath of nothing but clean air and closed her eyes to savor the strange and foreign bliss of the moment.

"Cecelia?" Her eyes flew open. She thought maybe she'd fallen asleep and Ethan was a nightmare, but no such luck. There he was in all of his appealing flesh. Cecelia burned at the memory of the bathroom. Had she really thought about kissing him? *That's what years of celibacy will do to you. Makes you want to get intimate with the first guy that stirs your pheromones.*

"Ethan," she said coolly, moving over so he could lean on the fence. He did just that and Cecelia noticed the mug of tea he had in his hands. Her heart stumbled over the picture he made, big beautiful cowboy with the mountains behind him, cradling a cup of chamomile tea.

Ethan was finding it difficult to say what he wanted to say because she was so damn striking in the moonlight. He'd watched for a moment before he'd approached. She had tilted her head back, arching that long throat, and when she took a deep breath, her stunning breasts had pressed against the denim shirt in a way that had Ethan gulping his tea and wishing it was something stronger.

"I have to say—" Ethan caught sight of Mark on his way to the barn and damned his brother for making him feel this guilt "—I haven't been very welcoming to you."

Cecelia looked up at him in blank-faced astonishment.

"I'm still not real happy you're here, but we both have to make the best of it." She began to frown. "I just don't have the time to be running after you making sure you don't get yourself killed. People like you don't belong up here." Cecelia's eyes narrowed.

He grinned and shook his head ruefully. "I've never met anyone who couldn't stay on Peaches." The grin turned into a smile, then a chuckle and before she could even huff, Ethan Cook was standing there, in the middle of the worst apology she had ever heard, laughing at her! Without thinking, Cecelia reached over and grabbed his thumb, pushing it toward his body like she learned in her self-defense class.

Ethan stopped laughing. "What the hell are you doing?" he asked. He tried shaking her off, but she kept twisting his thumb. Damn thing was beginning to hurt. "Let go of my thumb." Cecelia just stared at him.

Ethan knew it; all those exhaust fumes from the city were making her crazy. "Listen, Cecelia. I said I was sorry—"

She twisted with renewed force. "No, you didn't!"

Ethan started to shake his hand, trying to dislodge her

without hurting her. This was getting ridiculous. His knee trembled.

"Stop being a baby," she taunted, and that was the end of it. He knocked the teacup out of her other hand, threw his on the ground and with one sweep of his foot, he had her flat in the dirt, for the third time that day. Only now he was spread over her, his face inches from hers.

"You're absolutely out of your mind," he told her.

"There is no need to get violent," she said, dazed by her impact with the ground.

"You started it!" he shouted. And then it happened again—total sensory overload. All she was aware of, all she could feel was this man. Cecelia could only guess it was his proximity that had her in such a state. The last time she was under a man in this way was...well, during the Reagan administration, and that body had been nothing like the body that was flattening her now.

Ethan's hips pushed open her thighs until he was resting intimately against her, his chest pressed against her until all she could register was the hardness of his body against the softness of hers. It was delightful.

Cecelia's body short-circuited and with a kind of dreamy fascination she watched the mouth that was swearing at her for trying to break his thumb.

"...walk around here breathing and that hair of yours has got every man here in such a state of heat that—"

"I'm going to kiss you," Cecelia interrupted. Her self-edit mechanism had been squashed under the weight of his body.

"What?" he exclaimed. He looked a little scared of her. "Do you put your mouth right next to the tailpipe?"

Cecelia wasn't sure what that meant, but she didn't care. She slid her fingers into his hair and when he tried to rear back, she pulled a little until he stopped.

"Sit still, would you?" she murmured. She lifted her head off the ground and pulled on his hair until their lips met in a whisper of a kiss. She leaned back to end the kiss, but he followed. His soft and slightly chapped lips pressed against hers more firmly. She feathered her hands through his hair and pressed on his cheeks, relishing the rough textures of this man. Everything about him was proof of his work. As his lips rubbed gently across hers, she was dazzled by the thrill of being treated so tenderly by a man so tough.

"Thanks," she said when he lifted his head.

Ethan felt poleaxed. What would this woman do next? *First she breaks my thumb and then gives me two little kisses that I would give my grandmother and now she's thanking me.*

He told himself then and there that he needed to stay away from her. If she were on fire, he would tell somebody else to put water on her. He leapt to his feet, helped her up and walked away from her.

He looked back once and she lifted her hand in a limp wave goodbye. He growled under his breath, turned around and stalked back to her. The smile left her face, replaced by wariness and then fear as his growling became louder. "Crazy city people, radiation, cell phones making them infertile..." He stopped a breath from her, grabbed her head in his hands and kissed her in a way she had never dreamed of being kissed. He bit at her lip until she gasped and his tongue swept inside.

Ethan bit and sucked and charmed his way into the

kiss. Before she could register indignation, she was right in there with him. She grabbed on to the back of his shirt and held on for dear life. He manipulated her head, turning it so the kiss could go even deeper. Cecelia wrapped herself up in the shocking intimacy of this man. His scent, the tension in his back, the liquid heat of his mouth on hers.

Things spun loose in her, bones melted and in the center of her body there was a trembling. She pressed closer to him, molding herself as best she could to the lean, hard lines of his body.

Just as suddenly as he had come at her, he left her. He pulled back, looked at her with hooded eyes, opened his mouth as if to say something, shut it and walked away.

"Oh, my," Cecelia breathed.

5

THE NEXT MORNING everyone gathered at the corral to watch Mark break a stallion a man had brought from Billings. Mark's touch with animals was legendary and the entire ranch stopped operating to watch him with the stallion. Cecelia and Nate took a place next to Lis.

"Why is everyone so quiet?" Nate asked in a whisper. But it was more than quiet; the air was filled with nervous energy. The stillness of the thirteen people around the corral was tense.

"Mark shouldn't be doing this," Lis answered; her hands white-knuckled on the wooden fence. "The horse has been beaten." Cecelia looked closely at the giant horse and saw the old white scars that covered its flanks. "The man from Billings bought him that way, and the horse has been wild ever since. He's already hurt one man. Mark really shouldn't be doing this."

Cecelia marveled at the depth of emotion Lis had for this family.

How nice, she thought. *How wonderful to be so loved.*

When Cecelia was six, her parents and only aunt died in a car accident. There was no family left, so she was put into a series of foster homes. She was too old to be a desirable candidate for adoption and so she moved from foster home to foster home every couple of years.

Some were horrible, most were fine, but none were home.

She grew up an observer of families—invited, but not particularly welcome. Her childhood memories were of extended visits in rooms she shared, hand-me-down Christmas presents and lukewarm compassion.

As she grew up, her social worker said that she lacked social skills and that her interpersonal skills were non-existent: long periods of reserved, quiet behavior broken by fierce bouts of temper. But she was an excellent student. Somewhere in the part of her that remembered the way her mother smelled and the sound of her father's voice, she knew she couldn't blow off school. Education would save her when state-run programs could not. When she turned eighteen, the state turned her loose with few friends, no family, and a pamphlet on college scholarships for orphans.

Cecelia went to college, paying for it with a lot of loans, the meager grants and whatever scholarships she could get and hard work. The transition into college went almost unnoticed by Cecelia. She loved her first apartment with her own things, but her childhood did not prepare her for college, for making friends and dating boys. So she did what she learned as a child, bottled up her confusion and her curiosity and went about her life, observing.

Funny how life takes you places, she thought, watching the agonized concern on Lis's face. And for the millionth time in her life she wondered what would have happened if her parents hadn't died in that car accident.

The wild shrieking of a horse tore Cecelia from her thoughts. The abused stallion was rearing up, trying to get Mark off its back. Mark hung on, every muscle in his body straining for control. The horse took several leaping steps to the corral where the frantic, angry animal threw his body into the wooden fence and smashed Mark's leg between the post and the horse's own weight. Mark shouted once and then fell off the horse into a heap of dirt.

The entire corral burst into action. Ethan and Billy leapt over the fence. Billy crouched down next to Mark, while Ethan distracted the horse. Lis began to scramble over the fence, but Cecelia grabbed her. She may have been from the city, but she had the good sense to know Lis did not belong in the same place as a wild stallion.

"Did you see that, Cecelia?" Nate asked, his voice cracking in fear and excitement. "That horse almost killed him!"

Ethan went back to his brother while the other wranglers took over and herded the wild horse into an adjoining corral. He and Billy knelt over Mark, running their hands over his limbs, checking for broken bones. When Ethan gently laid hands on Mark's boot Mark groaned. His teeth gritted against the pain.

Billy said something and all three brothers smiled, albeit tensely. Ethan patted his brother on the shoulder, turned and yelled something to the other men and knelt down to his brother's ankle. Cecelia's heart tripped. That man, the competent one in charge, with the gentle hands and furrowed brow had kissed her last night.

Cecelia flushed hot then cold. She knew kisses were no longer an intimacy shared between two people who felt something for each other. These days a kiss was as personal as a handshake, the vague satisfaction of a lukewarm desire. But last night had not been vague or luke-warm, it had been wild and stirring. And she mourned the fact that she had shared that intimacy with a man she didn't like and who didn't like her.

As Cecelia watched Ethan bend to his brother, place a hand on his shoulder and smile, she felt the pressing ache of her solitary life.

Ethan and Billy hoisted Mark up. He looked ashen, brackets of pain around his mouth. The brothers began to hobble back to the house. As they passed, Lis took a step forward as if to join them, but she stopped. Her face twisted with a kind of sorrow Cecelia could truly sympathize with; the sadness of someone who wanted so badly to be welcomed and was never quite sure she was.

The men were nearly at the porch when Mark stopped and yelled to the men who were dealing with the stallion. "Leave him. I'm not done with him."

If anyone thought he was crazy, no one said it.

THEY TOOK Mark to the den and wrestled him to the couch. They tried to slide the boot off, but Mark was concerned it would cause more damage. The brothers decided they would have to cut off the boot, and Ethan quickly did so with a series of deft slices of his knife.

When the boot and sock came off, revealing the swollen foot and ankle, everyone swore. The skin was purple—so purple that in places it looked black. His toes were bright red and white as the blood tried to rearrange itself. The skin itself looked as if it might split wide open.

"It's not too bad," Billy assessed. Nate's jaw dropped.

"You'll probably be back on it in two days," Ethan offered. He tossed the pieces of boot in the trash. "Good thing those were a little too big. Could be a lot worse."

Nate looked at Mark's foot, which was close to the grossest thing he had ever seen and tried to imagine it worse.

"I'm serious about that horse, Eth," Mark said, grabbing on to his brother's forearm, grimacing when the motion jostled his ankle. "Don't let them take it." Ethan nodded his head, a promise the horse would stay.

"The stallion is ruined, Mark," Billy said. Mark just grimaced as he tried to wiggle his toes.

CECELIA HAD WALKED all over the house looking for the best reception on her cell phone and finally ended up in the side yard. It was time to pay the piper and call work. She took a deep breath and dialed her boss, Anita Brown. Anita had been in Cecelia's corner all along, but no one knew the precarious position the experimental program was in quite like Anita. Cecelia knew if Anita told her to bring Nate home, the program was done for; they simply could not afford setbacks like this.

Anita never pulled a punch and Cecelia returned the favor as she updated Anita on the situation.

"How's Nate?" Anita asked, after a pause.

"He smiled at me yesterday. He rode a horse without any kind of complaint, he helped with dishes and chores. Frankly, Anita, the boy is thriving." The line was silent and Cecelia held her breath and said silent prayers.

"You've never had a vacation, Cecelia," Anita finally said. "You've been here four years and you've accumulated a lot of time off."

"Anita, are you saying I could use my vacation days to stay here and help Nate stick it out? I have about three years' worth."

"Look. You put it on the line for this project and as long as you're there and the Cooks arrive soon, I don't see a problem. I'll pretend I never had this conversation with you. Why should I care where you take your vacation? Maybe you've always had a lust for cowboys." Cecelia almost dropped the phone. "I'm asking you if this is what you want to do with your vacation?"

Cecelia thought about the cruise she was halfheartedly planning and then she thought about Nate on that horse yesterday.

"Anita, this is the best chance for this kid," she said emphatically. "What kind of social worker would I be if I didn't do everything I could for him?"

Cecelia promised to keep Anita updated and when she hung up the phone she felt ecstatic about the way the broken pieces of her project had landed.

"You're giving up an awful lot for that kid." Cecelia whirled to see Ethan leaning up against the side of the house, slapping his gloves against his leg in a gesture of impatience. He used a finger to push up the brim of his hat so Cecelia could see his gray eyes. She felt burned by that gaze, nervous and burned.

"It's my job," Cecelia said defensively. "It's what I do."

"You don't have a family?" Ethan asked the question that had him up in the middle of the night. He had played pretty recklessly with Cecelia last night, not something he ever did with a woman he knew nothing about. She could be married and no matter what her feelings were about matrimony, he didn't kiss married women.

"No, I don't," she replied hotly. "I have a job I love and a lot of kids who need me." Cecelia found herself wondering what she had to justify to this man. Her life was her own and one kiss, no matter how heated, gave him no right to ask questions and make insinuations about her life.

"Hey, it's just a question." He threw up his hands.

Man alive, there was something about those dark eyes and the flash of color on her cheeks when she got ornery that twisted him up. He took a step toward her and checked himself. He had come out here to apologize for his behavior last night and here he was ready to replay it.

"Look, I'm staying out of your way and unless you have something to say, perhaps it would be best for you to stay out of mine." Cecelia was finding the situation, the man and the slow sizzle in her stomach highly uncomfortable.

"Settle down." He forced his forehead to relax and his hands to stop squeezing his gloves. This woman destroyed his good intentions. His will to be rational and adult about the whole stupid situation went out the window when she started talking with that briefcase voice. "I wanted to apologize for last night."

"For knocking me to the ground?" she asked. The discomfort in her stomach turned into an ache. She had no experience dealing with these situations and found it excruciating to have this conversation with Ethan.

"No, for the kiss. It was a mistake. Things are a lot different here than they are in Los Angeles. And I'm not sure if you were thinking of finding some kind of entertainment…''

"Entertainment?" Cecelia gasped, humiliation burned away by indignation. "Are you insinuating that…"

"I'm not insinuating anything, lady." He started jabbing his finger in her direction. "You kissed me first."

"A tiny little kiss. You're the one who gave me a thorough throat exam!"

"I've never met a woman who wanted that kiss more than you. You thanked me!" He took a step toward her, unsure whether his inclination was to kiss her or throttle her.

"That's hardly the point," she said. How exactly did modern women have these conversations? She was sure she should be doing something to put this man in his place. Should she slap him? A slap would feel great.

So would a kiss, some reckless, thoroughly crazy part of her whispered.

"You're right. The point is I'm sorry and you're sorry, now let's just steer clear of each other."

"Fine!" She stalked past him, glad that she wasn't the one left standing.

"Great!" he shouted at her retreating back, and stomped off toward the barn.

A breeze blew across the land, lifting the curtains to the window that had been open right above them.

MARK COOK sat on the couch in the den. He didn't feel the breeze that blew through the window, but he heard the conversation that had taken place just beneath it.

Mark's mysterious relationship with animals was nothing more than the sum of what he had learned by watching them. And he had seen enough mating dances and rituals to know that his brother and Cecelia were caught in the worst kind of heat—the kind you fought.

So, Ethan had given her a thorough throat exam. Mark laughed until the shaking hurt his ankle.

"Nothing like a nearly broken foot to make a man giggle," Billy said as he came into the room and sat on the arm of the chair across from Mark. "What's so funny?"

In hushed tones, Mark told him about the conversation he had just heard. He didn't know what was funnier, the story or Billy's reaction to it. Billy literally slipped off the chair, his mouth open and eyes wide.

"Ethan and Cecelia?" he kept repeating.

"It's not that unbelievable," Mark said, thinking. "She's attractive and single…"

"And our brother has been nothing but a jerk since she set foot on the ranch," Billy finished, unable to see where the attraction might lie.

"Maybe he's scared," Mark offered.

"He hasn't dated in four years." Billy crossed his arms and stroked his chin. "He works day and night. When was the last time he went into town?"

"Months," Mark answered.

"He's told us over and over again how he never means to have children, maybe he's decided that includes a relationship."

"You know, Billy, this is ridiculous. Cecelia's leaving in a couple of days, what kind of relationship could they have?"

"A fun one. A carefree one, without any of the guilt Ethan carries around with him," Billy answered. Mark thought about it and began to slowly nod. He had been watching his brother slowly empty out and tighten up, keeping his emotions to a minimum his entire life. Ethan was serious and dutiful. He took his life so seriously with no room for anything besides work. Perhaps some time spent in pleasurable pursuits would loosen him up. Maybe he and Billy could get their brother back for a little while.

"So," Mark started, "what are we proposing here?"

"A diversion," Billy answered, rather grandly.

"A brief encounter between two totally consenting and available people."

"A vacation from real life for Cecelia." Billy was really warming up to this idea.

"And a vacation from the past for Ethan," Mark finished on a somber note.

"I think…" Billy paused, considering the ramifications of what he was going to say. The last time Ethan had gone after him with murder in his eyes, Billy's nose had gotten broken. Thoughtfully, Billy put his hand up to his nose, rubbing a finger across the dent.

"He'll be pretty mad," Mark agreed, knowing exactly what his brother was thinking. "But…I have to say I find the urge irresistible."

"Mom always did say it ran in the family," Billy said, a spark of pure mischief in his eyes. A spark that matched the one in his brother's.

"We're a family of matchmakers," they said together in falsetto, a poor imitation of their mother's motto. They shook hands and the unsaid plan was immediately set in motion.

WHEN THE PHONE rang later that night Mark answered it before the first ring was over.

"Mom?" he whispered into the receiver.

"Hi, honey," she greeted brightly.

"Shhh!" he hissed into the receiver, looking around as if Ethan were lurking behind the couch.

"Honey? Why are you whispering?" she whispered into the phone.

With as much detail and as little volume as possible he told her what was happening with the beautiful social worker and her eldest son.

"A throat exam?" she squealed.

"Forget it, Mom. Let's just say they're seriously attracted to each other."

"Perfect," his mom said, full of pleasure and self-importance. It took a moment for the meaning of his mother's words to sink in. When they did he couldn't help chuckling.

"Mom, I tip my hat to you."

"How's Nate doing?" she asked.

Mark's powers of observation had noticed the progress Nate had been making. He told his mother about the smile, the eagerness for the horses, the willingness to help with chores. Well, willingness was a stretch, but he didn't sulk for very long.

"Wonderful," Mrs. Cook said. "You've got to get Ethan to spend some time with the boy." For the first time Mark had doubts about his mother's plan. Ethan's relationship with the boy was horrible. Ethan went out of his way to avoid Nate.

"That may not be the greatest idea, Mom," Mark said hesitantly.

"Trust me," his mother said emphatically, and it simply was not in Mark's nature to doubt the master. "Here's what we're going to do…"

THAT NIGHT dinner was, as usual, a riotous affair, despite the arctic breezes blowing between Cecelia and Ethan.

"Hey, Cecelia," Jesse, one of the youngest wranglers yelled across the table. Cecelia looked up at him with a smile. Although she had grown to expect the teasing among the men at the table, she still wasn't quite comfortable, but it was kind of fun. "You looked great on Peaches today. I'm sure she didn't mind you hugging her neck like that." The table erupted in laughter and Cecelia's cheeks turned pink. Billy had tried to get her back on the horse with serious coercion; of course it was Nate's "please" that worked.

"That horse is dangerous," she said with a rueful grin as the table erupted in more laughter. "She has you all fooled."

"Get her close to food and she's as dangerous as Renegade," Billy interjected to more laughter.

"About as dangerous as Trixie!" Jesse replied, referring to one of the ranch's dogs.

"The dog? Or the whore?" Max, the ranch's resident Casanova, asked.

"Watch it!" Lis warned, setting another bowl of mashed potatoes on the table. She sent a pointed look at Nate and all of the cowboys stopped laughing and looked guiltily at their plates, then at Cecelia.

Billy swiftly and skillfully changed the subject. "Speaking of horses and people with a real knack, did anyone see Nate on Bojangles today?"

"Sure enough. Kid sits well." Joe, the oldest man on the ranch gave the compliment to his plate full of food, but Nate heard it and Cecelia could see him sit up straighter and try to hide his grin of pleasure. Try, but not quite succeed.

This, Cecelia thought, *is absolutely marvelous.* Billy was proving an excellent companion to Nate. Eager and tireless. Billy had promised Nate a trail ride tomorrow and the boy seemed to hover over the ground.

Cecelia and Nate helped with dishes again and then Nate ran off to the bunkhouse in a fever of excitement. Cecelia quickly retired to her bedroom, anxious to avoid any more meetings with Ethan.

Ethan had the same thought and hid out in the barn. The virus in the barn was slowing down, having taken two horses and one of his mother's goats. He was determined, looking at Freddie, who lay sick and tired in the hay, that the death toll would end there.

He fiercely tied his mind to the task of caring for his horse, but as it had all day, his mind wandered to the social worker. He had done everything in his power to ignore her, avoid her and forget her, but his entire body was rebelling. His hands itched with the sensory memory of her hair and her skin. His body felt her under his, warm, strong and pliant and his mouth...

"Sick horse! Sick horse!" he said to himself in an attempt to retie the knots in his mind.

He should have gone with the boys into town last month. He had sworn off the easy women that hung out in the bars the cowboys frequented when he was eighteen. But it had been months since he left the Morning Glory. A few years ago he had a fairly consistent relationship with a woman from town, but when she began to allude to marriage and family, he slowly backed away, giving the same excuses he'd given to every other woman who had marriage on her mind. After that, he decided it almost wasn't worth the trouble and had stayed away from town and women and entanglements. Of course, now the first woman that came along he got the hots for. He hadn't felt this way since his one night with Trixie when he was eighteen.

His body didn't care that Cecelia was completely the opposite of what he wanted or needed. She was a city woman for crying out loud. She worked with kids on an everyday basis. She'd never been on a horse before and was so clearly not used to the life he loved that being attracted to her was ludicrous.

Still, it wasn't ludicrous the way his heart had pounded with grudging respect when she got back up on Peaches today. The woman had guts. And how she talked to all of the hands, even Toby who only had one eye and said some of the weirdest things ever, made him agonize with something like appreciation. It wasn't respect, he firmly told himself, but it felt like something close to it.

What really had him in a knot was how she woke up every morning and walked into the kitchen, sniffed appreciatively and smiled at everyone, especially that kid, and said, "Another great day to be in Montana." Then she went outside, closed her eyes, held out her arms like she was addressing the masses or trying to hug the entire ranch, and smiled. Smiled! As if she liked the place. Women from the city hated the ranch. It was a rule.

Then there was her behavior toward him. She ran as

hot and cold as they came. He had apologized. Twice! And she had all but jumped down his throat. She had bad news written all over her. Ethan looked back down at Freddie and forced himself to consider the issue at hand, which was a sick horse, missing parents, and a ranch to run. His lust ran a distant fourth.

6

MARK AND BILLY had a prebreakfast, prechore conference to discuss Mark's phone call with their mother and their matchmaking plan.

Mark, of course, was little help, second-guessing all of Billy's great ideas.

"I don't think accidentally locking them in the house is going to work, Billy," Mark said, shaking his head. "We have to eat."

"You're right," Billy agreed and resumed his pacing. "We could get Cecelia stranded on Sunnyside Mountain and Ethan would have to save her!"

"Billy, Ethan has been saving her for the past two days straight—it makes them surly, not romantic." Billy continued throwing out ideas and Mark continued to shoot them down, one by one.

"Come on, Billy. Space aliens?"

"Well, you're not coming up with anything!"

"How about jealousy?" Mark shrugged casually. "You know, make him a little jealous."

Billy stared at his brother and wondered how he could have hid his matchmaking light under a bushel for so long.

"Pure genius, Mark." Billy said.

BEFORE BREAKFAST, Billy rushed to meet Ethan in the barn to put the matchmaking plan in motion. He found Ethan in the barn checking up on his horse.

"Hey, Eth. Freddie looks good," Billy said, leaning up against the stall door. "Think he'll pull through?"

"He'll be fine," Ethan replied. He stroked Freddie's haunch once and stood up. "You're up pretty early." Ethan came out of the stall and shut the door behind him.

Billy tried to look as nervous as possible, he even shuffled his feet once for good measure. Ethan quickly caught on.

"What's up, Billy?" he asked, big brother concern oozing off of him.

For a second, Billy felt kind of bad for manipulating Ethan like this. He reached up to touch his nose, a small reminder of all the pain his big brother had put him through over the years. It was all the encouragement he needed.

"I've got a small problem." Billy paused for dramatic effect. "It's Cecelia."

"What did that woman do now?" Ethan growled and took off in angry strides for the door.

"No, Ethan. She hasn't done anything." He put out a hand to stop his brother from running out and paused again. *Man, I'd like to see Clint Eastwood do this better,* he thought. "I just…I just can't stop thinking about her."

"Join the… *What!*"

Billy was so pleased with the expression on his brother's face he almost started laughing. "She's just so pretty and smart and the way she is with Nate. It's…well, I think I…"

"Stop right there, Billy." Ethan could not find the source of this anger he was feeling, but it was enough to know that Cecelia was at the bottom of it. "Has anything happened…?" For some reason the words got stuck. The idea of that woman seducing his baby brother was unpardonable. It had nothing to do with jealousy; he just needed to protect his own. But where the hell did she get off kissing Ethan and then…

Forget it, he wasn't jealous.

"No! Nothing. I just like her is all. Do you think she would go for a younger man?"

"What are you talking about, Billy? She's here for a few days from the city. She's leaving."

"A lot can happen in a few days."

"You have nothing in common," Ethan continued as if Billy hadn't even spoken. "She's a social worker for crying out loud; she works with gangs and drug dealers. We work with cows. She's spent her whole life with kids and you hate kids."

"I love kids, Eth. Who are we talking about here?" Billy asked. He deserved some kind of Oscar award or something.

"The social worker and you. Don't do it. Whatever you're thinking about, don't do it!" Ethan walked away and Billy ducked into a stall to laugh.

The conversation with his brother had put Ethan in such a bad mood that not even coffee and sausage could cheer him up. Cecelia did her little "It's a good day to be in Montana" speech and Ethan wanted to shout at her for tempting his younger brother. For tempting him, for beguiling everyone on the damn ranch and being so damn pretty she hurt his eyes.

Her long, dark hair caught the light and shined brightly, reflecting almost blue highlights. Her smile and her eyes glowed with health and contentment. She helped herself to some coffee, sat down and talked to everyone at the table but him.

Every time she turned laughing eyes on Billy he wanted to jump up and shield Billy's eyes. Oh, she was a good one all right. Better than Trixie could even dream of being!

Nate ran into the room slipping and sliding across the floor. Instinctively Ethan put a hand up to steady the kid, but as soon as his hand touched Nate's shoulder the boy jerked away.

Ethan stabbed a sausage with such force his fork grated across the plate. Somehow these two strangers made him feel like an alien in his own home.

Nate filled up his plate, sat down and tried not to look at anyone. He was used to disappointment; he believed that the more you wanted something the more likely it was to be taken away. If Nate hadn't already learned this lesson in Los Angeles, he might have run up to Billy. But Nate was used to the smaller cruelties so he pretended today wasn't the day for the trail ride.

Nobody was fooled.

"Boy, you look like you've got something on your mind," Mark said, laughing.

"Billy and I might go on a trail ride today," he replied, shrugging.

"Well, we need to talk about that," Billy started. It

just about killed him to do this to the kid. He forced himself to remember the matchmaking mission.

I am a part of a long line of matchmakers, he thought. *I can't fail them now.* Besides, there was no way Ethan would let him and the kid down.

"With Mark down there's a lot of work to do around here and I really need to stick close." Billy had to look away from Nate, who, for a second, couldn't help but let the devastation show. Ethan, however, watched the proceedings with interest and his own conscience made an appearance.

"Billy," he said into the silence around the table, "you've got plenty of time for a ride."

"Hey, Ethan!" Billy exclaimed, ignoring what his brother said. "You could take him." Billy knew the logic was flawed, but he hoped no one noticed. In the ensuing dead silence, everyone turned uncomfortable eyes away from the tortured looks on both Ethan's and Nate's faces.

"I don't want to go on any stupid trail ride," Nate said to his plate.

"I've got to get back to the barn." Ethan left the table as if something were chasing him.

Mark and Billy looked after their brother with mixtures of shock, anger and disappointment.

"Nate," Cecelia said tentatively. She knew the physical pain she felt at this awkward turn of events was only a portion of how Nate felt. His dark eyes were shuttered. His lips, which were just beginning to learn to smile, turned down. So many disappointments in his young life and none of them seemed as painful as this one.

"Saddle up, buddy." Billy stood, finished the coffee

in his mug and set it down with a bang. "Ethan can kiss my boots."

"Really, Billy," Nate said as he took his nearly full plate to the sink. "I don't want to go anymore." He left the room with no complaint. No one could argue with the boy who seemed so much older than he should.

NATE SPENT the better part of the morning in his room, until Mark drew him out.

"Hey." He poked his head into the boy's room. "You smell that?" Both of them took deep sniffs. Nate's eyes told Mark that he recognized the smell. "Lis is making brownies. Now, my bet is those are for next week's lunches and she would have my hide if I tried to sneak a few right now. But you—" he pointed at the boy who was now sitting up in bed "—are small and fast and she probably wouldn't even notice if you snagged a few."

Nate spent the rest of the afternoon playing messenger and prankster for Mark. Mark had Nate rearrange Billy's room. Nate even agreed to pick flowers and put them on the kitchen table for Lis to find.

When he didn't think it would be too obvious, Mark sent Nate on the real mission.

"Hey, Nate, could you go ask Ethan about the stallion?" Mark could see the boy's hesitation and will to rebel.

"Really?" Nate asked, almost pleading with his new friend to think of something else.

"Yeah, I'm mighty concerned about that horse." It wasn't a lie and so Mark didn't feel guilty for ignoring the look in Nate's eye. Nate gave Mark one long, measured look and turned on his heel to go find Ethan. He finally found him in the barn with Freddie, the sick horse. The horse was standing in his stall and Ethan was grooming him, his back to Nate. Ethan looked so strong and big that Nate almost abandoned his mission. His mom was partial to big strong men like Ethan and he knew from experience that when one of those men got mad, things could get ugly.

He watched Ethan for a second and considered going back and telling Mark he couldn't find him. But as he stood there, Ethan started talking to the horse.

"Hey, buddy," he crooned, smiling at the horse as he ran the brush over his sleek flanks and belly. "You're going to be okay, aren't you? You and me are going to be okay."

"Ethan?" Nate's voice cracked and he wished he could start over. Startled, Ethan turned to the boy.

If there was one thing Ethan hated it was being reminded of his own mistakes and bad manners, and there was the boy trying to look so tough. Ethan felt like one big bully. What had happened at the breakfast table had stuck with Ethan all day and he knew if he ever wanted to look at his family or himself again, he had to try to make it right.

"Come on in," he said and Nate slipped into the stall. Ethan gave Freddie a little push. "Make room, pal."

"Is he better?" Nate asked, staying as close to the door as possible. Peaches was one thing, but Freddie was easily as big as Renegade and Nate had not forgotten that incident.

"Yep, he should be back to normal tomorrow." Ethan wasn't exactly being Mr. Rogers, but the kid wasn't shooting daggers at him or trying to run away.

"Is he yours?" Nate asked.

"Since he was a foal. I watched him being born."

"Gross!" Nate exclaimed before he could stop himself, but Ethan just chuckled and continued to brush Freddie's coat until it glowed.

"Mark wants to know about the stallion," Nate said, remembering his orders.

"Tell my crazy brother the stallion's waiting for him," Ethan replied. Nate nodded solemnly, watched Ethan for another second then turned and ran from the barn.

THE NEXT MORNING Ethan arrived at the kitchen later than usual. He flung open the screen door, stomped into the room and looked over everyone at the table like he was Julius Caesar addressing the senate. His stony gaze finally landed on Nate.

"You done eating?" Ethan barked at him.

Cecelia held her breath, ready to intervene at any moment, but to everyone's surprise Nate just looked down at what was left of his pancakes, shrugged and said, "Sure."

"Go get dressed. It's cold out and I need to check on some land." Somehow Nate took this as an invitation and got off his chair and carried his dishes to the sink.

Cecelia calmly stood up, caught Ethan's eye and jerked her thumb at the front door.

"A word with you, please," she said tersely and led the way to the front porch. As usual the scene outside the walls of the house had the ability to take her breath away. Mountains rose like specters, green and purple and black monsters reaching for a sky so big and so blue it hurt her eyes and pulled on her heart. But the issue at hand was enough to make her breath short and her heart ache.

"You must think I'm crazy," she said by way of starting shots.

"Undoubtedly," Ethan answered. "But you're not crazy for letting the boy go with me. He wants to go."

His flip answer had her seething. "He's scared to death of you!" She threw her hands in the air.

"You're right, and I'd like to change that. We don't need to be friends, but I don't need an eleven-year-old enemy with a criminal record around my barn."

"Do you think he would actually…?"

"No! C'mon, lady, it was a joke. Relax. I'm going to take the boy for a ride along the ridge. We'll be back in an hour." Ethan pushed his hat down harder on his head and made his way past her. He was down the steps before she stopped him.

"I don't think you're a kind man, Ethan Cook. I don't think it's in you." He turned to her. She stood on the top step, wearing denim and boots and an expression as unflappable as any he'd seen. The sun glowed from behind the house, caught between the mountains and the horizon and she was lit with some kind of light. She looked like a million of his own daydreams and fantasies. "But I am asking… I am begging you not to hurt that boy any more than he has been."

Those words hurt. They hurt and stung and he couldn't figure out why. He didn't want to care what this woman thought of him.

Cecelia did not look away from his level gaze. Finally,

after they measured the quality of each other, he nodded and left.

TWENTY-FIVE minutes later, Ethan seriously doubted the wisdom of his idea.

"What's that?" Nate asked for the millionth time.

"A tree," Ethan answered without looking.

"Yeah, but what kind of tree?" Nate's curiosity was alive in him. The park by his house had one lousy tree and it was usually covered in toilet paper. This forest was deep and dark with nothing but trees that smelled like the candles Cecelia always had in her office. Nate wanted to know this forest.

"Christmas tree," Ethan answered gruffly. The kid was driving him crazy.

Nate's enjoyment vanished, replaced by an eleven-year-old's anger.

"Hey, I didn't ask you to take me anywhere," he snarled at Ethan's back.

"You wanted to go!" Ethan snarled back.

Nate pulled on Peaches's reins, stopping. "Yeah, well, now I don't." Ethan stopped and turned Freddie around to face the bristling boy. They wore the same mutinous expressions as they stared each other down.

"Man." Nate's face screwed up with all the indignation he could muster. "I haven't done nothing to you."

"Kid..."

"My name is Nate Hernandez. Not kid or buddy. Nate."

"Okay, Nate. We're on a trail ride and trail rides are

quiet. You don't talk or ask questions while riding on a horse in the forest."

"I know you don't like me," Nate replied, shocking Ethan with his bluntness. "Why'd you ask me to go with you?"

It was in Ethan to be mean. He'd been mean for four solid days. It was even in Ethan to lie, sometimes that was easier, but it was also in him to be honest. And after a long moment, he chose honesty.

"I don't know." Ethan turned his horse around and continued through the forest. Nate considered the answer for a moment, shrugged and put his heels to Peaches, nudging her to follow.

They broke through the forest onto the ridge. Below them was a lush valley and the Morning Glory Ranch.

"Is that all yours?" Nate asked, awed by the size of the valley and the ranch nestled in its brilliant green folds.

"Part of it's Billy's and Mark's, most of it's Dad's, but that small section there—" Ethan pointed to an area above the ranch "—is mine." There was some kind of building on the land and Nate squinted to see it.

"How…ah…long have you known Cecelia?" Ethan asked, finding from somewhere in him a wealth of curiosity about the woman who was wreaking havoc in his life.

"Why do you care?' Nate shot at him, finding a wealth of protectiveness about the woman he had not let into his life.

Ethan dismounted, wrapped the reins around a low branch and took a small bag of food out of his saddlebag. He walked over to a log and sat down, making sure there was enough room for the kid, should he choose to follow. Nate did.

"She's living in my house, she works with my sister." Ethan shrugged and pulled out some jerky. "Just wondering, I guess."

"She's cool," Nate answered, taking the jerky Ethan offered.

"That why you're such a jerk to her?" Ethan asked, looking out over the valley, considering moving the cows to the northwest corner of the land.

"That why *you're* such a jerk to her?" Nate retaliated.

"Nope. I'm just a jerk," Ethan answered, his lip curled in a wry smile. After sniffing at it, Nate ate the beef jerky. "What happened that you got hooked up with her?"

Nate shrugged. "My brother got in trouble and then I got in trouble. My mom wanted me to get out of L.A.

"Do you ever get bored?" Nate asked, out of the blue. "Here. I mean it's cool and all, but you never see anyone."

Ethan thought about it, stunned by the question. Bored? He woke up in the morning and worked all day with just enough energy left to eat and fall asleep while reading a book at night. Once in a while he got twitchy, restless. So he went into town with the boys to drink and laugh and look at women.

Bored? No. Restless? Maybe.

"Too much work to get bored," he answered. "How about you, you get bored?"

Nate heaved a big sigh and thought for a moment. *He is such a serious kid,* Ethan thought, looking at him out of the corner of his eye. Briefly, Ethan wondered what the kid wasn't saying, which of his thoughts were the most private. But he shook off the curiosity and told himself he didn't care.

"Yeah," Nate finally said, "the city gets pretty boring."

They sat in silence for a few minutes, each looking at the land.

"We better get back," Ethan finally said, standing and stretching. He dusted off the seat of his jeans and tried not to smile when he saw Nate mimic him. The boy was so in need of a role model, he even chose Ethan.

"Hey?" the boy asked, his chin jutting out so far, Ethan thought he might fall over. "Could I ride Freddie back?"

Ethan laughed before he could stop himself.

CECELIA WAS WAITING for Ethan and Nate in the tack room. When Ethan sauntered in, he gave her a cool look and threw the saddle over its post. Cecelia tried to ignore the shift and pull of his muscles underneath his denim shirt.

"What happened?" Cecelia blurted out.

She had worked herself into a fit imagining the multitude of ways the trail ride could go wrong. She knew nothing about this man and she had left a vulnerable and volatile boy alone with him.

"We rode horses in the woods." Ethan's relaxed mood vanished. She was accusing him, every breath and every look told him she thought he was capable of hurting that boy. "What do you think happened?"

"Ethan, I don't want to fight with you," Cecelia said, trying to diffuse the suddenly tense situation. She took a step back and put her hands at her sides. She was weary of being at odds, and fighting with Ethan was filled with the pitfalls of her attraction to him.

"Nothing to fight about," Ethan answered. He let his gaze slide down her body, knowing it would disturb her. He didn't want her reasonable, not when he was so unreasonable.

Cecelia felt his gaze like a brand. She knew he was doing it to make her mad, to throw one more smoke screen between her, the ranch and him.

"When are your parents coming back?" Cecelia asked between gritted teeth.

"Two more days. They're fogged in in Atlanta."

"You talked to them?" Cecelia asked, aghast that she hadn't been told. She was in control of this project and the Cook family left out major details as if they were unimportant. Fireworks of tension and stress were exploding behind her eyeballs.

"Billy did," Ethan answered.

"Why doesn't anyone tell me anything!" she said. Her fingers flexed and she bounced on her toes, wanting to sink her teeth into a Cook.

"I didn't yell at the kid. I didn't beat him up. We rode horses, ate, looked at the land and came back. That's all. Your precious project and the boy are fine," he snarled and turned away, but Cecelia was having none of it.

Ethan had walked away from her once too often, and if he thought his sexy smoldering Marlon Brando looks were going to keep her away, he had another thing coming. Without Nate or Billy around to stop her, that thing was going to be loud and involve swear words.

"You overblown," she seethed, dashing around to face him, "oversexed—"

"Oversexed?" He would have laughed at the irony if it wasn't so damn depressing.

"—excuse for a man. Does it make you feel good to bully kids and women?"

Ethan grabbed her by the head and for a second neither of them knew what was going to happen next. Ethan overrode every shred of common sense and kissed her. Anger, desire and overwhelming confusion clawed him and he channeled it into this kiss. The explosion of hunger knocked them both off balance. She stumbled back and he followed, pressing her into the wall with the height and weight of his body.

He was hard, had been since he walked into the tack room with her and he ached to ease himself with her. The need to take those legs and wrap them around his waist, to urge that body to weep for his was out of control in him and it made him rough.

Cecelia couldn't find her way in this kiss, it was too aggressive and hurtful. She pushed him away, battered by his ferocity. He took three steps away and tried to get control of his breathing, his body and his whole damn life. He made the mistake of looking at her. She looked as tortured as he felt, leaning against the wall, her hands splayed as if she weren't aware of them. And her face...ah, the look on her face created a knot of shame in his chest. She was confused, and if he was honest, could be honest, hurt.

She raised a trembling hand to trembling lips. "I can't..." she started and trailed off.

I can't think, she could have said. *I can't remember*

*what we were fighting about. I can't keep kissing you
and hating you. I can't handle your anger and your passion. I'm not sophisticated enough.*

"I can't do this," she finally said.

Ethan looked at her, his chest heaving and his eyes
burning.

"Me, either," he agreed and walked into the stables.

7

THE NIGHT BEFORE the Cooks were to arrive home, Billy made an emergency phone call to his parent's hideout: The Weary Rancher Bed and Breakfast in Billings.

"I need a few more days," he told his parents in a whisper.

"I can't waste any more time here!" Mr. Cook exploded. "I have a ranch to run!"

"Dad, everything here is fine. You know that." He could hear the groans of frustration his father was smothering.

"But why do we have to stay away? It's not like we're going to ruin the mood...."

"First of all, Dad, you and Mom are legendary mood wreckers, as all of my prom dates can attest to, and second, the sooner you get back the sooner Cecelia has to leave."

"What about Cecelia?" Mac Cook asked, trying a different tactic to get out of his pink-ruffles-cats-and-weak-coffee-for-breakfast prison. "She can't stay there indefinitely."

"She's using up some vacation days," Billy answered. "I've never seen anyone more in need of a vacation than she is. She's like a different woman already, more relaxed, quick to smile. She and Ethan are at each other's throats all the time, but she and the kid are loving the ranch.''

There was a pause on the other line while both of his parents let out pent-up breaths.

''Wonderful,'' Missy finally said. ''We can give you two more nights.''

''That's a day and a half!'' Mac exclaimed. ''What are we going—''

''Shop,'' Missy cut in, answering the question before he could finish it.

''Son, stop messing around and get them together!'' Mac gave his last piece of advice before handing the phone to his wife while he sat down to consider his fate and the credit card bills.

Billy called out for Cecelia, knowing if she didn't talk to his parents herself, she would have a fit. He hated women in a fit. He passed the phone off to her when she came in.

''Mrs. Cook! How are you?'' she asked. The concern in her voice made the knot of shame in Billy's chest pull a little tighter. ''Oh, no, an airport strike?''

Ingenious mom, really top notch, Billy thought, mentally tipping his hat to his mother.

''A day and a half?'' Cecelia's voice trembled and cracked. ''I mean, that's wonderful!'' She smiled for Billy's benefit and laughed a little as if the prospect of three more days up here with Ethan Cook wasn't like getting ready to jump out of an airplane.

''We'll be fine. Thanks for calling,'' Cecelia said and set the phone back in its cradle.

''Airport strike,'' she said to Billy with a slightly pained expression on her face. He nodded a sympathetic and thoughtful nod. "Day and a half," she told him and then looked right at him, her stare piercing. He could actually see the wheels turning behind those sharp eyes of hers. She stood up straighter, threw her shoulders back and for a moment Billy thought she was going to call his bluff.

"No problem," she said and walked away like Patton returning to the field.

Billy and Mark had a lot of work to do.

AFTER THE PHONE CALL with the Cooks, Cecelia decided what she needed was a run to get rid of her tension. That had been two hours ago. She was lost. Really, really lost. A half-hour ago she had given up all pretense of running and had started to walk, looking for any clue as to where she was. Which, as she stopped walking and sat down on a boulder, was ridiculous. Trees were trees and since that's all there was, she could give up any hope of actually recognizing one of them.

As she sat, her feet and legs applauded loudly. She dug into the pocket of her reflective windbreaker vest and wrapped her hand around her mace. Any moment the Big Sky Country sun would sink behind a Big Sky Country mountain, leaving her to find the ranch by the reflective light of her Day-Glo vest and watch. Once again she considered the possibility of Big Sky Country bears and gripped her can of mace for reassurance.

Surely someone would come and look for her. Ethan kept close tabs on everyone at the ranch, especially her and Nate. He would send someone, or come himself if for no other reason than to laugh at her. That thought had her standing, ignoring the groans from her feet. She would not be found cowering behind a rock, clutching her mace and waiting to be rescued.

Since her last disastrous encounter with him she had decided to save herself future heartache and kill her attraction to the man by concentrating on all of his negative qualities. A highly unforgiving and rude thing she knew, but the alternative was unthinkable. She refused to get sexually involved with a man she didn't like.

She could see Ethan's exasperatingly smug grin and hear his childishly mean comments should he happen to find her in this particular predicament.

Which is why, when she heard a truck on the road behind her, she began to jog again.

When Ethan pulled up and kept pace beside her, she pretended for a moment that she was so focused she simply wasn't aware of his presence.

"You done running?" he asked bluntly. He was tired and pretty put out that he had been the one chosen to go find her. Of course, she would decide to go for a run in a forest she didn't know a few hours before dusk.

"Oh, Ethan. I didn't notice you there," she said, trying not to pant.

"You done running?" he asked again and she finally stopped. He tried to keep himself from noticing Cecelia's lower half. It was difficult, encased as it was, in spandex. He put the truck in Park and leaned out the window, pushing the rim of his hat up with a gloved hand.

It's those damn cowboy things that have me in such a dither, she thought. In her experience, men did not wear cowboy hats and leather gloves. Earlier today he had walked out into the yard in chaps. Chaps! She nearly melted into a pool of brainless, sex-driven female goo right there on the porch. Chaps *should* have looked stupid. On anyone else they would have been stupid. She simply was not attracted to men who might wear chaps. But Ethan had destroyed all of her previous conceptions about types of men and her attraction to them.

"If you're done running, I can give you a lift," he offered ungraciously.

"How far are we from the ranch?" she asked, as if she might consider running there.

"Eight miles."

She pretended to think it over. "I guess I've had enough." She walked over to the passenger side of the truck, yanked the door open and crawled in. As she sat, the can of mace slipped out of her pocket and rolled across the bench seat to hit Ethan in the thigh.

"You figuring on a lot of muggers in the woods?" he asked, picking up the can.

Whatever else he might say about this exasperating woman, she genuinely amused him.

"Bears," she mumbled, reaching out a hand for the mace.

"Pardon?" he asked, eyebrows climbing as if the inquiry were polite rather than deliberately embarrassing.

"I was figuring on bears!" she all but shouted at him. Ethan handed her the can and chuckled. Cecelia turned and fixed her gaze out the window as he put the truck in Drive and they bounced down the road.

"Since we're out this way, mind if we make a stop?" Ethan asked. He refused to look at her. Flushed skin, dilated eyes, a little sweat; the woman looked post-orgasmic.

"Whatever you like," she replied in a breathless, slightly husky voice. Ethan almost groaned.

"You training for a marathon or something?" he asked, trying to get his mind off the changing fit of his pants.

"Something like that," Cecelia said. "Where's the ranch from here?"

"We're on the crest of the ridge behind the ranch."

Cecelia nodded as if in complete understanding. Suddenly the road and trees stopped and Ethan drove up onto a cleared area next to a log cabin. The cabin faced the most spectacular view of the valley and surrounding mountains.

At this moment, with the sun setting in a blaze of pink, purple and blue, Cecelia doubted she had ever been in a place more beautiful.

"It does sort of take your breath away," Ethan murmured when he heard her gasp. He came up here every night for a reason. Sunset from this stretch of land was about the holiest thing he knew. He was filled with the reverence he had for this land he and his family called home. Ethan was not a man who prayed, he found actions far more suitable to making wishes and hopes come true, but looking over the edge of this ridge he felt like praying. Of sending out his dreams for the future, confident that the forces that had made this land and assured his presence here, would finish out the promise of life he had been taught to believe in. Home. Family. Legacy. Children.

The thought sent the familiar twist in his belly. That future was for his brothers, they would create the legacy, the children, the next generation of Cooks at the ranch.

He had tried once and the experience had burned him so badly that he swore he would never try again. Marsha had told him that he was a horrible husband and would be an unloving, uncaring father. Why should he risk that pain again? He would find all the joy he needed with the land and the work and the view from this butte.

Ethan got out of the cab and went around to the truck bed and began taking out the lumber he had brought up with him. He carried a load over to a pile he already had stacked and protected under a tarp. On his second trip, Cecelia hopped out of the truck and helped him. She was strong and quick and quiet. Traits that Ethan liked in everything: horses, dogs, brothers and women. It was tough to admit, but he found himself liking it in Cecelia.

"Are you building this house?" Cecelia asked dumping the last load of 2x4s.

"Rebuilding it." Ethan slapped the dust from his hands and propped a foot up on the stack of wood as he looked at the cabin. "This was my parent's first place. When the family got bigger, they built the house down there." Ethan jerked a thumb in the direction of the current Morning Glory. "It needs some work, but I should be finished by the middle of summer."

If he could keep up the backbreaking schedule he had been working under. Full days at the farm and then a couple of hours at night up here and then some more time with the sick animals and then to bed for a couple hours of sleep before doing it all again.

"Then what?" Cecelia asked. She couldn't even imagine the beauty of a life lived in this house, with this view and this family. Any family. She hoped he wasn't thinking of selling the house. Her mind leaping, she thought that perhaps the state could buy it and set up a permanent relocation sight....

"I'm going to live here," he replied, surprised by the question.

"Oh," she murmured and Ethan wondered why she looked vaguely disappointed.

It was still warm out and the peace and quiet and the view had diffused the animosity between them. So, Ethan decided to put to use the cold beers Billy had shoved in his hands as he walked out the door. When Ethan had looked at Billy blankly, Billy blurted out, "She'll be thirsty." Ethan thought that was as good a reason as any. He walked back to the truck and pulled a couple of bottles from beneath his seat.

When she saw him with two beers, she realized he did not just happen to run into her on that road.

"Mark sent me to find you," he explained, when he caught her eye. "I figured you'd be thirsty." He looked oddly sheepish and Cecelia took the beer out of his hand. She *was* thirsty.

Ethan walked up to the house and sat down on the porch steps, his bottle cradled in his hands. Cecelia followed and sat on the step below him. They watched the sunset and drank the beer in silence for a few minutes.

"I propose a truce," Cecelia said, smiling as she swiveled to look at Ethan. He was unbearably handsome and without a furrowed brow or scowl, his mouth was set in such an endearing crease. His eyes crinkled at the edge and it almost looked as though he might smile. "For the duration of the sunset, we will not fight," she said, holding up her beer as if she were giving a toast.

"Or kiss," Ethan added, his mouth curled in the half grin that set her heart skipping.

"Right," she agreed, ignoring the blush creeping up her cheek. "No fighting or kissing."

"What are we going to do?" he asked as he touched the lip of his beer bottle to hers.

"We will have a conversation, like normal people." She turned and rested her back against the stair railing, settling in. "Why do you want to move out of your parents' house?"

Ethan was unnerved. "I'm thirty-two years old, Cecelia," he replied by way of explanation. "Do you still live with your parents?" he asked wryly.

To Cecelia, who had only known independence and could not imagine the pitfalls of not having any, privacy was something she was so tired of she couldn't breathe for the loneliness of it. She carefully swallowed her mouthful of beer.

"No," she said evenly. "I don't."

"You probably don't sleep in the same bed you've had since you were twelve," Ethan replied, smiling a little and having no idea what was happening to Cecelia.

"Nope," she said in the same even tone. There had been so many beds the year she was twelve. Bunk beds, fold-out couches, cots in back rooms.

"Your mother probably doesn't put *Star Wars* sheets on your bed because she thinks it's funny," Ethan said, shaking his head and tipping his head back for a swig of beer. "I'm sure your father—"

It was ridiculous to let this conversation continue.

"Ethan, my parents are dead," Cecelia interrupted.

Ethan choked midswallow and lowered the beer bottle, his face blank in shock. She waited for the embarrassed stammer and patronizing hand on her shoulder that always followed her announcement.

"I didn't know. I'm sorry, Cecelia," he said.

Cecelia fought the urge to lower her eyes to avoid the pity she knew would be in his. But when she stubbornly met his eyes, she was surprised by the lack of pity in them. The quiet, unflinching earnestness of his apology had the old sadness and old tears carving a hollow spot in her stomach. She shrugged and took a sip of beer.

"It was a long time ago," she finally said, hoping to seem casual. Perhaps he might actually believe that time made her forget she had no parents.

Ethan felt the urge to run. The normal conversation she had mentioned had turned into something personal. The faint trembling in her hand and her over-bright dismissal of her parents' deaths had him fighting the painful desire to care, which, of course, brought on that gut reaction to run.

"How?" he asked lamely.

"Car accident. Ethan, please let's not dwell on this. People are orphaned every day." She even managed to laugh a little.

"Orphaned!" The sincerity turned into something resembling shocked horror. For a second Ethan's mind tried to erase the presence of his entire family. He couldn't. Not for a second could he understand what this woman knew as her life. All alone. He shook his head.

"Were you adopted?"

The questions were painful. Wondering in the silences between questions if he would drop the subject or want to know more was just prolonging an uncomfortable situation.

"I was not adopted." She told her abbreviated story in bright tones. "I was put into a series of foster homes until I was eighteen. I went to college, became a social worker and started working on my relocation project. I met your sister, met your family and took a strange trip into the wilderness of Montana—which I seem to be completely unsuited for—took a run, got a ride from you and here I am." She smiled, pleased she could make things light. She was relieved when Ethan's lip curled, too. "Soon to leave and find another kid to try and save."

They were silent for a moment and Ethan found himself reshuffling his perceptions of her. Looking at his reactions and words to her in a different light.

"It's important to you? This project?"

Cecelia took another drink of beer, the amber liquid sending a comfortable laxness to her system. A boneless, quiet comfort to her body that usually stood in angry indignation around this man. She tilted her head to the side, not because she was considering anything, but because it felt good to rest it against the smooth wood and peel the label from her bottle with her thumbnail.

"Yes." She looked at the small piece of paper on her nail. "When Nate first came to me I had him draw a picture." She continued to peel the label off her beer in a long strip. "A picture of anything he wanted, a car or a dog or a video game character, anything. He drew a picture of his brother." She turned sad, knowing eyes to Ethan. "That eleven-year-old boy has never seen a real horse, but his brother was killed in a jail riot. I know I can't change what he has seen or the sick reality of his life in the city, but I can show him that there is something else out there.''

She smiled at Ethan. A smile full of all the yearning and sadness in her heart. Ethan's breath caught for a moment in the clarity of that smile. ''I can show him the Cook family. I can show him the Morning Glory Ranch. And maybe the next picture he draws in my office will be of Billy or the mountains or Freddie.''

She rolled her head the other way and silently watched the last of the sun slip behind the mountain. The sky remained brilliant, illuminating the pale sliver of a moon. Past the most brilliant of the pink and purple clouds, the first stars of the night were visible.

Ethan tried to get his mind around this woman. He needed to sum her up in a nice package that would make wanting her less threatening. He had known beautiful women, and he had known smart women. He'd known women that could stand up to him and make him laugh. But he'd never met a woman that he particularly admired and as respect crept onto the edges of his feelings for her, he wondered why. Why her? When she couldn't be more wrong for him.

She turned to him again. ''Ethan, I know we started off on the wrong foot and I just want to tell you I'm so appreciative of the trail ride....''

To hear her thank him when he had done nothing, absolutely nothing to make her welcome, or to make her life easier, was the last straw. He set his beer down and leaned forward to frame her face in his rough hands. He looked, for one moment, into her eyes and saw all the doubt and hesitation inside the tough shell of this woman and almost didn't do it. Almost didn't take advantage of her warm mood and the sunset, but in the end he was still a bastard and kissed her because he didn't have the words to say she was an incredible woman doing an incredible job. He didn't have the words to tell her he was sorry.

The kiss was featherlight, a breath of touch across her lips. Unreal almost, and Cecelia sat transfixed by the tenderness. He turned his head, testing her, pressing his mouth more firmly into hers. Cecelia couldn't breathe, couldn't move. She did not push him away, but she didn't open her mouth to deepen the kiss.

The loveliness of this kiss, as pure as a first, as tender as the hundredth. Her head was filled with the radiance of the sunset, the colors seeping into her through that kiss. He leaned away from her, his eyes drinking in her face. He looked at her mouth and moved his thumb to trace the luxurious fullness of her bottom lip. He applied the smallest amount of pressure and her lips, trembling, separated. He leaned in for another kiss, the barrier of her lips broken.

The kiss deepened, but only their lips and his hands on her face touched. She was caught, suspended on a draft of warm air. The smell of his skin enveloped her. Carefully, scared to break the tenderness and find herself in another angry, fierce kiss, she reached out her hand to touch his. With a fingertip she traced the strength of the cords in his wrist. The fragility of the veins that carried his blood. Oh, the beauty of this kiss.

Ethan felt as if he was tracking a deer. Any kind of movement would send this woman running for safety. Carefully, he eased down so he was on her level and his hands slid deeper into her hair. Inches from him, Cecelia could feel the warmth of his body and leaned into it, running her palm up his arm, from her face to the solid muscle of his shoulder.

She sighed and he answered with a murmur. She told him everything was okay by pressing against him, he took what she offered and pulled her close. The tenderness of the kiss was soon to be swamped by the rising tide of need in both of them. She gasped again and in an attempt to urge him to more intimacies carefully sank her teeth into his bottom lip. He did the same. She sucked on his tongue, he did the same and Cecelia realized that Ethan would do nothing that she did not invite.

Up to this moment in her life Cecelia would not have been able to define the word erotic. But this moment, the surrender of this cowboy, the control over her own pleasure that he was giving to her was the most erotic thing in her experience. Her stomach did a somersault with the pleasure of it. She slowly ran her hands over the thin cotton of his shirt, sticking fingers in between the buttons to touch the hot skin and hair of his chest. She traced the place where the muscles of his back curled around his rib cage and found pleasure in his gasp.

She gasped in return when Ethan slid her vest off and slipped his hand under her shirt to pause at her waist. His big fingers spanning her skin from the waist of her tights to the bottom of her sports bra. When he stopped there Cecelia held her breath, waiting for the electric sensation of his hands pushing up the gray cotton of her bra and curling around her breasts.

Please, she thought. *Please,* she begged in the echo of her mind. *Please,* she whimpered silently as she twisted underneath his hands. Her body was begging, weeping for the next touch of Ethan's hands.

His leaned back, until their lips were a breath away, each gasp fanned the other's face. Slowly, afraid of what would happen should reality return, she opened her eyes. He was gazing at her with such intensity she could not breathe for the hunger she had for this man.

"Tell me," he breathed against her mouth, his tongue snaked out to lick at her lips. Cecelia gasped. "Tell me what you want." Cecelia found herself frozen against the words that were knocking at her teeth.

Throw me down, she wanted to shout. *Rip off my clothes. Kiss the parts of my body no one has kissed. Touch me everywhere. Put that mouth on every part of me. Make me come, make me scream.* Cecelia had never felt more like a woman, had never been aware of her body's desire to be filled by a man, by this man. But her teeth remained locked.

Reality had returned, seeping in with the cool night air. And the sad reality was she was not a woman who could kiss a man on a mountaintop while the stars woke up around her and forget about it the next day. She couldn't tease her soul with these romantic inclinations. Other women could probably call this a lark, but she couldn't. Loneliness gaped with a wide and toothless mouth, waiting to swallow her.

Slowly, she put her hand between them and applied pressure until he eased away, desire replace by confusion.

"Cecelia?" he asked.

"I told myself I wouldn't get involved with someone I didn't like and who didn't like me."

He bent his head for a moment and lifted it, his mouth open to say something, but Cecelia stopped him by putting a hand to his lips. His eyes said everything. He did like her and was sorry beyond words for the angry and mean things he had said.

She swallowed and sat up, using trembling hands to tuck her hair behind her ears. The shaking inside of her was rocking her; she couldn't remember why it was wrong to do this. She stood up and tried to find some distance, but the shaking was still inside her. The emptiness was still inside her.

"My life, ah..." She stopped, looked at him and found she couldn't see his swollen mouth and disheveled hair and still remember why self-preservation was more important than the feel of his hands on her. So she looked away, because her life was not one of self-indulgence. "My life is not big enough for this kind of affair."

The briefcase voice was back and Ethan could have ripped the stairs off with his bare hands. This woman ran hot and cold with cold-blooded efficiency.

"I don't," she was still talking, still explaining why she wouldn't let him near her again, "do this kind of thing and have no...I'm leaving and I don't believe in one-night stands."

Which wasn't exactly true. It wasn't as if she had a policy against brief affairs, but one had never landed in her lap. What she couldn't do was have a one-night stand with this man. Not now, when four days spent with this loving family had the bruise on her heart oozing fresh blood. Not now when the hunger in her for companionship and friendship was so overwhelming she wept with it. Not now when this man created in her a reminder of the womanhood she had forgotten about. She looked at his confused eyes and felt the same confusion. She would not be able to have an affair with this man, his life and, in effect, his family and be able to go home to her apartment, her life. The contentment she had found with her work would shatter; she could feel the cracks already.

"Please, take me back to the ranch," she said, forcing herself to look him straight in the eye.

Ethan watched her, weighing her resolve against the passion he felt in every tremble of her body. He weighed her resolve against the passion that had him hard and frustrated. Her resolve won.

"Okay," he said and led the way back to the truck.

8

————

BILLY MET MARK down by the south paddock. He looked around as if a part of a covert spy operation and lowered his hat so no one could read his lips should anyone be trying.

He felt like James Bond.

"We've got trouble," he said out of the corner of his mouth.

"I can't hear you when you mumble," Mark said, watching one of the wranglers work Renegade. The horse was getting better.

"I said, we've got trouble. Something happened last night and now Ethan and Cecelia are being *nice* to each other."

"So?" Mark pointed to the wrangler and directed him to run Renegade in a different direction. "That's what we wanted, right?"

"No! I mean they're being polite. Even Ethan."

"Polite?" Mark slowly turned to his brother, horror on his face. "Ethan's being polite?"

"I told you we had trouble."

NATE WAS NO DUMMY. He knew when something was up, and something was definitely up at the Morning Glory. Mark and Billy spent more time with lowered heads talking under the brims of their hats than they did ranching. Cecelia and Ethan were so polite to each other Nate almost wished that they would yell and throw things.

Nate watched with amazement as Ethan held a door open for Cecelia and she declined to go first, insisting Ethan go ahead of her. They actually argued about who would go first.

Nate couldn't figure out what was wrong with everyone. He climbed the porch stairs and dragged his feet into the kitchen. If no one was going to act normal he would find something to eat.

Lis was standing at the sink peeling potatoes. She looked at him over her shoulder when she heard him come in.

"Hey, Nate, why the long face?" she asked. Nate came to stand by her at the sink and Lis was surprised to see that the tough kid seemed to be pouting. She pulled a chair from the table, dragged it over to the sink and dug another peeler out of a drawer.

"Since you're here, why don't you give me a hand?" she asked, gesturing to the chair.

"I don't want to peel potatoes," he said, leaning his body against the cupboards next to Lis's legs. If it had been any other kid, she would say he was whining.

"Sure you do." Lis went back to peeling and tried not to smile as Nate grumbled and stood up on the chair. She gave him a quick lesson on how not to kill himself with the peeler and soon he was handling the potatoes like a pro.

"So, what's on your mind?" Lis asked after a few moments passed with nothing but the sound of peeling.

"Do you know what's going on around here?" Nate asked, taking Lis into his confidence.

"What do you mean?" Lis asked. She wished Cecelia were here so she could see how wonderfully normal this kid was acting.

"I mean with Mark and Billy and Cecelia and Ethan." Nate was surprised Lis didn't seem to know anything. Wasn't she paying attention?

"Oh, you mean the fact that Cecelia and Ethan are being so nice to each other it's enough to make you sick, especially when two days ago they were throwing things at each other. Or are you talking about Billy and Mark trying so badly to be matchmakers, when they obviously do not have the touch?" Nate watched in awe as Lis whittled a potato down to a sliver with increasingly angry strokes. "Or maybe it's the mysterious absence of the Cooks, or the late-night phone calls that Billy kills himself to answer before anyone else can. Or maybe I'm wrong and it's just that everyone on this ranch, with the exception of you and me," she waggled the peeler between them, "is acting like a two-year-old."

Lis and Nate whirled to face the applause coming from behind them.

"Very impressive," Mark said, laughing. He hooked his thumb into the pocket of his jeans and leaned against the doorway. He was in stocking feet. "I thought we were playing it pretty cool."

"So cool, Nate picked up on it," Lis said and Mark ducked his head.

"Well, that's what you get when you ask two cowboys to play matchmaker," he muttered.

"Why are you doing this, Mark?" Lis's smooth brow

knitted in confusion and concern. "It's not like you to meddle."

"I don't think it's so far-fetched. They're powerfully attracted to each other."

"But what do you want from it?" she asked. "Do you think they're going to fall in love in a week? Do you think they're going to get past all that they need to in just a week?"

"No, I just want Ethan to relax, to be like he was before this whole thing with Marsha happened."

"It's taken years for your brother to turn everything off like this. It can't be fixed in a week."

"My brother is in a world of hurt, Lis." He pushed himself away from the doorway and approached the two. Nate had no clue what was going on, but the vibe in the air was serious.

"So is Cecelia," Lis replied softly.

"Who hurt Cecelia?" Nate asked fiercely.

Mark put his hand on Nate's head, shaking it a little. "Nobody hurt her, Nate. She's just a sad woman."

Cecelia was a mad woman sometimes. Sometimes she could be mean, or funny or nice. Nate had never seen her real sad.

As Nate thought it over, the three of them stood in the sunny kitchen as if frozen in place: a man in his stocking feet with his hand cupping a boy's head and a woman with a broken heart.

AT THE MOMENT Cecelia wasn't sad; she was filthy dirty and confused as to how a person could tell the difference between a weed and a carrot. After pulling up the sixth premature carrot she was sure was a weed, she sat back in the dirt and blew her bangs out of her face in exasperation.

"I think you're ruining Lis's garden." Ethan tipped his hat back on his head and crouched down at the end of the row of carrots and weeds.

He's just so cowboy, she thought as a small frisson of awareness skittered though her body.

Since the kiss and the sunset two days ago, Cecelia felt as if she was hooked up to a battery and subject to random electrical shocks when Ethan was around. After a couple of hours of hyper-charged awareness she was jumpy and self-conscious. She wished he would go back to avoiding her instead of this new polite and friendly Ethan whom, she was sure, was going to kill her.

"She told me to weed the damn thing, but she didn't tell me what a weed looks like."

"Did you ask?" He raised an eyebrow and his lip curled slightly.

Oh, Cecelia thought, *why can't he just go hide in a barn?*

"No," she said with just a touch of a whine in her voice.

"Hmm," Ethan pretended to think about something. "What is it that they say about stubborn pride?"

"Stick it. They say stick it." They both smiled and Cecelia was subjected to another blast of electricity. "If you know the difference between a weed and a carrot please tell me or else take your smart-aleck self away from this garden."

Ethan spent a moment showing her what the vegetables looked like and then he stood, nodded at her and walked away.

Cecelia realized that the change in his attitude was due to the embarrassing spilling of the guts, which had accomplished what nothing else had. He had decided to respect her and what she was doing.

The change would have been welcome, but without the anger and distance she had nothing to keep her strong against the attraction she felt for him.

She spent a moment imagining her life in Los Angeles. She imagined her apartment, the tiny kitchen with the stove that only had one burner that worked. Her small table, with one side covered with mail and papers, magazines and catalogs. The other side was cleared with just enough room for her lonely dinners.

Unbidden, a picture of the Cook's kitchen superimposed itself with its giant, scarred table often far too overcrowded with food and people.

She shook her head to clear the image. She told kids when they felt scared or threatened to imagine a place where they always felt safe. She took her own advice and tried to find a retreat in the mental image of her living room. Her favorite room. Giant windows kept the room flooded with light. She had splurged and bought herself an oversize chair to sit and read in. She had a couch covered in books and clothes, which was fine because no one sat there. She only needed seating for one.

Suddenly that couch was covered in people, not clothes, and she was seeing the other night when she and Ethan had come home to find Lis, Nate, Mark, Billy and a couple of the cowboys in the den crowded on the couches and chairs spilling onto the floor passing around popcorn while they watched Barbara Walters interview everyone's hero, Clint Eastwood.

This exercise was not going as planned. Resolutely, she tried to banish the Cooks from her brain, concentrating instead on her bedroom in Los Angeles. She had painted it blue and yellow with matching covers on her bed. Of course, whom should her deviant little imagination place there but Ethan Cook, reclining on her pillows, wearing chaps.

And nothing else.

Exasperation gave way to despair as she realized she had lied to Ethan and worse, to herself, last night. She was wrong to think she could go back to her life as if she hadn't spent time with this family. Her life that couldn't allow The Ethan Cook Love Affair was already stretched out of shape.

She stood, dumping vegetables and weeds to the ground. An aching restlessness filled her as her brain struggled to ignore what her body already knew to be true.

Her life was about to get a whole lot bigger.

ETHAN DID what he could to make things as normal as possible. He wanted to understand Cecelia—part of him already did. Part of him knew her sense of self-preservation was what had gotten her as far as she had. And as much as he hated to admit it, part of him knew that an affair would be nothing but bad news for them.

So he was doing the wise thing and keeping his hormones to himself, but he couldn't go back to being taunting and mean after the other night. As yesterday had passed he wished he could go back to angry, sullen silences. Perhaps then he wouldn't find himself in the strange position of liking her. Not a lukewarm she's-okay kind of like, but a seek-her-out-for-a-few-laughs-and-see-what-she-was-doing-now kind of like. She had a way of looking at him while she was listening that made him feel like he was in high school again; giddy, a little foolish and very, very masculine.

Despite the few rough days at the beginning, she seemed to love ranch life now. She was slightly better on the horses and when the raccoon got onto the porch two days ago, instead of running and screaming she just screamed. Succeeding, of course, in scaring the creature away. She had been a little smug about that, as if that had been her plan all along, but no one was fooled.

Regardless, ranch life certainly loved her. Ethan hadn't heard the briefcase voice in a while, and she lost the puckered-up look she sometimes got around her mouth. She was relaxed and mellow and the sound of her laughing had the ability to make him stop and smile.

It was driving him crazy.

Ethan even noticed how her relationship with the boy had changed. They spent time with their heads bent looking at things Nate would find and bring to her. The boy sought her out and his smiles were ready and frequent.

"What's got you grinning?" Mark asked, snapping Ethan out of his thoughts. Mark was hauling a saddle into the tack room with the intention of fixing it.

Ethan watched his brother limp around the tack room looking for tools. "You sure you should be on that foot?" he asked, instead of answering his brother's question.

"Good as new." Mark barely winced when he bumped into a stack of old saddle blankets. He found what he needed and sat down to work, tearing some of the heavy leather stitches out of one side of the saddle.

"Mark?" Ethan clamped his mouth shut. *Am I crazy?* He couldn't tell his brother that he had a crush on the social worker. He and Billy would make his life hell!

"What?" Mark asked, not looking up from his repair work.

"Nothing, forget it." Ethan stood, yanked on his gloves and got as far as the door before turning around again.

"I have a problem," he blurted out. He was not by nature a blurter and it was one more thing that was different since Cecelia's arrival.

Now, he blurted.

"Hmm?" Mark hummed, looking up for a moment. "What's up, Ethan?"

The woman is driving me crazy, he thought about saying. *One second she's kissing the heck out of me, the next she tells me her life is too small for me, whatever that means. I've decided to be nice to her and now I like the woman, which is the last thing I want. Sex, yes. Like, no.*

"Ethan?" Mark prompted.

"Forget it." Ethan pushed open the door and walked out.

LIS SHOWED Cecelia the shortcut to the old house Ethan was working on. It was a ten-minute hike straight up the butte, but it beat the heck out of her two-hour run. Trying to appear as if she was on a friendly, news-bearing mission, she brought Ethan some dinner and the news that his parents would be home tomorrow night.

What he didn't know was that she was going to sneak up on his blind side, take off all her clothes and ask him to…well, to take it from there.

The trail opened up and she took a moment to get her bearings and calm her jumping stomach, but Ethan walked out onto the front porch and saw her, and her nervous system went haywire. They simply looked at each other before they both raised their hands in a limp greeting.

I'm going to seduce that man, Cecelia kept saying to herself, hoping that with repetition the idea would stop sounding so shocking. She walked to the landing and smiled up at him.

"I brought you dinner," she said.

I'm here to strip you naked, she thought.

"Chicken and some biscuits."

I'm here for crazy sex, she thought.

"I'll eat you up," and as Ethan's eyebrows skyrocketed and his mouth fell open Cecelia realized she had said it aloud. "I mean…hah…oops…ah you can just eat it up." She handed him the plastic container and fought the urge to run back down the trail.

Ethan took the container and fork from her hand. "Thanks," he said and sat down on the steps to eat.

"You've gotten a lot done," Cecelia commented nervously. "Haven't you?"

"Not really."

She looked at the horizon, hoping perhaps a skywriter would appear with some more asinine things for her to say, because she had exhausted her supply.

"Thanks for the food, you didn't have to bring it." Ethan was sure the silence was about to kill him. Before she arrived he had been pretending to fix the porch, but in actuality he had been staring at the sunset creating an interesting fantasy involving Cecelia and her incredible legs. He had just given up doing any work and was ready to pack up when she arrived on her previously fantasized-about legs, bringing him chicken. If there was an image to warm even the coldest man, that was it.

"Your parents are coming tomorrow," Cecelia told him. "They ah…yeah…tomorrow."

As she stuttered and stammered and looked about as uncomfortable as he felt, he wished she would leave so he could finish his sexual fantasies in peace and quiet.

"That's good," he said trying to fill the silence, "you can get back to your life in the big city."

No, she thought. *That's the last thing I want.*

He watched her take a few deep breaths and close her eyes.

"What are you doing?" he asked around a mouthful of chicken.

"Positive visualization," she answered, eyes still closed.

He choked, coughed and finally laughed. "Of what?"

She turned to him, dark eyes nervous in the half-light. "Of asking you to sleep with me."

He choked, coughed and choked again, unable to recover. Panicked she walked over to pound him on the back. The first whack knocked the container out of his hands.

"I'm okay, I'm okay," he assured her, catching her hands and holding them, before the second whack could dislocate his shoulder. "I'm wondering if I heard you correctly."

"You did," she said. She looked him straight in the eyes, her skin brushed with the gold of the setting sun. "I mean if you heard me…"

"I heard you. But what I'm wondering is why? Why now?" he asked, but he found in this moment that was so close to the fantasy he was having about her that he didn't care why she had changed her mind.

She had.

She was here.

Slowly, he leaned into her.

"I thought my life needed to be a little bigger," she whispered against his lips and in the next heartbeat they were kissing. Kissing as if they were lovers, long separated and afraid of being separated again. She twined her arms around his neck and held on as the lush tide of desire flooded her. Heat blossomed and grew as she dived into the kiss with heady abandon.

Ethan could taste the difference in this kiss and his body rejoiced. This was a woman coming to him with a clear conscience, who wanted him as much as he wanted her and was ready to test the depths of that desire. He couldn't help but smile in anticipation.

"What are you laughing at?" she asked, her mouth pressed to his. The hand he had in her hair would not let her retreat. She thought that a thoroughly sophisticated woman who had read the seduction rule book might break away from a man who laughed while kissing, but Cecelia felt an answering giggle rise in her own chest.

"You're standing in chicken and biscuits," he murmured. As if to compensate for his unprincely laughter, he picked her up and carried her into the half-finished house.

"I wasn't really thinking we would do this now," she said, when she could. "I mean I guess I was planning on a bed." He put her down in the middle of an empty room with nothing but four wooden walls around her. It was rustically charming, but she wondered how a sophisticated woman gently brought up an aversion to splinters in delicate parts of her anatomy. From the corner Ethan grabbed a sleeping bag and unrolled it with a quick flick of his wrist.

"Cecelia, we can't go back down there." He looked at her and noticed the appearance of doubt. "Since you crashed down my mountain a few days ago I've been wanting you. And frankly, right here and right now is exactly how I want you."

There was simply no arguing with that, so Cecelia followed her instincts and took the three steps that separated them.

"Right here and right now is how I want you, too." Cecelia kissed him with all the desire she never knew she had. His callused hands ran up under her thick sweater lighting little fires everywhere—the small of her back, her stomach, the electrified flesh just under her bra.

She hungered for the feel of him and relished the differences in their bodies in a way she had never done before with previous lovers. Well, lover.

Ethan was so strong. She trailed her fingers along every ridge of muscle in his torso. She was delighted when he moaned and his limbs trembled.

At the same time they reached for the hems of each other's shirts and pulled them off, tangled and laughing until the sight of each other's healthy, fit bodies brought their mouths back together and the heat between them escalated.

The sensation of skin on skin was like wrapping each other up in warm satin until that skin grew slick and their kisses feverish. They simply could not get enough of each other.

They grabbed for the waist of each other's pants.

"Here, just a second." He stopped her to lean down and untie his boots. She ran her fingers across his back and he knotted his boots in his haste.

"Hey, hold on…"

"No," she said, leaning down to press her lips to a long scar across his back. Her tongue flicked out to taste his skin. He was salty. She tasted him again.

"Okay," he groaned. He slid down onto the sleeping bag and took her with him. He tugged the rubber band out of her hair and groaned again when a yard of black satin fell around him.

Outside the large picture window the fading brilliance of the sunset was being replaced by moonlight. It fell on them clear and bright and etched their skin in tones of silver. Cecelia looked at Ethan and knew she had never seen a more beautiful man. As Ethan reached behind her to unclasp her bra, pulling simple cotton away from her curves, he sucked in a hot shaky breath. He was certain he had never seen a more beautiful woman.

He sat up, positioning his moonlit lover across his hips. Their eyes connected and burned as he reached up to gently touch her breasts and trace the trembling curves. He ran the back of his hand over her hardened nipple. When she gasped he did it again. She closed her eyes on a moan.

"Open your eyes." He whispered the command. "Look at me." Cecelia had no choice. Her body was hypnotized by his touch and her mind was slowly following.

"Watch what I do to you." She did and the sight stole her breath. "Look at your body," he said, almost to himself. "You're so damn perfect."

The sensation of this warm and supple woman lying on top of him had Ethan straining at the reins of his control. He wanted so badly to yank off her pants and drive into her. But he knew with each shuddering and tentative move she made that giving over to his hunger would be disastrous. He was surprised to realize he wanted nothing more than to drown in this woman's pleasure.

So he took care. His touch was soft and teasing as he undid her jeans and pulled them off along with her shoes. He rolled her to her back and eased down her body, stopping at her breasts.

"Look at these." His words blew air across her nipples and his groin tightened as she arched against him. "Do you want me to touch you?"

"Oh, yes," she groaned, putting her hands to his head and pulling his mouth to her breasts. He teased her: a lick here, a kiss there, until Cecelia was in agony. She knotted her hands in his hair and yanked. He rewarded her urgency by pulling her nipple into his mouth and sucking hard.

"Oh, yes," she gasped, satisfied by the roughness. He

continued his torment, until she was arching against him, her hands beating a frantic tattoo on his back.

"You okay?" he asked with a devilish grin and a long, slow lick across her lips.

"Come on, Ethan," she demanded, so close to begging. He chuckled and began a meandering journey down her torso. He reached the edge of her underwear and concentrated his efforts on the secrets inside. Through her underwear he traced the edges of her sex, first with his finger, then his tongue.

Cecelia held herself perfectly still, trying so hard to clasp this pleasure to her, to find its center and hold it, but it was huge and evasive and Ethan, with his clever tricks and clever mouth, had complete control.

Somehow her plan to seduce Ethan seemed laughable. She could only hold on and hope that her body and heart would be intact when he was done with her. His finger was inside the cotton underwear, slowly, so damn slowly, easing its way into the warmest part of her, only to reach it and retreat. Cecelia was desperate for the end of the teasing. Fire was running through her body, building to something powerful.

"What do you want?" he asked, a repeat of the question that had had her running two days ago.

"Touch me," she implored.

"Like this?" He eased inside of her, offering her his fingers, a shadow of the fulfillment she sought.

"Yes," she hissed, pressing her hips down as if to capture his hand in her flesh. He chuckled and slid out again.

Ethan Cook was the devil, Cecelia was sure of it.

"Do you want me to take these off?" He leaned down

and traced her with his tongue and teeth through her underwear.

She nodded frantically, past words.

"What will you do? Hmm? What will you do for me?" he murmured, easing the cotton down her restless legs. He tossed the panties over his shoulder and settled between her legs. He looked at her face. Her eyes were closed, lips parted for every panting moan.

She was perfect.

"Will you come?" he whispered against her agonized flesh. "Will you come for me?" With his thumbs he separated her flesh and with one slow lick of his tongue on the most agonized part of her body, she fell apart.

Ethan watched her shatter. She clasped his head in something close to a death grip while her body arched and swayed, trapped in the hurricane of pleasure that was almost pain. His hands flew to his pants, undoing the belt and fly. He got as far as pushing them down his hips before rational thought made an appearance, tapping at his shoulder and wagging a finger in disapproval.

He didn't have a condom.

With a curse he rolled away from Cecelia. He sat, hands gripping bent knees, his heart beating in his ears and tried to pull together his damaged control.

"What are you doing?" she whispered against his back. A long arm reached around to stroke his chest. Her touch was hot. So hot. He gritted his teeth, but he let her continue, unable to deny himself the scorching pleasure of her hands on him.

Both her hands came around to feather across the skin of his belly. She bit his back just as her hands found the pulsing length of his desire. He groaned and clapped a hand on hers, stopping their seduction.

"What's wrong?" Her voice was a breath across his shoulder.

"I have—" She pressed herself into him and the feel of her breasts against his back chased every thought from his head. She used his momentary lapse as a chance for her hands to continue their explorations. Against his will, his hips arched into her palms.

She chuckled and arranged herself so she cradled his body from behind with her own. "You have what?" she asked.

"No...ah...oh no." She eased her hands farther into the opened vee of his pants. He braced himself against the floor.

"Tell me what you need," she whispered into his ear. "I'll give it to you." She licked the sensitive spot behind his ear and with erotic precision bit his earlobe.

"Condoms," he finally managed to say. "I don't have any."

Cecelia grinned. The trip into town this afternoon had been worth it. She leaned back and with one hand found her pants, rifled through the pocket and found what she was looking for. She switched their positions so she was straddling him. The heat and wet of her pressed against the hard length of him and they both closed their eyes to savor the bliss.

"You don't need any." She looked him in the eye and held up the condom. One of thirty-six she had bought.

Explosions were going off in Ethan's head. He met

her level gaze with his own and after a moment smiled. "Thank you."

They both laughed and hugged each other hard before Ethan turned her to her back, pushed his pants off and slid into her.

They didn't think about it now, consumed as they were, but in the days that followed both would speculate on the feelings that blossomed in their chests as Ethan eased himself into Cecelia's weeping and welcoming body. Both of them would say it was the best sex of all time, but they would both wonder why that moment had felt, of all things, like coming home.

9

ETHAN BLINKED, but the stars flashing in front of his eyes didn't go away. He watched the small bursts of light on the edge of his vision and wondered why he couldn't feel his legs.

Cecelia brushed her hair from her face with a trembling hand. She braced herself on Ethan's shoulder and tried to push herself into a sitting position, but her hand slipped on his sweat-slicked skin and she ended up elbowing him in the throat.

He groaned in complaint and she tried to apologize, but all that came out was a scratchy rattle. She turned her head to the side, trying to get out of Ethan's armpit where she was wedged, and found it strange that her nose was only inches from the wall.

They had started in the middle of the room on a sleeping bag. She turned her head the other way and over Ethan's chest she saw the sleeping bag on the other side of the room.

Those splinters she was worried about were in Ethan's back and as far as she was concerned, well worth his pain.

"That," she finally managed to croak out, "was incredible."

"I can't feel my legs," was Ethan's response.

Cecelia went on, growing strangely invigorated, despite nearly two hours of rigorous activity. Sweat trickled between her breasts and she pulled her sticky hair off her neck and fanned herself with her hand.

"No tension, no stress." She let out an exuberant, well-pleased sigh. "You're better than a massage."

"Something's wrong with my eyes." Ethan squeezed his eyes shut and opened them again with no luck; starbursts still covered the ceiling. "Just my luck. Best orgasm of my life and I'll never be able to see or walk right again."

"Best of your life?" she asked, thrilled and hesitant. She had this crazy need in herself to grab him and hold tight. This enthusiasm for him made her uncomfortable.

He blinked at her and waited for the stars to clear.

She sat beside him, her hands in her hair, her beautiful breasts touched in silver. Her smile, full of loose, happy femininity and hesitant uncertainty, touched something inside of him and sparked that something to life.

He smiled before pulling her down on top of him, tangling his fingers in her hair. "Thank you," he whispered to the top of her head.

They lay still for a while, the sweat drying off their bodies. Ethan's vision returned to normal. They kissed whatever part of the other's body was available and kissable and generally enjoyed the quiet comfort of being happy. But soon it became cool and slowly they began to search out their clothes. As they dressed Cecelia grew uncomfortable with their new carnal knowledge of each other. She decided she simply wasn't sophisticated enough to handle crawling around on all fours searching for her underwear only to find it draped over one of Ethan's boots, without blushing.

They finished dressing and went outside in awkward silence. The empty plastic container and the chicken lay in the moonlight. For a moment Cecelia was terribly embarrassed.

Ethan put his arm around her and chuckled into her ear. "You really surprised the heck out of me." He pressed a kiss to her head and her embarrassment eased.

"Good," she replied and because he was irresistible, she put her arm around his waist and kissed him back, hitting the bottom of his chin.

Ethan closed his mouth against the words that might come out. He wanted to tell her she was sweet and fun and as sexually exciting as any woman, ever. For a split second he wished things were different between them. He wished he were a different man. And in that moment, he had the sensation of standing over a chasm, prepared to leap. His reaction was to search out the safety of their situation.

"You're leaving in a week," he said as a blunt reminder.

Cecelia was lost in her memories of the past few hours and his words, the reappearance of reality, was a cold breeze blowing through her.

"Yes, I am," she agreed.

"You're going back to the city. Your work." He kept talking and the distance between them kept growing. Suddenly, Cecelia clasped his lean cheeks in her hands.

"One week," she said, her life splitting wide open. "I'd like to do this again."

His smile was wide and grateful and blocked out the moon as he leaned down to kiss her.

THE NEXT DAY the ranch woke up early to prepare for the return of the Cooks. Lis was baking and the wranglers were making sure the barn and fences were as Mr. Cook had left them. In a word: perfect. The Cook brothers took extra pains cleaning up the evidence of their week and a half of bachelorhood in the house.

Cecelia tried to be as nonchalant about her new affair as possible, but she was convinced that everyone on the Morning Glory knew. It didn't help that every time she was left in the same room with Ethan she felt as if she was going up in flames and succeeded only in tripping and knocking things over.

"You okay?" Ethan asked, catching her as she caught her foot on the edge of a rug in the den.

"No!" she insisted. "I'm mortified."

"You're cute when you're mortified," he said, with a long slow smile that heated the air around them. He kissed her and putting aside her embarrassment, she melted into him and kissed him back with all the pleasure she felt.

MAC AND MISSY Cook arrived with appropriate fanfare. Laughter, stories and complete chaos reigned over a king's feast. It was easy to see why the Cook family held together so well. Mac and Missy treated everyone from Lis to the cowboys with respect and love. They greeted their sons as if they hadn't seen them in years. Missy kissed them all and Mac shook their hands and slapped their backs while complimenting them on not letting the place burn down while he was gone.

Missy greeted Nate and Cecelia right away. She ignored all of Nate's "don't touch me" signals and wrapped him in a hug. Cecelia was once again thrilled with her decision to see this out despite the setbacks.

Nate was eating himself sick when Mr. Cook finally sat down beside him. Nate wasn't sure how he was supposed to act in front of this man. Mac's white hair blew in the breeze and his brown eyes, nearly hidden in the creases and folds in his face, just stared at Nate. Nate wanted so badly to snarl "What are you staring at?" but Billy already told him it wasn't cool to do things like that. And because Billy said it, it was gospel.

So Nate waited, occasionally meeting Mr. Cook's eyes only to let them skitter away when it got to be too much.

When will the guy say something?

"So," the man growled, sticking out a hand about the size of the ham Lis had made for dinner, "you're Nate. I'm Mr. Cook."

"Yeah." Nate put his hand in the man's paw and shook it. When he pulled back the man held on to his hand until Nate was forced to look him in the eye.

"At the Morning Glory, you call me 'sir.'" The hand squeezed just a little to let Nate know he meant business. "My wife is 'ma'am.'" He cocked his head toward the woman who looked like Mrs. Claus in the books Nate read when he was a kid. "We're happy to have you here."

The man smiled and suddenly Nate wanted nothing

more than to make this man like him. He wanted, with eleven-year-old purity, to do well by this old cowboy.

"Yes, sir."

"Looks like Dad and Nate are getting acquainted," Billy noted, joining his brothers and mother at the far end of the table. They watched the nonconversation between the two and laughed when Mac wouldn't let go of Nate's hand.

"They'll be good for each other," Missy said. "Your father needs someone to lock horns with, since we've all been whipped into shape."

They all snorted at her sarcasm and got back to catching up.

"So, how is Cecelia adjusting?" Missy asked, pointedly not looking at anyone. She took a careful bite of Lis's baked beans and ignored her sons' clearing throats and smothered chuckles.

"I'd say she's doing pretty well," Billy answered. "What would you say, Mark?"

"She stopped screaming around the horses," Mark answered. "That's good."

"I haven't seen her sitting in horse crap in a couple of days," Billy added.

"She's good with that boy," Mark said.

"Nate or Ethan?" Billy asked with a wide smile.

"All right!" Ethan finally snapped. "What my brothers are trying to be so clever about is that Cecelia is fine, she is enjoying her time here and..." he trailed off, unsure how his wagging tongue had gotten him here.

"And?" his mother prompted.

"And it's nice having her here."

"What...?"

"I'm not talking anymore!"

"Fine." Missy took another bite of her beans. "How's Lis?"

CECELIA WAS WATCHING Mr. Cook and Nate with a careful eye. If she were a little bit closer she would have heard Nate call Mac Cook "sir" and she would have been able to rest easy knowing Nate Hernandez and Mac Cook were a match made in social-work heaven. But, she wasn't close enough, so she took a deep breath and charged in.

"Hello, Mr. Cook," Cecelia said, as she walked up to the two. "I hope you've recovered from your misadventure."

Mac laughed and took Cecelia's hand in two of his for a shake and a squeeze. Her fondness for him came back in a rush. This situation was worth all of her vacation time. Actually, last night had been worth all of her vacation time, but now was not the time to think about it.

"Nothing a bit of time in the saddle won't fix." Mac laughed. "I'm sorry for any trouble we might have put you through with all of this mess."

"Don't worry," Cecelia said, looking into Nate's unshuttered eyes. "It's been a lot of fun."

"I don't know what your plans are…"

"But you're welcome to stay as long as you like," Missy interrupted. She came up and put an arm around her husband's sturdy waist. "The boys have said you seem to be enjoying yourself."

"I am," Cecelia said, warmed by their generosity. She found herself wanting to say she would stay forever, caught in this bubble of family and friendship. "But I'm afraid duty will call at some point. The original agreement was that I would stay on for a week with you two and Nate. Since I have the clearance from work, I think I'll take that week."

I'll take that week, she thought, *and I'll take whatever your son can give me and I'll soak up enough of this home to last me when I get back to my life.*

"Good," Ethan answered from behind her. Cecelia turned to look at her lover and was gratified to see the approval in his eyes. It was nice to know he wanted more of her.

After dinner Mac took Nate to the barn and Cecelia lingered in the kitchen with Missy and Lis, laughing and gossiping until Cecelia figured it was safe to leave. With a rather dramatic yawn, which didn't fool either of the two women, Cecelia said she was going to go for a walk and then to bed.

She didn't say to where or with whom.

ETHAN WASN'T SURE if he should expect Cecelia or not. Perhaps, he thought, carrying lumber onto the porch with the firm idea that he would actually get some work done around here, her boldness had run out with the arrival of his parents. He hoped not. He really hoped not.

He felt as if someone had taken his life and thrown it up in the air. He was supposed to run around gathering the pieces and try to put it together the way it had been, but having found the Cecelia piece he was content to linger. It was strange, but it didn't require much examination, considering she was leaving. So he left it alone, determined to enjoy himself.

He would take this for as long as it was available and when she left, that was fine. He didn't expect any more, anything that stayed, that lasted and kept. It wasn't for him. He'd learned his lesson a long time ago.

CECELIA'S THOUGHTS were not that much different from Ethan's as she climbed the hill to his house. She would have been gratified and relieved to know his mind. She, too, would take what she could get.

This night, like the last, was idyllic for lovers; stars in plentitude, the air warm and the scent of pine and honeysuckle rolling down the mountains with the wind. She breathed deep and smiled; for the rest of her life juniper would remind her of seduction.

The sound of hammering beckoned and Cecelia was relieved that Ethan was here. She broke through the clearing and caught her breath at the sight of her lover's powerful body. He stood, wiped his face on his sleeve and caught sight of her.

"I thought my parents might have scared you off," he said, putting down his hammer and walking over to her.

"Well, your father took Nate to the barn, so I only had to get past your mom and she's about as scary as Mrs. Brady," she said dryly.

"Shows how much you know." Ethan put his hand to her hair, inordinately glad she had left it down. "When I was growing up she always had the uncanny ability to show up just when I was rounding third and heading for home with a girl."

"What?" Cecelia asked on a gust of laughter.

"Let's just say my mother's sudden and embarrassing

appearances in haylofts and truckbeds made me the oldest virgin laughingstock around these parts.'' He eased both hands into her hair, cupped her skull and marveled at all the toughness and bravery in this small woman.

''When did you finally get around to it?'' Cecelia asked, thoughts scattering with every gentle motion of his hands.

''What?'' he asked, distracted by the beauty of her skin in the moonlight.

''Losing your virginity,'' she said on a breathy sigh as he leaned down to taste the skin on her throat.

''Last night,'' he said into the curve of her collarbone.

She laughed until his hands took away her breath.

The urgency caught them both by surprise. The shelter of the house seemed like a million miles away and, in the storm of their feelings, completely unnecessary. In absolute accordance they fell to their knees in the grass and moonlight, their mouths and tongues fused.

He ripped open the buttons on her jeans and thrust his hands into them. She arched herself into his palm, while at the same time searching for the opening of his jeans, but he evaded her touch.

''Pay attention,'' he told her. ''Pay attention to what I do to you.''

There was no teasing here, his finger immediately found, and pushed into her. She ground her hips against him, and he added another finger to his first. She hissed and groaned and burned under his touch, she fought the rising tide of orgasm, wanting nothing more than to share this with him. To take him where he took her, a journey together into the red hot center of their passion.

"Please," she implored, forcing herself to open her eyes to stare into his. "Come with me."

He looked at her, took in her flushed face, full lips and eyes just on the verge of going blind with the pleasure he brought her. Without words he stripped them both of their clothes, and there in the tall grass he joined her, joined with her and fell apart in her arms.

THEY LAY side by side in the grass, their sweat cooling in the breeze. Cecelia started laughing first. Ethan, not sure what was so funny, but somehow finding all of it rather amusing, joined her.

"What's so funny?" he asked, after a moment. Which only had Cecelia laughing harder.

"I was engaged once," she told him when she got her breath back.

Ethan felt a low burning in his gut. He hated the fact that just the word "engaged" had the ability to affect him. He was a million years away from his mistakes. Why did they still make him ache with embarrassment and anger? He tried with supreme effort to push the memories away so as not to spoil his time with Cecelia.

"Really?" he asked, leaning up on an elbow at her side.

"Yep." She laughed again. "Norton was his name. He owned a deli."

"A meat man." That was funny to both of them, so they spent a few moments laughing into each other's shoulders.

"He had this thing with germs," she finally said. Because she was leaving in a week, there seemed to be a free license to share all, with no harm. The situation, to

Cecelia, made them immediate friends, with none of the strings and mystery involved in other relationships.

"Sterilization and all of that," she elaborated.

"I take it you and he never had sex in the dirt?" Ethan asked, rubbing some mud off of her collarbone where he had smeared it in his fever.

"Certainly not," she said. She had not known what she was missing having sex with Norton. Absently, she traced the curvature of the muscle in Ethan's shoulder. "He always had the air-conditioning blasting so we wouldn't get sweaty."

Ethan chuckled. "I once had this girlfriend who would only have sex with me if we had Bruce Springsteen playing on the radio."

"Oh, no." Cecelia laughed.

"I called it quits when she started to call me 'The Boss.'" Ethan smiled.

"That's a lot of pressure," Cecelia said, trying to empathize.

"You're telling me." He gently laid the palm of his hand over her breast and smiled when he felt her heartbeat trip and resume at a faster pace. "What do you say we go inside and do this again?"

"Why bother going inside?" she asked and pulled him down to her.

10

"LOOK." ETHAN PUT a hand on his hip and pointed his paintbrush at Cecelia. "If you're going to help," he shrugged and put on a pained expression, "you're going to have to get naked."

"Ethan!" Cecelia exclaimed. "Don't be ridiculous, I only want to help with the trim."

"Oh!" he said, as if she were clearing up a matter of confusion. "In that case, you'll just have to take off your shirt."

"Ethan, do you want help or not?" Considering this was their fourth night together, Cecelia was really fighting the urge to just take off her clothes, because she knew what was at the end of this game. But she played along because over the days she had come to expect and relish the teasing.

She had been helping Ethan every evening, working on the house with him until the teasing and companionship got to be too provocative and they retired to the bedroom. Tonight they were painting the newly constructed porch and Ethan was already hard at work and shirtless.

The sun was sinking, but it was still hot and the teasing glint in his eye turned challenging.

"Come on, Cec. We're all alone," he cajoled, absently stroking his chest.

"All right." She took the dare, pulling her shirt out of her pants. She wrapped her hands in the cotton and lifted it so he could see the flesh of her belly. "We'll have it your way." She whipped the shirt off and tossed it on the ground. The flash in his eyes made her very pleased that she had forgone a bra.

"Give me a brush," she said regally, holding out her hand, as if she weren't nearly naked. Ethan laughed and laughed until she could do nothing but join in.

And sadly, horribly, love him.

Age, apparently, burned away infatuation and fruitless lust leaving only Cecelia's inclination toward love. Here she was, a grown woman and for the first and, she was afraid, last time, she was in love.

She would leave in three days time and she would try with every heartbeat not to look back. Ethan Cook was a gift and she would not change any of the circumstances of their relationship for fear of losing what he gave so unknowingly: love, change, light where there was only dark, and memory where there had only been imagination.

"Here's your brush, you crazy lady." Ethan was holding out a brush to her and the look in his eyes warmed her to the bone. He may not love her, but he certainly liked and respected her. She would take it.

"Thank you." She took the brush with a small bow and got to work, sans shirt.

"The place is really shaping up, Ethan," Cecelia commented, after a moment.

"Thanks to you," Ethan answered, shouting from his

ladder as he worked on the eaves. "You've been a big help."

"Big inconvenience you mean," she said, laughing.

"We were able to order more windows. It's okay," Ethan reassured her for the hundredth time since she accidentally broke most of his windows two days ago.

They worked quietly until the sun went down and Ethan forgot about paint and brushes and led his shirtless, crazy lady into the house where he could truly thank her for her help.

No ONE at the ranch commented on Cecelia and Ethan's love affair. They kept quiet around Cecelia and she was able to convince herself that no one knew. And after Billy made the mistake of joking around with Ethan about the nightly construction on the ridge and Ethan went after Billy's nose with murder in his eyes, nobody said anything to Ethan, either. There was, however, plenty of talk and plenty of speculation.

Mark and Billy congratulated themselves on a job well done every time Ethan joked or teased Cecelia at the dinner table or lingered over coffee to continue a conversation instead of running out to the barn to work. Whenever they heard Ethan laugh they looked at each other and mentally tipped their hats.

Missy, however, was not ready to join in the party just yet. She watched carefully the heated and tender looks that passed between Ethan and Cecelia and thought long and hard about the old scars on Ethan's soul.

"Mac?" Missy was staring at the ceiling of their bedroom, long past the time she should have been asleep. "Are you sleeping?"

"Guhhh?" Mac grumbled and rolled over, pulling the blankets over his head.

"Mac?" She added an elbow to her query this time.

"Missy, what?" Mac was not and did not sound happy to be woken up.

"I'm worried about Ethan."

"Oh, come on, honey. He's thirty-two years old. Go to sleep." Mac pulled a pillow over his face.

Missy turned to her side and pulled both the blanket and pillow off her husband's head.

"What if this backfires and sets him back even further?" The agonized motherly concern in his wife's voice had Mac reluctantly opening his eyes and turning over to wrap an arm around her shoulders. "You remember how he was after Marsha left," Missy continued. "He shut down. It took years for him to even look at another woman."

"Honey, Ethan's had girlfriends before. He's not sixteen." Mac squeezed Missy to his side and pressed a sleepy kiss to her head. "He can take care of himself."

Missy was quiet for a few minutes and Mac mistakenly took that as an invitation to fall asleep again.

"It's been so nice this week, hasn't it?" she asked in a whisper. "Having Ethan back like this."

"Yes, it has," Mac agreed and curled his wife into the space in his body that was created just for her.

THE MORNING of the day before her departure Cecelia found Nate in the barn, combing and currying Peaches. Over the course of Nate's time here, Peaches had become his horse. Cecelia smiled when she heard Nate murmuring to the old horse like Ethan, Mark and Billy murmured to their horses.

"We're going to be okay, aren't we?" he asked the horse. The poignancy of the question gripped Cecelia's heart. "You and me, Peaches, we'll be just fine."

Cecelia stood for a moment relishing in the success of the Relocation Project. Nate's life had been filled with plenty since arriving at the ranch and Cecelia couldn't help but feel the warmth of pride as she considered her role in the transformation of this boy.

"Nate," she called, preserving his pride by pretending not to have heard him talking to his horse. "Where are you?"

"I'm in here with Peaches," he said quickly.

She turned the corner into the stall.

"Hey, Nate. How's it going?" she asked, a smile tugging at her lips.

"Good." He was still not a man of many words, but at least the ones he did speak weren't R-rated or mean-spirited.

"I'm leaving tomorrow," she said, coming right out with the reason for searching him out.

"What?" He stopped combing and looked up at her with undisguised shock. "I thought you would be staying."

"Why?" she asked.

"You and Ethan, I mean, you're like a thing, right?"

Cecelia felt as if the floor had dropped out from beneath her. *How in the world am I going to explain this?*

"We're friends, if that's what you mean," she answered tentatively.

"Give me a break, Cecelia." He shot her a dry look that told her to drop the act.

"Yes, we are a thing, but it doesn't change the fact that I have to get back to Los Angeles."

"Too bad for you," he said with a grin.

"I take it you don't want to go back?" She laughed. "'Cause you can, you know. It's part of the project, if you don't like it here you can come back with me."

He looked at her, square in the eye and shook his head. "I want to stay."

She told him she would be checking in with him every week and that he was required to keep a journal of his time here. He grumbled but she knew he would do it. He would not jeopardize his time here for anything.

"You're still writing your mom, right?" she asked, reminding him of another stipulation of his stay here.

"Every other day," he confirmed.

"Well, all right then..." she trailed off and found herself wanting to linger to talk to Nate. He had been her companion, as strange as it was, on this excursion and, akin to two people who survived things like plane crashes, they had a bond.

"It's cool, Cecelia," Nate said, smiling.

"You're right, Nate. It is cool." And somehow that said it all.

CECELIA LEFT the barn and headed back to the house to begin packing, and if she could be honest, begin steeling herself for the goodbye scene to come.

"Are you avoiding me, Cecelia?" Ethan asked, from behind her. She closed her eyes and fought the tears that just the sound of his voice saying her name brought to the surface. Carefully, when she was sure her face would not reflect any of what she felt, she turned toward him.

The naked pain on his face almost made her rush to him, and the flip answer she was going to give him died on her lips.

"I suppose I have been," she said honestly.

"Well, don't," he demanded gruffly. Cecelia was thrown by Ethan's grim countenance.

"I didn't think there was any point in a long drawn-out goodbye scene," she explained lamely, lifting a shoulder. The truth was she wasn't sure that she could look at Ethan without the words she didn't want to say spilling from her lips. She needed to get herself together in order to say goodbye and as much as she had been trying, she hadn't been able to do that yet.

"There is." He took the step that separated them and gripped the top of her arms. "There is always a point to goodbye. I'll meet you at the house tonight. Okay?"

She nodded, agreeing to Ethan's request and he pressed a dark, desperate kiss to her lips before he walked away.

It was a strange emotion that exploded in Cecelia's chest. Dread over the goodbye, relief that she wouldn't have to pretend her heart wasn't breaking, and hope, clean and true and bright that maybe Ethan wasn't going to be able to say goodbye to her.

Late at night, curled against Ethan's body, his arms around her, his sleeping breaths ruffling her hair, she had created a whole new life that she wanted for herself. A life with Ethan, in this house, with his children and his family filling the hole that her family left years ago.

She imagined her Relocation Project, only from the

receiving end. She would take these kids in, keep them in the house on the ridge and show them another world than the one they were used to. She and Ethan, together, would do that.

The last few nights she had fanned that little fantasy to life, sadly aware of the pain it would cause her when she was back alone in Los Angeles, but unable to stop herself.

Cecelia walked back to the house with a smile on her lips and hope burning a bright hole in her chest.

The Cooks were preparing a huge party in honor of Cecelia's departure. This would be her last night with Ethan and they were going to make it perfect if it killed them.

They even coerced Lis into getting involved.

"You're about the same size," Billy said. "She probably wants to get all dressed up but didn't bring anything besides jeans and that glow-in-the-dark vest."

"Yeah," Mark put in his two-cents worth, "women love dressing up."

"Oh, how would you know?" Lis asked, exasperated.

"You'd be doing her a favor, Lis. Really." Billy grinned and elbowed his brother in the side and Mark grinned, too. Lis was, and always would be, susceptible to the Cook boys when they turned into pleading cowboys.

"Oh, fine," she finally agreed.

She made sure everyone knew what a bad idea this was even as she climbed the stairs to Cecelia's room with one of her own skirts and blouses over her arm.

Cecelia answered Lis's tentative knock with a giant smile.

"Lis, don't tell me I gave you a bunch of weeds instead of vegetables," Cecelia said in mock horror, guessing Lis's visit was, in fact, a reprimand for her poor harvesting skills after Lis asked her to pick vegetables for the dinner salad.

"No, the vegetables are great. Thanks." Lis hesitated and looked down at the clothes in her arms. "I was just thinking that this was your last night and everything and maybe you might want to dress up. You can tell me to get lost, if you want."

Lis didn't have a lot of friends here. She loved her work and she loved the Cooks, but she realized when Cecelia smiled and clapped her hands like a fifteen-year-old at the sight of the skirt and blouse, she missed having a girlfriend.

"I've got some jewelry that goes with it," Lis offered, warming to the whole plot.

"You know, I didn't even bring so much as a tube of lipstick," Cecelia said, tickled by the prospect of wearing something pretty and feminine for Ethan. "You wouldn't happen to have any makeup, would you?"

"I don't have much, but you're welcome to what I have," Lis said. "Let's go to my room."

And the dress-up party was on.

MARK AND BILLY had emptied most of the contents of the kitchen drawers onto the floor when their mother walked in.

"What in the world are you two doing?" she shrieked, taking in the wreckage.

"Candles, Mom," Billy barked, his head buried in a cabinet. "We're looking for candles."

"Why?" she asked.

"We thought it would be a nice touch," Mark answered, throwing hundreds of paper napkins on the floor as he cleared her "paper napkin" drawer.

Missy reached over and pulled open the drawer closest to the door. The drawer her sons would have opened last in their search-and-destroy candle mission.

"You mean these?" She held out six long white tapers, which caused her sons to leap at her in excitement. She held up her hand and they stopped in their tracks.

"Clean up your mess," she said and left, candles in hand as ransom for a clean kitchen.

MAC AND NATE searched out Ethan in the barn.

"Now remember," Mac whispered out of the corner of his mouth to Nate, as they were about to enter the stall where Ethan was, "be cowboy."

"Right. Cowboy," Nate whispered, standing up a little straighter and walking with a strut in his step. Mac gave him his best all-business, tough-guy nod and tried not to crack up.

"Be cowboy" didn't mean anything to Mac, but Nate sure took it seriously.

They turned the corner just in time to see Ethan injecting a shot for red eye right into the eyeball of one of the cattle.

"Gross!" Nate shrieked, no trace of cowboy in him.

Ethan took a syringe out of the cow's eye and shared a laughing look with his father.

"Hi, guys," Ethan said. His father jerked his head in greeting and Nate followed suit. Ethan looked down at the cow to hide his grin.

"Son," Mac said, sobering, "why don't you go wash up?"

"Wash up? For what?" Ethan asked.

"For dinner." Mac cursed his meddling family. People should just let the forces of nature do their thing, but when the force of nature was Missy Cook there was no real point in arguing. "You know," he explained to his baffled son, "shower, shave, put on some clean duds."

"Clean duds?" Ethan repeated as if his father had asked him to strip naked and run around the barn.

"We're having a party for Cecelia," Nate burst in, getting to the point of things, "and no one wants you sitting at the table when you smell like a cow."

Ethan looked to his father for confirmation and when his father just nodded, a little abashedly, Ethan stood and dusted off his jeans.

"Well, I guess I'll go clean up."

BILLY AND MARK stood in the kitchen and admired their handiwork. The flickering candles lit up the kitchen in spots and, in the dark corners, flashlights pointed at the ceiling helped out.

"I think we're missing something," Billy said, scratching his chin.

"Ethan's showering, Cecelia's putting on makeup and we're already using every candle and flashlight on the ranch. What are we missing?" Mark asked, getting a little fed up with his brother's overactive matchmaking drive.

"Music."

"Music?"

"Yep, we need romantic music."

"Billy, I think I need to remind you that it's not going to just be Cecelia and Ethan at this table," Mark said. "Everyone is eating here tonight." As far as Mark could figure, fifteen people including dirty, raunchy cowhands and an eleven-year-old cowboy-in-training could pretty well ruin any kind of romance. Not to mention the presence of parents—and their parents were legendary romance killers.

"Yeah, I know, but I think music would be nice."

Billy stepped up to the old battered radio perched on the fridge. He flipped it on and searched through the static for the two stations they received clearly on the Morning Glory. One was broadcasting a Colorado Rockies game and the other was discussing cattle prices.

"We'll just have to go without music," Mark said, turning to go to his room and change clothes.

"Hey, Mark," Billy said in a tone of voice that had Mark stopping and shaking his head in denial of whatever crazy idea Billy had now. "Do you still have that guitar?"

"Yeah, but I haven't played in years."

"Who cares?" Billy's eyes were twinkling in the candlelight. "Play a few chords, 'Mary Had a Little Lamb,' it'll be perfect."

Billy clapped his brother on the shoulder and walked past him down the hallway, giving Mark no chance to argue as he hummed "Mary Had a Little Lamb" loudly.

"Perfect," Mark repeated skeptically.

"WHAT'S WITH THE LIGHTS?" Ethan asked, coming into the dark kitchen.

"Ask your brothers," said one of the dark blobs around the table that sounded like Jesse.

"Power is out," the Billy blob said.

"Fuse or something," Mark elaborated.

"Why doesn't someone…"

"Because we're hungry," Billy interrupted, "and it's nice eating by candlelight. Right?" There was a scuffle and a muffled groan before two hands—it sounded like Mitch and Abe—agreed.

From the far end of the table there was the scratch and sudden light from a match. Mac looked over the proceedings with an irritated eye.

"Nate?" Mac asked. "Could you turn on the hall light? Perhaps the fuse there is okay."

"But, Dad," Billy started arguing.

"I've got to see what I'm eating," Mac insisted. "Call me crazy." Nate did as he was told and the light from the hallway was perfect. Everyone could see and the candles still gave a touch of romance to the evening.

Just as all of the cowboys started applauding the new lighting, Cecelia walked in wearing a long, filmy skirt with a fitted denim shirt tucked into a wide leather belt.

As far as entrances went, it was perfect.

Cecelia, unsure of what was going on, blushed and looked embarrassed which only made everyone clap louder. Ethan found himself joining in and he didn't even try to stop his wide smile.

She was some woman.

Over the past few days he had been trying to ignore the strange desire he had to keep her. It didn't fit, or make sense, but he wanted to. He couldn't honestly say that he loved her, but the past few days had made the pain of years ago seem dim. She made the humiliation and distrust fade away.

But he knew who she was and where she belonged and sadly, as much as he might like to pretend otherwise, he knew who he was. A man that no woman wanted for a husband. So he smiled and clapped and even whistled for good effect, wishing the whole time that tonight wasn't goodbye.

Cecelia was amazed. In the glow of the lighting she could see the slicked-back hair and clean jaws of most of the men. She could also see the look in Ethan's eyes and it made her giddy enough to take a little bow.

She was overwhelmed by the amount of food and effort everyone seemed to go to for her. At her seat there was a pile of gifts. When she saw them and looked up at everyone with wonderment, the room stilled.

"What," she whispered, "what have you done?" She lifted some of the items, staring at them until the tears cleared from her vision.

"Well, some of them are reminders of your time here on the old Morning Glory," Jesse said with a laugh. She looked at all the wranglers with whom she had shared some of the most colorful meals of her life, and wished she could pack them into her suitcase and take them home with her.

"There's a map of the area with your route back to the airport clearly marked," Billy said with a grin. "Really, Cecelia, you shouldn't get lost."

"I put some seeds in those envelopes," Lis said, gesturing to the plain white envelopes marked with the names of some of the vegetables and flowers that filled the ranch's garden. "I don't know if you have any room where you live, but I thought you might..." When Lis's own eyes teared up, Cecelia couldn't help but grab on to her new friend and hold tight, riding out the powerful emotions.

So many gifts, just for her. Bought for her, given to her as jokes, as reminders, as tokens of gratitude. The tears she tried to hold back came out in a waterfall of joy and sadness.

"Thank you. Thank you everyone. I wish..." She let the sentence run out, because she simply lacked the power to put her wishes into words. She looked down at the pile of gifts and noticed the heavy-duty flashlight and laughed.

"Nate, just what we needed," she said, looking up for the boy.

"That's what I thought," he said grinning at her. Heedlessly, she reached over and hugged him. His own arms came around her and they stood there for a second, hugging and appreciating the place they had found together.

"Could I borrow that?" Billy asked, just before taking the flashlight, turning it on and placing it in the middle of the table, pointing up at the ceiling. "Now we can eat," he announced.

The dinner was loud and fun and the most bittersweet thing Cecelia had ever known. The entire time she was on the razor-sharp edge between laughter and tears, all the way through to coffee and chocolate cake.

Billy had been nudging Mark for the past half hour and for the past half hour Mark had been studiously ignoring him.

"Go get the guitar!" Billy muttered out of the corner of his mouth.

"No, it's a stupid idea," Mark whispered, turning his back on his brother.

"If you don't, I will," Billy threatened.

"Be my guest." Mark took a sip of coffee and gladly washed his hands of the whole affair.

Billy stood and conversations stopped.

"I think tonight calls for something special," he said almost sternly. "While some people might not think the departure of our new friend is an occasion," he looked pointedly at Mark, "I do."

Billy left the room and conversations resumed. When he returned with an old beaten-up guitar, conversations stopped again and everyone in the room shared puzzled looks.

"What are you doing with that?" Jesse asked, looking at Billy as if he had carried in a dead cow.

"I'm going to play it, and perhaps some people," he cast a meaningful glance at Ethan, "might like to ask a certain someone to dance." He jerked his head at Cecelia.

Billy sat down and began strumming into the complete silence.

"I think that boy has lost his mind," Jesse said in a loud whisper to Abe.

"I think everyone around here is a little loco," Abe agreed.

"I think," Mac stood and held a hand out to his wife, "that dancing might be the best idea yet."

Missy took his hand with a coy smile and Mac, displaying a grace nobody in the room knew he had, spun her into his arms. The two smiled at each other and danced as elegantly as they could in the light of flashlights and to the sweet, but strange, sounds of their son's ballad version of "Mary Had a Little Lamb."

"I think that's our cue," Ethan said to Cecelia. He stood, and, with eerie resemblance to his father, held out his hand.

Cecelia, thrilled and delighted and a little embarrassed, took the offered hand and slid into his arms as if she had been doing it for twenty years.

The sensation of holding Cecelia in his arms was a vivid tease. He concentrated on the curve of her back under his hand, the way his palm dwarfed hers, how perfectly her head rested just beneath his chin.

"You two look good together," Jesse said, laughing and nudging Abe at his side. "Ethan, see if you can hold on to her better than you did Marsha."

Billy's fingers fumbled over the strings, creating a discordant thrum, which reverberated in the silence. Abe slapped Jesse on the arm, Mac and Missy stopped dancing and Ethan's arms slowly dropped from Cecelia's body.

"Ethan?" Cecelia asked, confused by the strange turn of events.

Ethan laughed a bitter cold laugh that had Cecelia's stomach turning over.

"Good one, Jesse," Ethan said, his eyes opaque in the dim light. "Thanks for reminding me."

And with that Ethan walked out the front door into the night.

11
_____

THE PARTY atmosphere died and the hands all followed
Ethan out the door, mumbling their thanks and goodbyes.

Cecelia started to follow, but Mac stopped her.

"He's not going to want to talk to you just yet. Might
be better if you didn't go after him," he said. A confused
dread filled Cecelia. Standing in the chill of Ethan's departure, she wondered what secrets Ethan had held back
in the darkest part of the night when she had been spilling her guts.

Cecelia turned on the Cooks with fire in her eyes.

"What's going on here?" she demanded.

There was a long moment while the Cooks looked at
each other. Mac shrugged and nodded and Missy turned
to Cecelia.

"Have a seat," Missy said calmly.

"Just tell me what is going on!" Cecelia was getting
mad. Secrets were one thing, but Cecelia was getting the
feeling that the Cooks had been manipulating her. Their
harmless matchmaking had turned into something ugly.

"All right, stay standing," Missy conceded, seating
herself with a heavy sigh that revealed the sorrow and
pain that made her seem years older than she was.

"Ethan was married," Missy said.

"What?" Cecelia gasped, feeling like the floor had fallen out from beneath her.

"You could have tried for a little more subtlety, Ma," Billy said.

"This from the king of subtlety," Missy pointed out cryptically.

"What do you mean 'married'?" Cecelia asked.

"Marsha and Ethan were high-school sweethearts. Hell, they were kindergarten sweethearts," Mac answered. "Everyone knew they were going to get married, so much so that the kids didn't really have a choice about it. Well, after a few years of living on this ranch with a man who worked twelve hours a day, Marsha decided she didn't like it. They were young and both of them made mistakes, but Marsha started fooling around. A lot. And then when Ethan confronted her, she left."

"She just left?" Cecelia asked.

"Up and left," Mac answered, shaking his head sadly.

"Well, after that Ethan just about shut down. He never was the most open kind of person and this really set him back." Billy continued the story. "One night we were in town having a few drinks and Ethan looked at Mark and me and said, 'Never again, boys. It's up to you to have the families and keep this whole Cook legacy going' and that was it. He hasn't dated anyone seriously since. When you came along he seemed to go back to normal. You know, the way he was before Marsha left."

"What are you saying?" Cecelia asked, her heart breaking for Ethan.

"I'm saying, no matter what he says now, he cares," Billy told her.

The words fell into the room like gunfire on a quiet summer night.

"Why didn't anyone say anything?" Cecelia asked.

"Would it have mattered? I think you would have fallen in love all the same," Mark reasoned.

"I'm not...," Cecelia stuttered.

Missy put a hand on hers, clutching it like a lifeline. "Yes," she said, breathing power into Cecelia. "You are."

ETHAN STOOD on the ridge overlooking the valley and tried very hard to find the peace he knew was here. But tonight, when he needed the balm of the land, he was too angry and confused to be soothed.

Sadly, he was not surprised or happy to be aware of Cecelia's arrival on the trail behind him.

"I don't want you here," he said, before she could get closer to him.

"I know," she answered. He didn't turn, but every nerve was aware of the fact that instead of retreating she was now only inches behind him.

"I mean that, Cecelia."

"I know," she answered again. The touch of her hand on his back was a spark to the powder keg that had been lying in wait since Marsha left.

He turned on her then, ignoring the pity and pain on her face, instead only saw a target for his own blind rage. "What do I need to do to get rid of you?"

"Your parents told me about Marsha," she said, taking his insults with a minimum of pain.

Ethan stood in a blank moment of understanding.

"So?" he said, his lip curling.

"So." She paused, every counselor instinct told her to get out, to run, because this whole situation was too personal and she was bound to leave bloody if she didn't leave now. "I know why you're doing this."

He laughed, the same bitter, gut-wrenching laugh from earlier.

"You ever have someone run out on you, Cecelia?" Ethan asked. "Your parents dying, that had nothing to do with you. But Marsha leaving had everything to do with me."

"You were young."

"No, I was a bad husband. She told me so."

"Maybe you were just a bad husband for her."

"Pardon me, but I'm going to have to bow to Marsha's expertise here. She's the authority on being married to me. Look, Cecelia. I don't want a wife, I don't need a wife."

"You have to understand…"

"No," Ethan exploded. "The only thing that needs to be understood around here is, as I have tried to get across, I don't want you here."

"Ethan, don't do this. I can help you."

"Help me? What? Like counsel me?" His horror could not have been clearer.

"You need to talk to somebody," she said, lifting a hand in supplication.

"I don't need anyone, and frankly, honey, a woman from the city who is great in bed but useless on the ranch would be the last person I need."

Cecelia's shields and armor collapsed and his words, like swords and daggers, pierced her flesh and slid into the places in her heart she tried to keep safe. She gasped with the pain of this betrayal. He kept talking, ignoring her pallor, her eyes filling with tears.

"This," he gestured to the space between them as if it held their fragile and breaking relationship, "was nothing, Cecelia. It wasn't permission to know or ask about my life. It wasn't going to turn into anything or last past you getting in that car and driving down that mountain."

She took stumbling steps away from him, shaking her head as the knives he had pushed into her twisted.

"Ethan, I know this isn't you talking. I know you don't mean these things…"

He chuckled, shaking his head in a derisive kind of pity.

"You love me, don't you?" he asked and Cecelia's silence was answer enough for both of them. "That's your problem," he told her cruelly and turned his back on her.

Cecelia had known that she wouldn't leave this mountain with her heart intact, but she didn't think Ethan would take a hammer to it. She stood there for a moment shaking with the pain he had given her and then turned and ran blindly back down the path she had come up.

At the ranch no one asked her anything. One look at her face and they knew that everything had backfired and the price had been Cecelia's heart.

Cecelia spent a sleepless night torn between berating herself for her stupidity and foolishness and wishing with everything in her that Ethan loved her back, just a little. Just enough to walk into her room and apologize, to take her in his arms and take back all the horrible things he had said to her.

Every sound outside her door had her jumping, sitting up in bed and waiting for her door to slide open and Ethan to step in, hat and heart in hand.

Dawn came and she was still waiting.

In the chill of the sunrise she finished packing, concentrating on shoving the pain and heartache into the same small dark place in her heart where she kept the memories of her parents. She had to maintain control, gather it in and conquer it, or she would never make it off this mountain.

Missy Cook was already in the kitchen, sitting at the table with a cup of coffee in her hands, sending steam into the pale, early-morning light.

"Coffee's on," she said. Cecelia wanted to feel pity for the woman who sat looking years past her age, but she had no energy to spare for her. It took all of her will simply to stay standing under her own crushing sadness.

"I'm just going to leave," Cecelia said, hoisting her bag onto her shoulder. "Nate knows what he needs to do and you can contact me if there are any problems. Thank Jesse for fixing my car."

"Cecelia?" The look on Missy's face begged Cecelia to drop the act, to stop pretending she had everything under control. Cecelia looked her in the eye and ignored sympathy's call.

"Thank you for your hospitality." She walked past the older woman, out onto the front porch where the familiar beauty of the land teased the lock on her control. She went down the steps to the lawn and crossed it to her car.

"Cecelia?" Missy called from the porch. Cecelia turned, putting her hand up to shade her eyes from the sun. "Ethan loves you. I know it and so does he. That's why he's doing this."

"No, he doesn't, Missy," Cecelia said. "He made that very clear."

She turned and got in the car. She wiggled the gearshift, yanked on the wheel and turned the key twice and when the car started she began her trip down the mountain and the process of leaving her broken heart on the Morning Glory Ranch.

She turned her second corner, leaving the house out of sight and to say she was surprised to see Ethan in the middle of the road on Freddie would be an understatement.

Her heart stopped.

He was blocking the whole road, so she had no choice but to stop. For a brief moment she considered pushing on the accelerator and sending Ethan and his horse down the mountain the fast way, but Freddie had been nothing but sweet to her, so she sat in the stopped car and glared at Ethan.

He dismounted and Cecelia was sickened by herself as she opened the car door and got out to meet him. Her broken heart was beating again with new hope.

"What do you want, Ethan?" she demanded, crossing her arms and trying to look as irritated and unhurt as possible.

He stopped a few feet from her and when his eyes met hers the grief and confusion in the gray depths almost melted her. "I wanted to tell you…"

Ethan trailed off, unable to find the way out of his misery. He had sat up all night trying to come to grips with his old grief and guilt. He knew he needed to let the past go and the more he thought about Marsha and their marriage the looser the knot in his chest became. It wasn't gone, but he could breathe without the constant reminder of being played for a fool by his wife.

Every time he had closed his eyes last night, he remembered Cecelia's face when he told her that loving him was her problem. He hadn't meant that. The last thing he wanted was to hurt this beautiful, strong woman in front of him. But he had. He knew there was something else driving him, too, an emotion stronger than any other, one he'd repressed for so long he didn't know what to do with it.

Cecelia waited for him to finish his words, hoping against hope that he had come here to tell her he didn't want her to go. Perhaps he was standing in front of her to tell her that he loved her, too.

"I wanted to tell you I was sorry," he finished.

That's a start, she thought.

"And," he continued, "I didn't want you to leave without telling you that I…" He paused again and Cecelia could actually hear the blood pounding in her veins. She smiled at him, tears of gratitude and understanding welling in her eyes. How she loved this big, beautiful cowboy.

"I had a really good time," he concluded, looking earnest.

The tears dried up in her eyes and the pounding became deafening in her rage.

"Had a good time?" she repeated slowly.

"Yeah, a really good time."

"Oh," Cecelia said, nearly laughing, "a *really* good time. Well, that's just great, Ethan. I'm glad. I'm glad that you had a good time. You want to know why? I'll tell you, because in one fell swoop here you have taken everything good out of this time up here with you and your family. You have taken that and replaced it with horse crap!'' She was working herself into a wild state, she could feel her eyes bugging out and the cords in her neck straining. Steam, she was sure, was coming out of her ears.

''You'll excuse me if I don't return the compliment, Ethan. Now, please move yourself and your horse, I'm trying to get off this mountain.'' She got back in her car and slammed the door so hard that it didn't catch and bounced back open. She had to repeat the slamming process. She waggled the gearshift with vicious intent, grabbed on to the wheel and nearly tore it off as she turned it, pretending for a brief, joyful moment that it was Ethan's head. The car started on the first try and when she looked up to be sure Ethan was out of her way, he was nowhere to be seen.

On the drive to the airport Cecelia had to pull over twelve times because she was crying too hard to see the road.

ONE MONTH LATER Samantha dialed her parent's number from her desk at work and waited impatiently for someone to answer.

''What did you guys do up there?'' she whispered into the phone when someone finally picked up.

''What? Sweetie?'' Her father was baffled. Samantha took a deep breath and reined in her temper for someone who really deserved it.

''Hi, Dad. Is Billy around?''

"Of course. Are you okay, honey? Do you need money?"

"Dad, I'm fine." She couldn't help but laugh. She was twenty-three and had been living in the city on her own for two years. Still, her father asked her if she needed money every time she talked to him. "I'm just a little angry with my brothers right now."

"So, what else is new?" He chuckled. He shouted for Billy and passed the phone to his son, who had no idea what he was in for.

"Hello," Billy said.

"What did you guys do?" Samantha demanded.

"Whoa, hold on a second. What are you talking about?" Billy asked.

"I'm talking about the fact that I sent a wonderful woman up there a month ago and you guys sent back a wreck."

"Is Cecelia okay?" Billy felt bad, as bad as he'd ever felt about anything, for the way his whole matchmaking debut had turned out.

"No!" Samantha shouted and then looked around to see if anyone had heard. "She is not okay," she continued in a hushed tone. "She's working herself to death. I don't think she's eating, she refuses to talk about anything that happened and I've caught her crying her eyes out in the women's bathroom on numerous occasions. Now, tell me what happened."

"I really don't know," Billy explained. "Things were going well and then Jesse opened his big mouth and Ethan flipped out and the next thing I know Cecelia's gone and Ethan's acting crazy."

"What do you mean crazy?" Samantha asked.

"I mean lunatic. He works all the time. I don't think he sleeps. He does full days down here and then, I swear, he works all night on that house. He doesn't talk to anyone except to yell at them. And yesterday, Nate, the poor kid, just mentioned Cecelia's name and you'd think by the way Ethan acted that the boy had spit on Freddie. It's weird."

"Ah-ha," Samantha murmured speculatively.

"Hey, wait a second, whatever that 'ah-ha' means, you can forget it. It was just that kind of thinking that got us here in the first place," Billy said, trying to stem the uncontrollable tide of matchmaking.

"No, it wasn't," Samantha said, sitting up straight and taking on the tone of someone who knows exactly what she is talking about. "What started this whole thing is my firm belief that Cecelia and Ethan are perfect for each other."

"Are you telling me…? No way!"

"Yes way. Now, I worked really hard to get those two together for a few days and whatever you did ruined it all."

"So, what are we going to do now?"

Samantha saw Cecelia coming out of the washroom with a telltale red nose and puffy eyes.

"I've got to go, but you guys better think of something and you'd better make it good." With those words, Samantha hung up on Billy.

THAT NIGHT after dinner at the Morning Glory there was a family meeting of sorts. Ethan wasn't there, but Lis and Nate were standing in his place.

"So," Billy was saying, swirling around the coffee in

the bottom of his mug, "Samantha is pretty angry about us ruining her work to get them together."

"I have to say I'm with Mac on this," Lis chimed in, putting the pot of coffee down in the center of the table where everyone could grab it. "You guys hurt two people with your manipulating. You should just leave this alone."

"No way! I agree with Mom." Mark leaned up and grabbed the coffee and poured some in his cup. "I think all this stuff that's going on with Cecelia and Ethan only proves how strongly they feel for each other."

"That's all fine and good," Missy took the pot of coffee and added some more to her mug and to her husband's, "but what are we going to do to get them back together?"

The kitchen was quiet while everyone thought about the predicament and then, as if Nate had grown two heads, all eyes slowly turned to him.

"Hey, Nate," Billy said, "how would you like it if Ethan stopped making you muck out the stalls at dawn every morning?"

"Are you kidding me? I'd love it," Nate answered. He wasn't sure what that had to do with getting Cecelia and Ethan back together, but to get out of mucking stalls, he'd do just about anything.

12

"NATE, SLOW DOWN." Cecelia pinched the bridge of her nose and wondered, briefly, why people did that. Pinching the bridge of her nose never made her feel better, it just gave her bruises.

"Look, Cecelia, just come and get me, okay?" Nate demanded in a sullen, angry tone that Cecelia thought she would never hear from him again.

"Nate, I don't understand. A month ago you loved it there."

"Yeah, well, now I hate it." Nate looked over at the doorway where most of the Cooks were gathered listening to the conversation. He shrugged and looked quizzically at them and they all gave him enthusiastic thumbs-up.

"So, come and get me," he said in his most angry voice and then smiled at the Cooks who all beamed at him. *This,* he thought, *is kind of fun.*

"Nate, I can't just come and get you. You have to tell me what happened."

Nate put his hand over the receiver and shot a panicked look at the doorway of Cooks.

"She wants to know what happened," he said in a loud stage whisper.

"Shit," Billy murmured and Lis smacked him in the shoulder.

"He hit me," Nate said into the receiver, thinking Lis was giving him a cue.

"No!" Billy yelled and Mark hit him.

"He hit me twice," Nate said smugly into the phone.

There was a long tense pause while Cecelia assimilated the information.

"Who hit you?" she asked in a deadly voice.

"Ethan," Nate answered. As one unit the Cooks groaned and sagged against the wall. Their brilliant plan was falling apart.

"I'll be there tomorrow," she said and hung up.

Nate hung up the phone and smiled triumphantly at the Cooks.

"She'll be here tomorrow," he said and with his nose in the air he breezed past his audience.

ETHAN SPED all the way to the airport. He sped and cursed and tried to control his impulse to do violence to Cecelia Grady.

That woman had some nerve yanking Nate out of the Morning Glory this way. It made him even angrier as he thought about the boy's devastated face earlier that morning.

"She wants me to go back," Nate had said, sulking into his sausage.

"Why?" Ethan had asked. He looked around at his family, but they all shrugged and shook their heads looking like someone had come down and stolen Christmas right out from under their noses.

When it came time for someone to meet her at the

airport Ethan had volunteered for the job. He was so angry with this woman that he couldn't wait to lay into her. It would be just like a woman to use this boy as a way to get back at Ethan for ending the affair the way he did. Just the thought of it brought up memories of Marsha's manipulations and sneaky dealings.

What really poured salt in the wounds was that he had himself convinced that Cecelia was different, some kind of angel of womanhood. Then she went and pulled a stunt like this. Ethan was left with all the old bitterness, only worse because in the month she had been gone, he'd convinced himself that he loved her. Loved her!

Well, he thought, making a tight turn into an airport parking space, that was the end of that. He would stop that nonsense.

He got out of the truck, slammed the door good and hard and walked to the building with long angry strides. People stopped and stared, mothers pulled their children close and couples in his direct path walked quickly to get out of the way of the crazy man as he stormed into the terminal.

Ethan didn't notice the attention he was getting, his mind was on one thing—strangling Cecelia with her own hair.

CECELIA HAD SPENT the better part of the night imagining exactly what she was going to do to Ethan Cook when she got her hands on him. While part of her was ready to tear him limb from limb, the other part of her was in shock. That the tender lover who had held her and loved her so gently all those nights would actually raise a hand to Nate was unbelievable.

Part of her, the part that wept in the women's bathroom, the part that still loved him, couldn't actually see him doing it. But then all she had to do was remember Ethan the first few days she knew him, and the way he had so coldly and blithely dismissed her when she left.

She had told him once that she didn't think there was any kindness in him, which, she had sadly learned, was the truth. It was her fault that she had forgotten.

Cecelia wasn't sure who would pick her up, but Samantha had assured her that someone would be there. Ethan, leaning nonchalantly against the wall, was the last one she expected. She stopped, caught in a horrible moment of heartbreak—he was so handsome, his features so familiar. She felt her face flush hot, then cold, and then her temper flared out of control and she charged toward him.

It was impossible to miss the woman storming through the terminal, and for a split second Ethan was reminded of how incredibly exciting this woman was when she was passionate. But that moment passed and when she finally got to him, his anger was just as great as hers.

"What the hell do you think you're doing?" they yelled at the same time. They paused, regrouped and tried again.

"You've got some kind of nerve," they said in unison once again. Before they could do it for the third time Cecelia clapped a hand over his mouth.

"I'm not going to listen to you. I'm not going to talk to you. You hit that boy." She shook her head at him in disbelief and disgust. "You hit him and I'm getting him away from you."

"What are you talking about?" Ethan asked, dodging her hand.

"You hitting a little kid."

"I didn't hit Nate," he replied hotly.

"Don't bother lying."

"Lying?" Ethan barked. "You are accusing me of lying? That's a good one. Let's say we cut the crap and you tell me why you're really here."

"I am here because you hit Nate!"

"You're here because you're mad."

"Mad?"

"Yeah, you're mad at me and you're taking it out on the kid."

"You're right, Ethan." Sarcasm oozed from her words. "I am taking him back because I'm mad at you. Mad at you for hitting him!" she yelled. People were beginning to stare, so Ethan grabbed this infuriating woman whom he used to love and started to drag her down the hall. But he should have known Cecelia would make it difficult. She dug in her heels and started yelling at the top of her lungs.

"You hit him and now you're kidnapping me," she hollered. She pulled away from him with all of her weight and lowered her body so she was almost sitting on the floor, but he wouldn't let go.

"Help!" she screamed. Everyone was staring, but no one was helping. "Somebody help me!"

"Ethan?" A grizzled old man sitting in front of an airport coffee shop stood up. "You need some help with that girl?" he asked.

With nothing left at his disposal, Ethan did what he did best and treated Cecelia like a cow. He dipped his

shoulder, yanked on her arm and before she could say
"Beg your pardon" she was riding across his shoulders
like a new calf.

"Good one, Ethan." A young man in a cowboy hat
walked past and gave Ethan the thumbs-up.

"Ethan, I am warning you," Cecelia yelled into his
ear and pushed her hair out of her eyes.

"No, sweetheart, I'm warning you. If you can't keep
it quiet, I'm going to stuff you in a garbage can and
leave you, got it?"

Cecelia didn't dignify that with a response.

Ethan got her out into the parking lot and dumped her
into the passenger seat of his truck. He crawled in the
other side, got one look at her face and wished he had
dumped her in a garbage can. She was one angry
woman.

"You left me no choice, Cecelia," he said reasonably.
"You were creating a scene."

"Oh, really?" She laughed dangerously. "You want
to see a scene, wait until I haul your entire family into
court for this."

"Cecelia, if you take Nate away because you want to
get back at me for the way things went sour, that's one
thing, but if you involve my family…"

"Get back at you?" Cecelia interrupted. "Where did
you get that idea?"

"Why else would you be doing this?" He started the
car and pulled out of the airport parking lot.

"Because you hit Nate!"

"Cecelia," he said seriously, beginning to think there
was something else going on here. "I never touched that
boy."

There was a moment of silence.

"Nate said you hit him," Cecelia told Ethan. She looked at him in time to see his jaw clench and eyes shut. Part of her, the part that loved him and cried in bathrooms, laughed and said *I told you so* to the part that had caused the scene back at the airport.

"The boy is lying." Ethan looked her right in the eye and Cecelia had to believe him.

"But why would he…" She trailed off.

"Billy!" they said in unison as lightning struck and the whole situation became clear.

"Your whole family has been in on this from the beginning," Cecelia said, shaking her head in amazement. "That whole candlelight dinner thing, the dancing and now this." Cecelia was torn between anger and relief that Nate had not been hurt.

"They pulled out all the stops here. They even called in the kid," Ethan said and out of the corner of his eye he watched Cecelia.

Suddenly, without the anger that had been pushing him through this reunion, he was reminded of what the last month had done to his feelings for her. He loved her. And as she sat in the truck with him, biting her lip and shaking her head, his feelings burst in him like thunder.

He fought the urge to pull over on the side of the road and let the whole thing spill out; all of his dreams of marriage and family and living up on that ridge with her and whatever stray kids she wanted to save. He wanted all of that, the whole scenario. A month and a half ago if he had told her how he felt he could be reasonably assured that she returned his feelings, but now after a month had passed, after the horrible way he had botched their goodbyes—both of them—he didn't know what to do.

She was sitting there, not saying anything, not looking at him and he wondered if maybe he had blown it so bad with her that all of her feelings for him were gone. He remembered how she'd looked when he said those words he didn't mean, every word that hurt her.

He couldn't really blame her. He had screwed up royally.

"What are you going to do?" he asked when the silence in the car continued to stretch.

"With Nate?" Cecelia asked.

"Yeah."

"I'll leave him here, but not until I have a very explicit conversation with your family about professional behavior," she said in her briefcase voice, and certain parts of his body surged in response.

"You can't really blame them. They were just trying to help out."

"By costing my program money? By yanking me out of my office in the middle of the week? By forcing me into this situation with you?" She stopped abruptly and Ethan watched her get herself under control.

"I was done with you, Ethan," she whispered roughly. "I didn't want to see you again."

"I know," he said and pushed away the words he wanted to say.

"Is the house done?" Cecelia asked, breaking the silence. They were almost at the turnoff to Ethan's house.

"Yeah, for the most part," he answered.

"I want to see it," Cecelia said abruptly.

Ethan looked at her profile and slowed the car down to take the turn. They bounced over rocks and holes until the road opened up and the house was visible.

"Oh, Ethan. Look at what you've done." The truck wasn't completely stopped and Cecelia was out of it, gazing at the house with a smile and shining eyes. Ethan's heart contracted and then broke and the pain pushed the words right out of his mouth.

"I love you," he said.

Cecelia's back was to him, but he could tell by her incredible stillness that she had heard him. He continued; the dam broken, he was unable to stop.

"It's like a living thing inside me. This past month I've been going crazy, driving everyone else crazy because I didn't want to let this out. But I have to. You're back and I know that you'll go again. I know that what I said and how I acted was wrong and cruel, but I've got to say it." He stopped, shaking with his feelings. "I love you."

"Is this supposed to change things?" she asked after a moment.

"Yes. No. Look, I don't know." He stopped, unable to continue conversing with the back of her head. He grabbed her shoulders and turned her around. She was crying. Silently, tears fell in silver trails down her smooth cheeks. He ached with this pain he was causing her. He traced the trails with his thumbs, trying to erase them. Trying to erase the pain.

"I know I was letting the past ruin my future. I knew it all along, but I had never felt strongly enough about a woman to risk it again. I gave Marsha everything I had and she threw it back in my face. It's not easy doing that again.''

"Is that what you're doing?" Cecelia asked. "Giving me everything?"

"I'm trying to," he said with all the honesty in him.

"Are you going to give me this house?" The tears spilled faster, but the pain in her eyes was fading, replaced by the same fragile emotion he had in his own eyes.

"I'll share it with you," he said solemnly.

"Are you going to give me children?"

"As many as you want." It was a vow, and his eyes told her so.

"Are you going to give me your family?"

"You can have them." Ethan smiled and Cecelia laughed and finally after a month apart and the longest car ride in the history of the world, Ethan took her in his arms and kissed her. And the broken heart in his chest healed and Cecelia felt her own scars vanish in the healing power of this kiss.

"Wait." She pulled away but kept her arms linked around his shoulders. "I have one more question."

"Whatever," he said grandly, trying to pull her in closer, but she continued to resist.

"I'm serious."

"Me, too. Whatever you want I'll give you."

"I want to bring kids from the city up here. I want to run the Relocation Program from up here and I want to be a host for kids like Nate."

Ethan didn't have to think about it. "Absolutely."

He began walking her backward toward the house. "Now, let me tell you what I want."

She smiled at him, so dazzled by her love for him and the promise of their future that he had in his eyes that she would have promised him anything. Her life, her heart, every tomorrow that was hers she wanted to share with this man.

"I want to show you my bed."

"Your bed?" she asked, amazed. It was sad but true that all of their lovemaking had happened in mud, on the floor or on a mattress that he had put on the floor in one of the rooms in this house.

"Yes, a big one."

"I can't wait," she said. And meant it with all of her heart.

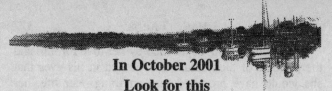

In October 2001
Look for this
New York Times bestselling author

BARBARA DELINSKY

in

Bronze Mystique

The only men in Sasha's life lived between the covers of her bestselling romances. She wrote about passionate, loving heroes, but no such man existed...til Doug Donohue rescued Sasha the night her motorcycle crashed.

AND award-winning Harlequin Intrigue author

GAYLE WILSON

in

Secrets in Silence

This fantastic 2-in-1 collection will be on sale October 2001.

HARLEQUIN®
Makes any time special ®

*Harlequin truly does make any time special. ...
This year we are celebrating weddings in style!*

A
Walk
Down
the Aisle
WEDDING CELEBRATION

To help us celebrate, we want you to tell us how wearing the Harlequin wedding gown will make your wedding day special. As the grand prize, Harlequin will offer one lucky bride the chance to **"Walk Down the Aisle" in the Harlequin wedding gown!**

There's more...

For her honeymoon, she and her groom will spend five nights at the **Hyatt Regency Maui.** As part of this five-night honeymoon at the hotel renowned for its romantic attractions, the couple will enjoy a candlelit dinner for two in Swan Court, a sunset sail on the hotel's catamaran, and duet spa treatments.

A HYATT RESORT AND SPA®   Maui • Molokai • Lanai

To enter, please write, in, 250 words or less, how wearing the Harlequin wedding gown will make your wedding day special. The entry will be judged based on its emotionally compelling nature, its originality and creativity, and its sincerity. This contest is open to Canadian and U.S. residents only and to those who are 18 years of age and older. There is no purchase necessary to enter. Void where prohibited. See further contest rules attached. Please send your entry to:

Walk Down the Aisle Contest

In Canada
P.O. Box 637
Fort Erie, Ontario
L2A 5X3

In U.S.A.
P.O. Box 9076
3010 Walden Ave.
Buffalo, NY 14269-9076

You can also enter by visiting www.eHarlequin.com
Win the Harlequin wedding gown and the vacation of a lifetime!
The deadline for entries is October 1, 2001.

HARLEQUIN®
Makes any time special ®

PHWDACONT1

HARLEQUIN WALK DOWN THE AISLE TO MAUI CONTEST 1197
OFFICIAL RULES
NO PURCHASE NECESSARY TO ENTER

1. To enter, follow directions published in the offer to which you are responding. Contest begins April 2, 2001, and ends on October 1, 2001. Method of entry may vary. Mailed entries must be postmarked by October 1, 2001, and received by October 8, 2001.

2. Contest entry may be, at times, presented via the Internet, but will be restricted solely to residents of certain geographic areas that are disclosed on the Web site. To enter via the Internet, if permissible, access the Harlequin Web site (www.eHarlequin.com) and follow the directions displayed online. Online entries must be received by 11:59 p.m. E.S.T. on October 1, 2001.

    In lieu of submitting an entry online, enter by mail by hand-printing (or typing) on an 8½" x 11" plain sheet of paper, your name, address (including zip code), Contest number/name and in 250 words or fewer, why winning a Harlequin wedding dress would make your wedding day special. Mail via first-class mail to: Harlequin Walk Down the Aisle Contest 1197, (in the U.S.) P.O. Box 9076, 3010 Walden Avenue, Buffalo, NY 14269-9076, (in Canada) P.O. Box 637, Fort Erie, Ontario L2A 5X3, Canada.

    Limit one entry per person, household address and e-mail address. Online and/or mailed entries received from persons residing in geographic areas in which Internet entry is not permissible will be disqualified.

3. Contests will be judged by a panel of members of the Harlequin editorial, marketing and public relations staff based on the following criteria:

    - Originality and Creativity—50%
    - Emotionally Compelling—25%
    - Sincerity—25%

    In the event of a tie, duplicate prizes will be awarded. Decisions of the judges are final.

4. All entries become the property of Torstar Corp. and will not be returned. No responsibility is assumed for lost, late, illegible, incomplete, inaccurate, nondelivered or misdirected mail or misdirected e-mail, for technical, hardware or software failures of any kind, lost or unavailable network connections, or failed, incomplete, garbled or delayed computer transmission or any human error which may occur in the receipt or processing of the entries in this Contest.

5. Contest open only to residents of the U.S. (except Puerto Rico) and Canada, who are 18 years of age or older, and is void wherever prohibited by law; all applicable laws and regulations apply. Any litigation within the Province of Quebec respecting the conduct or organization of a publicity contest may be submitted to the Régie des alcools, des courses et des jeux for a ruling. Any litigation respecting the awarding of a prize may be submitted to the Régie des alcools, des courses et des jeux only for the purpose of helping the parties reach a settlement. Employees and immediate family members of Torstar Corp. and D. L. Blair, Inc., their affiliates, subsidiaries and all other agencies, entities and persons connected with the use, marketing or conduct of this Contest are not eligible to enter. Taxes on prizes are the sole responsibility of winners. Acceptance of any prize offered constitutes permission to use winner's name, photograph or other likeness for the purposes of advertising, trade and promotion on behalf of Torstar Corp., its affiliates and subsidiaries without further compensation to the winner, unless prohibited by law.

6. Winners will be determined no later than November 15, 2001, and will be notified by mail. Winners will be required to sign and return an Affidavit of Eligibility form within 15 days after winner notification. Noncompliance within that time period may result in disqualification and an alternative winner may be selected. Winners of trip must execute a Release of Liability prior to ticketing and must possess required travel documents (e.g. passport, photo ID) where applicable. Trip must be completed by November 2002. No substitution of prize permitted by winner. Torstar Corp. and D. L. Blair, Inc., their parents, affiliates, and subsidiaries are not responsible for errors in printing or electronic presentation of Contest, entries and/or game pieces. In the event of printing or other errors which may result in unintended prize values or duplication of prizes, all affected game pieces or entries shall be null and void. If for any reason the Internet portion of the Contest is not capable of running as planned, including infection by computer virus, bugs, tampering, unauthorized intervention, fraud, technical failures, or any other causes beyond the control of Torstar Corp. which corrupt or affect the administration, secrecy, fairness, integrity or proper conduct of the Contest, Torstar Corp. reserves the right, at its sole discretion, to disqualify any individual who tampers with the entry process and to cancel, terminate, modify or suspend the Contest or the Internet portion thereof. In the event of a dispute regarding an online entry, the entry will be deemed submitted by the authorized holder of the e-mail account submitted at the time of entry. Authorized account holder is defined as the natural person who is assigned to an e-mail address by an Internet access provider, online service provider or other organization that is responsible for arranging e-mail address for the domain associated with the submitted e-mail address. **Purchase or acceptance of a product offer does not improve your chances of winning.**

7. Prizes: (1) Grand Prize—A Harlequin wedding dress (approximate retail value: $3,500) and a 5-night/6-day honeymoon trip to Maui, HI, including round-trip air transportation provided by Maui Visitors Bureau from Los Angeles International Airport (winner is responsible for transportation to and from Los Angeles International Airport) and a Harlequin Romance Package, including hotel accomodations (double occupancy) at the Hyatt Regency Maui Resort and Spa, dinner for (2) two at Swan Court, a sunset sail on Kiele V and a spa treatment for the winner (approximate retail value: $4,000); (5) Five runner-up prizes of a $1000 gift certificate to selected retail outlets to be determined by Sponsor (retail value $1000 ea.). Prizes consist of only those items listed as part of the prize. Limit one prize per person. All prizes are valued in U.S. currency.

8. For a list of winners (available after December 17, 2001) send a self-addressed, stamped envelope to: Harlequin Walk Down the Aisle Contest 1197 Winners, P.O. Box 4200 Blair, NE 68009-4200 or you may access the www.eHarlequin.com Web site through January 15, 2002.

Contest sponsored by Torstar Corp., P.O. Box 9042, Buffalo, NY 14269-9042, U.S.A.

PHWDACONT2

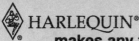